PRAISE FOR

Abarat
DAYS OF MAGIC, NIGHTS OF WAR

"Clive Barker has made his mark as one of the best fantasy writers since C.S. Lewis."

—*The Midwest Book Review*

"Fantastically complicated and dreamlike, sensations intensified by the elaborate sonorous imagery. All the threads are pulled together in a splendidly apocalyptic finale of cinematic scope."

—*Kirkus Reviews*

"You're eager to love this beautiful book. And, thankfully, it is easy to love."

—*The Guardian*

"Fantastic and often spine-chilling."

—*KLIATT* (starred review)

"Will keep readers on the edge of their seats."

—ALA *Booklist*

ALSO BY CLIVE BARKER

CLIVE BARKER

ABARAT

DAYS OF MAGIC, NIGHTS OF WAR

JOANNA COTLER BOOKS

An Imprint of HarperCollinsPublishers

Library of Congress Cataloging-in-Publication Data

Barker, Clive, date.

Days of magic, nights of war / Clive Barker.— 1st ed.

p.   cm. — (Abarat ; bk. 2)

Summary: Candy Quackenbush's adventures in the Abarat continue as she
makes a startling realization as to who she is, and the forces of Night begin plans
for war.

ISBN-10: 0-06-059638-4 — ISBN-13: 978-0-06-059638-5

[1. Fantasy.] I. Title.

PZ7.B25046Day 2004   2003024166

[Fic]—dc22   CIP

                                                                        AC

Typography by Neil Swaab

❖

First Harper Trophy edition, 2005

First rack edition, 2006

For my mother, Joan

I dreamed I spoke in another's language,
I dreamed I lived in another's skin,
I dreamed I was my own beloved,
I dreamed I was a tiger's kin.

I dreamed that Eden lived inside me,
And when I breathed a garden came,
I dreamed I knew all of Creation,
I dreamed I knew the Creator's name.

I dreamed—and this dream was the finest—
That all I dreamed was real and true,
And we would live in joy forever,
You in me, and me in you.

C. B.

CONTENTS

PART FOUR: THE SEA COMES TO CHICKENTOWN

PROLOGUE

HUNGER

Here is a list of fearful things:
The jaws of sharks, a vulture's wings,
The rabid bite of the dogs of war,
The voice of one who went before.
But most of all the mirror's gaze,
Which counts us out our numbered days.

—Righteous Bandy,
the nomad Poet of Abarat

OTTO HOULIHAN SAT IN the dark room and listened to the two creatures who had brought him here—a three-eyed thing by the name of Lazaru and its sidekick, Baby Pink-Eye—playing Knock the Devil Down in the corner. After their twenty-second game his nervousness and irritation began to get the better of him.

"How much longer am I going to have to wait?" he asked them.

Baby Pink-Eye, who had large reptilian claws and the face of a demented infant, puffed on a blue cigar and blew a cloud of acrid smoke in Houlihan's direction.

"They call you the Criss-Cross Man, don't they?" he said.

Houlihan nodded, giving Pink-Eye his coldest gaze, the kind of gaze that usually made men weak with fear. The creature was unimpressed.

"Think you're scary, do you?" he said. "Ha! This is Gorgossium, Criss-Cross Man. This is the island of the Midnight Hour. Every dark, unthinkable thing that has ever happened at the dead of night has happened right here. So don't try scaring me. You're wasting your time."

"I just asked—"

"Yes, yes, we heard you," said Lazaru, the eye in the middle of her forehead rolling back and forth in a very unsettling fashion. "You'll have to be patient. The Lord of Midnight will see you when he's ready to see you."

"Got some urgent news for him, have you?" said Baby Pink-Eye.

"That's between him and me."

"I warn you, he doesn't like bad news," said Lazaru. "He gets in a fury, doesn't he, Pink-Eye?"

"*Crazy* is what he gets! Tears people apart with his bare hands."

They glanced conspiratorially at each other. Houlihan said nothing. They were just trying to frighten him, and it wouldn't work. He got up and went to the narrow window, looking out onto the tumorous landscape of the Midnight Island, phosphorescent with corruption. This much of what Baby Pink-Eye had said was true: Gorgossium *was* a place of terrors. He could see the glistening forms of countless monsters as they moved through the littered landscape; he could smell spicy-sweet incense rising from the mausoleums in the mist-shrouded cemetery; he could hear the shrill din of drills from the mines where the mud that filled Midnight's armies of stitchlings was produced. Though he wasn't going to let Lazaru or Pink-Eye see his unease, he would be glad when he'd made his report and he could leave for less terrifying places.

There was some murmuring behind him, and a moment later Lazaru announced: "The Prince of Midnight is ready to see you."

Houlihan turned from the window to see that the door on the far side of the chamber was open and Baby Pink-Eye was gesturing for him to step through it.

"Hurry, hurry," the infant said.

Houlihan went to the door and stood on the threshold. Out of the darkness of the room came the voice of Christopher Carrion, deep and joyless.

"Enter, enter. You're just in time to watch the feeding."

Houlihan followed the sound of Carrion's voice. There was a flickering in the darkness, which grew more intense by degrees, and as it brightened he saw the Lord of Midnight standing perhaps ten yards from him. He was dressed in gray robes and was wearing gloves that looked as though they were made of fine chain mail.

"Not many people get to see this, Criss-Cross Man. My nightmares are hungry, so I'm going to feed them." Houlihan shuddered. "*Watch*, man! Don't stare at the floor."

Reluctantly, the Criss-Cross Man raised his eyes. The nightmares Carrion had spoken of were swimming in a blue fluid, which all but filled a high transparent collar around Carrion's head. Two pipes emerged from the base of the Lord of Midnight's skull, and it was through these that the nightmares had emerged, swimming directly out of Carrion's skull. They were barely more than long threads of light; but there was something about their restless motion, the way they roved the collar, sometimes touching Carrion's face, more often pressing against the glass, that spoke of their hunger.

Carrion reached up into the collar. One of the night-mares made a quick motion, like a striking snake, and delivered itself into its creator's hand. Carrion lifted it out of the fluid and studied it with a curious tender-ness.

"It doesn't look like much, does it?" Carrion said. Houlihan didn't comment. He just wanted Carrion to keep the thing away from him. "But when these things are coiled in my brain they show me such delicious horrors." The nightmare writhed around in Carrion's hand, letting out a thin, high-pitched squeal. "So every now and then I reward them with a nice fat meal of fear. They love fear. And it's hard for me to feel much of it these days. I've seen too many horrors in my time. So I provide them with someone who *will* feel fear."

So saying, he let the nightmare go. It slithered out of his grip, hitting the stone floor. It knew exactly where it was going. It wove across the ground, flick-ering with excitement, the light out of its thin form illuminating its victim: a large, bearded man squatted against the wall.

"Mercy, my Lord . . ." he sobbed. "I'm just a Todo miner."

"Oh, now be quiet," Carrion said as though he were speaking to a troublesome child. "Look, you have a visitor."

He turned and pointed to the ground where the nightmare slithered. Then, without waiting to see what happened next, he turned and approached Houlihan.

"So, now," he said. "Tell me about the girl."

Thoroughly unnerved by the fact that the nightmare

was loose and might at any moment turn on him, Houlihan fumbled for words: "Oh yes . . . yes . . . the girl. She escaped me in Ninnyhammer. Along with a geshrat called Malingo. Now they're traveling together. And I got close to them again on Soma Plume. But she slipped away among some pilgrim monks."

"So she's escaped you twice? I expect better."

"She has power in her," Houlihan said by way of self-justification.

"Does she indeed?" Carrion said. As he spoke he carefully lifted a second nightmare out of his collar. It spat and hissed. Directing it toward the man in the corner, he let the creature go from his hands, and it wove away to be with its companion. "She must at all costs be apprehended, Otto," Carrion went on. "Do you understand me? *At all costs.* I want to meet her. More than that. *I want to understand her.*"

"How will you do that, Lord?"

"By finding out what's ticking away in that human head of hers. By reading her *dreams*, for one thing. Which reminds me . . . *Lazaru!*"

While he waited for his servant to appear at the door, Carrion brought out yet another nightmare from his collar and loosed it. Houlihan watched as it went to join the others. They had come very close to the man, but had not yet struck. They seemed to be waiting for a word from their master.

The miner was still begging. Indeed he had not ceased begging throughout the entire conversation between Carrion and Houlihan. "Please, Lord," he kept saying. "What have I done to deserve this?"

Carrion finally replied to him. "You've done nothing," he said. "I just picked you out of the crowd today because you were bullying one of your brother miners." He glanced back at his victim. "There's always fear in men who are cruel to other men." Then he looked away again, while the nightmares waited, their tails lashing in anticipation. "Where's Lazaru?" Carrion said.

"Here."

"Find me the dreaming device. You know the one."

"Of course."

"Clean it up. I'm going to need it when the Criss-Cross Man has done his work." His gaze shifted toward Houlihan. "As for you," he said. "Get the chase over with."

"Yes, Lord."

"Capture Candy Quackenbush and bring her to me. Alive."

"I won't fail you."

"You'd better not. If you do, Houlihan, then the next man sitting in that corner will be *you*." He whispered some words in Old Abaratian. "*Thakram noosa rah. Haaas!*"

This was the instruction the nightmares had been waiting for. In a heartbeat they attacked. The man struggled to keep them from climbing up his body, but it was a lost cause. Once they reached his neck they proceeded to wrap their flickering lengths around his head, as though to mummify him. They partially muffled his cries a little, but he could still be heard, his appeals for mercy from Carrion deteriorating into shrieks and screams. As his terror mounted the night-mares grew fatter, giving off brighter and brighter flashes of sickly luminescence as they were nourished. The man continued to kick and struggle for a while, but soon his shrieks declined into sobs and finally even the sobs ceased. So, at last, did his struggle.

"Oh, that's a disappointment," Carrion said, kicking the man's foot to confirm that fear had indeed killed him. "I thought he'd last longer than that."

He spoke again in the old language, and—nourished, now, and slothful—the nightmares unknotted themselves from around their victim's head and began to return to Carrion. Houlihan couldn't help but retreat a step or two in case the nightmares mistook him for another source of food.

"Go on, then," Carrion said to him. "You've got work to do. *Find me Candy Quackenbush!*"

"It's as good as done," Houlihan replied, and without looking back, even a glance, he hurried away from the chamber of terrors and down the stairs of the Twelfth Tower.

PART ONE

FREAKS, FOOLS AND FUGITIVES

Nothing

After a battle lasting many ages,
The Devil won,
And he said to God
(who had been his Maker):
"Lord,
We are about to witness the unmaking of Creation
By my hand.
I would not wish you
to think me cruel,
So I beg you, take three things
From this world before I destroy it.
Three things, and then the rest will be
wiped away."

God thought for a little time.
And at last He said:
"No, there is nothing."
The Devil was surprised.
"Not even you, Lord?" *he said.*
And God said:
"No. Not even me."

—From *Memories of the World's End*
Author unknown
(Christopher Carrion's favorite poem)

1

PORTRAIT OF
GIRL AND GESHRAT

L ET'S GET OUR PHOTOGRAPH taken,"
Candy said to Malingo. They were walking down a
street in Tazmagor, where—this being on the island of
Qualm Hah—it was Nine O'clock in the Morning. The
Tazmagorian market was in full swing, and in the
middle of all this buying and selling a photographer
called Guumat had set up a makeshift studio. He'd hung
a crudely painted backcloth from a couple of poles and
set his camera, a massive device mounted on a polished
wood tripod, in front of it. His assistant, a youth who
shared his father's coxcomb hair and lightly striped
blue-and-black skin, was parading a board on which
examples of Guumat the Elder's photos were pinned.

"You like to be pictured by the great Guumat?" the
youth said to Malingo. "He make you look real good."

Malingo grinned. "How much?"

"Two paterzem," said the father, gently pressing his
offspring aside so as to close the sale.

"For both of us?" Candy said.

"One picture, same price. Two paterzem."

"We can afford that," Candy said to Malingo.

"Maybe you like costumes. Hats?" Guumat asked them, glancing at them up and down. "No extra cost."

"He's politely telling us we look like vagabonds," Malingo said.

"Well, we *are* vagabonds," Candy replied.

Hearing this, Guumat looked suspicious. "You can pay?" he said.

"Yes, of course," said Candy, and dug in the pocket of her brightly patterned trousers, held up with a belt of woven biffel-reeds, and pulled out some coins, sorting through them to give Guumat the paterzem.

"Good! Good!" he said. "Jamjam! Get the young lady a mirror. How old are you?"

"Almost sixteen, why?"

"You wear something much more ladylike, huh? We got nice things. Like I say, no extra charge."

"I'm fine. Thank you. I want to remember this the way it really was." She smiled at Malingo. "Two wanderers in Tazmagor, tired but happy."

"That's what you want, that's what I give you," Guumat said.

Jamjam handed her a little mirror and Candy consulted her reflection. She was a mess, no doubt about it. She'd cut her hair very short a couple of weeks before so she could hide from Houlihan among some monks on Soma Plume, but the haircut had been very hurried, and it was growing out at all angles.

"You look fine," Malingo said.

"So do you. Here, see for yourself."

She handed him the mirror. Her friends back in Chickentown would have thought Malingo's face—with his deep orange hide and the fans of leathery skin to either side of his head—fit only for Halloween. But in the time they'd been traveling together through the islands, Candy had come to love the soul inside that skin: tenderhearted and brave.

Guumat arranged them in front of his camera.

"You need to stand very, very still," he instructed them. "If you move, you'll be blurred in the picture. So, now let me get the camera ready. Give me a minute or two."

"What made you want a photograph?" Malingo said from the corner of his mouth.

"Just to have. So I won't forget anything."

"As if," said Malingo.

"Please," said Guumat. "Be very still. I have to focus."

Candy and Malingo were silent for a moment.

"What are you thinking about?" Malingo murmured.

"Being on Yzil, at Noon."

"Oh yes. That's something we're sure to remember."

"Especially seeing *her* . . ."

"The Princess Breath."

Now, without Guumat requesting it, they both fell silent for a long moment, remembering their brief encounter with the Goddess on the Noon-Day island of Yzil. Candy had seen her first: a pale, beautiful woman in red and orange standing in a patch of warm light, *breathing out* a living creature, a purplish squid.

This, it was said, was the means by which most of the species in the Abarat had been brought into Creation. They had been breathed out by the Creatrix, who had then let the soft wind that constantly blew through the trees and vines of Yzil claim the newborn from her arms and carry them off to the sea.

"That was the most amazing—"

"I'm ready!" Guumat announced from beneath the black cloth he'd ducked under. "On the count of three we take the picture. One! Two! Three! Hold it! Don't move! Don't move! *Seven seconds.*" He lifted his head out from under the cloth and consulted his stopwatch. "Six. Five. Four. Three. Two. One. That's it!" Guumat slipped a plate into his camera to stop the exposure. "Picture taken! Now we have to wait a few minutes while I prepare a print for you."

"No problem," Candy said.

"Are you going down to the ferry?" Jamjam asked her.

"Yes," said Candy.

"You look like you've been on the move."

"Oh, we have," said Malingo. "We've seen a lot in the last few weeks, traveling around."

"I'm jealous. I've never left Qualm Hah. I'd love to go adventuring."

A minute later Jamjam's father appeared with the photograph, which was still wet. "I can sell you a very nice frame, very cheap."

"No, thanks," said Candy. "It's fine like this."

She and Malingo looked at the photograph. The colors weren't quite true, but Guumat caught them looking like a pair of happy tourists, with their brightly colored, rumpled clothes, so they were quite happy.

Photograph in hand, they headed down the steep hill to the harbor and the ferry.

"You know, I've been thinking . . ." Candy said as they made their way through the crowd.

"Uh-oh."

"Seeing the Princess Breath made me want to *learn* more. About magic."

"No, Candy."

"Come on, Malingo! Teach me. You know all about conjurations—"

"A little. Just a little."

"It's more than a little. You told me once that you spent every hour that Wolfswinkel was asleep studying his grimoires and his treatises."

The subject of the wizard Wolfswinkel wasn't often raised between them: the memories were so painful for Malingo. He'd been sold into slavery as a child (by his own father), and his life as Wolfswinkel's possession had been an endless round of beatings and humiliations. It had only been Candy's arrival at the wizard's house that had given him the opportunity to finally escape his enslavement.

"Magic can be dangerous," Malingo said. "There are laws and rules. Suppose I teach you the wrong things and we start to unknit the fabric of time and space? Don't laugh! It's possible. I read in one of Wolfswinkel's books that magic was the beginning of the world. It could be the end too."

Candy looked irritated.

"Don't be cross," Malingo said. "I just don't have the right to teach you things that I don't really understand myself."

Candy walked for a while in silence. "Okay," she said finally.

Malingo cast Candy a sideways glance. "Are we still friends?" he said.

She looked up at him and smiled. "Of course," she said. "Always."

2

WHAT THERE IS TO SEE

AFTER THAT CONVERSATION THEY never mentioned the subject of magic again. They just went on with their island hopping, using the time-honored guide to the islands, *Klepp's Almenak*, as their chief source of information. Every now and again they'd get a feeling that the Criss-Cross Man was closing in on them, and they'd cut short their exploring and move on. About ten days after they'd left Tazmagor, their travels brought them to the island of Orlando's Cap. It was little more than a bare rock with an asylum for the insane built on its highest point. The asylum had been vacated many years before, but its interior bore the unmistakable signs of the madness of its occupants. The white walls were covered with strange scrawlings that here and there became a recognizable image—a lizard, a bird—only to dwindle into scrawlings again.

"What happened to all the people who used to be in here?" Candy wondered.

Malingo didn't know. But they quickly agreed that

this wasn't a spot where they wanted to linger. The asylum had strange, sad echoes. So they went back to the tiny harbor to wait for another boat. There was an old man sitting on the dock, coiling a length of frayed rope. He had the strangest look on his face, his eyes all knotted up, as though he were blind. This wasn't the case, however. As soon as Candy and Malingo arrived, he began to stare at them.

"You shouldn't have come back here," he growled.

"Me?" Malingo said.

"No, not you. Her. *Her!*" He pointed at Candy. "They'll lock you away."

"Who will?"

"*They* will, soon as they know what you are," the man said, getting to his feet.

"You keep your distance," Malingo warned.

"I'm not going to touch her," the man replied. "I'm not that brave. But I see. Oh, I *see.* I know what you are, girl, and I know what you'll do." He shook his head. "Don't you worry, I won't touch you. No sir. I wouldn't do a damn-fool thing like that."

And so saying he edged around them, being sure to keep his distance, and ran off down the creaking dock, disappearing among the rocks.

"Well, I guess that's what happens when you let the crazy folks out," Malingo said with forced brightness.

"What was he seeing?"

"He was crazy, lady."

"No, he really seemed to be seeing something. The way he was staring at me."

Malingo shrugged. "I don't know," he said. He had

his copy of the *Almenak* open and used it to nimbly change the subject. "You know I've always wanted to see Hap's Vault," he said.

"Really?" said Candy, still staring at the rocks where the man had fled. "Isn't it just a cave?"

"Well, this is what Klepp says—" Malingo read aloud from the *Almenak.* "'*Huffaker*'—Hap's Vault's on Huffaker, which is at Nine O'clock in the Evening—'*Huffaker is an impressive island, topographically speaking. Its rock formations—especially those below ground—are both vast and elaborately beautiful, resembling natural cathedrals and temples.*' Interesting, huh? You want to go?"

Candy was still distracted. Her yes was barely audible.

"But listen to this," Malingo went on, doing his best to draw her thoughts away from the old man's talk. "'*The greatest of these is Hap's Vault*' . . . blah, blah, blah . . . '*discovered by Lydia Hap*' . . . blah, blah, blah . . . '*It is Miss Hap who was the first to suggest the Chamber of the Skein.*'"

"What's the Skein?" Candy said, becoming a little more interested now.

"I quote: '*It is the thread that joins all things—living and dead, sentient and unthinking—to all other things—*'"

Now Candy *was* interested. She came to stand beside Malingo, looking at the *Almenak* over his shoulder. He went on reading aloud. "'*According to the persuasive Miss Hap, the thread* originates *in the Vault at Huffaker, appearing momentarily as a kind of flickering light before winding its way invisibly through the Abarat . . . connecting us, one to another.'"* He closed the *Almenak.* "Don't you think we should see this?"

"Why not?"

The island of Huffaker stood just one Hour from the Yebba Dim Day, the first island Candy had ever visited when she'd come to the Abarat. But whereas the great carved head of the Yebba Dim Day still had a few streaks of late light in the sky above it, Huffaker was smothered in darkness, a thick mass of clouds obscuring the stars. Candy and Malingo stayed in a threadbare hotel close to the harbor, where they ate and laid their plans for the journey, and after a few hours of sleep they set out on the dark but well sign-posted road that led to the Vault. They'd had the foresight to pack food and drink, which they needed. The journey was considerably longer than they'd been led to expect by the owner of the hotel, who'd given them some directions. Occasionally they'd hear the sound of an animal pursuing and bringing down another in the murk, but otherwise the journey was uneventful.

When they finally reached the caves themselves, they found that a few of the steep passageways had flaming torches mounted in brackets along the cold walls to illuminate the route. Surprisingly, given how extraordinary the phenomenon sounded, there were no other visitors here to witness it. They were alone as they followed the steeply inclined passageway that led them into the Vault. But they needed no guide to tell them when they had reached their destination.

"Oh Lordy Lou . . ." said Malingo. "Look at this place."

His voice echoed back and forth across the vast cavern they had come into. From its ceiling—which was so far beyond the reach of the torches' light as to be in total darkness—there hung dozens of stalactites. They were immense, each easily the size of an inverted church spire. They were the roosts of Abaratian bats, a detail Klepp had failed to mention in his *Almenak*. The creatures were much larger than any bat Candy had seen in the Abarat, and they boasted a constellation of seven bright eyes.

As for the depths of the cavern, they were as inky black as the ceiling.

"It's so much bigger than I expected it to be," Candy said.

"But where's the Skein?"

"I don't know. Maybe we'll see it if we stand in the middle of the bridge."

Malingo gave her an uneasy look. The bridge that hung over the unfathomable darkness of the Vault didn't look very secure. Its timbers were cracked and antiquated, its ropes frayed and thin.

"Well, we've come *this* far," Candy said. "We may as well see what there is to see."

She set a tentative foot on the bridge. It didn't give way, so she ventured farther. Malingo followed. The bridge groaned and swayed, its boards (which were laid several inches apart) creaking with every step they took.

"Listen . . ." Candy whispered as they reached the middle of the bridge.

Above them they could hear the chittering of a chatty bat. And from far, far below the rushing of water.

"There's a river down there," Candy said.

"The *Almenak* doesn't—"

Before Malingo could finish his sentence, a third voice came out of the darkness and echoed around the Vault.

"As I live and breathe, will you look at that? *Candy Quackenbush!*"

The shout stirred up a few bats. They swooped from their roosts down into the dark air, and in doing so they disturbed hundreds of their siblings, so that in a matter of a few seconds countless bats were on the move; a churning cloud pierced by shifting constellations.

"Was that—?"

"Houlihan?" Candy said. "I'm afraid it was."

She'd no sooner spoken than there was a footfall at the far end of the bridge, and the Criss-Cross Man stepped into the torchlight.

"Finally," he said. "I have you where you cannot run."

Candy glanced back along the bridge. One of Houlihan's stitchling companions had appeared from the shadows and was striding toward them. It was a big, ill-shapen thing, with the teeth of a death's head, and as soon as it set foot on the bridge the frail structure began to sway from side to side. The stitchling clearly liked the sensation, because it proceeded to throw its weight back and forth, making the motion more and more violent. Candy grabbed hold of the railings, and Malingo did the same, but the frayed ropes offered little comfort. They were trapped. Houlihan was now advancing from his end of the bridge. He had taken the flaming torch from the wall and held it ahead of him as he advanced. His face, with its criss-crossed tattoos, was gleaming with sweat and triumph.

Overhead, the cloud of bats continued to swell, as events on the bridge disturbed more and more of them. A few of the largest, intending perhaps to drive out these trespassers, swooped down on Candy and Malingo, letting out shrill shrieks. Candy did her best to ignore them: she was much more concerned with the Criss-Cross Man, who was now no more than seven or eight feet away.

"You're coming with me, girl," he said to her. "Carrion wants to see you in Gorgossium."

He suddenly tossed the torch over the railing, and with both hands free he raced at Candy. She had nowhere left to run. "What now?" he said.

She shrugged. Desperate, she looked around at Malingo. "We may as well see—"

"What is there to see?" he replied.

She smiled, the tiniest smile, and then, without even glancing up at their pursuers again, they both threw themselves headfirst over the rope railing.

As they plunged into the darkness, Malingo let out

a wild whoop of exhilaration, or perhaps fear, perhaps both. Seconds passed, and still they fell and fell and fell. And now everything was dark around them and the shrieking of the bats was gone, erased by the noise of the river below.

Candy had time to think: *If we hit the water at this speed we'll break our necks,* and then suddenly Malingo had hold of her hand, and using some trick of acrobatics he'd learned hanging upside down from Wolfswinkel's ceiling, he managed to flip them both over, so that they were now falling feet first.

Two, three, four seconds later, they hit the water.

It wasn't cold. At least not icy. Their speed carried them deep, however, and the impact separated them. For Candy there was a panicky moment when she thought she'd used up all her breath. Then—God bless him!—Malingo had hold of her hand again, and gasping for air, they broke surface together.

"No bones broken?" Candy gasped.

"No. I'm fine. You?"

"No," she said, scarcely believing it. "I thought he had us."

"So did I. So did *he.*"

Candy laughed.

They looked up, and for a moment she thought she glimpsed the dark ragged line of the bridge high above. Then the river's current carried them away, and whatever she'd seen was eclipsed by the roof of the cavern through which these waters ran. They had no choice but to go wherever it was going. Darkness was all around them, so the only clues they had to the size of caverns through which the river traveled was the way the water grew more tempestuous when the channel narrowed, and how its rushing din mellowed when the way widened again.

Once, for just a few tantalizing seconds, they caught a glimpse of what looked like a bright thread— like the Skein of Lydia Hap's account—running through the air or the rock above them.

"Did you see that?" Malingo said.

"Yes," said Candy, smiling in the darkness. "I saw it."

"Well, at least we saw what we came to see."

It was impossible to judge the passage of time in such a formless place, but some while after their glimpsing of the Skein they caught sight of another light, a long way ahead: a luminescence which steadily grew brighter as the river carried them toward it.

"That's starlight," Candy said.

"You think so?"

She was right; it was. After a few more minutes, the river finally brought them out of Huffaker's caverns and into that quiet time just after nightfall. A fine net of cloud had been cast over the sky, and the stars caught in it were turning the Izabella silver.

Their journey by water wasn't over, however. The river current quickly carried them too far from the dark cliffs of Huffaker to attempt to swim back to it and bore them out into the straits between Nine and Ten O'clock. Now the Izabella took charge, her waters holding them up without their needing to exert themselves with swimming. They were carried effortlessly out past Ninnyhammer (where the lights burned bright in the cracked dome of Kaspar Wolfswinkel's house) and south, into the light, to the bright, tropical waters that surrounded the island of the Nonce. The sleepy smell of an endless afternoon came off the island, which stood at Three O'clock, and the breeze carried dancing seeds from the lush slopes of that Hour. But the Nonce was not to be their destination. The Izabella's currents carried them on past the Afternoon to the vicinity of the island of Gnomon.

Before they could be delivered to the shores of that island, however, Malingo caught sight of their salvation.

"I see a sail!" he said, and started yelling to whoever might be up on deck. "Over here! *Here!*"

"They see us!" Candy said. "They see us!"

3

ON THE *PARROTO PARROTO*

THE LITTLE VESSEL MALINGO'S sharp eyes had spotted wasn't moving, so they were able to let the gentle current carry them toward it. It was a humble fishing boat no more than fifteen feet in length and in a very dilapidated condition. Its crew members were hard at work hauling up onto the deck a net full to bursting with tens of thousands of small mottled turquoise-and-orange fish, called smatterlings. Hungry seabirds, raucous and aggressive, wheeled around the boat or bobbed on the water close by, waiting to snatch up those smatterlings that the fishermen failed to get out of the net, onto the deck and into the hold of their boat quickly enough.

By the time Candy and Malingo were within hailing distance of the little vessel, most of the hard labor was over, and the happy crew members (there were only four on the boat) were singing a song of the sea as they folded the nets.

> *"Fishes, feed me!*
> *Fishes fine!*
> *Swim in the nets*
> *And catch the line!*
> *Feed my children!*
> *Fill my dishes!*
> *That's why I love you,*
> *Little fishes!"*

When they were done with the song, Malingo called to them from out of the water.

"Excuse me!" he yelled. "There are still two more fishes down here!"

"I see you!" said a young man among the crew.

"Throw them a line," said the wiry bearded man in the wheelhouse, who was apparently the Captain.

It didn't take very long for Candy and Malingo to be brought up over the side of the boat and onto the stinking deck.

"Welcome aboard the *Parroto Parroto*," said the Captain. "Somebody get 'em some blankets, will you?"

Though the sun was still reasonably warm in this region between Four O'clock in the Afternoon and Five, their time in the water had chilled both Candy and Malingo to the bone, and they were glad of the blankets and the deep bowls of spicy fish soup that they were given a few minutes later.

"I'm Perbo Skebble," said the Captain. "The old man is Mizzel, the cabin girl is Galatea, and the young fellow there is my son Charry. We're from Efreet, and we're heading back there with our hold full."

"Good fishin'," Charry said. He had a broad, happy face, which fell naturally into an expression of easy contentment.

"There'll be consequences," Mizzel said, his own features as naturally joyless as Charry's were naturally happy.

"Why do you always have to be so *grim*?" Galatea said, staring contemptuously at Mizzel. Her hair was shaved so close to her scalp, it was little more than a shadow. Her muscular arms were decorated with elaborate tattoos. "Didn't we just save two souls from drowning? We're all on the Creatrix' side on this boat. Nothing bad's going to happen to us."

Mizzel just sneered at her, rudely snatching the empty soup bowls from Candy and Malingo. "We've still got to get past Gorgossium," he said as he headed down into the galley with the bowls. He cast a sly, faintly threatening glance back at Candy as he departed, as though to see whether he'd succeeded in sowing the seeds of fear in her.

"What did he mean by that?" Malingo said.

"Nothing," said Skebble.

"Oh, let's tell the truth here," said Galatea. "We're not going to lie to these people. That would be shameful."

"Then you tell 'em," Skebble said. "Charry, come, lad. I want to be sure the catch is properly stowed."

"What's the problem?" Candy said to Galatea, when the father and son had gone about their work.

"You have to understand that there's no ice on this boat, so we've got to get the catch back to Efreet before the fish go rotten on us. Which means . . . let me show you."

She led them to the wheelhouse, where there was an old and much-weathered map pinned up on the wall. She pointed a well-bitten fingernail at a place between the islands of Soma Plume and Gnomon.

"We're about here," she said. "And we've got to get . . . up to here." Their destination lay past the Twenty-Fifth Hour, way to the north of the archipelago. "If we had more time, we'd take the long way back, hugging the coast of Gnomon and then passing the Nonce and heading north between Ninnyhammer and Jibarish, and rounding the Twenty-Fifth till we get back to our village."

The Twenty-Fifth, Candy thought: she'd been there briefly with the women of the Fantomaya. She'd seen all kinds of visions, including one that she'd dreamed of many times since: a woman walking on a sky full of birds, while fish swam in the watery heavens around her head.

"There's no chance you could drop us off at the Twenty-Fifth, is there?" Candy said.

But even as she spoke she remembered the dark side of life on the Twenty-Fifth. She'd been pursued there by a pair of monsters called the Fugit Brothers, whose features moved around their faces on clicking legs.

"You know what?" she said. "Maybe that's not such a good idea after all."

"Well, we can't do it anyway," Galatea told her. "It'll take too long. The fish'll rot."

"So which way are we going?" Malingo said.

Candy had guessed already, from looking at the map.

"We're going between the Pyramids of Xuxux and Gorgossium."

Galatea grinned. Every other tooth in her mouth was missing. "You should be a-fishing, you should," she said. "Yep, that's where we're going. Mizzel thinks it's a bad plan. He says there's all manner of things that live on the island of Midnight. Monsterosities, he says. Horridy things that will come flapping over and attack the ship."

"Why would they do that?" Candy asked.

"Because they want to eat the fish. Or else they want to eat us. Maybe both. I don't know. Whatever it is, it ain't good news. Anyhow, we can't be squibbies about this—"

"Squibbies?" said Candy.

"Cowards," Malingo said.

"We gotta sail past Midnight whether we like it or not," Galatea went on. "Either that or we lose the fish, and a lot of people will go hungry."

"Not a good choice," said Skebble as he climbed out of the hold. "But like the girl says, we got no choice. And . . . 'fraid you got no choice but to come with us. Either that or we dumps you in the water again."

"I think we'd rather stay on board," Candy said, giving Malingo an anxious look.

They headed north, out of the bright afternoon waters of the straits between Four and Five into the dark seas that surrounded Midnight. It wasn't a subtle change. One minute the Sea of Izabella was glittering with golden sunlight and they were warm; the next, waves of darkness covered the sun and a bitter cold swept in to surround them. Off to their port side they could see the immense island of Gorgossium. Even from a considerable distance they could pick out the windows of the thirteen towers of the fortress of Iniquisit and the lights that burned around the Todo mines.

"You want a closer look?" said Mizzel to Candy.

He passed her his battered old telescope, and she studied the island through it. There seemed to be immense heads carved from some of the stony outcrops of the island. Something that looked like a wolf's head, something that looked vaguely human. But far more chilling were the vast insects she saw crawling around the island: like fleas or lice grown to the size of trucks. They made her shudder, even at such a safe distance.

"Not a pretty place, is it?" Skebble said.

"No, not really," said Candy.

"Plenty of folks like it though," the Captain went on. "If you've got a darkness in your heart, that be the place you go, huh? That be the place you feel *at home*."

"Home . . ." Candy murmured.

Malingo was standing beside her and heard her speak the word.

"Homesick?" he said.

"No. *No*. Well . . . sometimes. A little. Just about my mom, really. But no, that wasn't what I was thinking." She nodded toward Gorgossium. "It's just strange to think of somebody calling that dismal place their home."

"*Each to their Hour,* as the poet wrote," Malingo said.

"Which is your Hour?" Candy asked him. "Where do you belong?"

"I don't know," Malingo said sadly. "I lost my family a long time ago—or at least they lost me—and I don't expect to see them again in this life."

"We could try and find them for you."

"One day, maybe." He dropped his voice to a whisper. "When we don't have so many teeth nipping at our heels."

There was a sudden explosion of laughter from the wheelhouse, which brought the conversation to an end. Candy wandered over to see what was going on. There was a small television (which had red curtains to either side of the screen, like a little theater) placed on the floor. Mizzel, Charry and Galatea were watching it, much entertained by the antics of a cartoon boy.

"It's the Commexo Kid!" Charry said. "He's so wild!"

Candy had seen the Kid's image many times now. It was hard to go very far in the Abarat without meeting his perpetually smiling face on a billboard or a wall. His antics and his catchphrases were used to sell everything from cradles to coffins, and all that anybody would want in between. Candy watched the flickering blue screen for a little while, thinking back to her encounter with the man who had created the character: Rojo Pixler. She'd met him on Ninnyhammer, briefly, and in the many weeks since she'd half expected to see him again at some turn in the road. He was part of her future, she knew, though she didn't know how or why.

On screen the Kid was playing tricks, as usual, much to the amusement of his little audience. It was simple, knockabout stuff. Paint was spattered; food was thrown. And through it all jogged the relentlessly cheerful figure of the Commexo Kid, dispensing smiles, pies and "just a li'l bit o' love" (as he would round off every show saying) to the world.

"Hey, Miss Misery," said Mizzel, glancing around at Candy. "You don't laugh!"

"I just don't think it's very funny, that's all."

"He's the best!" Charry said. "Lordy Lou, the things he says!"

"Happy! Happy! Happy!" said Galatea, perfectly copying the Kid's squeaky voice. *"That's what I is! Happy! Happy! Hap—"*

She was interrupted by a panicked shout from Malingo. "We've got *trouble!*" he yelled. *"And it's coming from Gorgossium!"*

4

THE SCAVENGERS

CANDY WAS THE FIRST out of the wheelhouse and back on deck. Malingo had Mizzel's telescope to his eye and was studying the threatening skies in the direction of Gorgossium. There were four dark-winged creatures flying toward the fishing boat. They were visible because their innards glowed through their translucent flesh, as though lit by some bitter fire. They gibbered as they approached, the chatter of mad, hungry things.

"What are they?" Candy said.

"They're zethekaratchia," Mizzel informed her. "Zethek for short. The ever-hungry ones. They can never eat enough. That's why we can see their bones."

"Not good news," Candy guessed.

"Not good news."

"They'll take the fish!" Skebble said, appearing from the bowels of the ship. He'd apparently been attending to the engine, because he was covered with oil stains and carried a large hammer and an even more sizeable wrench.

"Lock down the holds!" he yelled to his little crew. *"Quickly, or we'll lose all the fish!"* He pointed a stubby finger at Malingo and Candy. *"That means you as well!"*

"If they can't get to the fish, won't they come after us?" Malingo said.

"We have to save the fish," Skebble insisted. He caught hold of Malingo's arm and pressed him toward the brimming holds. "Don't argue!" he said. "I don't want to lose the catch! And they're getting closer!"

Candy followed his gaze skyward. The zethek were less than ten yards from the boat now, swooping down over the twilight sea to begin their scavenging. Candy didn't like the idea of trying to protect herself against them unarmed, so she grabbed hold of the wrench in Skebble's left hand. "If you don't mind, I'll take that!" she said, surprising even herself.

"Take it!" he said, and went to help the rest of the crew with the labor of closing the holds.

Candy headed for the ladder on the side of the wheelhouse. She put the wrench between her teeth (not a pleasant experience: it tasted of fish oil and Skebble's sweat) and clambered up the ladder, turning to face the zethek once she reached the top. The sight of her standing on the wheelhouse, the wrench in her hand like a club, had put a little doubt in them. They were no longer swooping down on the *Parroto Parroto* but hovering ten or twelve feet above it.

"Come on down!" Candy yelled to them. "I dare you!"

"Are you crazy?" Charry hollered.

"Get down!" Malingo called to her. *"Candy, get—"*

Too late! The closest zethek took Candy's bait and swooped down, its long, bone-bright fingers reaching to snatch at her head.

"Good boy!" she said. "Look what I've got for you."

She swung the wrench in a wide arc. The tool was heavy, and in truth she had very little control over it, so it was more by accident than intention that she actually struck the creature. That said, it was quite a blow. The zethek dropped out of the sky as if shot, striking the boards of the wheelhouse so hard they cracked.

For a second he lay still.

"You killed him!" said Galatea. "Ha-ha! Good for you!"

"I . . . don't *think* he's dead. . . ." Candy said.

What Galatea couldn't hear, Candy could. The zethek was *growling*. Very slowly he raised his gargoylish head. Dark blood ran from his nose.

"You . . . hurt . . . me. . . ."

"Well, come over here," Candy said, beckoning to the beast across the fractured boards of the roof. "I'll do it again."

"The girl's suicidal," Mizzel remarked.

"Your friend is right," the zethek said. "You *are* suicidal."

Having spoken, the zethekaratchia opened his mouth *and kept opening it, wider and wider*, until it was literally large enough to bite off the top of Candy's head. In fact, that seemed to be his intention, because he lunged forward, leaping across the hole in the roof and throwing Candy down on her back. Then he jumped on top of her. The wrench flew out of her hand; she had no time to pick it up. The zethek was upon her, his mouth vast—

She closed her eyes as a cloud of the beast's breath broke against her face. She had seconds to live. And then suddenly Skebble was there, hammer in hand.

"Leave the girl alone," he hollered, and brought the hammer down on the zethek's skull, delivering it such a calamitous blow that he simply fell backward into the wheelhouse through the hole in the roof, dead.

"That was brave, girl," he said, hauling Candy to her feet.

She patted the top of her head just to be sure it was still there. It was.

"One down," said Candy. "Three to—"

"Help, somebody!" Mizzel yelled. *"Help!"*

Candy turned around to find that another of these wretched things had caught hold of Mizzel and was pinning him to the deck, preparing to make a meal of him.

"No, you don't!" she yelled, and ran for the ladder.

Only when she was halfway down did she remember that she'd left the wrench on the roof. It was too late to go back for it.

The deck, when she reached it, was slick with fish oil and water, and instead of running she found herself sliding over it, completely out of control. She hollered for someone to stop her, but there was no one close enough. Straight ahead was the hold, its door already

opened by one of the beasts. Her only hope of stopping herself was to reach out and grab the zethek that
was assaulting Mizzel. But she'd have to be quick,
before the opportunity slid by. She put out her hand
and made a grab for the beast. The zethek saw her
coming and turned to ward her off, but he wasn't fast
enough: she caught hold of his hair. He squawked like
an enraged macaw and struggled to free himself, but
Candy held on. Unfortunately, her momentum was too
great to bring her to a halt. Quite the reverse. Instead,
the creature came along with her, reaching up to try
and untangle her fingers from his ratty locks even as
they both slid toward the gaping hold.

Over the edge they went and down among the fish.
Luckily it wasn't a long fall; the hold was almost filled
with smatterlings. But it wasn't a pleasant landing, a
thousand fish sliding beneath them, cold and wet and
very dead.

Candy still had her grip on the zethek's hair, so that
when the creature stood up—which he did instantly—
she was hauled to her feet too.

The creature wasn't used to being held by anybody,
especially some scrap of a girl. He writhed and raged,
snapping at her with his over-sized mouth one
moment, the next attempting to shrug her loose by
shaking his body so violently that his bones clattered.

Finally, apparently despairing of escape, the zethek
called to his surviving comrades: *"Kud! Nattum!
Here! In the hold! Now!"*

A few seconds after the call had gone out, Kud and
Nattum appeared over the edge of the hold.

"Methis!" Nattum said, grinning. "You have a girl for me!"

So saying, he opened his mouth and inhaled so powerfully that Candy had to fight to keep herself from being pulled straight into the maw.

Kud wasn't interested in such tricks. He shoved Nattum aside. "I take her!" he said. "I'm hungry."

Nattum shoved back.

"So am I!" he growled.

While she was being fought over, Candy took the opportunity to yell for help.

"Somebody! *Malingo? Charry?*"

"Too late," said Kud, and leaning over the edge of the hold he caught hold of her and pulled her up. He was so quick and violent that Candy lost her grip on Methis. Her feet slid over the slimy fish for a moment; then she was in the air, being hauled toward Kud's mouth, which now also opened like a toothed tunnel.

The next moment everything went dark. Her head—much to her horror—was in the mouth of the beast.

5

THE SPEAKING OF A WORD

THOUGH HER ENTIRE SKULL was suddenly enclosed by the zethek's mouth, Candy was still able to hear one thing from the outside world. Just one stupid thing. It was the squeaking voice of the Commexo Kid, singing his eternally optimistic little song.

"Happy! Happy! Happy!" it squealed.

She offered up a little prayer in that dark moment, to ask any God or Goddess, of Abarat or the Hereafter, who would listen. It was a very simple prayer. It simply said: *Please don't let that ridiculous Kid be the last thing I hear before I die—*

And, thank the divinities, her prayer was answered.

There was a dull thud directly above her, and she felt the tension of Kud's jaws relax. She instantly pulled her head out of his mouth. This time the slickness of the fish beneath her was to her advantage. She slid across the carpet of smatterlings in time to see Kud collapse among the fish. She took her eyes off him and looked up at her savior.

It was Malingo. He was standing there with Skebble's hammer in his hand. He smiled at Candy. But his moment of triumph was short. In the next instant Kud rose up roaring from his slimy bed of fish and pulled the legs out from under Malingo, who fell down on his back.

"Ah-*ha*!" Kud yelled, laying eyes on the hammer that slipped out of Malingo's hand when he fell. Kud snatched it up and got to his feet. The brightness in his bones had become a furious blaze in the last few minutes. In the sockets of his skull, two dots of scarlet rage flickered as he turned his stare toward Candy. He looked like something from a ghost-train ride. Wielding the hammer, he raced at Candy.

"*Run!*" Malingo yelled.

But she had nowhere to run to. There was a zethek to the left of her and one to the right, and behind her a solid wall. A skeletal smile spread over Kud's face.

"Any last words?" he said as he lifted the hammer above his head.

"Come on," he growled. "You must have something in your head."

Curiously, she did have something in her head: a word she could not even remember hearing until this moment—

Kud seemed to see the confusion in her eyes.

"*Speak!*" he said, striking the wall to the left of her head with the hammer. The reverberations echoed all around the hold. The dead smatterlings convulsed, as though they'd been given a spasm of life. "*Talk to me!*" Kud said, striking the wall to the right of

Candy's head. Showers of sparks erupted from the spot, and the fish jumped a second time.

Candy put her hand up to her throat. There was a word there. She could feel it, like something she'd eaten but not quite swallowed. It wanted to be spoken. That she was certain about. *It wanted to be spoken.*

And who was she to deny it its ambitions? She let the syllables rise up, unbidden. And spoke them.

"Jassassakya-thüm!"

she said.

From the corner of her eye she saw Malingo sit bolt upright on the bed of fish.

"Oh Lordy Lou . . ." he said, his voice hushed with awe. "How do you know that word?"

"I don't," Candy said.

But the *air* knew it. The *walls* knew it. No sooner were the syllables out of her lips than everything began to vibrate in response to the sound of whatever Candy had said. And with each vibration the air and the walls repeated the syllables in their own strange fashion.

> *Jassassakya-thüm!*
> *Jassassakya-thüm!*
> *Jassassakya-thüm!*

"What . . . have . . . you . . . done . . . girl?" Kud said.

Candy didn't know. Malingo, on the other hand, did.

"She's uttered a Word of Power," he said.

"I have?" Candy replied. "I mean, *I have*. That's what I've done."

"Magic?" Kud said. He began to retreat from her now, the hammer sliding out of his fingers. "I knew there was something about you from the beginning. You're a witch-girl! That's what you are! A witch-girl!"

As the zethek's panic grew, so did the reverberations. With each repetition they gathered strength.

Jassassakya-thüm!
Jassassakya-thüm!
Jassassakya-thüm!

"I think you should get out of here now," Malingo yelled to Candy as the din climbed.

"What?"

"I said: *Get out! Out!*"

As he spoke he stumbled toward her through the fish, which were also vibrating in rhythm with the words. The zetheks paid no attention to him, nor to Candy. They were suffering from the effects of the word. They had their hands clamped over their ears, as though they were afraid it was deafening them, which perhaps it was.

"This is *not* a safe place to be," Malingo said when he got to Candy's side.

She nodded. She was beginning to feel the distressing influence of the vibrations herself. Galatea was there to lift her up onto the deck. Then both girls turned to help Malingo, reaching down to catch hold of his long arms. Candy counted:

"One, two, three—"

And they hauled together, lifting him up with surprising ease.

The scene in the hold had become surreal. The Word was making the catch vibrate so violently that at first glance the fish seemed to be alive again. As for the zethek, they were like three flies caught in a jar, propelled back and forth across the hold, slamming against the sides. They seemed to have forgotten all about the possibility of escape. The word had made them crazy, or stupid, or both.

Skebble was standing on the opposite side of the hold. He pointed to Candy and yelled at her: *"Make it stop!* Or you're going to shake my boat apart!"

He was right about the boat. The vibrations in the hold had spread throughout the vessel. The boards were shaking so violently nails were being spat into the air, the already cracked wheelhouse was rocking to and fro, the rigging was vibrating like the strings of a huge guitar; even the mast was swaying.

Candy looked over at Malingo.

"See?" she said. "If you'd taught me some magic I'd know how to turn this *off.*"

"Well, wait," Malingo said. "Where did you learn that word?"

"I didn't learn it."

"You must have heard it somewhere."

"No. I swear. It just appeared in my throat. I don't know where it came from."

"If you two have quite finished chatting?" Skebble hollered over the din. "My boat—"

"Yes!" Candy shouted back. "I know, I know!"

"Inhale it!" Malingo said.

"What?"

"*The Word!* Inhale the Word!"

"Inhale it?"

"Do as he says!" Galatea yelled. "Before the boat sinks!"

Everything was now shaking to the rhythm of the Word. There wasn't a board or a rope or a hook from bow to stern that wasn't in motion. In the hold the three zetheks were still being pitched around, sobbing for mercy.

Candy closed her eyes. Strangely enough, she could *see* the word that she'd uttered in her mind's eye. There it was, clear as crystal.

Jass . . . assa . . . kya . . . thüm . . .

She emptied her lungs through her nostrils. Then, still keeping her eyes tightly shut, she drew a deep breath.

The word in her mind's eye *shook.* Then it cracked, and it seemed to fly apart. Was it just her imagination, or could she feel it coming back into her throat? She swallowed hard, and the word was gone.

The reaction was instantaneous. The vibrations died away. The boards dropped back into place, peppered by nails. The mast stopped lurching to and fro. The fish stopped their grotesque cavorting.

The zetheks quickly realized that the attack had ceased. They unstopped their ears and shook their heads, as though to put their thoughts back in order.

"Go, brothers!" Nattum said. "Before the witch-girl tries some new trick!"

He didn't wait to see that his siblings were doing as he suggested. He started to beat his wings furiously and climbed into the air, weaving a zigzag course skyward. Methis was about to follow; then he turned to Kud.

"Let's ruin their catch!"

Skebble let out a howl of complaint. *"No!"* he yelled. *"Don't—"*

His cry was ignored. The two creatures squatted down among the fish, and the vilest smell Candy had ever smelled in her life rose up from the hold.

"Are they—?"

Malingo nodded grimly.

"The catch! The catch!" Skebble was howling. "Oh, Lord, no! No!"

Methis and Kud thought all this was hugely amusing. Having done their worst, they beat their wings and lifted off.

"Damn you! Damn you!" Skebble yelled as they flew past.

"That was enough fish to feed the village for half a season," Galatea said mournfully.

"And they poisoned it?" Malingo said.

"What do you think? Smell that stink. Who could ever eat something that smelled like that?"

Kud had by now escaped into the darkness, following Nattum back to Gorgossium. But Methis was so busy laughing at what they'd just done that he accidentally clipped the top of the mast with his wing. For a moment he struggled to recover himself but lost his momentum and fell back toward the *Parroto Parroto*, hitting the edge of the wheelhouse roof and bouncing off onto the deck, where he lay unconscious.

There was a moment of surprised silence from everybody on deck. The whole sequence of events— from Candy's speaking of the Word to Methis' crash—had taken at most a couple of minutes.

It was old Mizzel who broke the hush.

"Charry?" he said.

"Yes?"

"Get a rope. And you, Galatea, help him. Tie up this burden of filth."

"What for?"

"Just do it!" Mizzel said. "And be quick about it, before the damn thing wakes up!"

6

TWO CONVERSATIONS

"So," said Mizzel, once the stunned zethek was firmly secured. "You want to know my plan?"

They were all sitting at the bow of the boat, as far from the stink of the hold as they could get. Candy was still in a mild state of shock: what she'd just witnessed herself doing (speaking a word she didn't even know she knew) needed to be thought about very carefully. But now was not the time to do the thinking. Mizzel had a plan, and he wanted to share it.

"We're going to have to dump out all the smatterlings. Every last fish."

"A lot of people are going to go hungry," Galatea said.

"Not necessarily," Mizzel replied. He had a sly expression on his scarred and weatherworn face. "To the west of us lies the island of Six O'clock. . . ."

"Babilonium," Candy said.

"Precisely. Babilonium. The Carnival Island. Masques and parades and fairs and bug wrestling and music and dancing and *freaks*."

"Freaks?" said Galatea. "What kind of freaks?"

"Every kind. Things that are too small, things that are too large, things with three heads, things with no head at all. If you want to see freaks and monsters, then Babilonium's the place to find them."

While the old man was speaking, Skebble had gotten up and gone to the door to study the bound zethek.

"Have you *seen* these freak shows on Babilonium?" he said to Mizzel.

"Certainly. I worked in Babilonium in my youth. Made a lot of money too."

"Doing what?" said Galatea.

Mizzel looked a little uncomfortable. "I don't want to go into details," he said. "Let me just say it involved . . . um, bodily gases . . . and flame."

Nobody said anything for a moment or two. Then Charry piped up. "You farted fire?" he said.

Everybody subdued their amusement with a great effort of will. All except for Skebble, who let out a whoop of laughter. "You did!" he said. "You did, didn't you?"

"It was a living," Mizzel said, staring fiercely at Charry, his ears bright red. "Now can I *please* get on with my story?"

"Go on," said Skebble. "Get to the point."

"Well, it seems to me if we could sail this damn boat to Babilonium, we would sure as certain find somebody to buy that zethek and put him in one of them freak shows."

"Would we make much money from a deal like that?"

"We'll make sure we do. And when we've done the

deal we'll sail to Tazmagor, get the hold scrubbed out and *buy* a new supply of fish."

"What do you think?" Candy said to Skebble.

He glanced out at the bound creature, scratching at his tatty beard.

"No harm in trying," he replied.

"Babilonium, huh?" Candy said.

"What, you have a problem with this?" Skebble said testily. It had been a grim and eventful couple of hours. He was obviously weary, his energies exhausted. "If you don't want to come with us—"

"No, no, we'll come," said Candy. "I've never been to Babilonium."

"The playground of the Abarat!" Malingo said. "Fun for all the family!"

"Well, then . . . what are we waiting for?" said Galatea. "We can dump the smatterlings as we go!"

By chance Otto Houlihan was on Gorgossium at that time, waiting for an audience with the Lord of Midnight. It was not an appetizing prospect. He was going to have to report that though he came very close to capturing the girl in Hap's Vault he had failed, and that she and her geshrat companion had most likely thrown themselves to their deaths. The news would not make Carrion happy, he knew. This made Houlihan nervous. He remembered all too well the feeding of the nightmares he'd witnessed in the Twelfth Tower. He didn't want to die the same way as the wretched miner had died. In an attempt to put these troubling thoughts from his mind, he slipped away to a little inn called The Fool in Chains where he could drink some Hobarookian vodka. Perhaps it was time—he thought as he drank—to cease his life as a hunter and find a less risky means of making money. As a bug-wrestling promoter, perhaps; or a knife juggler. Anything, as long as he never had to come back to Gorgossium and *wait.* . . .

His clammy meditations were interrupted by the sound of laughter from outside. He staggered out to see what all the fuss was about. Several customers, many in states of inebriation as bad or worse than his own, were standing in a rough circle, pointing to something on the ground in their midst.

The Criss-Cross Man went to see. There in the dirt was one of the uglier occupants of Gorgossium: a large zethek. He had apparently collided with a tree and had fallen to earth, under which he was now standing, looking very confused, picking leaves out of his hair and spitting out dirt. The drunkards just kept laughing at him.

"Go on, *laugh at me!*" the creature said. "Kud seen a thing you be way afraid of. A terrible thing I seen."

"Oh yeah?" said one of the drunks. "And what was that?"

Kud spat out one last mouthful of dirt. *"A witch-girl,"* he said. *"Does bad magic on me. Almost kills me with her Word."*

Houlihan elbowed his way through the crowd and grabbed hold of the zethek's wing so that he wouldn't try to escape. Then he peered into his broken, confounded face. "You said you *fought* with this girl?" he said.

"Yes."

"Was she alone?"

"No. She was with a geshrat."

"You're sure?"

"You saying I don't know what a geshrat looks like? I've been drinking their blood since I was a baby."

"Never mind about the geshrat. Talk to me about the girl."

"Don't shake me! I will not be shaken. I'm—"

"Kud the zethek. Yes, I heard. And I'm Otto Houlihan, the Criss-Cross Man."

The moment Houlihan offered up his name, the crowd that had been pressing around Kud suddenly melted away.

"I've heard of you," Kud said. "You're dangerous."

"Not to my friends," Otto replied. "You want to be my friend, Kud?"

The zethek took but a moment to think on this.

"Of course," the creature said, bowing his head respectfully.

"Good," said the Criss-Cross Man. "Then back to the girl. Did you catch her name?"

"The geshrat called her—" He frowned. "What was it? Mandy? Dandy?"

"Candy?"

"Candy! Yes! He called her Candy!"

"And on what island did you last see this girl?"

"No island," Kud replied. "I saw her on a boat, out there—" He pointed behind him, toward the lightless waters of the Izabella. "You go after her?"

"Why?"

Kud looked nervous. "Magic in her," he said. "Monstrous. She's monstrous."

Houlihan didn't remark on the oddity of a creature like Kud calling Candy a monster. He simply said: "Where do I find her?"

"Follow your nose. We spoiled their catch by befouling their hold."

"Very sophisticated," Houlihan said, and turned his back on the befuddled beast to consider his options. If he stayed on Gorgossium he would eventually be admitted into Carrion's presence and be obliged to explain how once again the girl had outmaneuvered him. The alternative was to leave Midnight and hope he would be able to find Candy and get some answers *from* her *before* Carrion summoned him back and demanded answers. Yes! That was better. A lot better.

"Are you finished with me?" the zethek growled.

Houlihan glanced back at the wretched thing.

"Yes, yes. Go," he said. "I've got work to do, following your *stink*."

7

SOMETHING OF BABILONIUM

THE SHORT VOYAGE TO the Carnival Island quickly took the *Parroto Parroto* out of the darkness that surrounded Gorgossium. A golden glow on the horizon marked their destination, and the closer they came to it the more boats appeared in the waters around the little fishing boat, all making their way west. Even the most unremarkable of vessels was decorated with flags and lights and streamers, and all were filled with happy people on their way to celebrate on the island ahead.

Candy sat in the bow of the *Parroto Parroto*, watching the other vessels and listening to the singing and the shouts that echoed across the water.

"I don't see Babilonium yet," she said to Malingo. "All I see is mist."

"But do you see the lights in that mist?" Malingo said. "That's Babilonium for sure!" He grinned like an excited kid. "I can't wait! I read about the Carnival Island in Wolfswinkel's books. Everything you ever wanted to see or do, it's there! In the old days, people used to come over from the Hereafter just to spend time in Babilonium. They'd go back with their heads so stuffed with the things they saw, they had to make up new words to describe it."

"Like what?"

"Oh. Let me see. *Phantasmagoric. Cathartic. Pandemonical.*"

"I never heard of *pandemonical.*"

"I made that one up." Malingo smirked. "But there were hundreds of words, all inspired by Babilonium."

As he spoke, the mist began to thin out and the island it had been concealing came into view: a glittering, chaotic conglomeration of tents and banners, roller coasters and sideshows.

"Oh. My. Lordy. Lou," Malingo said softly. "Will you look at that?"

Even Charry and Galatea, who were working on building a makeshift cage of timbers and rope to contain the captured zethek, stopped work to admire the spectacle.

And the closer the *Parroto Parroto* came to the island, the more extraordinary the sight seemed to be. Despite the fact that the Hour was still early and the sky was still light (showing just a few stars), the lanterns and lamps and myriad little fires on the island burned so brightly that they still made the island shimmer with their light. And by that light the crowds could be seen, busy about the happy labor of pleasure. Candy could hear their contented buzz, even over a considerable expanse of water, and it made her heart quicken with anticipation. What were these people seeing that made them so giddy with bliss? They chatted, they whooped, they sang, they laughed; more than anything they laughed, as though they'd only just learned how.

"This is all *real*, isn't it?" Candy said to Malingo. "I mean, it isn't a mirage or something?"

"Your guess is as good as mine, lady," Malingo said. "I mean, I've always assumed it was perfectly real, but I've been wrong before. Oh . . . speaking of that . . . of being wrong, if you're still interested in learning whatever magic I got out of Wolfswinkel's books, I'd be happy to teach you."

"What made you change your mind?"

"What do you think? The Word of Power you uttered."

"Oh, you mean *Jass*—"

Malingo put his finger to Candy's lips. "No, lady. Don't."

Candy smiled. "Oh yes. That might spoil the moment."

"You see, what did I tell you in Tazmagor? There are laws to magic."

"And you can teach me those laws? At least some of them. Stop me from making a bad mistake."

"I suppose I could try," Malingo conceded. "Though it seems to me you may know more than you think you know."

"But how? I'm just—"

"—an ordinary girl from the Hereafter. Yes, so you keep saying."

"You don't believe me?"

"Lady, I don't know any other ordinary girls from the Hereafter besides you, but I'd be willing to bet none of them could take on three zetheks and come out the winner!"

Candy thought of the girls in her class. Deborah Hackbarth, Ruth Ferris. Malingo was right. It was very hard to imagine any one of them standing in her shoes right now.

"All right," she said. "Supposing I *am* different, somehow? What made me that way?"

"That, lady, is a *very* good question," Malingo replied.

After much maneuvering through the flotillas of boats and ferries and people on water bicycles that thronged the harbor, Skebble brought the *Parroto Parroto* in to dock at Babilonium. Though the catch had been dumped in the straits several miles back, the stink of the zetheks had permeated their clothes, so their first task before they ventured onto the crowded walkways was to purchase some sweeter-smelling outfits. It wasn't difficult. Over the years a number of enterprising clothes merchants had set up their stalls close to the dock, realizing that many of the visitors would want to shuck off their workday clothes as soon as they arrived on Babilonium and buy something a little more appropriate to the air of the Carnival. There were perhaps fifty or sixty establishments in this chaotic little bazaar, their owners all singing out the virtues of their wares at the tops of their voices. Shoemakers, boot makers, cane makers, breeches makers, petticoat makers, bodice makers, suit makers, hatmakers.

Needless to say, there were a lot of very garish and outlandish outfits for sale—singing boots, aquarium hats, moonbeam underwear—but only Charry (who did buy the singing boots) gave in to the merchants' relentless salesmanship. The rest all chose comfortable clothes that they could wear without embarrassment when they eventually moved on from Babilonium.

The Carnival Island was all Candy and Malingo had hoped it would be, and more. It attracted people from right across the archipelago, so there were all kinds of shapes and faces, garments, languages and customs. The visitors from the Outer Islands, for instance—from Autland and Speckle Frew—were dressed simply and practically, their sense of Carnival limited to a new waistcoat or a little fiddle playing as they walked. Celebrants from the Night Islands, on the other hand—from Huffaker and Jibbarish and Idjit—were dressed like escapees from a magician's dream, their masks and costumes so fantastic that it was hard to know where the audience ended and the entertainment began. Then there were the travelers from Commexo City, who favored a certain cool modernity in their outfits. Many wore small collars that projected moving images up around their faces—masks of color and light. More often than not it was the Commexo Kid whose adventures were playing on the screens of these faces.

Finally, of course, there were those creatures—and

there were many—who, like Malingo, needed neither paint nor light to make them part of this prodigious Carnival. Creatures born with snouts, tails, scales and horns, their forms and their voices and their behavior a fantastical show unto itself.

And what had all these Carnival-goers come to see?

Whatever, in truth, their eager hearts and spirits desired. Mycassian Bug Wrestling in one tent, subtle-body dancing in another; a seven-ring circus, complete with a troupe of albino dinosaurs, in a third. There was a beast called a fingoos, who put its snout right through your head to read your mind. Next door to that, a thousand-strong choir of mungualameeza birds were singing excerpts from Fofum's *Bumble Bees*. Everywhere you looked there were entertainments. The Electric Baby, who had a head full of colored lights, was on display here, as was a poet called Thebidus, who recited epic poems with candles perched on his pate, and a thing called a frayd, which was billed as a beast that had to be seen to be believed: not one but many creatures, each devouring the other to make a "living testament to the horrors of appetite!"

Of course, if you didn't wish to go into the tents, there was plenty to do in the open air. There was a dinosaur on display—"lately captured by Rojo Pixler in the wilds of the Outer Islands"—and a hoofed beast the size of a bull delicately walking a high wire, and of course the inevitable roller coasters, each claiming to be more heart-stopping than the competition.

The air was filled with the mingled smells of a thousand things: pies, caramel, sawdust, gasoline, sweat, dog's breath, sweet smoke, sour smoke, fruit nearly rotten, fruit *beyond* rotten, ale, feathers, fire. And if happiness had a smell, that too was in the air of Babilonium. In fact, it was the fragrance that hovered behind all the other fragrances. Nor did the island ever seem to exhaust its surprises. There was always something new around the next corner, in the next tent, in the next arena. Of course, any place that boasted such brightness and wonderment had its share of shadows too. At one point the group made a turn off the main thoroughfare and found themselves in a place where the music wasn't quite as upbeat and the lights not quite so bright. There was a more sinister, serpentine magic at play here. There were colors in the air, which made half-visible shapes before dissolving again; and music coming from somewhere that sounded as though it was being sung by a choir of irate babies. People peeped out from behind curtains of booths to the right and left, or flew over them, their shapes changing as they somersaulted against the sky.

But they'd come to the right place, no doubt of that. Right up ahead was a large canvas sign that read FREAK SHOW, and under it a brightly colored row of banners on which a variety of outlandish creatures had been crudely painted. A creature with a fringe of arms and tentacles around its huge head; a boy with a body of a reptile; a beast that was a bizarre compendium of pieces thrown together carelessly.

Seeing all of this, Methis the zethek quickly realized what was being planned on his behalf. He began to fling himself around his cage, cursing obscenely.

The crudely made cage looked as though it might break beneath his assault but proved stronger than the creature's fury.

"Should we feel a little sorry for him?" Candy asked.

"After what *he* did?" said Galatea. "I don't think so. He would have murdered you in cold blood if he'd had the chance."

"I suppose you're right."

"And destroying the fish like that," said Malingo. "Pure malice."

The zethek knew he was being talked about and fell silent, his gaze going from one person to the next, hatred in every glance.

"If looks could kill," Candy murmured.

"We should leave you to make the sale," Malingo said to Skebble when they were within a few yards of the freak show.

"You should have a little coin for yourselves," Mizzel said. "We could never have caught the creature if not for you. Especially Candy. My Lord! Such courage!"

"We don't need any money," Candy said. "Malingo's right. We should leave you to sell the creature."

They paused a few yards shy of the entrance to the freak show to make their farewells. They hadn't known one another very long, but they'd fought for their lives side by side, so there was an intensity in their parting that would not have been there if they'd simply gone out sailing together.

"Come to the isle of Efreet one Night," Skebble said. "We never see the sun up there, of course, but you're always welcome."

"Of course, we got some fierce beasts live up there," Mizzel said. "But they stay to the south side of the island mostly. Our village is on the north side. It's called Pigea."

"We'll remember," Candy said.

"No, you won't," said Galatea with half a smile. "We'll just be some fisherfolk you met on your adventuring. You won't even remember our names."

"Oh, she remembers," Malingo said, glancing at Candy. "More and more, she remembers."

It was a curious thing to say, of course, so everyone just ignored the remark, smiled and parted. The last time Candy looked back, the quartet was dragging Methis' cage through the curtains into the freak show.

"You think they'll sell him?" Candy said.

"I'm sure they will," Malingo replied. "It's ugly, that thing. And people pay money to see ugly things, don't they?"

"I guess they do. What did you mean when you talked about my remembering?"

Malingo looked at his feet and chewed on his tongue for a little time. Finally he said: "I don't know exactly. But you're remembering *something,* aren't you?"

Candy nodded. "Yes," she said. "I just don't know what."

8

A LIFE IN THE THEATRE

IT WAS THE FIRST time on their journey together that Candy and Malingo had realized that they had different tastes. Up until now they'd traveled in step with each other, more or less. But faced with the apparently limitless diversions and entertainments of Babilonium, they found they weren't quite so well matched. When Malingo wanted to see the green werewolf star juggler, Candy was itching to go on the Prophet of Doom ride. When Candy had been Doomed six times, and wanted to sit quietly and gather her breath, Malingo was ready to go take a ride on the Spirit Train to Hell.

So they decided to separate, to follow their own fancies. Occasionally, despite the incredible density of the crowd, they would find each other, as friends will. They'd take a minute or two to exchange a few excited words about what they'd seen or done, and then they'd part again, to find some new recreation.

On the third time this happened, however, Malingo reappeared with the leathery flaps he had on his face standing proud with excitement. He was wearing a cockeyed grin.

"Lady! Lady!" he said. "You *have* to come and look at this!"

"What is it?"

"I can't really describe it. You just have to come!"

His excitement was infectious. Candy put off going to watch the Huffaker Snail Tabernacle Choir and followed through the throng to a tent. It was not one of the huge circus-sized tents, but it was large enough to hold several hundred people. Inside there were about thirty rows of wooden benches, most of them filled by an audience that was roaringly entertained by the play that was being performed onstage.

"Sit! Sit!" Malingo urged her. *"You have to see this!"*

Candy sat down on the end of a crowded bench. There was no room for Malingo anywhere nearby, so he remained standing.

The setting of the play was a single large room stuffed to over-capacity with books, antique ornaments and fanciful furniture, the arms and legs of which were carved with the scowling heads and tremendous talons of Abaratian monsters. All of this was pure theatrical illusion, of course; most of the room was painted on canvas, and the details of the furniture were painted too. As a result, none of it was very solid. The whole set shook whenever a cast member slammed a door or opened a window. And there was plenty of that. The play was a wild farce, which the actors performed with abandon, yelling and throwing themselves around like clowns in a circus ring.

The audience was laughing so hard that many of the jokes had to be repeated for the benefit of those who didn't hear them the first time. Glancing along the row in which she was sitting, Candy saw people with tears of laughter pouring down their faces.

"What's so funny?" Candy said to Malingo.

"You'll see," he replied.

She went on watching. There was a shrill exchange going on between a young woman in a bright orange wig and a bizarre individual called Jingo (that much she heard), who was running around the room like a crazy man, hiding under the table one moment and hanging from the swaying scenery the next. To judge by the audience's response this was about the funniest thing they'd ever seen. But Candy was still lost as to what it was all about. Until—

—a man in a bright yellow suit came onstage, demanding rum.

Candy's jaw fell open. She looked up at Malingo with an expression of disbelief on her face. He smiled from ear to ear and nodded, as if to say: *Yes, that's right. It's what you think it is.*

"Why are you keeping me here, Jaspar Codswoddle?" the young woman demanded.

"Because it suits me, Qwandy Tootinfruit!"

Candy suddenly laughed so loudly that everybody else around her stopped laughing for a moment. A few puzzled faces were turned in her direction.

"Qwandy Tootinfruit . . ." she whispered. "It's a very funny name. . . ."

Meanwhile, onstage: "You're my prisoner," Codswoddle was saying to Qwandy. "And you're going to stay here as long as it *suits* me."

At this, the girl ran to the door; but the Codswoddle character threw an elaborate gesture in her direction, and there was a flash and a puff of yellow smoke, and a large grotesque face appeared carved on the door, snarling like a rabid beast.

Jingo hid under the table, blabbering. The audience went wild with appreciation at the stage trickery. Malingo took a moment to lean over and whisper to Candy.

"We're famous," he said. "It's our story, only sillified."

"Sillified?" she said. It was a new word, but it nicely described the version of the truth that was being played out on the stage. This was a sillification of the truth. What had been a frightening experience for both Candy and Malingo was enacted here as an excuse for pratfalls, word games, face pullings and pie fights.

The audience, of course, didn't care. What did it matter to them whether this was true or not? A story was a story. All they wanted was to be entertained.

Candy beckoned to Malingo, who squatted down on his haunches beside her.

"Who do you suppose told the playwright about what happened to us?" she whispered to him. "It wasn't you. It wasn't me."

"Oh, there's plenty of spirits on Ninnyhammer who could have been listening."

By now the play was heading for its big conclusion,

and events onstage were getting more and more spectacular. Tootinfruit had stolen a volume of Codswoddle's magic, and a battle of wild conjurations ensued, with the stage set becoming a fourth actor in the play. Furniture came to life and stalked around the stage; Codswoddle's yellow-suited ancestors stepped out of a painting on the wall and tap-danced. And finally Qwandy used a spell to open up a hole in the floor, and the malevolent Codswoddle and all his train of monstrous tricks were snatched away into what Candy assumed was the Abaratian version of hell. Finally, to everybody's delight, the walls of the house folded up and were dragged away down the same infernal hole, leaving Qwandy and Jingo standing against a backcloth of sparkling stars, free at last. It was all strangely satisfying, even for Candy, who knew that this version was very far from the truth. When the crowd rose to give the bowing actors a standing ovation, she found herself rising to join in the applause.

Then the painted red curtain came down, and the crowd began to disperse, talking excitedly and repeating favorite lines to one another.

"Did you enjoy it?" Malingo asked Candy.

"In a weird way, yes. It's nice to hear that laughter. It—"

She stopped for a moment.

"What's wrong?" said Malingo.

"I thought I heard somebody calling out my name."

"Here? No, I—"

"There! Somebody is calling my name." She looked over the crowd, puzzled.

"Maybe one of the actors," Malingo said. Looking back toward the stage. "Perhaps you were recognized?"

"No. It wasn't one of the actors," Candy replied.

"Who then?"

"Him."

She pointed across the rows of benches toward a solitary figure who was standing close to the flap of the tent. The man was instantly recognizable, even though they were just catching glimpses of him through the departing crowd. The colorless skin, the deep-set eyes, the designs on his cheeks. There was no mistaking him.

It was Otto Houlihan, the Criss-Cross Man.

9

AGAIN, THE CRISS-CROSS MAN

"**H**OW DID YOU FIND us?" Candy asked.

Otto Houlihan smiled that joyless smile of his. "I followed the trail of stinking smatterlings," he said. "It wasn't hard to figure out where you'd gone. You're not all that clever, whatever you might think."

"But how—"

"—did I know you were making a getaway on a little fishing boat?"

"Kud told him," Malingo said.

"Good guess, geshrat," Otto replied. He didn't look at Malingo. He concentrated his chilly gaze on Candy. "My, but you've become so much more famous since last we met." He glanced toward the stage. "Apparently your life is now the stuff of bad comedy. Imagine that."

"Why don't you give up the chase?" Candy replied. "We're never going to let you take us. You know that."

"If I had my way," Houlihan replied, raising his hands as he started to approach her, "you would be buried right here. But Carrion wants you alive. And so alive I must take you."

If any of the departing audience had heard this, they decided to ignore it. Now everyone had departed. The Criss-Cross Man didn't bother to look around at the empty auditorium. He had all his attention focused on Candy.

"Run . . ." Malingo murmured to her.

Candy shook her head and stood her ground. She wasn't going to let Houlihan think that she was afraid. She refused to give him the satisfaction.

"Please, lady," Malingo said. "Don't let him—"

"Ah!" said a ripe, rounded voice from the direction of the stage. *"Fans!"*

With a little growl of frustration, Houlihan dropped his hands, still a stride or two away from Candy. The man who had just played Jaspar Codswoddle had appeared from backstage. He was nowhere near as fat or as tall as the character he had just portrayed. The illusion had been created with a false stomach, a false bottom and leg extensions, some of which he was still wearing. In fact he was a diminutive man, and beneath his makeup—most of which he'd wiped off—he was bright green. The robes he'd thrown on offstage were more theatrical than anything he'd worn during the play. Behind him came his entourage of two: a highly muscled woman in a florid dress and what looked like a five-foot ape in a coat and carpet slippers.

"Who wants an autograph then?" the little green actor said. "I'm Legitimate Eddie, in case you didn't recognize me. I know, I know, it was an uncanny transformation! Oh, and this young lady behind me is Betty Thunder." The woman curtsied inelegantly. "Perhaps you'd like an autograph from Betty? Or from my play-wright, Clyde?" The ape also bowed deeply. Candy glanced around at Houlihan. He had retreated a step or two. Obviously he didn't like the idea of doing anything violent in front of these three witnesses. Especially when one of them—Betty Thunder—looked as though she could break his nose with one punch.

"I'd *love* an autograph," Candy said. "You were wonderful."

"You thought so?" Legitimate Eddie replied. "Wonderful?"

"Really."

"You're too kind," he protested with a sly smile of satisfaction. "One does one's best." He quickly pro-duced a pen from behind the rolls of his stomach fat.

"You have something for me to sign?" he said.

Candy pulled up the sleeve of her jacket. "Here!" she said, proffering her bare forearm.

"Are you sure?"

"I won't *ever* wash it off!" Candy said. She caught Malingo's eye as she spoke, and with a couple of dart-ing looks to left and right, instructed him to look for a quick exit.

"What shall I write?" Eddie wanted to know.

"Let me see," Candy said. "How about: *To the real Qwandy Tootinfruit*."

"That's what you want? Well, all right. *To the real . . .*" He had barely written two words when the significance of what he'd been asked to write struck him. He very slowly raised his head to look at Candy. "It can't be," he breathed softly.

Candy smiled. "It is," she said.

From the corner of her eye, she could see Houlihan was now approaching again. He seemed to have realized something was wrong. At lightning speed, Candy snatched the pen out of the actor's hand and then swung around behind him, putting her shoulder against his back and shoving him toward the Criss-Cross Man. The padding made him unstable. He stumbled forward and fell against Houlihan, who also lost his balance. Both men fell to the ground, with Legitimate Eddie on top.

Houlihan roared and raged—*"Get off me, you fool! Let me up!"*—but by the time he had got himself out from under Eddie, Malingo had already led Candy to a gap in the wall of the tent.

"You're not going to escape me, Quackenbush!" Houlihan yelled as Candy slipped away.

"Which way?" Malingo said when they got outside.

"Where are the most people?" He pointed off to their left. "Then let's go!" she said.

As they made their way toward the crowd, she heard Houlihan's voice behind her and glanced over her shoulder to see him appearing from the tent, a look of insane fury on his face.

"You're mine, girl!" he yelled. "I've got you this time."

Though there were only about six strides between the pursuer and pursued, it was enough to give Candy and Malingo a head start. They plunged into the throng and were quickly hidden by the parade of people and animals.

"We should split up!" Candy said to Malingo as they took refuge behind a line of booths.

"Why?" said Malingo. "He'll never find us in this chaos!"

"Don't be so sure," Candy said. "He has ways—"

As she spoke, Houlihan's voice rose above the clamor of the celebrants. "I'm going to find you, Quackenbush!"

"We have to confuse him, Malingo," Candy insisted. "You go that way. I'll go this."

"Where will we meet again?"

"At the freak show. I'll meet you there in half an hour. Keep to the crowds, Malingo. It'll be safer."

"We'll never be safe as long as that man's on our heels," Malingo said.

"He won't be on our heels forever, I promise."

"I hope you're right. *Vadu ha,* lady."

"*Vadu ha,*" Candy said, returning the wishes in Old Abaratian.

With that they parted. For Candy the next few minutes were a blur. She pressed through the crowds, trying all the while to get the sound of Houlihan's voice out of her head, but hearing him every step of the way, repeating the same dreadful syllable.

"Mine! Mine! Mine!"

Hundreds, perhaps thousands of faces moved before her as she proceeded, like faces in some strange dream. Faces masked with cloth or papier-mâché or painted wood; smiling sometimes, astonished sometimes; sometimes filled with a strange unease. There were a few faces she recognized among the masks.

The Commexo Kid appeared in a hundred different versions; so did the faces of Rojo Pixler and even Kaspar Wolfswinkel. There were others to which she could put no name that nevertheless drew her attention. A young man danced past her wearing a black mask streaming with bright red dreadlocks. Another man had a face that had erupted into bright green foliage, in which flowers like daisies bloomed; yet another was tattooed from head to foot with golden anatomy but wore on his chest a cleverly painted hole, which seemed to show her his mechanical heart.

And every now and then among these bright, strange creatures there would be a naysayer: a serpent in this Eden, preaching the Coming Apocalypse. One of them, dressed in a ratty robe that exposed his stick-like legs, even had a fake halo attached to his head and pointed at the people as they passed, saying they would all perish for their crimes, at the End of Time.

But his bitter words could not destroy the magic of this place, even now. Everywhere she looked there was beauty.

A swarm of miniature blue monkeys the size of hummingbirds fluttered up in her face and clambered into the sky, up invisible ropes disappearing in a cloud of violet smoke. A dozen balloons floated past her, pursued by a quiverful of needles, which caught up with their quarry and pierced them, liberating a lilting chorus of voices. A fish of elephantine proportions, with bulging eyes that looked like twin moons, floated past, trailing a scent of old smoke.

In this confusion of wonders Candy had long ago

lost all sense of direction, of course. So it came as a total surprise when she turned the corner and found herself in the very backwater that they'd first come down with the zethek in his cage. Straight ahead of her lay the freak show, its brightly colored banners depicting the cast of monsters to be found inside.

She glanced back down the alleyway, just in time to see Houlihan come into view. Hoping to avoid his eye, she shrank back into the shadows, and for a moment she thought she was going to be lucky.

But then, just as he was about to disappear into the crowd again, he seemed to sniff her, and with a chilling certainty he turned his head in her direction and peered down the darkened alleyway. There was no more shadow for Candy to shrink into. She could only hold her breath and wait.

Narrowing his eyes as though trying to pierce the shadows, the Criss-Cross Man began to push his way through the crowd toward the alleyway. The smallest of smiles had appeared on his face. He knew where she was.

Candy had no choice. Clearly he'd seen her. She had to retreat. And there was only one place to go: into the freak show.

She broke out of the shadows and started to run. She didn't bother to look over her shoulder. She could hear how close Houlihan was now: the sound of his feet sticking and unsticking on the garbage-strewn ground, the raw rasp of his breath.

She parted the canvas curtains and flung herself through them into the backstage area of the freak show. The smell that met her was almost overpowering: the mingled stench of rotting hay and some sickly sweet perfume that had perhaps been splashed around to cover up the other smells. There were three large cages close by, the largest containing a thing that looked like a pony-sized slug. It let out a pitiful mewling at the sight of Candy, and it pushed its eyes between the bars of its cage on fleshy horns. They scrutinized Candy for a long moment. Then the thing spoke, its voice soft and well-educated.

"Please let me out of here," it said.

The creature had no sooner uttered these words than they were echoed from the other two cages (one of which contained what looked like a four-hundred-pound porcupine-woman; the other, one of the creatures Candy had seen advertised on the billboards outside the show: a hybrid boy, with scaly flesh and a pointed tail). The same cry, or a rough variation of the same, escaped them both: *"Let us out!"*

It was now rising from other directions too. Some of the voices were high-pitched squeals, some low rumbling, some just scrawls of sound.

And then, just as she thought the cacophony could not get any louder, she heard Houlihan out in the alleyway, whistling for her like a man who'd lost his pooch in the crowd.

Quietly cursing him, she backed away. Any minute, she guessed, the Criss-Cross Man was going to step into view. The sooner she was out of here the better. . . .

Meanwhile there was a roll of drums from the show itself, followed by an announcement delivered by a woman's voice, which managed to be both coarse and pompous.

"Welcome, ladies and gentlemen, to Scattamun's Emporium of the Malformed. You are guests in the largest collection of freaks, grotesques, inverts, miscreations, mutants, monsters, tetragogs and fiends in the Abarat; plus, of course, the one and only Eye in a Box! Be prepared to be *appalled* at the horrors Creation has made in the name of Life; at the Horrors that Evolution in all its Cruelty has brought forth! They were made for our amusement! Feel free to mock them! Spit at them! Poke them a little if you dare! And be grateful you are not in their shoes!"

"Please—" the giant slug mewled. "Let me out."

After hearing Mrs. Scattamun's horrendous speech, Candy had no doubt of what she should do. She pulled open the bolts on the creature's cage. The slug leaned its weight against the door, which swung open with an ill-oiled creak. Meanwhile Candy moved on to liberate the porcupine-woman, followed by the hybrid boy. None of them lingered. The very moment the bolts were drawn they were out, hollering and howling with joy at their liberation.

The freaks nearby heard this joyous din, of course, and started to raise a chorus of their own. Soon the whole wooden platform upon which the freak show stood was shaking with their demands of freedom. Candy might have gone to find them and set them free, but at that moment the curtains were pulled apart, and Otto Houlihan came through, gloating.

"There you are!" he said, advancing on Candy. "I

knew you couldn't escape me forever."

Before he could catch hold of her, the porcupine-woman intervened, stumbling between them in her ambition to be free. In so doing she blocked the Criss-Cross Man's path for a few vital seconds, preventing him from getting hold of Candy. She pulled aside a second rotting canvas and stepped into a much more brightly lit area. Here there were twenty cages and tableaux arranged for the viewing pleasure of the paying customers, of which there were several dozen. Everybody seemed to be having a fine time watching the Scattamuns' poor captives as they shook their cages. The louder the freaks sobbed and complained, the more they laughed.

Candy was revolted by the whole spectacle and felt a spasm of guilt at the sight of Methis, who had been quickly elevated to the status of The Most Terrifying Freak in Captivity. He didn't look particularly terrifying. He sat at the back of his cage with his head in his hands, his eyes downcast. A little boy with cotton candy all around his mouth was kicking the bars of Methis' cage, trying to get a response from him. When he failed, he started to spit at the zethek.

"Did *this* one pay, Mrs. Scattamun?" said a tall bony man, pointing down at Candy.

Mrs. Scattamun swept on over, her gray dress raising a little cloud of dust. She had spiky painted eyelashes and cherubic lips. Her nose and cheeks bore the unmistakable bloom of a very heavy drinker.

"No, I didn't sell a ticket to this one, Mr. Scattamun."

"Did you not, Mrs. Scattamun?"

"I did not."

The pair of them wore hats, which were morbid variations on the aquarium hats that were apparently such a rage in Babilonium. Instead of housing living fish, however, the Scattamuns' hats were filled with dead, withered creatures.

"Did you come here to look at the freaks?" Mrs. Scattamun said.

"Yes . . ." Candy said.

"But you didn't *pay* to look."

"I came in here by mistake," Candy said.

Mrs. Scattamun put out her empty palm. "Mistake or no mistake, everybody *pays*. That'll be six zem." She leaned forward and the withered thing on her head bobbed in its formaldehyde.

Before Candy could reply, there was a fresh eruption of noise from the back room, and Houlihan started shouting again.

"Out of my way!" he yelled. "All of you! Out of my way before I slit your throats."

Hearing this outburst, the audience began to beat a hasty retreat, which did not please Mrs. Scattamun.

"Mr. Scattamun," she said. "Kindly discover what's going on back there. *And stop it!* Well? Don't just look at me!" She gave her husband a very unloving shove. *"Go!"*

Reluctantly Mr. Scattamun crossed to the curtain and stepped through. Two seconds later he was thrown backward through the curtain at great speed. He was followed by the man who'd pushed him: Otto Houlihan.

Mrs. Scattamun let out a shrill shriek. "Get up and get that yellow monster out of here!" she demanded. "You heard me, Mr. Scattamun."

Obediently Mr. Scattamun got to his feet, but Houlihan kicked him in the chest and down he went again, knocking over several small cages as he did so.

"Where's the girl?" Houlihan demanded.

Candy had taken refuge behind a cage that contained a beast three times her size, which seemed to have completely rubber limbs. It bawled like a baby. Candy told it to hush, but it responded by bawling even more loudly.

Its din drew Mrs. Scattamun's attention to Candy.

"The girl's back there!" she said to Houlihan. "I can see her from here! She's hiding behind the fetteree!"

"I see her," Otto said.

"Don't hurt my children!" Mrs. Scattamun said. "They're our bread and butter, they are."

Houlihan drew a long-bladed knife out of his belt and headed toward the cage containing the bawling fetteree. Candy ducked down as low as possible and crawled behind the cages, keeping her head down so as to make as small a target as possible.

Suddenly there was a growl in the shadows, and she looked up to find herself face-to-face with a creature she knew.

"Methis!"

The zethek was wearing the most pitiful of expressions, and Candy couldn't help but feel another spasm of guilt. The creature was no doubt feeling claustrophobic, locked up in a little cage. After all, he had wings.

Wait: wings! Methis had wings!

"Listen to me," she said to the zethek.

Before she could get any further, somebody grabbed hold of Candy's collar and hauled her to her feet.

"You leave our freaks alone, girl!" Mrs. Scattamun snarled. She stank of old liquor and cheap perfume. "Hey, you!" she yelled to the Criss-Cross Man. "I've got your girl! You want to come and take her away?"

10

"THE FREAKS ARE OUT! THE FREAKS ARE OUT!"

C ANDY HAD TO THINK quickly. Houlihan
was no more than ten strides away. He wouldn't let her
slip through his lethal fingers this time. She glanced at
Methis, who was looking up at her with a forlorn
expression. The zethek was still dangerous, she knew.
Still hungry. Could she possibly make an ally out of
him? After all, they both wanted the same thing right
now, didn't they? To be out of this place. He out of
reach of the Scattamuns, she out of reach of Houlihan.
Could they perhaps do together what they could not do
apart?

It was worth a try.

Wrenching herself free from Mrs. Scattamun, she
reached around the side of the cage and hauled the
heavy iron bolt open. Methis didn't seem to understand what she'd done, because he didn't move, but
the horrendous Mrs. Scattamun understood perfectly
well.

"You wretched girl!" she seethed, catching hold of

Candy again and shaking her violently. In so doing she knocked Candy against the cage, and the unbolted door swung open.

Methis looked lazily over his shoulder.

"Move!" Candy said to him.

Mrs. Scattamun was still shaking her and calling for her husband while she did so.

"Mr. Scattamun! Fetch your whip! Quickly, Mr. Scattamun! The new freak is escaping!"

"Hold the girl!" Houlihan yelled to Mrs. Scattamun. *"Hold her!"*

But Candy had had quite enough of being shaken, thank you. She gave the Scattamun woman a good elbow in the ribs. She expelled a sour breath and let go of Candy. Then she stumbled backward. The Criss-Cross Man was directly in her path. The woman fell against him—much to his irritation—blocking his route to his intended victim.

Candy quickly reached through the bars and gave Methis a nudge, telling him again to *move.* This time he seemed to understand. He pushed the cage door open and quickly slipped out. Before he could get out of reach, Candy threw herself forward and caught hold of one of his front limbs, pulling herself toward him. As she did so, she glanced back to see an irritated Houlihan knocking off Mrs. Scattamun's hat as he scrambled to his feet. The hat smashed as it hit the ground. The stink of formaldehyde sharpened the air. Mrs. Scattamun let out a keening sound.

"My chitterbee!" she shrieked. "Neville, this man's broken my chitterbee!"

Her husband was in no mood for consolations. He had picked up his freak-taming whip and now raised it, preparing to strike out at Candy. Methis spread his wings with a swooping sound. Then he ran down the passageway between the cages, flapping his wings, with Candy still hanging on to him.

"Fly!" she yelled to the zethek. *"Or he'll have you back in the cage! Go on, Methis! FLY!"*

Then she pulled herself onto Methis' back and held on for dear life.

Candy heard Scattamun's whip crack. His aim was good. She felt a sting of pain around her wrist and glanced down to see that the whip was wrapped around her wrist and hand three or four times. It hurt like crazy, but more than that, it made her mad. How dare this man take a whip to her? She glanced back over her shoulder.

"You . . . you . . . *freak!*" she yelled at him. She caught hold of the whip in her hand, and by sheer luck at the same moment Methis' wing beats carried them both up into the air. The whip was jerked out of Scattamun's grip.

"Oh, you stupid, stupid man!" Mrs. Scattamun shouted, and caught hold of the trailing handle of the whip, while Candy unwrapped the other end from her wrist. As Candy and Methis rose into the air, Mrs. Scattamun stumbled after them between the cages, unwilling to let the whip go. After a few steps one of the freaks casually put his foot out and tripped her up. She fell heavily, and Candy let the whip drop on top of the sprawled figure. She was still shrieking at her husband, her curses getting more elaborate by the syllable.

Since there was no roof on the Scattamun's empire of malformations, Candy and Methis were able to rise freely in a widening spiral until they were maybe fifty feet above the island. The scene below was becoming more chaotic by the moment. The three escapees from the backstage area had by now come into the freak show and were going among the cages, opening them up with their teeth and fingers, even their agile tails.

It was very satisfying for Candy to watch the escalating pandemonium as the members of Scattamun's bestiary threw open their cages and escaped, repeatedly knocking their sometime captors over in their haste to be at liberty. From her elevated position Candy was able to see how news of the escape was spreading through the crowd out on the boardwalk. Children were gathered into the arms of fretful parents as the shout went up: *"The freaks are out! The freaks are out!"*

As they continued to ascend, Candy heard a strange noise coming out of Methis and thought for a moment that he was sick. But the noise he was making, strange as it may have sounded, was simply laughter.

Malingo, meanwhile, had taken refuge behind Larval Lil's Beer and Sweet Potato stand, where he had kept out of sight for a while, until he was certain that there was no danger of being apprehended by the Criss-Cross Man. He had persuaded one of the cooks to bring him a mug of red ale and a slice of pilgrim's pie, and he was sitting among the garbage cans happily washing the pie down with ale when he heard somebody nearby talking excitedly about a girl he'd just seen, flying overhead in the grip of some monster or other.

That's my Candy, he thought, and finishing off the last of the pilgrim's pie, he scanned the glowing clouds. It didn't take more than a minute or two for him to locate his lady. She was hanging on to the back of the zethek as they flew north. He was very happy, of course, to see that she hadn't fallen victim to Houlihan (whose whereabouts he'd long since given up on), but watching his friend get smaller and smaller as Methis bore her away toward twilight made him fearful. He hadn't been alone in this world since he'd escaped from Wolfswinkel's house. He'd always had Candy at his side. Now he would have to go and look for her on his own. It was not a happy prospect.

He watched the girl and her winged mount steadily eroded by the gentle gloom of dusk. And then she was gone, and there were just a few stars, glittering fitfully in the sky low over Scoriae.

"Take care, lady," he said to her softly. "Don't worry. Wherever you are . . . I'll find you."

PART TWO

THINGS NEGLECTED, THINGS FORGOTTEN

The Hour! The Hour! Upon the Hour!
The Munkee spits and thickets cower,
And what has become of the Old Man's power
But tears and trepidation?

The Hour! The Hour! Upon the Hour!
Mother's mad and the milk's gone sour,
But yesterday I found a flower
That sang Annunciation.

And when the Hours become Day,
And all the Days have passed away,
Will we not see—yes, you and me—
How sweet and bright the light will be
That comes of our Creation?

—Song of the Totemix

11

TRAVELING NORTH

THE BRIGHTNESS OF BABILONIUM'S Infinite Carnival didn't light up every corner of the island, Candy soon discovered. The zethek carried her up a gentle slope, on the other side of which the garish lights of the pomps, parades, carousels and psychedelias gave sudden way to the hazy blue of early evening. The din from the crowds and from the roller coasters and from the barkers at the sideshows grew more remote. Soon only the occasional gust of wind brought a hint of that din to Candy's ears, and after a little while, not even that. All she heard now was the creaking of the zethek's wings and the occasional charmless rasp of the creature's labored breathing.

Beneath them, the landscape was little more than a wilderness of reddish dirt dotted with a few solitary trees, all spindly and undernourished, which threw their long shadows eastward. Now and again she saw a farmhouse, with a couple of cultivated fields beside it, and cattle settling down after their evening milking. Though of course it was *always* dusk here, wasn't it?

The evening stars were always rising in the east; the flowers opening to meet the moon. It would be a very pleasant Hour to live in, with the day almost ending but the night not yet begun. It had been different, she thought, in the Carnival. There the lights had lent the sky a false brightness, and the din had driven out the aching hush that was all around her now. Perhaps that was why Six O'clock had been chosen as a place to put the razzmatology of the Carnival: it was a kind of defense against the darkening Hour, a way of delaying the darkness with laughter and games. But it couldn't be put off forever. The farther north they traveled, the longer the shadows became, and the red of the earth darkened to purple and to black as the light steadily faded from the sky.

Candy did her best to be an undemanding passenger. She didn't move too much, and she kept her mouth shut. Her greatest fear was that the zethek would realize that he was in no danger of being recaptured and would swing around and head back to Gorgossium. But so far the beast seemed content to fly on northward. Even when they cleared the coast of Babilonium and began to cross the straits between Six and Seven, he did not show any sign of wanting to turn. But he did swoop down toward the water and skim it, looking, Candy guessed, for fish to scoop up out of the water. Candy hoped he didn't actually catch sight of anything, because if he plunged his head into the water she would almost certainly be thrown off his back. Luckily the gathering darkness and the wind ruffling the surface of the water made fish spotting difficult, and they flew on over the murky straits without incident.

The island of Scoriae was visible ahead, with the magnificent, ominous cone of Mount Galigali at its heart. She knew very little about this Hour, beyond the few facts she'd read in *Klepp's Almenak*. It had mentioned, she remembered, that there had once been three beautiful cities on the island—Gosh, Mycassius and Divinium—and that an eruption of Mount Galigali had destroyed all three cities, leaving no survivors, or so she thought she remembered. She had no idea how long it was since the eruption had occurred, but she could see that the larval paths had marked the island like wide black scars, and no seed had sprouted on them nor house been built since the liquid rock had cooled.

There was only one place, at the westbound edge of the island, where the gloom and sterility were relieved somewhat. There, a bank of pale, pliant mist had gathered, as though nestling the spot, and rising from this gently moving cloud was a forest of tall trees. They had to be a particularly Abaratian species, Candy reasoned; no trees in the Hereafter (at least none she'd ever been taught about in school) thrived in a place where there was only the last blush of sunlight in the sky. Perhaps these were trees that fed not on sunlight but on the light of the moon and stars.

Fatigue, and perhaps hunger, were now taking a serious toll on Methis' flying skills. He was rocking from side to side as he flew, sometimes so severely that one or the other of his wing tips would graze the tops of the waves. His feet plowed the water too, on occasion, throwing up a cold spray.

Candy decided this was the time to break her silence and offer a few words of encouragement.

"We're going to make it!" she said to him. "We've just got to get to the shore. It's no more than a quarter of a mile."

Methis didn't reply. He just flew on, his flight becoming more erratic with every wing beat.

Candy could hear the waves splashing on the shore now, and her view of the mist-shrouded trees was better and better. It looked like a place she might lay down her head and sleep for a while. She had lost track of how long it was since she'd enjoyed a good long sleep.

But first they had to reach the shore, and now with every yard they covered that seemed to be a more and yet more remote possibility. Methis was laboring hard; his breath was raw and painful.

"We can do it!" Candy said to him. "I swear . . . *we can.*"

This time the exhausted creature responded to her.

"What's with this *we*? I don't see *you* flapping *your* wings."

"I would if I had wings to flap."

"But you don't, do you? You're just a burden."

As he spoke, there was a surge of surf in front of them and a massive creature—not a mantizac, but something that looked more like a rabid walrus—lunged out of the water. Its snaggle-toothed maw snapped just inches from Methis' snout, then the monster fell back into the sea, throwing up a great wall of icy water.

There was a panicky moment or two when Methis was flying blind through the spray, and all Candy could do was cling to him and hope for the best. Then she felt a strong wind against her face and shook the water from her eyes to see that Methis was climbing steeply to avoid a second attack. She slid down over his wet back and would surely have lost her grip and fallen had he not quickly leveled off again.

"Damn gilleyants!" he yelled.

"It's still below us!" Candy warned.

The gilleyant was breaching again, this time roaring as it threw its immense bulk out of the water. Then it came back down again with another great splash.

"Well, it's not getting *us*," Methis said.

The encounter had put some fresh life into the zethek. He flew on toward the island, keeping his new elevation, at least until they were so close to the shore that the water was no more than three or four feet deep. Only then did he swoop down again, making an inelegant landing in the soft amber sand.

They lay there on the beach for a while, gasping with relief and exhaustion. It didn't take very long for Candy's teeth to begin to chatter. The gilleyant's cavorting had soaked her to the skin, and now the wind was chilling her.

She got to her feet, wrapping her arms around herself. "I have to find a fire or I'm going to catch pneumonia."

Methis also got up, his expression as miserable as ever.

"We won't see each other again after this, I daresay,"

he said. "So I suppose I should wish you luck."

"Oh, well, that's nice—"

"But I'm not going to. It seems to me you're just a troublemaker, and the more luck you have the more trouble you'll make."

"Who for?"

"For innocent beasts like me," Methis growled.

"Innocent!" Candy said. "You came to steal fish, remember?"

"Oh, stop the self-righteous talk! So I was going to steal a few fish. Big deal! For that I get beaten around by you and your magic, put in a cage and sold to a *freak show*, and then made to carry you on my back! Well, you know what? You can freeze to death *right here* for all I care." He flapped his wings hard, deliberately aiming the icy draft in Candy's direction. She shuddered.

"Enjoy yourself," he said with a sneering smile. "If you're lucky, maybe Galigali will explode. That'll keep you warm."

Candy was too cold to waste words on a reply. She just watched while the zethek flapped his wings violently to reach takeoff velocity and then ascended gracelessly into the air. He took a moment to fix the direction of Gorgossium, then he headed off across the water, staying close to the waves as he went, in the hope, presumably, of spotting an unlucky fish.

In less than a minute, he had disappeared from sight.

12

DARKNESS AND ANTICIPATION

AT JUST ABOUT THE same time that Methis was heading back toward the Midnight Isle, a small vessel—the kind that no zethek would attack, hungry though they always were—was departing from Shadow Harbor, on the eastern flank of Gorgossium. The vessel was a funeral barge, beautifully appointed from bow to stern with black sails and blackbird plumage surrounding the place where the deceased would normally be laid. This was a funeral barge without a body, however. In addition to the eight oarsmen who labored to propel the vessel through the icy waters at a very nonfunereal pace, there was a small contingent of stitchling soldiers, who sat around the edges of the vessel, prepared to ward off any attacker. They were the best of troops, every one of them ready to give up his life for his master. And who was that master? The Lord of Midnight, of course.

He stood dressed in voluminous robes of thrice-burned silk (the blackest, most portentous; the silk of all melancholias) and studied the lightless waters of the Izabella as the barge sped on. Besides the soldiers and the oarsmen, he had two other companions on this vessel, but neither of them spoke. They knew better than to interrupt Christopher Carrion while he was in the midst of his meditations.

At last he seemed to put his thoughts aside, and turned to the two men he had brought with him.

"You may be wondering where we are heading today," he said.

The men exchanged glances but said nothing.

"Speak. One or the other."

It was Mendelson Shape (whose ancestors had been in the employ of the Carrion dynasty for generations) who chanced a reply. "I *have* wondered, Lord," he said, eyes downcast.

"And have you by now guessed?"

"I think perhaps we're on our way to Commexo City. I heard a rumor that Rojo Pixler is planning a descent into the deepest parts of the Izabella to see what lives down there."

"I heard the same rumor," Carrion said, still studying the dark waters. "He spies down into the depths and has made contact with the beasts that live in the trenches."

"The Requiax," Shape said.

"Yes. How do you know of them?"

"My father claimed he saw the body of one of their sort, Lord, washed up on the beach near Fulgore's Cove. Huge it was, even though it had been mostly eaten and rotted away. Still . . . its eye or the hole where the eye had been . . . was so big that my father could have stood inside it and not touched the top."

"Then our Mr. Pixler is going to have to be careful down there," Carrion said, still not taking his eyes off the black waters. "Or he's going to leave the Commexo Kid an orphan." He chuckled to himself at the thought.

"So that's not where we're going?" Shape said.

"No. That's not where we're going," Carrion replied, turning his attention to the other passenger who was with him on the funeral barge. His name was Leeman Vol, a man whose reputation went before him, just as Carrion's did. And for much the same reason: to see him was to be haunted by him.

Nothing about Vol was pleasant or pretty. He did not like the company of his fellow bipeds much, preferring to enjoy the fellowship of insects. This in itself had gained him a measure of infamy around the islands, not least because he bore on his face more than a few mementos of that intimacy. He had lost his nose to a spider many years before, the creature having injected his proboscis with a toxin so powerful that it had mortified the skin and cartilage in a few agonizing minutes, leaving Vol with two slimy holes in the middle of his face. He had fashioned a leather nose for himself, which effectively masked the mutilation but still made him the target of taunts and whispers. Not that the nose was the sole reason that people talked about him. There were other facts about Vol's appearance and personal habits that made him noteworthy.

He had been born, for instance, with not one but *three* mouths, all lined with bright yellow teeth that he had meticulously sharpened to pinprick points. When he spoke, the mingling and interwoven sounds of these three mouths was uncanny. Grown men had been known to block their ears and leave the room sobbing because the sound put them so much in mind of their childhood nightmares. Nor was this second grotesquerie all the vileness that Vol could boast. He had claimed from his childhood that he knew the secret language of insects and that his three mouths allowed him to speak it.

In his passion for their company, he had made his body into a living hotel for members of the species. They seethed over his anatomy without check or censure: under his shirt, in his trousers and over his scalp. They were everywhere. Miggis lice and furgito flies, threck roaches and knuckle worms. Sometimes they bit him, in the midst of their territorial wars, and often they burrowed into his skin to lay their eggs; but such were the small inconveniences that went with being a home for such creatures.

"Well, Vol?" Carrion said, watching a line of yellow-white miggis lice migrate across the other's face. "Where are we headed? Any ideas?"

"The Pyramids at Xuxux, perhaps?" Vol said, his three mouths working in perfect unison to shape the words.

Carrion smiled behind the circling nightmares in his collar.

"Good, Vol. Exactly so. The Pyramids at Xuxux." He returned his gaze to Mendelson Shape. "You see now why you were invited to join me?"

Poor Mendelson didn't reply. Fear had apparently seized hold of his tongue and nailed it to the roof of his mouth.

"After all," Carrion went on, "we wouldn't be here, preparing to get into the Pyramids, if you hadn't crossed over into the Hereafter to get the Key."

He slid his gloved hand into the folds of his robe and slowly brought into view the Key that Shape had pursued, along with its thieves, John Mischief and his brothers, across the forbidden divide between the dimension of the Abarat and that of the Human World. It had not been an easy chase. In fact, Shape had ended up returning to the Abarat on the heels of the girl to whom Mischief had given the Key: Candy Quackenbush. It had not been he, in the end, who'd got the Key back. It had been the wizard Kaspar Wolfswinkel, into whose hands Candy had later fallen. But Mendelson could see by the appreciative smile on his Lord and Master's face that Carrion knew his servant had done the cause of Darkness no little service in his pursuit. Now Carrion had the Key back. And the Pyramids of Xuxux were to be unlocked.

"Well . . . will you look at that?" said Vol.

The six Pyramids were appearing from the murk of the Night Hour, the largest of them so tall that clouds formed around its summit. The Hour here was actually One O'clock in the morning, and the sky was completely lightless. The Sea of Izabella was not, however. As the funeral barge approached the steps of the Great Pyramid, its presence (or more correctly, the presence of its most powerful passenger) summoned to the hull a vast number of tiny creatures, specks of crude and unthinking life, that were somehow drawn to be near a great force such as Carrion. They each flickered with their own tiny bud of luminosity, and perhaps it was this fact—that they had been made as carriers of light, while Carrion was a Prince of Darkness, light's smotherer—that made them so attentive to him. Whatever the reason for this uncanny assembly, they came to see the barge in such numbers that they threw a garish radiance up out of the water. And as though this weren't strange enough, there now came a din out of the Pyramids, such as might have been made by an orchestra of demons, warming up for some monstrous overture.

"Is that noise really coming from the Pyramids?" Shape said.

Carrion nodded.

"But they're *tombs*," Shape said. "The royal families were laid to rest there."

"And so were their slaves and their eunuchs and their horses and their cats and their sacred serpents and their basilisk."

"And they're dead," said Shape. "The serpents and the eunuchs and the . . . whatever. They're all dead."

"All dead and mummified," Carrion replied.

"So . . . *what's making all that noise*?"

"It's a good question," said Carrion. "And given that you will be seeing for yourself in a few minutes, there's no reason why you shouldn't know. Think of the dead as flowers."

"Flowers?"

"Yes. What you hear is the noise of insects, drawn to those flowers."

"Insects? Surely not so loud a noise, Lord, would come out of *insects*?" Shape made a stumbling laugh, as though he thought this was a joke. "Anyway," he went on, "what would inspire them to make such a sound?"

"Explain to him, Vol."

Vol grinned and grinned and grinned.

"They make that noise because they smell us," he said. "Especially you, Shape."

"Why me?"

"They sense that you're close to death. They lick their lips in anticipation."

Shape grew contemptuous now. "Insects don't *have* lips," he said.

"I doubt . . ." said Vol, approaching Shape, ". . . that you've ever looked closely enough."

Vol's three yellow smiles were too much for Shape. He pushed the man away with such force that many of the insects living on his skull fell off and pattered into the water. Vol let out a sob of quite genuine distress and spun around, leaning over the edge of the barge and reaching down into the water close to the steps, scooping his infestation up.

"Oh, don't drown, little ones! *Where are you?* Please, please, please, *please* don't drown." He loosed a low moan, which began in his bowels and climbed up through his wretched body until it escaped his throat as a howl of rage and sorrow. *"They're gone!"* he yelled. He swung around on the murderer. *"You did this!"*

"So?" said Shape. "What if I did? They were *lice* and *worms*."

"They were my children!" Vol howled. "My *children*."

Carrion raised his hands. "*Silence*, gentlemen. You may continue your debate when we have finished our business here. Do you hear me, Vol? Stop sulking! There'll be other lice, just as adorable."

Leaving the two men staring at each other in sullen silence, Carrion went to stand in the bow of the barge. During the argument the unmelodious din from inside the Pyramids had ceased. The "bees"—or whatever else had been making the noise—had hushed in order to listen to the exchange between Vol and Shape. Now both the occupants of the Pyramids and their visitors were silent, each listening for some telltale noise, each knowing it was only a matter of time before they laid eyes upon one another.

The barge came alongside the flight of stone steps that led up to the door of the Great Pyramid. The vessel nudged the stone, and without waiting for the stitchlings to secure the barge, Carrion stepped off the deck and began his ascent of the stairs, leaving Mendelson Shape and Leeman Vol to hurry after him.

13

THE SACBROOD

IT HAD TAKEN A great deal of organization—and more than a little bribery—to arrange Carrion's visit to the great Pyramids of the Xuxux. They were, after all, sacred places: the tombs of Kings and Queens, Princes and Princesses; and in their humbler chambers, the servants and animals belonging to the mighty. The royal dead had ceased to be laid there several generations ago, because all six Pyramids had been filled with the deceased and their belongings. But the Pyramids had continued to be carefully guarded by soldiers working for the Church of Xuxux. They circled the Pyramids on a fleet of vessels elaborately decorated with religious insignia, and they were armed with weapons of fearsome firepower. Furthermore, they had the complete freedom to use their weaponry in defense of the Pyramids and the royal remains that were contained therein. But Carrion had arranged to have the patrol interrupted for a time so that his funeral barge could slip in, unnoticed, to the steps of the Great Pyramid.

As he approached his destination, however, his thoughts were not upon the difficulties of arranging this journey, nor on what lay inside the Pyramid to which he had spent so much trouble getting the Key. They were upon the girl whose presence in the Abarat had come about because she had accidentally interrupted the thief of the Key and his pursuer. In other words, on Candy Quackenbush.

Candy Quackenbush!

Even the name was ludicrous, he told himself. Why did he obsess about her the way he did? She was here because of a fluke of circumstance, nothing more. Why then could he not get her wretched name out of his head? She was a girl from some forsaken little town in the Hereafter, nothing more. Why then did she haunt his thoughts the way she did? And why—when thoughts of her *did* arise—were there other images following on after her? Images that troubled him deeply; that sickened and shamed him. Images of a bright Afternoon on the Nonce, and bells ringing in jubilation, and every flower, as if by some unspoken understanding of the Hour's flora, becoming white for a marriage ceremony . . .

"Sickening," he said to himself as he ascended the Pyramid steps. "She's nothing. *Nothing.*"

Shape overheard his master's mutterings.

"Lord?" he said. "Are you well?"

Carrion glanced back at his servant. "I have bad dreams, Shape," Carrion told him. "That's all. Bad dreams."

"But why, my Lord?" Shape said. "You're the most

powerful man in the Abarat. What is there in this world that could possibly be troubling to you? As you yourself said: *She's nothing.*"

"How do you know what I was talking about?"

"I just assumed it was the girl. Was I wrong?"

"No . . ." Carrion growled. "You weren't wrong."

"Mater Motley could surely deal with her for you," Shape went on, "if you don't care to. Perhaps you could share your fears with her?"

"I have no desire to share *anything* with that woman."

"But surely, Lord, she's your grandmother. She loves you."

Carrion was becoming irritated now. "My grandmother loves nothing and nobody except *herself,*" he said.

"Maybe if I told her—"

"Told her?"

"About your dreams. She would prepare something to help you sleep."

At this, Carrion let out a raw noise of rage and caught Shape by the windpipe, drawing him so close that his face was pressed against the sweaty surface of Carrion's collar. The nightmares seething in the fluid on the other side came to peer at him, tapping their bright snouts against the glass.

"I warn you, Shape," he said. "If you ever say *anything* to my grandmother about my bad dreams . . . your life will *become* one."

Mendelson scrambled to be free of his master's hold, his good leg pushing Carrion away from him, while his peg leg shook rhythmically in the air.

"I—I—I am loyal to you, Lord," Shape sobbed. "*I swear*, liege, by all that's dark."

As quickly as Carrion had picked Shape up, he let the terrified man go. Shape dropped from his hands like a sack filled with stones and lay splayed on the step, his terror giving off an unmistakable smell.

"I wouldn't have killed you," Carrion remarked lightly.

"Thank . . . thank you . . . Prince," Shape said, still watching his Lord from the corner of his eye as though at any moment the coup de grâce might still fall and his unhappy life be summarily ended.

"Come on now," Carrion said with a brittle brightness in his voice. "Let me show you how much *trust* I have in you. Get up! Get up!"

Shape got to his feet. "I'm going to give you the Key to the Pyramids," Carrion said. "So that you can have the honor of opening the door for me."

"The door?"

"The door."

"Me?"

"You."

Shape still looked queasy about all this. After all, who knew what lay on the other side of that door? But he could scarcely refuse an invitation from his Prince. Especially when the Key was there in front of him, shimmering and seductive.

"Take it," Carrion said.

Shape glanced over Carrion's shoulder at Leeman Vol, who was staring at the Key. He wanted it badly,

Shape could see. If he'd dared, he would have snatched it out of Carrion's hand, run to the door and opened it up, just to say that he'd been the first to see what lay inside.

"Good luck," Vol said sourly.

Shape made an attempt at a smile—which failed—and then went to the door, drew a deep breath, and slid the Key into the lock.

"Now?" he said to Carrion.

"The Key is in your hand," Carrion replied. "Choose your own moment."

Shape took a second deep breath and turned the Key, or at least made an attempt to do so. But it would not move. He leaned against the door, grunting as he attempted to force the Key to turn.

"No! No! No!" Carrion ordered him. *"You'll bruise the Key, imbecile. Step away from the door! Now!"*

Mendelson obeyed instantly.

"Now calm yourself," Carrion instructed him. "Let the Key do the work."

Shape nodded and limped back to the door. Again he put his hand on the Key, and this time—though he was barely pressing upon it—the Key turned in the lock all on its own. Astonished, and not a little terrified, Shape retreated from the door, his work done. The Key was not only turning in the lock, it was slipping deeper into the door as it did so, as if to deny anyone a change of heart. In response to the turning of the Key, an entire area of the door around the lock—perhaps a foot square—began to grind and move. This was no ordinary mechanism: as its effect spread, waves of energy came off the Pyramid like heat from a boiling pot. The door was opening, and its shape echoed that of the building itself: an immense triangle.

A stench came out from the darkness on the other side. It wasn't the smell of the long dead or the spices in which they had been preserved. Nor was it the smell of antiquity; the dull dry fragrance of a time that had been and would not come again. It was the stink of something very much alive. But whatever the life-form that was sweating out this odor, drooling it, weeping it, it was nothing any of the three had ever encountered. Even Carrion, who had a weary familiarity with the world in all its corruptions, had never smelled anything quite like this before. He stared into the darkness beyond the door with an odd little smile on his face. Mendelson, on the other hand, had decided that he'd had enough.

"I'll wait in the barge," he said hurriedly.

"No, you don't," said Carrion, grabbing hold of his collar. "I want them to meet you."

"Them?" said Leeman Vol. "Are . . . are there *many* of them?"

"That's one of the things we're here to find out," the Lord of Midnight replied. "You can count, can't you, Shape?"

"Yes."

"Then go in there, and bring out a number!" Carrion said, and pressing Shape in the direction of the door, he gave his servant a shove.

"Wait!" Shape protested, his voice shrill with fear. *"I don't want to go alone!"*

But it was too late. He was already over the threshold. There was an immediate response from the interior; the din of an infinite number of carapaced things roused from invertebrate dreams, rubbing their hard, spiny legs together, unfurling their stalked eyes. . . .

"What have you got in there?" Vol wanted to know. "Hobarookian scorpions? A huge nest of needle flies?"

"He'll find out!" Carrion said, nodding in Shape's direction.

"A light, Lord!" Shape begged. "Please. At least a light so I can find my way."

After a moment's hesitation, Carrion seemed to soften, and smiling at Shape, he reached into his robes, as if he intended to produce a lamp of some sort. But what came out appeared to be a small top, which he set on the back of his left hand.

There it began to spin, and in spinning threw off waves of flickering light, which grew in brightness.

"Catch!" Carrion said, and flipped the top in Shape's direction.

Shape made an ungainly attempt to catch hold of it, but the thing outwitted him, spinning off between his fingers and hitting the ground. Then it spun off into the Pyramid, its luminescence growing.

Shape looked away from the top and up into the space that its ambitious light was filling. He let out a little sob of terror.

"Wait," Leeman Vol said. "There can only be one insect that gives off a stench such as this."

"And what would that be?" Carrion said.

"Sacbrood," Vol replied, his voice ripe with awe.

Carrion nodded.

"Oh, Gods . . ." Vol murmured, advancing a few steps toward the door to get a better view of the multitudes within. "Did you put them in here?"

"I sowed the seeds, yes," Carrion replied. "Countless years ago. I knew we would come to be in need of them in time. I have a great purpose to put them to."

"What purpose is that?"

Carrion smiled into the soup of his nightmares. "Something mighty," he replied. "Believe me. Something *mighty*."

"Oh, I can imagine," Vol said. "Mighty, yes . . ."

As he spoke, a limb perhaps eight feet long, and divided into a number of thorny segments, appeared from the shadows.

Leeman loosed a cry of alarm and backed away from the door. But Carrion was too quick for him. He caught hold of Vol's arm, stopping him in his stride.

"Where do you think you're going?" he said.

In his panic Vol's three voices trod on one another's tails. "They're *moving—oving—ving*."

"So?" said Carrion. "We're the masters here, Vol, not them. And if they forget, then we have to remind them. We have to control them."

Vol looked at Carrion as though the Lord of Midnight was crazy. "Control *them*?" he said. "There are tens of thousands of them."

"I will need a *million* for the work I want them to do," Carrion said. He pulled Vol closer to him, holding him so tight Vol had to fight for breath. "And believe me, there *are* millions. These creatures are not just in the Pyramids. They've dug down into the earth beneath the Pyramids and made hives for themselves. Hives the size of cities. Every one of them lined with cells, and each one of those cells filled with eggs, all ready to be born at a single command."

"From you?"

"From us, Vol. From *us*. You need me and my power to protect you from being slaughtered when the Last Day comes, and I need your mouths to communicate with the sacbrood. That seems fair, doesn't it?"

"Y—y—yes."

"Good. Then we understand each other. Now you listen, Vol: I'm going to let you go. But don't try running off. If you do I won't take kindly to it. You understand?"

"I—I—I understand."

"Good. So . . . let's see what our allies look like up close, shall we?" he said. He let Leeman Vol go. Vol didn't attempt to make a run for it, even though his soles itched to do so.

"Shield your eyes, Leeman," Carrion instructed him. "This is going to be very bright."

He reached into the folds of his robes and took out perhaps a dozen of the luminous tops. They flew in all directions, spinning and blazing brightly. Some rose up into the heights of the Pyramid, others dropped away through holes that had been opened in the floor of the Pyramid, still others flew off left and right, illuminating other chambers and antechambers. Of the

Kings and Queens who had been laid to rest here in the Pyramids with such panoply, there was nothing left. The sarcophagi that had housed their revered remains had gone, as had the holy books and scrolls that contained the prayers that were written to soothe them to paradise; nothing was left. The slaves, horses and sacred birds slaughtered so that their spirits might escort the royal souls on the Eternal Highway had also gone. The sacbrood's appetite had devoured everything: gold, flesh, bone. The great devouring tribe had taken it all. Chewed it up, digested it.

"Look!" Carrion said as he surveyed the occupants of the Pyramid.

"I see," Vol said. "Believe me, I see."

Even Vol, who had an encyclopedic knowledge of the world of insects, was not prepared for the horror of these creatures' forms; nor for the limitless variety of those forms. Some of the sacbrood were the size of maggots and surrounded by great puddles of stinking life, their bodies hissing as they writhed against one another. Some seemed to have a hundred limbs and scuttled in hordes over the ceilings, occasionally turning on one of their number and sacrificing it to their appetite. Some were flat as sheets of paper and slid over the ground on a film of slime.

But these were the least. There were sacbrood here the size of obese wrestlers, others as huge as elephants. And in the shadows behind these enormities there were greater enormities still, things that could not be comprehended by a single glance of the eye, because their vastness defied even the most ambitious gaze. None seemed afraid of the lights burning in their midst, even after being so long in darkness. Rather they sought out the brightness with a kind of hunger, so that it seemed as though the entire contents of the Pyramid was moving toward the door, revealing their terrible anatomies with more and more clarity. Limbs snapping like scissors, teeth chattering like maddened monkeys, claws rubbing together like the tools of a knife sharpener. There was nothing in their shapes that suggested kindness or compassion: they were evildoers, pure and simple.

"This is greater than I imagined," Carrion said with a perverse pride. "What terrors they are."

As he spoke, a creature the size of ten men emerged from the great mass. Numberless parasitic forms, like lice, crawled over its restless body.

"Do they want to kill us?" Vol wondered aloud. The insects on his head had taken refuge in his collar. He looked strangely vulnerable without their darting company.

"It will tell us, I daresay, when it has a mind to," Carrion said, watching the great creature with a mingling of respect and caution.

Finally it spoke. The language it used, however, was not one that Carrion knew. He listened carefully, and then turned to Leeman Vol for assistance; Vol, whom the Brood-beast seemed to recognize as one who would comprehend it. Indeed he did. He began to translate, a little cautiously at first.

"They . . . *it* . . . welcomes you. Then it tells you: *We are growing impatient.*"

"Does it indeed?" Carrion said. "Then tell it from me: soon, very soon."

Vol replied to the Brood-beast, which went on immediately to speak again, its voice thick and undulating.

"It says that it's heard there are trespassers among the islands."

"There are one or two," Carrion said. Vol's three mouths provided a translation of this. "But nobody will get between us and our Great Plan."

Again the Brood-beast spoke. Again, Vol translated.

"It says: *Do you swear?*"

"Yes," said Carrion, plainly a little irritated that his honesty was being called into question by this monster. "I swear." He looked defiantly at the creature. "What we have planned will come to pass," he said. "No question of it."

At that moment the Brood-beast revealed that it knew more about the craft of communication than it had been displaying, because the creature now spoke again, but in a recognizable fashion. It spoke slowly, as though piecing the words together like the fragments of a jigsaw; but there was no doubting what it said.

"*You . . . will . . . not . . . cheat . . . us, Car-ri-on,*" it said.

"Cheat you? Of course not!"

"*Many . . . years . . . in . . . dark-ness . . . we . . . have . . . waited.*"

"Yes, I—"

"*Hungry!*"

"Yes."

"HUNGRY! HUNGRY!"

The chorus was taken up from every corner of the Pyramid, and from the tunnels and hives many thousands of feet below, and even from the other Pyramids of the six where sacbrood had also bred over the years, and awaited their moment.

"I understand," Carrion said, raising his voice above the din. "You're tired of waiting. And you're hungry. Believe me, I do understand."

His words failed to placate them, however. They moved toward the door from all directions, the horrid details of their shapes more apparent by the moment. Carrion was no stranger to the monstrous—the pits and forests and vermin fields of Gorgossium boasted countless forms of the ghastly and the misbegotten— but there was nothing, even there, that was quite as foul as this loathsome clan, with their fat, wet clusters of eyes and their endless rows of limbs clawing at the rot-thickened air.

"Lord, we should take care," Vol murmured to Carrion. "They're getting closer."

Vol was right. The sacbrood were getting far too close for comfort.

Those overhead were moving the fastest, skittering over one another's bodies in their unholy haste and shedding living fragments of their bodies as they did so, which twitched on the ground where they'd fallen.

"They do seem *very* hungry," Mendelson observed.

"What do you suppose we should do about that, Mr. Shape?" Carrion wondered.

Shape shrugged. "Feed them!" he said.

Carrion reached out suddenly and caught hold of Shape by the nape of his neck. "If you're so concerned about their well-being, Mr. Shape, maybe you should sacrifice your own sorry flesh to their appetite, huh? What do you say?"

"No!" said Shape, trying to wriggle free.

"You say *no*?"

"Yes, Lord, please, Lord. I'd be more use to you alive, I swear."

"In truth, Shape, I can't imagine *any* state in which you'd be of use to me."

So saying, Carrion shoved Shape away. The man stumbled on his stump and fell to his knees in the shadow of the Brood-beast that had been talking to Carrion. For a fleeting moment the thing looked down at him with something close to *pity* on its misshapen face. Shape turned from it, and getting up, he fled across the littered ground, not caring that he was going deeper into the Pyramid, only determined to avoid both Carrion and the creature. As he hobbled away, he heard a sound above him. He froze on the spot, and in that instant a barbed, ragged form—wet and sinewy, and attached by a knotty length of matter to the ceiling—dropped on top of him. Shape cried out as it eclipsed him; then the living cord by which the thing was attached to the roof hauled on its freight, and the creature was taken back into the shadows, with Shape in its grip. He called out to his master one last time, his voice muted by the beast in whose maw he was caught. There was a final series of pitiful little kicks.

Then both cries and kicks stopped, and Shape's life ceased.

"They're feeling murderous," Leeman Vol said to Carrion. "I think we should go."

"Maybe we should."

"Do you have anything else you need to speak with them about?"

"I've said and seen all I need to," Carrion replied. "Besides, there will be other times." He went back to the door, calling to Vol as he did so. "Come away."

Even now Vol watched the creatures with the fascination of a true obsessive, his head twitching left and right, up and down, in his eagerness to see every last detail.

"Away, Vol, away!" Carrion urged him.

Finally Vol made a dash for the door, but even now he paused to glance back.

"*Go!*" Carrion yelled to him, pulling the door shut. "Quickly, before they get out!"

Several of the brood, who were within a few yards of the threshold, made a last desperate attempt to reach the door and block it before it closed, but Carrion was too quick. The Pyramid door closed in the same bizarre fashion that it had opened, and he quickly turned the Key in the lock, sealing the sacbrood in their prison hive. They shook the stones of the Pyramid's walls in their frustration and loosed such a din of rage that the stone steps on which Carrion and Leeman Vol stood vibrated beneath their feet. Still, it was done. Carrion reverentially removed the Key from the lock and slipped it into the deepest recesses of his robes.

"You're shaking," he said to Vol, with a little smile.

"I—I—I—never saw such things before," Vol conceded.

"Nobody has," the Lord of Midnight replied. "Which is why when I choose my moment and set them free, there will be chaos and terror in every corner of the Abarat."

"It'll be like the end of the world," Leeman said, retreating down the steps to the funeral barge.

"No," Carrion said as he followed Leeman down. "There you're wrong. It will be the beginning."

14

LAMENT (THE MUNKEE'S TALE)

CANDY DIDN'T WASTE TIME shivering on the shore. It had been clear even from a distance where on the island she might find some place of relative comfort: in the mist-shrouded forest that lay a quarter mile along the beach. A light, warm breeze was coming out of the trees, its balm both welcoming and reassuring. Occasionally one of its gusts seemed to carry a fragment of music: just a few notes, no more, played (perhaps) on an oboe. A gentle, lilting music that made her smile.

"I wish Malingo was with me," she said to herself as she trudged along the beach.

At least she wasn't alone. All she had to do was follow the sound of the music and she'd surely find the music maker, sooner or later. The more of the melody she heard, the more bittersweet it seemed to be. It was the kind of song her grandfather (her mom's dad, Grandpa O'Donnell) used to sing when she was little. Laments, he called them.

"What's a lament?" she had asked him one day.

"A song about the sad things in the world," he'd told her, his voice tinged with a little of his Irish roots. "Lovers parted, and ships lost at sea, and the world full of loneliness from one end to the other."

"Why'd you want to sing about sad things?" Candy had asked him.

"Because any fool can be happy," he'd said to her. "It takes a man with real heart"—he'd made a fist and laid it against his chest—"to make beauty out of the stuff that makes us weep."

"I still don't understand. . . ."

Grandpappy O'Donnell had cupped her face in his big, scarred hands. He'd worked on the railroad most of his life, and every scar had a story. "No, of course you don't," he said with an indulgent smile. "And why should you? A sweet slip of a girl like you, why should you have to know anything about the sorrow of the world? You just believe me when I tell you . . . there's no way to live your life to the full and not have a reason to shed a tear now and again. It's not a bad feeling, child. That's what a lament does. It makes you feel happy to be sad, in a strange way. D'you see?"

She hadn't seen. Not really. The idea that sadness could somehow make you feel good was a hard idea to fathom.

But now she was beginning to understand. Abarat was changing her. In the brief time she'd been traveling among the Hours, she'd seen and felt things she would never have experienced in Chickentown, not if she'd lived there a thousand years. The way the stars seemed to move when a traveler passed over the boundary between one Hour and the next, and whole constellations fell slowly out of the sky; or when the moon, falling brightly on the sea, called up slow processions of fish from the purple-blue deeps of the Izabella, all showing their sad silver eyes to the sky before they turned and disappeared into the darkness again.

Sometimes just a face she passed by, or a glance someone would give her—even the shadow of a passing bird—would carry a kind of melancholy. Grandpappy O'Donnell would have liked it here, she thought.

She was close to the edge of the misty trees now, and just a little way ahead of her a pathway began, made of mosaic stones that depicted a pattern of interwoven spirals, winding into the forest. It was a strange coincidence that her feet should have brought her precisely to the spot where this path began, but then her time in the Abarat had been filled with such coincidences; she wasn't surprised any longer. And so she simply followed the pathway.

The people who had laid the mosaic had decided to have some fun with the design. Dancing in and out of the spirals were the likenesses of animals—frogs, snakes, a family of creatures that looked like green raccoons—which seemed ready to scamper or slide away as soon as a foot fell too close to them.

She was so busy studying this witty handiwork that she didn't realize how far she'd come. The next time she looked up, the beach had gone from sight behind her, and she was entirely surrounded by the immense trees, their canopy alive with all manner of Night birds.

And still she heard the lament, somewhere off in the distance, rising and falling.

Beneath her feet the spiral designs of the pathway were getting stranger by the step, the species of creatures that had been woven into the design becoming ever more fantastical, as though to alert her to the fact that her journey was about to change. And now ahead of her she saw the threshold of that change: a massive doorway flanked by elegant pillars stood between the trees.

Though the hinges were still in place, and the remains of a hefty iron lock lay on the ground, the door itself had been eaten away by some rot or other. Candy stepped inside. The absent door had guarded a building of exceptional beauty. On every side she saw that the walls were decorated with exquisite frescoes, depicting happy, magical scenes: landscapes in which people danced so lightly they seemed to defy gravity and rise into the sky; or where creatures possessed of an unearthly beauty appeared from the cavorting waters of silver rivers.

Meanwhile the lament continued to play, its melody as bittersweet as ever. She followed the music through the grandiose rooms, every footfall now echoing off the painted stones. The palace had not been left untouched by the forest that surrounded it. The trees, possessed of a feverish fluidity that gave them greater strength than ordinary trees, had pushed through the walls and the ceiling, the mesh of fruit-laden branches so like the intricately carved and painted panels that it was impossible to see where dead wood ended and living began, where paint gave way to leaf and fruit or vice versa. It almost seemed as if the makers of this place, the carvers and the painters, must have known that the forest would invade at last and had designed the palace so that it would swoon without protest into the arms of nature.

She could almost bring to mind the people who had worked here. It seemed easy to picture their furrowed faces as they labored at their masterpiece; though of course it was impossible that she could really know who they were. How could she remember something she hadn't witnessed? And yet the images persisted, growing stronger the deeper she traveled into the palace. She saw in her mind's eye men and women working by the light of floating orbs like little moons, the smell of newly cut timbers and paint freshly mixed sharpening the air.

"Impossible," she told herself aloud, just to be clear about this once and for all.

After a while she realized somebody was keeping pace with her, nimbly moving from shadow to shadow. Now and again she'd catch a tiny glimpse of her pursuer—a flash of its eyes, a blur of what looked like striped fur. Eventually curiosity overcame her. She called out: "Who are you?"

Surprisingly, she got an immediate guttural reply.

"The name's Filth."

"Filth?"

"Yeah. Filth the munkee."

Before she could respond, the creature appeared from between the trees and came to stand, bow-legged, in front of her. He was indeed a monkey, as he had claimed, but he had a decidedly human cast to his crooked face. His eyes were slightly crossed, and his wide, preposterous mouth housed an outrageous assortment of teeth, which he showed whenever he smiled, which was often. He was dressed in what looked to be the remnants of an old circus costume: baggy striped pants held up by a rotting belt, an embroidered waistcoat in red, yellow and blue, and a T-shirt on which was written I'M FILTH. The entire ensemble was caked with mud and pieces of rotted food. The smell he gave off was considerably less than fragrant.

"How did you find your way in here?" he asked Candy.

"I—I followed the music."

"Who are you, anyhow?"

"Candy Quackenbush."

"Daft name."

"No dafter than Filth."

The ape-man raised a grimy finger and without any preamble put it in his nose, pressing it into his nostril and hooking it around so that the top came out of the other hole. Candy did her best not to look appalled in case it encouraged him.

"Well, then we're both daft, aren't we?" he said, wiggling his finger.

Candy was no longer able to disguise her revulsion. "Do I disgust you?" he asked her cheerfully.

"A little," she admitted.

The munkee tittered. "The King used to be most amused when I did that."

"The King?"

"King Claus of Day. This was his Twilight Palace, this place. These are the borderlands of his domain, of course. By the time you get halfway up Galigali, it's Night."

Candy looked around at the remnants of the fine building with new respect.

"So this was a *palace*."

"It still *is*," Filth said. " 'Cept it don't have Kings or Queens in it no more."

"What happened to them?"

"Weren't you taught no history at school?"

"Not Abaratian history, no."

"What other kind of history is there?" Filth said, giving Candy a strange look from the corner of his eye. He didn't wait for an answer. "Actually, the palace was really built for Claus' daughter, Princess Boa. And when she died, her father told everybody— his courtiers, his cooks, his maidservants, his fool— *me*—to just go our various ways and find happiness any way we could."

"But you didn't go?"

"Oh, I went for a while. I tried being a nun, but I didn't like the hats." Candy laughed at this, but Filth's expression remained perfectly serious, which somehow made the joke even funnier.

"So you came back?" Candy said.

"Where else was I going to go? What's a fool to do

without a King? I was nothing. Nobody. At least here I had the *memory* of being happy. *She'd* made us happy, you see. She could do that."

"*She* being—?"

"Princess Boa, of course."

Princess Boa. It was a name Candy had heard spoken several times, but always in whispers.

"Claus had two children," Filth said, "Prince Quiffin and Princess Boa. They were both fine, beautiful creatures—that's Quiffin over there." He pointed to a portrait of a fine-featured young man, with his dark hair and beard coiffed into delicate curls. "And the girl gathering the arva blossoms, over there? That's my sweet Princess when she was eleven. She was something special, even then. Another order of being, she was. There was this *light* in her . . . in her eyes. No. *In her soul.* It just shone out of her eyes. And it didn't matter how grumpy or down in the mouth you were feeling, you only had to be with her for a minute or two and everything was good again." He fell silent for a few seconds, then very quietly repeated himself: "Everything . . . was . . . good."

"Was it a sickness that killed her?"

"No. *She was murdered.*"

"Murdered? How horrible."

"On the day of her wedding. Right there in the church, standing beside the man she was going to marry, Finnegan Hob." Tears were brimming in the munkee's eyes. "I was there. I saw it all. And I never want to see anything so terrible again as long as I live. It was as if all the light went out of the world in one moment."

"Who murdered her?" Candy asked.

Filth's face was completely motionless, except his eyes, which flickered back and forth like panicked prisoners in the cells of his skull.

"They said a dragon did it. Well, a dragon *did* do it; at least the killing part. And Finnegan killed the thing right outside the church, so that was an end to that. But the real villain . . ." His eyes closed for a moment. When they opened again he was looking directly at Candy. "The Lord of Gorgossium," he said, very quietly. "That's who made it happen. Christopher Carrion."

"Why wasn't he arrested?"

The munkee made a bitter laugh. "Because he's the Prince of Midnight. Untouchable by the laws of Day. And nobody on the Nightside would bring him to law; how could they? Not when he was the last Carrion! It makes me crazy to think about it! He has her blood on his hands, her *light* on his hands. And he goes free, to cause more mischief. There's no justice in this world!"

"You know this for certain?" Candy said. "That he's guilty of her murder?"

After a moment's musing, Filth said: "Put it this way: if he was standing here right now, and I had the means to do away with him . . . I would." The munkee snapped his fingers. "Like that! There are some things you don't need evidence for. You just *know*. In your heart. I don't know *why* he did it. I don't really care. I only know he did." Now he fell silent, and in the lush breeze the lament returned.

"Sad music," Candy said.

"Well, this isn't a place of dancing. Not anymore. Will you excuse me for a while? I don't feel in the mood to go on talking."

"Oh yes, of course. I'm sorry. I shouldn't have—"

"The number of times I've told myself: do your best to be happy. You can't change the past. She's gone forever. And that's all there is to it. But I suppose there's a little corner of my heart that refuses to believe that."

He gave Candy one last, mournful glance, and then he headed off into the blue shadows. As he went he said: "The musician's called Bilarki, by the way. He doesn't talk anymore, so don't try and get a conversation out of him; you'll be wasting your time."

15

THE PURSUER

TWO SUMMERS BEFORE, THERE had been a tragedy in Chickentown that could have matched the tale of Princess Boa for sadness. A young man called Johnny Morales had come into town for his sister Nadine's wedding, and the night before had been killed in an automobile accident. The young man's passenger, who was the bridegroom-to-be, had also been killed. They'd been drinking heavily at the groom-to-be's bachelor party, and laughing together (according to a survivor of the wreck) when Morales had lost control of his car and run off the highway into a tree. The double tragedy had been too much for Nadine. Having lost her brother and her beloved in one terrible moment, she gave up on life. Two and a half months later she checked into a rundown motel on the outskirts of town and took enough of her mother's sleeping pills to make sure she never woke up again. The pain, the sadness, the meaninglessness of her life without her brother and her almost-husband had over-whelmed her.

Candy had known Nadine just a little; she had worked as a checkout girl at the supermarket where her mother, Melissa Quackenbush, had shopped. She'd always seemed the kind of person Candy could never imagine herself being: always smiling, always helpful.

Her death had affected Candy deeply. For reasons she couldn't really understand, she'd felt profoundly sad. Sadder even than what she'd felt when Grandpappy O'Donnell had passed away.

She'd dreamed about being at the wedding many times after that, in a huge church filled with the kind of flowers you'd only ever see in a dream. Sometimes she'd been a guest at the wedding (though in reality nobody from the Quackenbush family had been close enough to any of the bride's or bridegroom's families to be invited). Sometimes she'd been the bride. She hadn't told anybody the dreams. She'd felt a little foolish about having them; after all, she really had no *right* to them. It wasn't her tragedy. Why then had it moved her so deeply?

She sat in the chamber with the portraits of Prince Quiffin and the young Princess Boa and turned the puzzle over, looking for some way *in* to it. She felt a connection here in the Twilight Palace: the sadness of Nadine Morales and that of Princess Boa joined by a bridge of her *own* feelings, her *own* thoughts. But why? What was the purpose of that bridge?

And while she was asking herself these questions, it was probably worth also asking why fate had dropped her here in the palace in the first place. As Methis had carried her toward the Hour of Seven and the mist-shrouded trees had come into view, she'd had the distinct impression that there was something here that was significant; though at the time she hadn't known what. Now she did. These empty, lament-filled rooms were what had drawn her. Those, and the story she had just heard.

Now, having heard it, she wanted to leave. The munkee's story had brought back the thoughts of Nadine Morales, and she wanted to put those out of her head. But there was still a large part of the palace she hadn't seen. She couldn't leave here (possibly to never come back) without investigating further. So, as the invisible Bilarki continued to play his laments (a different melody now, but no less sad than those that had preceded it), she ventured deeper and deeper into the palace. The light diminished as she went, and the darker it got the easier it was to imagine how these rooms might have been when the palace had still been in its glory. What an amazing place it must have been! The walls bright with color, the air full of laughter and the smell of good food. If only she'd been here to see it. In a way, she thought, she'd come to the Abarat too late; its days of fine palaces and great Kings and Queens were over. The Abarat had become a chaotic place, overshadowed by murder and bad magic, by sadness and freak shows and the ever-present laughter of the Commexo Kid.

The sheer weight of Bilarki's music was beginning to take its toll. The farther she went, the more tired she became. Her limbs began to feel heavy. Soon she wanted to lie down and sleep for a while. And why not? She was as safe here as any other place. Safer, probably. She found herself a chaise lounge that looked reasonably comfortable and sat down on it. Up in the branches of the trees Bilarki moved like a ghost, trailing his laments as he walked through the trees.

Her lids were like lead; they soon closed. In a few seconds her head was filled with voices, rising up out of the walls around her. Somebody seemed to call her, as if from the past.

"Come here, dear one!" he said.

"The stars are so bright tonight," a young woman's voice replied. *"I wonder what they say?"*

"Don't ask! Never ask."

"Why not?"

"Because you might not like the answer."

She heard somebody laughing at this and turned her dream sight around, looking for whoever it was who was so amused, and she found a man with a large gray beard standing at the opposite end of the room. Even if he hadn't been wearing a crown, Candy would instantly have recognized him as the King. He looked directly at her in the dream, and there was such love in his eyes, such deep, unspoilable love, that it made Candy want to cry with pleasure. She could never remember her father looking at her in such a way.

"What's this, child?" Claus said. *"Please, no tears."*

Candy put her hand up to her face. Her cheeks were wet. The King approached her, opening his arms as he approached.

"There's nothing in the world to be sad about, darling."

"I was only thinking of how different things will be when I'm married" came the reply. It was her voice she heard speaking, but it was subtly changed. It had a richness in it that wasn't in Candy's voice, a kind of lilting music. She made a note to herself to remember this when she woke from this dream.

"He loves you," King Claus said to her. *"He loves you, my darling, with all his heart. If he did not, I would not allow him to marry you and take you away from me."*

Claus smiled and gently stroked her face. She half expected his fingers to be cold—reaching as he was from the past—but no, they were warm and soft. He spoke again, now almost whispering.

"Finnegan is a child of both Night and Day," he said. *"There has never been a man like him in the history of the islands. At least none that we know of. It is a gift of the Gods that you two should find each other and fall in love. Together you will heal a breach that has divided these islands for generations."* In Claus' eyes she could see how this prospect delighted him. *"You'll have the most beautiful children the Abarat has ever seen, and this palace will be the perfect place for them to live, because it stands at the spot where the Dark Hours meet the Light.*

"Smile," he said again, oh so softly.

She put her hand up and covered his, interweaving their fingers.

Before she could make the smile he wanted to see,

she heard somebody shouting, far off.

"What is that?" she said.

King Claus was still looking at her with that sweetly loving expression, as though he hadn't heard her ask the question. The shouting became louder, but no more coherent. Whoever it was who was doing the yelling, he was in a state of panic.

She looked around, but there was no sign of an intruder. The room she was in was bright and happy, like the people in it.

Then she realized: the panicker wasn't here with her in this dream. He was outside, in the waking world!

"I have to go," she said to Claus. It was strange to be talking this way to somebody in a dream, but he'd been so kind to her that she didn't want to offend him.

"Where are you going?" King Claus said. *"You belong here. Always. Always."*

"I have to wake up!" she said.

He looked at her with a puzzled expression on his face. *"Wake up?"* he said. *"But you're not dreaming—"*

"Yes, I am. I am! Listen to that shouting!"

"I can't hear anything," King Claus said gently. *"Is this a joke?"*

"No—" she said, stepping away from him. *"I have to go."*

His fingers were still interwoven with hers; he didn't want to let her go. Nor, in a way, did she want to lose contact with him. She could have happily bathed in the King's voice and words for another hour.

Still, she *had* to go. The panicked voice was close. And now she recognized it.

"Filth!" she said.

"The munkee?" Claus replied.

"Yes. Yes, the munkee!" Candy replied. *"He's in trouble. I have to go to him!"* She pulled her hand from the King's hand, and as they broke contact she felt herself rising up out of the waking dream. *"I'm sorry,"* she said to the King as his face grew dimmer before her. *"I'm sure I'll—"*

She didn't have a chance to finish the sentence. At that moment she woke, and the dream disappeared in a heartbeat.

Filth was at her side, his eyes crazier than ever.

"We gotta problem!" he hollered. "We gotta *big* problem!"

"What is it?" said Candy, rubbing her eyes.

"I went down to the beach to get some fresh air, and this boat came in with four stitchlings rowing. You know what stitchlings are?"

"Oh yes. I'm afraid I do."

"These weren't your normal stitchlings, though. These were bigger, stronger. And they had these helmets—"

"Mires. They're called mires," Candy said grimly. "I assume they weren't alone?"

"No."

"There was a man with criss-cross tattoos on his cheeks leading them?"

"Yes, there was."

"His name's Otto Houlihan, sometimes called the Criss-Cross Man."

"I've heard of him. He's—"

"A hunter. He works for the man who killed your Princess—"

"Christopher Carrion."

"Exactly."

"And now Houlihan's coming after you?"

"Yes."

"Why?"

"I guess Carrion thinks I'm trouble."

Filth tilted his head, a look of bemusement on his face. "Why would he think that?"

"Long story."

"The short version."

"Well . . . I came from the Hereafter. By accident. *I think . . .*"

"Go on," said Filth.

"There are some people in Gorgossium who think I'm here to spoil their plans."

"What kind of plans?"

"I don't know."

"So you're not—"

"Not what?"

"Here to spoil their plans?"

"No. I don't even know what their plans are."

"So they're barking up the wrong tree."

"Yes. But I just happen to be *up* in this tree, and it doesn't seem to matter to them that I'm innocent."

"They'll take you anyway."

"Probably."

"Huh." Filth considered all this for a moment. "Fascinating," he remarked. Then: "Gotta go."

"You're leaving?"

"Yes. Well, I'm—"

"—a busy munkee!"

"A coward."

Candy laughed, despite the grimness of her situation.

"At least I'm honest," said Filth. "Good-bye. It was really nice knowing you."

There was a loud crash from the direction of the palace entrance, followed by Houlihan's voice.

"Candy Quackenbush," he yelled. "Show yourself! Give yourself up! Do you hear me?"

Filth gave Candy a cheesy grin, then fled, bounding through a window that was set too high in the wall for Candy to follow him through.

"Thanks a bunch, munkee!" she called softly after him.

Houlihan, meanwhile, was following his nose through the labyrinth of the palace, his voice getting louder all the time.

"You've nowhere left to run," he shouted. "Just throw yourself down on the ground and wait for me."

Candy did her best to put the Criss-Cross Man out of her head and instead concentrated on how to avoid her pursuer. There were plenty of doors, but where did they lead? If she took the wrong turn, the passageway might lead her back into Houlihan's hands.

While she was pondering all this, the breeze that had first come blowing along the beach out of the trees came once more against her face, carrying Bilarki's music. She would follow it, she decided, and hope that it would lead her to safety. Where was it coming from? She held her breath, listening closely. Ah, *there*!

Through the door off to her right, with the clouds carved into the dark frame.

She didn't linger. Slipping off her shoes, she hurried to the door and pushed it open. The breeze was waiting on the other side, and so was Bilarki's music. She followed it, fleet footed, praying to herself that it would lead her to safety.

One thing was certain: the chase was leading her into rooms which she had so far not discovered; rooms that became more miraculous in appearance the farther she traveled. One room had walls that looked as though they'd been carved from green ice (though the walls were quite warm); another was cunningly decorated with an open window through which a forest could be seen that threw down a shadow made of light. But she had no time to admire any of these places for more than a moment. The sound of Houlihan's approach was never very far off, and sometimes his stitchlings set up a hellish howling which echoed through the palace as though it were some terrible madhouse. Luckily, she still had Bilarki's music. Just as she felt certain she had come around in a circle and was going to be delivered into Houlihan's grip, she would find that the music had led her into a completely new part of this extraordinary labyrinth.

Her good fortune couldn't go on forever, however. By degrees the sound of her pursuers became louder, and more than once as she slipped out of one door she saw their shadows crossing the threshold of another.

"I see you . . ." the Criss-Cross Man called after her.

"I told you, Candy Quackenbush. *There's nowhere left to run. . . .*"

She glanced back, and he was there, finally, his face the same sickly yellow she remembered, his eyes fetid with hatred. For a moment his gaze fixed upon her and she was held by it, as though he had somehow rooted her feet to the floor. It took a great effort of will to unglue herself, but she managed it. She turned away from him and scanned the wall ahead in search of an exit. At first she could see no door: only a fresco depicting a purple landscape, its horizon lit by a constellation of lantern stars, where animals that looked like escapees from some gossamer circus paraded and leaped.

But her eyes were sharp, even in the half-light of the Twilight Palace. There *was* a door in the wall. It was just so cunningly incorporated into the elegant painting that it was at first not apparent.

Now she saw it; and ignoring another warning from Houlihan, she fled through it, and into the Twilight Palace's strangest chamber.

16

THE WUNDERKAMMEN

IN THE MIDDLE OF the room was a tree whose ambitious branches had pierced the roof of the chamber. Sitting at the base of the tree on a large toadstool was the musician whose laments had drawn Candy to this palace of strange wonders in the first place: Bilarki. He was a relatively commonplace-looking individual, except for the tendrils of spiraling matter that grew out of his head and his back, swaying to the rhythm of the music that he played. His instrument was not an oboe, as Candy had first guessed; it was something far more Abaratian, and the notes that arose from it were woven strands of green and turquoise and orange.

She was loathe to distract him from his music making, but the situation was dire.

"Excuse me," she said to him. "Is there a way out of here? Besides the way I came in, I mean."

He opened his eyes, which had been closed in pleasure, and looked at her sideways. She could tell by the expression on his face that he understood what she was saying to him, but instead of responding he just continued to play. Or did he? Was the playing somehow a *way* of responding to her? The music had shrugged off its sadness completely now and was getting increasingly urgent. She attended closely. What was he saying?

"There *is* another way, isn't there?" she said.

Bilarki played on. He was almost in a frenzy by now. Clearly he wasn't going to reply to her.

She glanced back toward the door through which she'd come. On the other side of it she could hear the sound of objects being broken, furniture being overturned. Clearly Houlihan was prepared to trash the entire palace rather than let her slip through his fingers again as she had on Ninnyhammer, Soma Plume, Huffaker and Babilonium. With the music adding fuel to her fire, she began to search along the walls, high and low, looking for some sign of another door.

The scene painted on the wall—which showed two monkish characters (one human, one Abaratian) carrying staffs that bloomed into leaves and stars—made the search more difficult, its elaborate beauty constantly distracting her from the simple business of finding a handle, or a switch, even a narrow crack that would offer some clue to the location of an exit. Still, she was thorough, keeping her palms pressed to the wall while she systematically moved around the room.

The music was losing its agitation, she noticed. What was it telling her? That she was getting *cold*. Yes! Glancing up at Bilarki, she reversed the direction of her search, and sure enough the music from the trees above regained its momentum, urging her on in the direction she was going. She reached the corner of the room, looking along the wall ahead of her. It didn't look too promising. There was no sign of any crack or fissure along the wall, however insignificant. But still the music urged her on, and she obeyed its urgent instruction, investigating this wall as carefully as she had the last.

She didn't waste a moment looking back toward the door. She didn't need to. She could hear the sound of destruction getting steadily louder as Houlihan and his monsters searched the room behind her. It was only a matter of time before they found the door through which she'd come. A minute or two if she was lucky. Seconds, more likely.

And then, without warning, the music changed again. The urgent music suddenly gave way to a slow steady chord, which seemed to catch at her heart. She pressed at the wall in front of her with renewed intensity, as the chord Bilarki was playing became more powerful. Was it her imagination, or was there a faint *reverberation* in the wall? No, she wasn't imagining it. The painted wall *was* trembling, as though it knew a secret and it was shaking with the anticipation of sharing what it knew.

The din from behind her was suddenly terrifyingly loud. And this time she couldn't help herself: she glanced back. To her great surprise, she saw Filth the munkee ducking through the door, obviously doing his best to look as small as possible as he ran. He kept running until he reached Candy, at which point he did his best to hide behind her skinny legs.

"You came back," she said, smiling down at him.

"Ssh!" he replied, nervously fingering his booger-filled nostrils. "They're right outside the door."

He had no sooner spoken than several things happened at the same moment. First, the tremulous chord that Bilarki had been playing resolved itself into some final state, and the wall beneath Candy's palm churned and shook and opened up. She heard Filth gasp, and she looked down to see an expression of awe on his simian face.

"Will you look at that?" he said.

Candy followed the line of his gaze. She had perhaps four seconds to marvel at the unveiling of the room. Then she heard the sound of her pursuers squabbling to be the first through the door, and Houlihan's voice cutting through the argument.

"I see you, Candy Quackenbush!"

Again she looked back. Houlihan's face had grown brighter since she'd looked at him a few minutes before. Now it cast a jaundiced luminosity on the mire-stitchlings who surrounded him with a most unflattering light, revealing them in all their terrible emptiness, like living scarecrows dragging their rotted carcasses through these exquisite chambers in pursuit of her.

"Bring her to me!" the Criss-Cross Man cried.

At his instruction the stitchlings came lumbering across the room, all reaching out to be the first to lay their cold hands on her.

"Quick!" Filth said. *"Move yourself before it's too late!"*

He pulled on her arm and hauled her through the opening in the wall.

The room on the other side wasn't like any other room that she'd found in the palace. There was nothing in it made for human comfort: no chairs, no table, no bed. There were shelves on three of the four walls, built from floor to ceiling, but there was nothing *on* those shelves that might have been for the entertainment of the palace's occupants, such as books. Instead the place was filled, every available inch of it, with objects that had nothing in common with one another.

Hanging from the ceiling on a web of rusty chains was a stuffed reptile of some kind, which possessed six pairs of petite but brightly colored feathered wings and a seventh, much larger wing, which grew from the crown of its long-snouted head. A mummy sitting in a chair looking thoroughly bored. On the shelves behind the desiccated giant were dozens of jars, urns, flasks and other odd vessels in which were pickled a bizarre cross section of objects both natural and unnatural. In one was a bird with a baby's head (or a baby with a bird's body), wearing a pretty pink lace bonnet. In another was a creature with a halo of tentacles, posed against a painted seascape. Many of the objects weren't even things she could name, odd encrusted forms that might have been the rusted parts of some ancient clockwork machinery or the fossilized remnants of some ancient crustacean or the curious mingling of the two.

On another wall, a collection of masks had been hung in no particularly artful arrangement; and among them, dolls in wedding dresses, their once-virginal lace yellowed by time.

"This is the *Wunderkammen*," the munkee explained. "I think that's a word that comes from the Hereafter. It means a Cabinet of Wonders." It was the oddest collection Candy had ever seen and utterly arbitrary: as though somebody had simply assembled in one room every strange and unusual thing he had ever laid his hands or eyes upon. The centerpiece was an Abaratian totem pole carved of wood and garishly painted: a tribe of creatures sitting one on top of the shoulders of another, some squatting comfortably, others balanced precariously. The pole was too tall to be accommodated by the room. A hole had been cut in the ceiling, and the totem rose another eight or nine feet beyond.

Despite the need to move on before Houlihan caught up with them, the pole was too extraordinary for Candy to just pass it by.

"What is it?" she asked Filth.

"It's a tribe," he replied. "A whole tribe, frozen together."

"Why?"

"Punishment. They're called the Totemix. And they're *troublemakers*, let me tell you."

Candy's eyes flicked up and down the Totemix, going from face to face. There were all manner of peculiarities in the assembly: wild men and crazy women, cross-eyed children and face-pulling dogs. She was still looking at this incredible collection when she heard the Criss-Cross Man's voice behind her.

"Well, well . . ." Houlihan said. "Look at this!

You've got a nose for objects of power, Quackenbush!"

"I do?"

"First the Key—"

"That wasn't me."

"Now King Claus' private collection of astonishments, huh? His Wunderkammen. I would never have
found it if I hadn't had you to follow. Carrion will be
very pleased. Very pleased. He might even decide not
to have you executed." Houlihan smiled. "Though I
doubt that," he said, putting on a passable imitation of
regret. "Nuth! Yitter! Take her away. But be careful
with her, you understand me?"

The two largest stitchlings growled their response
and approached Candy with a strange caution, as
though they were afraid of her or something in her
vicinity.

But just as they laid their hands on her, the munkee
unleashed a screech so sudden and so loud that it made
the stitchlings lose their grip on their quarry. Candy
was quick. She ducked past their outstretched fingers
and made a rush for the door. Houlihan blocked her
way, a smug smile on his checkered face.

"Not this time," he said.

He casually shoved her back into the room, and she
fell against a table on which was laid a group of carved,
brightly painted Gods and Goddesses. The statues fell
to the floor, and Candy went down among them. As she
fell, she could have sworn she heard voices nearby,
speaking as it were through fixed expressions.

"Lordy-Lou!" somebody said.

"*Down she goes!*" said another.

"*Clumsy, ain't she?*" a third remarked.

She picked up one of the statues by its wooden legs and peered at it.

"Did you speak?" she said to it.

The statue stared back at her with dead eyes. *No, it hadn't spoken.* So what had?

"Take her!" Houlihan yelled to his stitchlings, and the bigger of the two came rushing at her. She attempted to defend herself with the statue, but Yitter—if Yitter it was—simply snatched the carving out of her grip and struck her a blow that flung her halfway across the room. She landed at the base of the totem pole.

Houlihan sauntered toward her.

"*It's over, girl,*" he said. "You're mine."

He was interrupted by a dark blur that dropped down from the ceiling. It was Filth. The momentum threw the Criss-Cross Man backward as Filth beat him with his fists.

"*Get this ape off me!*" Houlihan yelled.

"I'm not an ape!" Filth screeched. "*I'm a munkee! MUN! KEEEE!*"

Candy knew she only had a few seconds' grace before the stitchlings pulled Filth off Houlihan. She reached up and caught hold of the totem, intending to pull herself to her feet. The moment she made contact with the object, however, she felt a shock in her hand which ran up her arm, through her shoulder, up her neck and into her head, where it erupted in a strangely pleasurable burst of feeling. Though there was chaos everywhere, her thoughts were cool and comfortable. She looked down at the palm of her hand and saw to her astonishment that it was bright, almost *golden*; in fact, the map of her anatomy—bones and nerves and all the rest—was suddenly visible to her. It wasn't upsetting to see her hand this way. Quite the reverse. It was wonderful. In a timeless space where there was no Criss-Cross Man, nor stitchlings, she stared down at the intricacies of her palm with sweet wonderment.

The vision didn't last long. Not wanting to lose it, she put her hand back on the totem, hoping the renewed contact would ignite that golden fire a second time. And it did! As soon as she touched the carvings, a fresh wave of feeling passed up through her hand and blossomed in her head.

She felt a rush of energy against her face, like a breath exhaled. And with it the sound of voices—the same voices that had spoken so unflatteringly when she'd fallen down but that now were speaking what sounded like a single multisyllabled word, from which she could pick out only a few recognizable sounds.

"*—camunanotafreexamalesatacpolastafan—*"

She looked up at the pole, and her mind, which had been struggling with the mystery of things half remembered since she'd stepped over the palace threshold, was suddenly granted a rush of comprehension.

Totemix! Filth had said *Totemix!* That was the name of the creatures who were gabbling right now. They were a tribe called the Totemix! And they were there in the pole, being stirred from their slumbers by the touch of her palm!

She saw them moving now, shifting in their skin of paint, their eyes flickering, their mouths widening, parting, smiling as the spell of life moved up the pole from the spot where Candy had made contact. With every few inches it crept, a new limb or organ would be granted life. An arm extended itself, a foot wriggled its three-jointed toes, a trio of eyes focused on the world they had woken to. There were none among the Totemix that were completely human; but then there were none that were completely animal either.

One, she saw, was a long-limbed, round-bodied creature with a single horn on its head; another had three vaguely feline heads, but wore a fancy suit; a third and fourth were joined at the head, their features indistinguishable.

The first creatures to escape this strange prison were the birds, or those of vaguely birdlike form. They leaped out of their solid state with grateful cries, instantly climbing up to the heights of the chamber and circling the vaulted ceiling. Their voices seemed to be a call to life; it speeded up the waking of the other Totemix. A creature with a serpentine body and vermilion wings flew up to join the congregation of birds; a creature with a nose that could be played like a violin came out making his own strange music. A woman bristling with white fur threw herself at the wall and did a somersault off it. Everywhere there were jubilations and astonishments, whoops of joy and shouts of delight.

None of the creatures looked angry or ready to do any harm, but the Criss-Cross Man kept his distance nevertheless. Again he ordered the stitchlings to move in and bring Candy to him, but even they were reluctant to get too close to the awakening Totemix.

Meanwhile the resurrection continued, as living things jumped and flew from every part of the pole. In some places so many creatures had been cunningly woven together that when they came to life it was like upending a jug of living things and letting the contents spill out. Tiny rodents uncurling themselves as they tumbled, piglike animals that possessed squeals out of all proportion to their diminutive size, long-limbed apes no bigger than Candy's hand. And while this rain of tiny marvels fell, much greater beasts rose up from the column like bathers emerging from a warm bath: sluggish at first, but invigorated by the first gust of cool air that came against their faces.

Candy sat in the midst of this springing up of life with tears of joy and amazement in her eyes. She had seldom felt so happy as she did right now.

Houlihan was *not* happy. It pleased him not at all to see this spectacle of conspicuous happiness, of golden light and joyful birdsong, of things coming forth into the living world with yelps of bliss. It disgusted and revolted him. Most of all, he was revolted by the Quackenbush girl, who was sitting at the heart of all these birthings wearing tears and an idiotic smile. Twice now he had ordered the stitchlings to venture into the chaos of light and life and bring her to him. But the stitchlings, even the mires, were stupid, superstitious creatures. They were intimidated by the flux of power that surrounded the girl. The only way he was going to be able to finish this wretched business off, Houlihan knew, was for him to venture into the tribe of Totemix and seize Candy with his own hands.

He wasn't entirely weaponless. He had bought from a man in Huffaker a Star-Striker, a four-foot-long bat, which had been used in the ancient and brutal sport of Star-Striking. Strikers were *moral* things. They knew the difference between good and bad and chose to favor one or the other. The striker that Houlihan carried with him had been owned by a line of fearsome Star-Strikers, who had played the great game with brutal, and often lethal, efficiency. In other words, he carried a bat that had not only struck falling stars out of the air but had killed many innocents along the way. He liked its heft. It gave him confidence. It had all the authority of an executioner's ax. He lifted it up and let it fall weightily on his shoulder. Then, doing his best to ignore all the brouhaha of the Totemix, he focused his attentions upon the girl from the Hereafter.

"Count the seconds, Candy Quackenbush," he said. Something had cracked inside him, as he'd watched Candy among the Totemix. Whatever Carrion's orders had been, he would not be bringing Candy back to Gorgossium alive. With the Star-Striker held tight in his hand he went in pursuit of the girl, determined to bring an end to her and her corruptions once and for all.

17

THE STAR-STRIKER

BEING IN THE MIDST of the loosing of the Totemix was like nothing Candy had ever seen or felt before. The golden light that she'd first seen in her own hand now filled the air all around her, a great vortex in which many of the resurrected creatures still cavorted as though simply for the sheer pleasure of it. Was this what the beginning of the world had been like, she wondered? A kind of bright spiral-dance?

She wanted to be a part of that dance. She got to her feet and began to spin around in the middle of the light, laughing as if she were half crazy. Maybe she was. Maybe this whole adventure was a kind of mad dream, which she was inventing as she went along. If so, she didn't want to wake up from it. There was too much to see, to much to—

Wait! As she spun around she caught an unwelcome glimpse of an interloper in this magic dance. The Criss-Cross Man had left his refuge by the door and was coming toward the center of the room, wielding a weapon of some kind. Arcs of blue-black lightning sprang from it, hitting the walls and even, on occasion, the ceiling. The weapon gave off a smell of burning sugar mingled with something fouler. The waves of golden power flowing from the Totemix recoiled from the weapon, as though in disgust at its essential nature.

To judge by the expression on Otto Houlihan's face, he was pleasurably surprised at the weapon's efficiency. He wielded it with two hands, cutting a dark swathe through the golden veils of life, hacking his way in Candy's direction.

"It's over, girl," he said. "This is the end! The end!"

Candy stopped dancing and focused on Houlihan as best she could, looking for some way to slip past him.

"Filth!" she yelled.

"Over here!" the munkee replied.

Filth had clambered up a stack of shelves and was now squatting at the top.

"Get out of here!" Candy called to him. *"And get all the Totemix out too!"*

"Why?"

"Him!" Candy said, nodding toward the Criss-Cross Man.

Filth got the message immediately. Candy watched him start to scramble down the shelves, then she returned her attention to the enemy.

Houlihan had raised the dark weapon above his head.

"Star-Striker! Star-Striker!" Candy heard Filth yell. "Watch out, he's got a Star-Striker!"

She glanced over her shoulder, wondering how far she had to retreat. Not very far, as it turned out. The eruption of power from the unleashing of the Totemix had thrown over a great mass of furniture; she would have to turn her back on Houlihan to clamber over it all, leaving her exposed to attack.

But what other option did she have? It was either that or remain standing here in the midst of the light, and letting him—

The light. Of course: the light.

She opened her hands and stared down at her palms. The golden glow she'd seen there was still shining as bright as ever. Motes and scraps of brightness were drawn to her fingers from the air.

It's all part of the dance, she thought; the dust, her hands, the light that was spiraling around her: *it's all part of the same wonderful dance. And I'm in it.*

She reached down and closed her hand around the bright air, then tugged at it. There was weight in the luminescence, and strength. It was like pulling on a piece of fabric; she could feel the light folding around her fingers, eager to make itself more intimate with her.

If Houlihan guessed what she was up to, she knew he would rush to quicken her end. But he was too intent on his weapon at that moment; his gaze was turned up lovingly toward the Star-Striker.

Candy had room in her heart to feel a little pang of sorrow for him, that he would never feel the joy that had been granted to her in the time she had explored the mysteries of the Abarat. He had chosen evil and darkness; poor, sad man that he was . . .

All the while that she was shaping these thoughts,

she was working at the light with her hands, subtly gathering it to her body. It came more easily by the moment; like attracting like. She could feel a comforting cocoon of light assembling around her, and the golden luminescence from her hands was now spreading up her arms. It was spilling off her face too, she knew; she could see it lightening the air in front of her. What must she look like, she thought? Perhaps a little *terrifying*?

Oh, to have the chance to walk the streets of Chickentown like this! Or better still, to go home to Followell Street and find her father sitting slumped in front of the TV, surrounded by beer cans and the stink of cigarettes. He would look up and see her standing there, shedding brightness. Maybe that would wake him out of his stupor!

She was momentarily distracted by the thought of her father, and in those few seconds Houlihan stepped forward to cut her down. In fact it almost seemed that the Star-Striker was doing the leading. The blow was just a heartbeat away. She drew a desperate breath. The light flooded her body, pouring inside her, filling her with its strength.

The next moment the Star-Striker came slicing down. Candy was there to meet it, a net of light spread between her hands. The weapon struck the net, and she saw the two opposing forces break against each other like two tremendous waves, light shattering dark shattering light shattering dark—

She felt the impact immediately, saw the needles of the Star-Striker's force speeding toward her. But the light was her ally. It gathered around her to ward off the blow and keep her from harm, driving the needles back at their deliverer without even scratching her.

In the middle of this confrontation, her point of view was suddenly changed. She saw the room from someplace high above her head. Everything in the room was picked up by the powers that were unleashed there, picked up and carried into the same delirious flux. The objects that had been neatly arranged in the room when she'd first stepped into it were now thrown into fantastic confusion, spun around by the currents of the warring energies. Gigantic shells, strange musical instruments, carved mirrors, flowers of immense size, two pairs of jewel-encrusted boots, several shrunken heads, a spindly skeleton dressed in rags, a doll's house of exquisite elaboration (its doors and windows thrown open in the storm, adding a hundred rooms' worth of Lilliputian furniture to the dance), and a great deal else Candy could not have put a name to. Then there were the Totemix, who were also whirling around, most of them laughing for the sheer joy of this ride; holding on to their tails so that they rolled around like airborne wheels, or surfing the tide of warring powers as though it was the greatest game in Creation.

Perhaps it was, Candy thought. Perhaps this struggle between light and dark was at the very heart of why she was here in the Abarat: the Night-world and the Day-world in a conflict that would in time draw everything into one tremendous, world-changing maelstrom.

She had lost sight of Houlihan for a time, but now she saw him again at the center of the swirling chaos. He was still holding on to the Star-Striker with both hands, but the expression on his face was no longer quite so confident. He seemed afraid. And with good reason. Every dark wave of power that the Star-Striker emitted was being thrown back by the light. He twisted and turned as he attempted to avoid the needles of darkness that flew his way.

"Let go of your weapon!" Candy yelled to him over the din of the vortex. *"Do you hear me, Houlihan? LET IT GO!"*

He heard her. But he couldn't obey. His hands shook violently, as though he was genuinely attempting to make them release the weapon, but they refused to let it go. The Star-Striker was in control of his muscles. The murderous power he'd brought in his heart to help him execute Candy had turned against him. He was its victim now.

His face, which had never worn anything but a scowl or a smug smirk, was suddenly full of fear, his mouth open in the shape of a wordless howl. Unable to escape, all he could do was fling himself back and forth in his panic. At last he seemed to make a decision to try and break the Star-Striker. He raised it above his head and brought it down in a quick arc to hit the ground. But it did not break. Instead, it sent up a wave of darkness greater than any that had preceded it, which in turn drew down a fist of golden light to counter it. Had Houlihan been able to let go of the Star-Striker, he might have escaped the calamity. But he was caught in its midst, the two forces meeting where he stood.

It was more than his body and spirit could endure. He threw back his head as shards of power, flung off the darkness that was pouring from the Star-Striker, pierced him.

"No, please no!" he cried. *"Help me!"*

His cry became a shriek. Then, abruptly, it stopped.

The light of life, which had always burned with uncanny strength in Otto Houlihan's stare, went out of him.

The very moment that his heart ceased to beat, the Star-Striker seemed to lose its power over his anatomy. His grip on the lethal bat loosened, and he fell to the ground like a dropped doll.

As for the Star-Striker itself, it held its position in the air for a few seconds, then it became subject to the very process it had helped unleash. A wave of knotted energies struck it, and it spun across the room, crashing into several orbiting objects before striking the wall and becoming impaled there.

And so, in a hail of darkness and light, the lethal battle of the Wunderkammen—and along with it, Houlihan's pursuit of Candy—came to an end.

18

DEPARTURE

"WELL, THAT'S NOT SOMETHING you see very often," Filth remarked. He was standing in the doorway, the fur all over his body standing on end thanks to the energies unleashed in the room. Sparks ran off the tips of the longer hairs and crackled in the air.

All around the Wunderkammen, objects were coming to a rest, gently dropping out of the air and landing in the confusion of things that already littered the floor. Some of the Totemix were already rooting through the litter, especially the simpler creatures, whose first cogent thought upon being awakened from their frozen state was to fill their bellies. They soon realized that a stuffed reptile or a painted fan made very unnourishing repasts and quickly began to venture out of the Wunderkammen in search of something more filling. None of them left, however, without first coming over to Candy and inclining their heads, paying their respects to their liberator. Only then did they hurry away.

"Shall we go?" Filth said.

Candy nodded.

Outside the door they found the Criss-Cross Man's stitchlings. They had beaten a hasty retreat as soon as things inside the Wunderkammen had become too crazy, but they lay close to its threshold now, face-down on the palace tiles. All motivation had apparently been sapped from them once their leader had perished.

At the door Candy looked back at the Star-Striker, which was still buried to half its length in the wall. A thin veil of blue-black smoke rose from the weapon, and occasionally a large pearl of darkness formed on the handle, which immediately drew the attention of wandering barbs of light. They closed upon these last fragments of darkness and burned them away in a heartbeat.

"Do you think it's safe to just leave it here?" she said.

"Well, personally I don't fancy touching it," Filth said. "Not after what it did. Besides, nobody comes here. . . ."

"Somebody'll come looking for *him* eventually," Candy said, nodding toward the sprawled body of the Criss-Cross Man.

"Maybe," Filth replied. "Maybe not. If it was Carrion who sent him—"

"It was."

"Then he probably already knows his agent's dead. And he won't care about burying the body, will he? He'll leave the carcass here for the filch crows and the mange hounds to take. After all, if anybody believes in the natural order of decay, it's a man called *Carrion*."

"So you think I should just leave it all like this?"

"I would. You've got more important business right now than burying evil men. You have quite a power inside you, girl. If I were you, I'd be wondering why. There's only one soul I ever knew who had that kind of capacity inside her, and she's—"

He stopped in midsentence and looked at Candy with a most peculiar expression on his face.

"What's wrong?" she asked him.

"I should stay out of this business," Filth said, almost as though he was instructing himself. "It's too mighty for the likes of me. There may be rituals to be performed, sacred poems to be spoken. I should be very careful."

Candy saw the anxiety on his face and knew that it would be unfair to press him to speak anymore.

"I understand," she said.

"Really?"

"Really," she said. "You're saying I've got to go and finish this magical business myself."

"Well . . . yes. I'm just a fool, me. A dead King's jester. I'm good for a joke and a pie in the face. But not magic . . ."

The song that had brought her here was being played again. But this time there were words with it; or at least she heard words. Perhaps they were in her head, in her memory.

Whichever, they made a strange kind of sense to her.

> *"What a voyage this has been,*
> *This life of mine!*
> *Every Hour I wake*
> *To find some new blossom*
> *Hanging in the trees over my head!*
> *Blossoms the shape of clouds,*
> *Blossoms the shape of fire*
> *Blossoms the shape of love.*
> *All that has already passed away*
> *And all that is still to come*
> *On this long strange road."*

Off many Hours to the west of Scoriae, on the south side of Odom's Spire, the Twenty-Fifth Island, three women of the Fantomaya—Diamanda, Mespa and Joephi—sat with a bottle of brandy, some of the most pungent furini cheese ever made, along with a fresh loaf of twice-thatched bread, and watched the gray-blue expanse of the Izabella.

Things had been strange of late, they all agreed. Nor did they have much argument about why there was such a hiccup in the usual flow of the Abarat's energies.

"Candy," Joephi said, without the least doubt. "This is all because of Candy."

"Well, we can scarcely blame her without also blaming ourselves," Mespa said. "We should have talked to her *earlier*, while she was still in the Hereafter, instead of leaving her to discover things for herself."

"Personally, I think it's better she discovers them for herself, and learns how to deal with them, than that we simply *instruct* her," Diamanda said. She was much the oldest of the three, and today she felt it. The responsibilities of what they had together unleashed on the Abarat weighed heavily upon her. "No girl of her age is going to take well to instruction from us, or anybody," she went on. "And it's not as if she were an ordinary girl. She's got powers moving in her—"

"Exactly!" said Joephi. "Exactly! *She has powers moving in her.* And we're letting her wander the islands unsupervised? It's playing with fire, Diamanda. It's a very dangerous game."

Diamanda got up and walked down to the water, where the little waves broke against the stony shore. She rubbed her aching back as she stared at the sea.

"Damn these old bones of mine," she said. Then, returning to the subject in hand: "From the very beginning of this enterprise we have been risking a great deal. We've always known that. There could have been terrible consequences at just about every stage of our endeavor. And now . . . now I begin to fear that things will get very much worse before they get better."

"Is that a prophecy?"

"Call it an informed guess," Diamanda said, turning back to face her sisters. "At times like this—times of change, I mean—we have to plan for the very worst of eventualities. We have to hope and pray that they don't happen, but we still have to plan . . ."

"What are you talking about?" Mespa said, rising from the stone on which she'd been sitting.

"Well . . . if anything were to happen to any of us . . ."

"You mean to you," Joephi said. "That's what you

mean, isn't it? You've been having bad dreams, haven't you?"

"A few," Diamanda admitted. "Hopefully they don't mean anything and we'll all live to see what we planned all those years ago come to fruition. But if something *should* happen to one of us, I want us all to promise that we'll let the girl make her own choices. Goodness knows she may not do exactly what we want her to do. She's got a will of her own—"

"More than one," Mespa said dryly.

"True." The thought put the tiniest of smiles on Diamanda's face. "That may be the saving of her, of course," she said. "It may be the saving of us *all*."

She looked up at the sky over Odom's Spire. It was a curious sight. Light and dark were inverted there, proof of the unique power of the Twenty-Fifth Hour. The stars were pinpoints of blackness against a pallid heaven. Diamanda studied the spectacle, looking for some further sign of what the future held. But apparently she found nothing.

"I know we'd like to think that destiny holds the reins in all of this," she said softly. "That somewhere fate has laid out a happy future. But, sisters, I think Candy will confound our expectations, whatever they may be, and however fondly we may hold them. We must let her be her own creature, for better or worse."

"Goddess forgive us for what we did," Mespa murmured.

"You regret it, don't you?" Joephi said to Mespa. "You wish we'd never done it."

"We interfered with the natural order of things,"

Mespa said. "I don't believe that was wise."

"But it's done," Diamanda said forcefully. "And there's no taking it back. There's no trying to bend her to our will if we disagree with the choices she makes. She's not our toy."

"She learned quickly," Joephi said. "And there's a lot of anger in her. Probably from the father. Perhaps if she forgave him—"

"There, you see," Diamanda said. "You still want to manipulate her." She made a grim smile. "As if we could. Her, of all people."

"I'm only saying that the combination of rage and power makes for a dangerous force. And here's you saying we shouldn't try to *control* that force. Let her learn, you say. But what happens *while* she's learning, Diamanda? Think of the damage she could do."

"Think of the good," said the old lady. "Think of why we did this in the first place. What we wanted to *preserve*."

"Well, it's a terrible risk we're taking," said Joephi. "I just hope we don't live to regret it."

There was a little silence. Then Mespa said: "Can't we at least give her a clue or two?"

"Well . . . I don't see how," Diamanda replied. "Where would we begin?"

"On that night. The rain. Her mother."

"Well, you see, there's another thing, now that you mention it," said Joephi. "The mother."

"What *about* her?" said Diamanda.

"We gave her a piece of the mystery. She accepted it. She birthed it. She nursed it."

"So?"

"So has it ever occurred to you that maybe she'd been touched by magic too?"

Diamanda waved the troublesome notion away. "She was just a vessel. There's no power in her."

"I'm just telling you, Diamanda, if we're looking for the future to surprise us, we should look *beyond* the girl. Look to those she's touched."

"And *will* touch," Mespa said grimly. "*Is* touching even now. I think Joephi's right. We must be vigilant. Look everywhere for signs."

As if to prove the point Mespa was making, one of the stars that trembled at the Spire's zenith chose that moment to perish, exploding with the hushed grace of a dandelion disintegrating before a gust of wind.

All the women looked up and watched as the dark flakes of star stuff fell and fell and were extinguished. The three were silent for a while after the show was over. But finally Mespa said: "And what did that signify, do you suppose?"

Diamanda drained her brandy glass. "At a guess?" she said. "Nothing at all."

19

LIFE AND DEATH IN CHICKENTOWN

IN A WORLD VERY remote from the place where Joephi, Mespa and Diamanda were exchanging their thoughts and fears—in Chickentown, Minnesota—life went on very much as it always had. Which was not to say that Candy Quackenbush's disappearance had not caused a good deal of gossip around town. It had. Especially because there had been some bizarre details attached to the story.

According to one rumor, for instance, the Quackenbush girl had been seen the day that she'd disappeared by old Mrs. Lavinia White (aka the Widow White), who lived on Lincoln Street, at the very edge of town. In an interview with a reporter from the *Chickentown Courier*, the Widow White claimed she had seen Candy walking in the direction of the open prairie, and she had been staring up at the sky.

"Had there been anything to stare at?" the Widow White had been asked.

"Just a few clouds," the widow replied. "But later on . . ."

"What happened later?" the reporter had asked.

"It was strange . . ." Lavinia said. "About half an hour after she'd passed by, my bedroom window began to rattle."

"What did you do?"

"I opened the window up."

"Did it stop rattling?"

The Widow White had given the man a look of profound contempt, as though she could not imagine why he would ask such a thing when there was so much more to be talked about.

"*I could smell the sea,*" she told the reporter. "I know how crazy that sounds, but I did. I swear. I smelled the ocean. All salty and cold."

"That's impossible," the reporter had replied.

"Are you trying to imply that I'm crazy?"

"No . . ."

"Because I'm not. I may be old, but I'm *not* crazy. I smelled seawater, I'm telling you."

Not wishing to offend the old lady, the journalist had gently asked Lavinia when exactly she'd last been near the ocean.

"On my honeymoon," the Widow White had replied. "Seventy-two years ago."

"Is it possible that perhaps your memory is a little shaky?" the reporter had mildly suggested.

Lavinia had fixed the poor man with a gaze whose sharpness had not been blunted by the passage of years. "Are you suggesting that I don't remember what happened *on my own honeymoon?*" she said.

Her outrage did her no good. When the report appeared in the *Courier*, it was accompanied by the observation that "Lavinia White's claims that she smelled the sea that day are a sad comment on the frailty of old age."

The reporter (along with the editor of the newspaper) quickly came to regret voicing an opinion on the matter. There were two hundred and eleven calls to the *Courier* that day, all from people in town who said that they too had smelled the ocean on the day that the Widow White had smelled it. Maybe it was some freak wind condition, some suggested, but it wasn't the Widow White's imagination.

As a result of these complaints the editor dispatched a photographer and another reporter to comb the area where the Quackenbush girl had disappeared. There was some kind of broken-down tower out there, according to the police, but that was about all.

This soon turned out to be only part of the truth. The *Courier* photographer did indeed get pictures of the tower, which looked like a lighthouse on the prairie, but he also found and photographed the rotted remains of a long wooden jetty. This was strange, the *Courier* commented. Who would have built a jetty out there in the middle of nowhere when there was no water for miles?

And once the area was examined more closely, it turned out that there were still stranger phenomena to report. In the waist-high grass around the jetty, the photographer came upon a bizarre array of objects. So many, in fact, that the editor of the *Courier* demanded, in print, that the police make a search of the location. Pleading a lack of manpower, the police brought in the Chickentown Boy Scouts, issued them forensic gloves and three sizes of plastic garbage bags, instructed them to collect all the "evidence" from the vicinity and sent them on their way to pick it up.

They found all kinds of oddities. The desiccated remains of hundreds of fishes that had certainly never swum in any Minnesota lake; a number of dead birds, also of unknown species; innumerable shells; a glass eye (green); a leather tail (blue); a wooden instrument carved in the shape of a snake that when blown produced a single note of eerie beauty; seven shoes, none of them making a pair; and several more bags of stuff that had been so corrupted by its time in the water as to be unrecognizable.

There was also a single living survivor of whatever body of water had been here. Under a large rock beneath the jetty, two of the boys found a creature that looked not unlike an enormous turquoise lobster. The creature wriggled so violently that it loosened itself from its old barnacle-encrusted armor. The tender-shelled beast then fled away through the long grass, and was gone.

All of this was duly reported in the pages of the *Courier,* under the headline "Weird Sights Seen Close to Town Limits."

If that had been the end of the weirdnesses, the folks of Chickentown might have decided to forget the reports and get on with their commonplace lives.

But it was not the end. It was just the beginning.

* * *

In the middle of town, at the Comfort Tree Hotel, Norma Lipnik (who had given Candy a tour of the hotel just before the girl's disappearance) had some oddities of her own to deal with; events she was determined to keep out of the pages of the *Courier* for purely commercial reasons (she didn't want to scare away customers) but which were soon going to become public knowledge anyway.

The Comfort Tree Hotel had a ghost. Most of the time this was of no great concern. In fact, when Candy had been here, Norma had taken her up to the old section of the hotel—to Room Nineteen—where this phantom was reported to reside, and had proudly given her a history of his sad life. His name was Henry Murkitt, and according to hotel legend he had committed suicide in Room Nineteen one melancholy Christmas many years ago. He'd had his reasons. Norma knew two of them. His beloved wife, Diamanda, had walked out on him, the story went, leaving for unknown destinations. That was the first reason. And the second? The city council had decided in December of 1947 to change the name of the town (which had until that time been called Murkitt, in honor of Henry's ancestors, who'd founded the community eighty years before) to Chickentown.

Henry had taken these blows very hard. So hard indeed that he had simply decided that his life wasn't worth living. He'd locked himself up with a gun and a whiskey bottle and said good-bye to life. But according to many of the hotel staff, poor Henry had never quite been able to let go of the world that had caused him so much pain. He still haunted the stale air of

Room Nineteen. He was an entirely benign presence. He'd never attempted to frighten any of the Comfort Tree's staff; nor had he done anything destructive to the fabric of the hotel.

Until now, that is.

Now Norma was standing in the doorway of Room Nineteen, staring at the opposite wall. On it, somebody had scrawled two words.

HIGHER GROUND

Norma didn't like having to accept that this was the handiwork of a deceased man, but she had little option. Her staff were all honest, hardworking folks; none of them would have played a trick like this.

Which left only one person, Norma reasoned. The graffiti was the work of Henry Murkitt. But *what did it mean*? That was the question Norma tussled with as she stared at the two words scrawled into the plaster. Had the ghost in Room Nineteen simply gone a little crazy over the years, or was he attempting to communicate something?

She went over to the wall and tentatively ran her fingers over the letters. The gouged plaster was cold, unnaturally so. She quickly withdrew her hand, the tiny hairs on the back of her neck prickling. Was he there in the room with her right now? She snatched a furtive, frightened glance over her shoulder. Then, taking a deep breath, she said: "Are . . . you in here, Henry?"

At first there was no response. No sound, not the merest scratching. Nothing to signify that there was any presence here at all. Norma began to turn back toward the door. But as she did so, she caught sight of movement from the corner of her eye. She froze, not really wanting to look. But her curiosity was stronger than her fear, and she slowly turned to look back in the direction of the movement.

It was just the drape!

She expelled the rest of her breath, shaking her head at the foolishness of all this. Just a moth-eaten drape caught in the breeze, that was—

Wait now. Breeze? What breeze? The window was closed and locked, and yet the gray curtain was billowing as though a gust had caught it from behind.

"Oh my Lord . . ." Norma said.

As she spoke, the lamp that hung in the middle of the room, its shade yellowed with age and nicotine, began to swing.

And by its giddying light she saw the filthy fabric of the drape suddenly twitch, as though it had been caught by an invisible hand, and in its folds she saw a face, no doubt of that; its features were simplified by the fabric: just two pits for eyes, a vague lump for a nose and a wide-open mouth.

It was more than Norma wanted to see. She let out a short shriek, which she muted with her fingers, and retreated to the door. She was afraid the thing was going to come toward her, but it didn't move. It just stayed there in the fabric while the lamp flickered overhead. Suddenly the lamp brightened and burned out. That was Norma's cue. She turned and pulled open the door, slamming it hard behind her.

* * *

It took her a few minutes, and six fumbled cigarettes, to calm herself down. But when she did, she quickly came to realize the ghost in Room Nineteen had probably meant no harm with its appearance. After all, she'd called it, hadn't she? All the ghost of Henry Murkitt had done was answer her call, probably the only way he could. So now the question: what should she do about it? She decided that she was too flustered to disguise the fact that something had happened from her staff. They knew her too well. So she assembled everyone in the kitchen and explained as best she could what she'd seen on the wall, and in the drapes, of Room Nineteen.

"He's trying to send a message of some kind," Ethel Bloch, who was in charge of the housekeeping, said.

"All right," Norma said testily. "Suppose he is. What then?"

"You should tell people. About what you saw. And the words."

"Ha! People will think you're crazy," Ed Farrow, who looked after the hotel kitchen, warned. "Nobody will ever come to this hotel again. I'm tellin' you, folks are weird about this stuff. Remember that suicide over at McEnroe's Motel? Ol' Mick McEnroe thought he was going to get more business out of that than he could deal with. He had them darn-fool hats made 'n' all. And what happened? Place closed down in two months. Nobody wants to be reminded of death when they're out havin' a good time."

The staff generally seemed to agree with Ed Farrow, and the meeting finished with everyone agreeing to keep all this under wraps, at least until Norma could make some enquiries about what Henry Murkitt and his message on the wall was really about.

Unfortunately, somebody in that assembly couldn't keep his or her mouth shut. Word of what Norma had witnessed soon spread through town, and by the early evening there was a small group of townspeople standing outside the hotel, apparently trying to work out which of the windows belonged to Room Nineteen. Norma didn't waste time accusing anybody. What was done was done. She decided in the middle of the evening that she would go out and talk to the assembled crowd. It turned out that three people already possessed blurred but perfectly decipherable photographs of the scrawlings in Room Nineteen, though they refused to name the person who'd let them into the hotel to take them. Finally Norma had decided simply to own up to what she'd seen. If she'd been hoping that this would bring an end to the matter, she was sadly mistaken. The crowd instead grew larger as news about *"the words on the wall"* spread through town. By the end of the day there were three hundred people in the street outside the hotel. Norma felt as though she were in a state of siege. Just after midnight a couple of the rowdier members of the crowd decided that they wanted to get into the hotel and see what Henry Murkitt had written on the wall for themselves. They attempted to force an entrance. Norma had had enough. She called the police. Five minutes later there were three squad cars outside, and the crowd was being gently dispersed.

* * *

At the edge of the prairie, the Widow White sat by her window and listened to the sirens drifting through the streets from the middle of town. She'd heard from her daughter-in-law Vivien about what was going on down at the Comfort Tree Hotel, and it made her curse her old age with especial vehemence. She wanted to be down there, mingling with the crowd, finding out what was happening.

Something of significance was in the air, that she didn't doubt. She heard the wind gusting against the window and the glass creaking as the gusts came against it. She wheeled herself over to the window and made a frustrated attempt to open it. The wood had warped during the winter freeze, and now her arthritic fingers had difficulty getting the darn thing open.

But she struggled on, defying the pain in her finger joints, determined to have a sniff of that wind. At last the latch succumbed to her efforts, and she pushed the window open. The sweet scent of prairie grass came to meet her from the darkness.

She thought of the report she'd read in the *Courier*, about what they'd found out there on the prairie: the tower, the garbage and the dead fish littered in the grass as though at a high-water mark.

A high-water mark!

"Oh, saints in heaven preserve us," she said softly, and she stared out into the night.

Hadn't Vivien told her that the phantom message writer in Room Nineteen had written HIGHER GROUND?

It was a warning. Of course it was. *Higher Ground!*

Higher Ground! How could everyone (herself included) have been so dense? The ghost in the Comfort Tree Hotel knew what it was talking about! There was water out there, somewhere. Maybe an underground river of some kind locked in the rock, straining to be free. Or maybe something stranger? It didn't really matter now. What mattered was to spread the warning, beginning with Vivien.

She turned her wheelchair away from the window. Her breath was suddenly hard to catch, and her arms felt leaden.

"Calm down, Lavinia," she told herself quietly. "Just . . . calm yourself down; you're having a panic attack. Breathe, Lavinia. Breathe."

But the advice did no good. A terrible burning pain had begun in the middle of her chest, like the worst heartburn imaginable. She let out a little sob of complaint and threw her desperate gaze back toward the open window, wondering if there was any way she could call for help from there. It was certainly closer than the telephone. But her arms were suddenly too heavy to lift. And the pain in her chest was unendurable. She just wanted it to stop, even if that meant her long life was now at an end. Better that than a moment more of this unendurable agony.

"Enough," she said through gritted teeth. "Please . . . enough."

Her heart heard her words, and it did her the great kindness of obeying. The pain went out of her as suddenly as it had come. She issued one last, grateful breath. Then she was gone.

20

MALINGO ALONE

IN THE WEEKS SINCE Candy had helped Malingo slip out of Kaspar Wolfswinkel's clutches and escape the prison island of Ninnyhammer, the geshrat had scarcely ever been without her company. And he'd been very grateful for that fact. Even in dreams they'd been close. It was a cornerstone of geshratian belief that sleep did not separate friends and loved ones, but instead brought their slumbering souls closer to one another. Hence the familiar geshrat wishes as they parted for bed; not "good night" or "sweet dreams," but *"See you sleeping."*

Now, however, Candy had gone, and Malingo was left alone. Not literally, of course. He had people pressing in on him from every side—singing, dancing, hooting and hollering, all having the time of their lives. But their high spirits only served to make Malingo feel lonelier. For the first couple of hours after Candy had disappeared into the darkening sky in the grip of the zethek, he stood at the edge of the bustling crowd, pressed against the fence that kept the unwary from stepping over a cliff and falling into the sea. Behind him, people pushed and shoved, eager to be on to the next attraction.

"Rude, rude, rude," Malingo muttered to himself. "If Candy were here, we wouldn't be knocked around like this!"

Finally he became so irritated by the way people were pushing he decided to find himself a more comfortable place to stand. With great difficulty he turned against the living tide and attempted to press through the crowd. On the far side of the throng he could see food stalls. He imagined buying a thick slice of Spakean flan at one of them, sprinkled liberally with sugar-loon spice, and his appetite made him impatient. He raised his voice:

"Can I get through, please? I just want to— *Please!* Will you all just GET OUT OF MY WAY!"

His shouting drew a few irritated stares, but the crowd continued to surge on by, preventing him from taking so much as a single step away from the fence. He knew from his weeks traveling with Candy what she would do in such a situation. She'd just press on forward, and not take *no* for an answer. So that was what he did. He put his hands together and took a deep breath, as though he were about to take a dive, then pressed into the crowd of people.

He chose a bad moment. Three large Hobarookians, all wearing big purple noopus furs as waistcoats, and striped hats, were swaggering past, and they didn't take kindly to anybody getting in their way.

"Hey, geshrat-dog! Don't you even think of steppin' there."

"You tell him!"

"I hate geshrats!"

"Hate 'em!"

"Didn't you hear us, idjit? You're in our way."

All thoughts of Spakean flan had gone out of Malingo's head. All he could think of now was the way he was being treated by these bullies. It made his blood boil.

"All right," he said, deliberately standing in the Hobarookians' path, his fists raised. "Which one of you is going to be first?"

The trio laughed, and the smallest of the three (who was still six inches taller than Malingo) gave him a hefty shove in the middle of his chest. He stumbled backward, coming within reach of the largest of the thugs, who also gave him a shove.

"How 'bout we just knock the li'l twitch around?" the big one said. "Me, den Spittel, den Slegm, den me again."

"Oh yeah," said Slegm, the short one. "You mean like a *game*! Good one, Snut!"

The crowd had quickly cleared to give the Hobarookians plenty of space to torment their new toy. Nobody raised a voice, much less a hand, to stop this thuggery. Snut pushed Malingo back into the embrace of Spittel, who turned him around, punched him and then threw him back to Slegm, who slapped him back and forth across his face. None of the blows were particularly hard, but they reminded Malingo of his time under Kaspar Wolfswinkel's cruel thumb, when every day brought blows and insults and humiliations. Candy had saved him from all of that, of course. And it was Candy who'd taught him that he need never live in fear again.

"I have faith in you," she'd said to him, over and over. She'd meant it too.

"Wot you doin', geshrat?" said Snut.

"He's finkin', dat's wot he's doin," Spittel said. "He's finkin' 'bout how much his nose hurts."

In fact Malingo was doing more than thinking. He was conjuring. At the back of his head he turned over some secret words that he remembered from a book in Wolfswinkel's library: *Essential Conjurations for Hand-to-Hand Combat.*

How did the rhyme begin? Something about feathers. No, not feathers. Feather-steel! That was it —

Spittel kicked Malingo's legs from under him, and down he went. Face to the dust, he spoke the conjuration in a whisper.

> *"Cover me from*
> *Scalp to sole,*
> *In the feather-steel*
> *That—"*

Oh Lordy Lou, the rest of the words escaped him. What were they? Meanwhile, the Hobarookians had become bored with their game of Pass the Geshrat. Slegm started to kick Malingo. A small crowd had finally started to form around the four figures. People were treating this as though it were just another entertainment. And still the Hobarookians kicked and kicked. Malingo tried to put the pain out of his head and concentrate on the conjuration. How did it finish?

> "Cover me from
> Scalp to sole,
> In the feather-steel . . ."

What about the feather-steel? What about it?

Then the words leaped onto his lips, out of nowhere.

"—That Nazrat stole!"

"What did you say?" said the Hobarookian called Spittel. He caught hold of Malingo and hauled him to his feet. "What *was* that?"

"Nothing," Malingo said.

"Nothing?" said the Hobarookian. "I'll give you nothing! Hit him, Snut!"

"Well, hold him still."

"He *is* still. Hit him."

Snut delivered a blow to Malingo's stomach. But the conjuration was in place. It was feather-steel he struck, and it was enough to break all the bones in his hand. He yelled and fell to his knees, nursing his broken digits. In the moment of confusion Malingo spoke a second spell:

> "Hear the hatred?
> Hear the drums?
> On your own heads,
> The beating comes."

Nobody heard him utter a word. The crowd was too busy shouting. One little child, raised up on his father's shoulders, started to chant:

"Blood! Blood! Blood! Blood!"

Slegm, meanwhile, had caught hold of Malingo and yelled to Spittel. "They want blood! Let's give 'em blood."

Spittel grinned. "My pleasure," he said, and threw a blow in Malingo's direction. Somewhere between its origin and its destination, however, it got turned around and came right back at the brute, who found himself being pounded by his own fist.

He let out a howl as the blows landed, one after the other. The crowd was very amused.

"You're doing this!" Slegm said, pushing Malingo from him. "You filthy magic man." He threw two punches of his own at Malingo, but both landed on his own jaw.

"This is better than the shows!" Somebody in the crowd laughed.

The three Hobarookians, even the wounded Snut, were so furious at this humiliation that they began to throw blows willy-nilly, all of which came back and struck them. The crowd cheered every blow and laughed at every new bruise. They were too interested in the violence to notice Malingo creeping away. Nor did they notice a length of blue fabric that dropped out of the sky, unfurling close to the geshrat.

"Quickly!" said a woman's voice.

He turned around and for a moment he seemed to see a face there in the folds of the blue fabric.

"Move yourself!" the woman's voice said. *"Grab hold of the cloth!"*

He didn't need telling twice. As he did so, he looked back at the crowd to find that Slegm had finally shaken off the force of Malingo's enchantment and was making his way toward Malingo, spitting blood along with oaths of the foulest kind.

"I'm ready!" Malingo said to the woman in the blue cloth.

"Hold on," she said. "This is going to be quite a ride!"

At that moment Slegm reached out and caught hold of Malingo's shirt.

"Gotcha!" he yelled.

The blue cloth was meanwhile wrapping itself more tightly around Malingo's hand and wrist, solidifying its hold.

And then it lifted him into the air.

Slegm held on for the first ten feet of the flight. Then Malingo's shirt began to tear, and with one final curse he let his quarry go and dropped back down to the ground.

Malingo didn't look down. He just hung on to the billowing fabric as it rose like a great blue sail. He could hear the din of the crowd below him—exclamations of surprise and disbelief. But after a little time the makeshift kite he was clinging to changed direction, and the crowds and the light and the noise faded away, and the only sounds he could hear were the whistle of the wind and the woman's voice, humming some calming song.

21

NIGHT CONVERSATIONS

CHRISTOPHER CARRION HAD RETURNED from the Pyramids of Xuxux to the fortress of Iniquisit on Gorgossium with a great deal to occupy his thoughts. It was clear from his encounter with the sacbrood in the tombs that the hive he'd created was volatile. Not only were the sacbrood intelligent, but they were ambitious too, and their egg-laying capabilities made them formidable. Naively he had assumed that they would be passive players in the deadly game he was about to play and would be easily manipulated. But now he saw the error of that assumption. They had their own agenda. He could no more trust them than he could trust Leeman Vol, who had spent the voyage back to Gorgossium plucking tiny red lice from his scalp and whispering to them. Carrion didn't ask what he was talking to them about, much less whether they were answering him.

Vol revolted him. Had he not needed the man's skills as a translator, he would undoubtedly have thrown him overboard and not thought twice about it.

But he could not afford to lose Vol from his entourage, especially now that he had seen how powerful and numerous the sacbrood had become. It would be a different story when the war was over and won. Not only did he plan to exterminate every last occupant of the sacbrood hives, he would make sure Vol perished too.

He did his best to put thoughts of Vol and the sacbrood out of his head once he got back to the Twelfth Tower. Here, where the walls were covered with doodlings and carvings he'd made as a child, he felt comforted. He sent for his loyalist servants, Baby Pink-Eye and Lazaru, to fetch his map of the islands. It was duly brought and laid out in the room. The map was round, and designed to be precisely the circumference of the tower, covering every inch of the floor of the High Chamber, thus allowing Carrion to stride over water and land like a colossus. He walked from island to island, crouching down now and then to examine the shape of a particular bay or the slope of a particular hill, all the while planning his plans.

His meditations were interrupted by the sound of barking birds, followed by an eruption of martial drums that echoed back and forth between the towers. He got up and went to the window. Far below him (thirty-seven stories, in fact), a mighty procession, illuminated by innumerable lights, was winding over the rocky landscape and through the arches that lay between the Twelfth and Thirteenth Towers. About halfway down the length of this procession, borne high on a throne set on the severed wrist of an immense mummified hand, which had somehow been given animation, was Carrion's grandmother Thant Yeyla Carrion, commonly known as Mater Motley. She was not wasting her precious time while she traveled but was hard at work sewing by the light of flickering torches. The Prince didn't need to wonder what she was working on; it was always the same obsessive labor. She was sewing together the skins of stitchlings, half-human sacks into which the living mud from the Todo Mines would be poured. By this means a vast army was being assembled that would in time be used to destroy the bright powers of Day, and whatever forces Day might in time assemble. It was an endeavor that had so far lasted many years, but his grandmother had let it be known that the great labor was coming to an end, and very soon the army of stitchlings would be entirely assembled. The Lord of Midnight would be their generalissimo, but their Creatrix was Mater Motley.

He descended the cold stone stairs with uncommon haste. He knew better than to leave his grandmother waiting at the tower door. Even in the best of moods she was an evil-tempered woman, quicker to take offense than he was, and quicker to punish offenders. Her presence had immediately created a state of flustered chaos in the Twelfth Tower, and it irritated him to see how many of his supposedly loyal servants had fled into the caves beneath the tower rather than risk being where Mater Motley's homicidal gaze might alight upon them. Even the various subspecies that haunted the crawl spaces of the tower, the offspring of gargoyles and wild dogs, of snake-apes and lightning, had sought the comfort of the dungeons rather than chance being seen.

Only a youth called Letheo, a fifteen-year-old Carrion had found wandering the mud mines a year or so back and had taken under his protection, remained at the front door, unintimidated. The boy had spat on his palm, attempting to plaster back an errant lock of hair.

"Aren't you afraid, Letheo? The old witch is dangerous. Don't you know that?"

Letheo smiled at his savior. "I ain't afraid of *her*," he said. "I got you to protect me, boss. Anyhow, I want to see what all the fuss is about."

"So you've never laid eyes on my lovely grandmother?"

Letheo shook his head, and the lick of black hair fell over his forehead again.

"Well then, you should go and let her in," Carrion said. "It's time you met the wickedest woman in the Abarat."

"Is she really the wickedest?"

"Oh yes," Carrion said, without a trace of a smile. "She's the worst. The worst of the worst. You can't have a reputation like hers without doing harm to deserve it. Patricide. Matricide. She's committed them all."

"What *are* all those things? Patri—"

"—cide. The murder of your father. Matricide. The murder of your mother."

"She did that?" Letheo said, his voice softened by awe.

"Trust me . . . that's the least of it."

"What could be worse?"

"Infanticide?"

"Infanti— *The murder of children?*"

"See what a quick learner you are!"

"Amazing."

"But you remember—"

"What?"

"—where your allegiance lies, boy."

Letheo bowed respectfully. "You are my Prince," he said. "Always. To the end of the world."

Carrion grinned his skeletal grin. "It's agreed then," he said. "To the end of the world. Take my hand on it."

Letheo was flattered to be shaking the hand of his Lord. He took it eagerly. "To the end of the world."

"Now. Get the door. Let the wicked woman in before she poisons our doorstep."

Letheo went to the door and, with the silent tread of one who was born to do some harm or other, opened it. Not a moment too soon. Standing there on the tower step, her gloved hand raised in readiness to knock on the door, was one of Mater Motley's countless maid-servants, a middle-aged woman whose headdress was draped with the holy colors of scarlet and gray and whose face was marked with tattoos like shadows. All this marked her out as one of Mater Motley's inner circle, a member of the Sisterhood of the Thread. In witching circles, this was a powerful woman.

"The Queen Mother Thant Yeyla Carrion calls on her grandson. Will you tell him—"

"I'm here, Lady Putrith," Carrion said, stepping out of the shadows.

The tiny gray Lady Putrith proffered a tiny gray smile, which showed her sharpened teeth. "Prince," she said, inclining her head. "Your grandmother awaits you." She then stood aside, sweeping her voluminous cloak back with theatrical flourish, so that Carrion had easy passage.

"Letheo," Carrion said. "Come with me."

Boy and man stepped out into the cold darkness, Letheo trotting to keep up with Carrion as he strode along the line of Mater Motley's drummers and incense burners and earth beaters until he reached the platform on which the old woman's great throne was elevated. Vessels of purple-black fire, in which she occasionally soaked her needle-pricked fingers to quicken them, hovered to the left and right of her.

"This is a pleasant surprise," Carrion said, his tone carrying not the least hint of genuine pleasure.

Mater Motley seemed to be equally unmoved to be in the presence of her grandson. She took her left hand out of the flames and picked up the sewing that lay on her lap.

"You never come to see me anymore," she said, not looking at Carrion. "So I am obliged to come and see *you*." Her voice was as unlovely as her expression, harsh and joyless. "You are ungrateful, Carrion."

"I am *what*?"

After a long moment the hag's eyes lifted from the rhythm of the needle and thread and fixed on him. "You heard me," she said. "The Sisterhood toils Night upon Night upon Night to make an army for you—"

"For *us*, Grandmother," Carrion said, refusing to be

intimidated by Mater Motley's stony stare. "This is *our* great work. Our dream."

Mater Motley unleashed a sigh of epic gravity. "I'm too old for dreams," she said. "You're the one who'll lord it over the islands when the great work is done."

Carrion shook his head. He'd heard this all before. She was always the victim, always the martyr. "And of course you don't have the strength to do harm to anybody, do you?" he said. "You're just a weary, poorly served old lady who will be dying soon in a blaze of sainthood." He laughed. "You are ridiculous."

"And you are cruel," she said. "And one day you will suffer for it."

"Yes, yes," Carrion said. "One day, one day. Now leave your needle awhile," he said. "Let's walk together in some quiet place."

The old woman's lip curled. "You think you're so clever, Carrion. Just because you lived and all your brothers and sister perished. But who was it saved you?"

"It was you, Grandmother. And not an hour passes without my giving up a prayer of gratitude."

"Liar," the Hag said coldly. She slipped her needle and thread into the pincushion hanging from her waist and put aside the stitchling she was working on. Then she uttered a little word of Old Abaratian— *yethasiha*—and a gaseous staircase spilled from the front of the platform. She rose and descended it.

She was wearing, as always, a dress of eerie luxury and magnificence, the length of which was decorated with what might have been dolls, or the remains of dolls, when in reality they were the shrunken remains of her victims, reduced to plaintive scraps and sewn onto the dress in place of silky bows.

"You look wonderful, Grandmother."

"And you look haggard. What's wrong with you? Lovesick?"

"Lovesick? Me? Who would I be sick with love over?"

"I don't know, you tell me. Come, we'll walk, and you can confess to me."

22

A DEATH SENTENCE

TOGETHER CARRION AND HIS grand-mother walked along the lip of the mine working, and as they walked they talked of the future.

"Just so you know, I didn't believe a word of what you were saying back there," Carrion remarked to his grandmother. "You want to control the islands every bit as much as I do. Maybe more. After all, you've had rather longer to covet them."

Mater Motley stopped walking and stared at her grandson without a trace of affection.

"And what if I have coveted them?" she said. "Don't you think I *deserve* an empire after all that I've suffered?" Her face bore the unmistakable signs of that suffering, even by the forgiving light of a Gorgossian moon. Her skin was riddled with lines. Rage was in them, and envy; and most of all hatred, endless hatred.

"You deserve whatever you can get," Carrion said to her. "I'm not questioning that. The question is: how do we *get* this empire?"

"In the long term, we'll have to take the Twenty-Fifth Hour. Occupy it, root out its secrets."

"And if it doesn't want to give up its secrets?"

"Destroy it."

"That can be done?"

"Well, it won't be easy, but yes, *anything* can be done if we have the will to do it. First, however, we have to get the troublemakers out of our way. Which brings me to the matter at hand. Shall we walk a little farther?"

A wall of acrid smoke rose up out of the pit of the mine ahead of them, as the mud was mixed with various toxic agents in preparation for its being piped into the bodies of the stitchlings. The heat and stink were practically overwhelming, but Mater Motley was untouched by either. She led Carrion on through the oppressive smoke as though she were wandering in a sunlit field.

"Who's the boy, by the way?" Mater Motley asked Carrion. "The one following us."

"His name's Letheo. He wants to be an assassin when he grows up. So he came to me for some schooling."

"Sensible child. There's never a time when a good assassin can't find employment. You've heard about Houlihan, I suppose?"

"What about him?"

"You sent him on a mission to find the girl from the Hereafter, yes?"

"Yes. I sent him after Candy Quackenbush. The last I heard—"

"He's dead, Carrion."

"What?"

"I don't have any of the details yet. But I heard from one of my spies on Scoriae. A very reliable source. The Criss-Cross Man is dead. And the girl did it."

Carrion turned his back on his grandmother, while an image of the girl appeared in his mind's eye, standing with one foot planted on Houlihan's chest.

"She has to die, Carrion."

"Yes?"

"Yes! We've underestimated her somehow. She's no simpleton schoolgirl from the Hereafter. She's some kind of crazy incantatrix."

"Impossible."

"You sound very sure."

"I . . . researched her. . . ." Carrion said somewhat uncomfortably.

"What induced you to do that?"

Carrion turned back to his grandmother. "She . . . intrigued me," he said lightly.

"And what did these researches of yours turn up?"

"Not much. She's here by mistake; I think that much is clear. I had sent Mendelson Shape—"

"The *late* Mendelson Shape," Mater Motley said.

"You hear everything, don't you?"

"Where death's concerned, I have an ear. Go on. You were saying, you sent Mendelson Shape—"

"To get the Key to the Pyramids, which had been stolen."

"By John Mischief and his brothers."

"Yes. And having stolen it, they fled. To the Hereafter.

At the moment that Shape caught up with them, the girl appeared in the vicinity. Pure accident. Mischief passed the Key over to her—lodged it in her mind—thinking, I suppose, that he'd collect it later."

"But it didn't happen that way?"

"No. The tide picked them all up and carried them back here."

"The way you tell it, it all sounds perfectly innocent."

"But you don't think it is?"

"No! Of course not! You listen to me. This girl is *not* some innocent bystander. You'd see that if you could only get a clear perspective on her. Put any tender thoughts about her aside. You do *have* tender thoughts about her, don't you?"

Carrion averted his eyes and stared into the poisonous pit.

"Answer me," the old woman said, her voice like iron nails on slate.

"How could I have any tender feelings for her? I've never even met the damn creature."

"So then you won't feel bad about killing her."

"No. Of course not."

"Don't send one of your minions to do the job, or he'll end up the same way as the Criss-Cross Man. Remember, Houlihan was good. But somehow she bested him."

"A fluke," Carrion said.

"Maybe."

"You're not trying to suggest that this girl is actually a threat to us, are you?"

Mater Motley sighed, her patience thin. "My point is that her presence here is not an accident."

"But the Sea—"

"Yes, let's just consider the Sea, shall we? Why did the Sea of Izabella go to the Hereafter? Because *somebody called it*, Carrion. Who was it? Not Mendelson Shape."

"No. No, of course. Shape wasn't capable of that kind of magic. He was a functionary. Nothing more."

"What about Mischief and his brothers? Are they trained in magic?"

"I doubt it."

"So do I. And yet the Sea was summoned to the Old Shore, Carrion. Who summoned it?"

"I don't think there's any great mystery there," Carrion said. "There's a lighthouse left over from the Days of Empire."

"Yes, but somebody had to make that beacon *burn* to bring the Sea, Carrion. And again I ask you: *who*?"

The Lord of Midnight didn't answer this time. At least not immediately. His hands went up to his collar, and he tapped his fingers against it. As he did so, the nightmares came up from the shadows and rubbed their intestinal lengths against the glass, as though seeking their creator's reassurance, and he theirs.

"So we're back to the girl again," Carrion said.

"Who else?" the old woman said. Though Letheo was standing a respectful distance away from the conversation and could not have heard the debate over the din of the diggers below, Mater Motley nevertheless drew closer to Carrion and spoke in a near whisper.

"We are more vulnerable than I would like right now, Carrion. If the Grand Court of the Hours were to get even a sniff of what we're plotting, we would be stripped of all titles, all possessions and—if they felt so predisposed—of our very lives."

A thrill of fear—or even some perverse excitement—must have passed through Carrion at that moment, because the nightmares threw out threads of lightning, which illuminated his face all the way through his flesh to his corrugated bone.

"Nobody would dare," he said.

"You think Princes are beyond harm?" She took one of her spare needles from the sleeve of her dress and raised it in front of his face. "Don't you remember how this hurt?"

The nightmares became more agitated than ever. They remembered. So did Carrion. How could he ever forget? How she had meticulously stitched up his lips for speaking the word *love*. And how the rage had flared up in his soul while he was muted, so that it seemed sometimes he would surely *catch fire*.

"All right," Carrion said. "So I'm not beyond harm. Thank you for the reminder."

"Now, just get rid of the girl. The sooner she's dead, the happier I'll be. And I know you only live to make me happy."

Carrion smiled. "How right you are."

"But be sure the thing is done in absolute secrecy."

"Of course. I may take Letheo. He can help me work."

"You warn him, though," Mater Motley said,

throwing a sideways glance at the youth, "that if he gives me *any* reason to suspect his loyalty, he will not be able to count on your protection to save his hide."

"I'll tell him," Carrion said. "You said the girl is on Scoriae?"

"Last I heard. Somewhere in the vicinity of the old Twilight Palace. But she won't be there for long, I can guarantee it. So be quick, Carrion."

"I will. I will."

"Good."

Mater Motley had no more to say to him and wasn't going to waste valuable breath on pleasantries. Turning her back on her grandson, she followed the path along the edge of the mine, slipping her beloved needle back into her sleeve as she went.

23

DREAMER TO DREAMER

WHEN CANDY EMERGED FROM the Cabinet of Wonders—her heart still pounding ferociously as a consequence of all that she'd witnessed, all that she'd done—she went to sit down in a spot under the trees. Hopefully the gentle sound of the breeze in the mist-draped branches would soothe her, and she'd be able to make some sense of what had just happened.

Filth, meanwhile, scampered up the tree and sat in the branches, watching his visitor with a new nervousness.

She glanced up at him. "It's all right," she said, trying to sound reassuring. "I'm not going to go crazy or anything."

As she said this, she remembered standing on the dock at Orlando's Cap, with Malingo, and the old man with the knotted eyes pointing at her.

"They'll lock you away." Isn't that what he'd said? *"They'll lock you away."*

Another piece of this puzzle was in those words. It was all connected. What had happened here, what had happened on the *Parroto Parroto*, and the warning she'd heard on the dock. All these things were part of one huge mystery.

"Do I frighten you?" she asked Filth.

He just gave her an anxious munkee smile, his lips curled back until the mottled pink of his gums showed.

"Yeah," she said. "Well, if it's any comfort, I frighten myself a bit too."

"Huh." Filth's finger went to his nose and dug deep, his digging accompanied by the sound of comforted grunts. "What you did in there . . ." he said. "It was extraordinary."

"I didn't think about it," Candy said. "I just did what seemed . . . natural."

"Which makes it even more extraordinary."

"I suppose it does."

Filth cocked his head. "What was that grumbling noise?"

"That was my stomach. I'm hungry."

"Why didn't you say so?" Filth complained. "The palace has got an enormous kitchen. I could cook us something." He seemed relieved to be able to do something that might please her; soothe her even.

"Only if you promise to wash your hands first," Candy replied.

While Filth went to the kitchen, Candy stayed under the tree, still turning over all that had happened, though nothing resembling a solution to the puzzle presented itself to her, just the pieces; everywhere she looked, pieces. Right back to the event that had brought her here, now that she thought of it. Her in the light-house back in the Hereafter, with Shape limping up the stairs to kill her, and her somehow knowing, *knowing without knowing why she knew,* how to light the lamp that would bring the Sea of Izabella to claim her. So many signs. So many clues. But what did it all mean?

After maybe twenty minutes, there was a call from the munkee: the food was ready. She followed the smell of cooking and found her way into the cavernous kitchen, where Filth was perched on a tall stool preparing a number of dishes. He'd already fried up a good portion of what looked like spiral-shaped dough-nuts and had opened a selection of jars of fruit in syrup. Now he was taking the bones out of a large pickled fish, noisily sucking the meat off before toss-ing them over his shoulder.

Candy hadn't realized quite how hungry she was until she was standing in the presence of all this food. Without even bothering to sit down, she started to eat, and she'd soon tasted just about everything that Filth had prepared for her and was starting to feel a warm glow of fulfillment. A distinct sense of sleepiness was also creeping upon her.

"You should go and lie down," the munkee said. "Get a little shut-eye."

"Mmm, maybe I will."

"There's a small bed in the corner over there," Filth went on. "It's where the cooks used to take a snooze. Lie down. I'll wake you up if something interesting happens."

"Thank you," Candy said. Her limbs were pleasantly

heavy, as were her eyelids. She went over to the low, narrow bed and pulled back the antiquated quilt. Underneath were no sheets, just a couple of threadbare blankets. She lay down, and her grateful limbs sank into the softness of the old mattress. She reached down and lifted up the quilt. She was in the process of pulling it up over her body when sleep overtook her.

She dreamed she was sitting on the stairs in Followell Street; but it was a different sensation than simply dreaming it, she felt somehow that she was *there*, in spirit. She could hear her brothers fighting upstairs, their voices shrill, their insults as crude as they'd ever been.

"Fat butt!"

"Ape brain!"

"Dog breath!"

"Cow's ass!"

Now there came a third voice, this one slurred by too much beer.

"Will you shut the hell up, or do I have to come up there and beat the livin' daylights outta you? Which is it goin' to be?"

Candy looked down the stairs and saw her father standing in the shadows below, his face damp with sweat. She remembered how intimidating and unpredictable he was in moods like this. How the whole house seemed to hold its breath in anticipation of his next outburst.

"Well?" Bill Quackenbush yelled up the stairs. "Which is it to be?"

"We'll be quiet, Dad," Don said meekly.

"You're damn right you'll be quiet, because if you're *not* quiet I'm gonna make you wish you'd never been born, you hear me? NEVER BEEN BORN!"

There was complete silence now from the boys. Not even a footfall. They knew from painful experience how cruel their father could be when he got into one of his drunken furies.

Growling something under his breath, Bill Quackenbush turned around and went back to the beer-stained splendor of his easy chair.

Even though she knew her father couldn't see or hear her right now, Candy instinctively did as she had long ago learned to do whenever her father got into a mood like this. She sat very still and said nothing for a while. Only when it seemed his rage had quieted did she go in search of her mother.

Where was she? The kitchen was empty, but the back door was open, and Candy headed out, glancing up at the clock above the fridge as she went. It was 4:05 P.M. In Abarat, she'd be in Gnomon at this hour. But time ran differently here, in the world she'd called home for so long. Soon the sun would begin to slide down toward the horizon, and evening would settle in. All she had to do was stay still here, and the hours would slip on by. That idea seemed a little odd to her now. She'd become quite used to the notion that Time was a place, a spot on the map that you went to visit, just as you would any other place.

One day, she thought, *I'm going to come back to Chickentown, to this house, to my mom and dad and my brothers*. And thinking of that, she made a mental note to start collecting some souvenirs of Abarat to bring back with her. They couldn't be things she could ever find in the Hereafter. They'd have to be totally Abaratian. A copy of *Klepp's Almenak*. A compass watch like one she'd seen in the marketplace at Tazmagor, which showed you when was where, or where was when, or both. Maybe some photographs of the wilder flora and fauna of the Hours. *Evidence*, in short. Things she could show to people that would be incontestable proof that there was another, more wonderful place where gossip and beer and chicken production were not the only things that mattered.

She'd walked to the far end of the yard as she planned her evidence collecting, and there, sitting in a rusted garden chair with her back to the house, was her mother.

"Oh, Mom . . ." Candy said softly.

Candy half expected Melissa Quackenbush to sense her daughter's presence and turn and smile at her. But she didn't move.

"Mom?" Candy said again.

She was close enough now to be able to hear her mother's soft rhythmic breathing. Was she asleep? Moving very cautiously, so as not to wake her, she took a step around the chair. The sight of her mother's face made Candy want to cry. Melissa looked so weary, so drained. Her eyes were closed, her mouth turned down, her freckled brow marked by a deep frown.

"Candy?" she murmured in her sleep. "Is that you?"

Her eyes wandered back and forth beneath her blue-veined lids as though attempting to make sense of some dreamed sight or other. The sorrowful expression on her mother's face made Candy want to turn away. But when she did so, she found her mother standing just a few yards away from her, in the middle of the unkempt lawn. Confused, Candy looked back at the woman sleeping in the rusted chair, and again at her mother's twin.

"I don't get it," Candy said. "Why are there two of you?"

"One dreaming, one awake," Melissa said, as though it was the easiest idea in the world. "I'm over in that chair, dreaming. And I guess you're somewhere else too, asleep."

"So we're meeting each other in our dreams?" Candy said.

Melissa nodded. "It's so good to see you, honey," she said. "Where have you been? Did you hitchhike somewhere? Did you go to Minneapolis?"

"No."

"Where then? Where *are* you?"

"I'm a long, long way from Chickentown, Mom."

"Oh, God. Did somebody kidnap you?"

"No," Candy said with a grin. "I've just been traveling, that's all."

"Well, why didn't you call me and tell me you were safe?" Melissa replied, her relief souring into anger. "How could you be so selfish? I imagined all kinds of things. And of course your dad was sure you'd gotten into trouble with some boy, or with drugs."

"No boy. No drugs."

"What then?"

"Oh, Mom . . . if I told you what's happened to me . . . I swear, you'd say I was crazy."

"I don't care: *I want to know.*"

In her sleeping state, Melissa was becoming agitated. Candy reached down and gently laid a soothing hand on her mother's shoulder.

"Mom, I'm sorry," she said. "I had no way of contacting you."

"Don't be silly. Nobody's that far away."

"I was. I am."

"Then tell me," Melissa said.

"Tell you what?"

This time the sleeping Melissa and the waking one spoke together. *"Everything!"* they said. *"Tell me everything!"*

"Huh. Everything. Well, where do I start?" Candy thought about the question for a moment, and then, finally, she said: "Who am I, Mom?"

"You're my daughter, of course. You're Candy Quackenbush."

"Where was I born?"

"You know where you were born. Here in Chickentown."

"You're sure?"

"Of *course* I'm sure."

Candy studied Melissa's face, looking for some sign of doubt. She saw it too, a little flicker in her mother's eyes.

"Was there anything strange about the way I came into the world?" Candy said.

This time Melissa looked away. "I don't know why you're asking these silly questions."

"I'll tell you why," Candy replied, her voice very calm. "Because though we're dreaming that we're in the same world, Mom, we're not. I'm in a place called the Abarat. It's nowhere on any map that you've ever looked at."

"That's ridiculous."

"No. It isn't. It's the truth. And I think you know it's the truth."

She paused to give her mother an opportunity to contradict this, if she was going to, but she said nothing, so Candy went on.

"Right now I'm sleeping on an island called Scoriae, at the Hour of Seven in the Evening. Every Hour has its own island here, you see. You can sort of time travel by hopping from island to island. I'm actually in what's called the Twilight Palace. It was built for a Princess, a long time ago. . . ."

Melissa still didn't answer, though she was shaking her head very, very slowly, as if this was all too much to take in. But Candy went on telling her story, watching her mother's face all the while. "When I first came here, I thought: this is new; this is like nothing I've ever seen before. But I was wrong. As the weeks have gone on, more and more I've had the feeling that this *isn't* the first time I've been here." The doubt in her mother's face deepened. *"I've been in the Abarat before, Mom,"* Candy said. "I don't know how that's possible, but I have."

She paused again for a moment, to collect her thoughts, and then she went on.

"And it seems to me that if *I* know something about the Abarat, then probably you do too, because you've been with me all through my life, right from the very beginning."

Again Candy gave her mother a moment to think about this. Then she said: "Do you, Mom? Do you know something?"

Almost in a whisper, Melissa replied: "Maybe."

"Tell me. Please. Whatever it is. Tell me."

Melissa took a deep breath. Then, very softly, she said: "The night you were born, it was raining *so* hard it was like there was going to be a second Flood. I never saw rain like it. But I had to get to the hospital, rain or no rain, because you were suddenly ready to be born, and you weren't going to be delayed." She made a little smile. "You were willful, even then," she said. "So your dad bundled me into the truck and off we went. But once we're on the highway, guess what? We run out of gas. So your dad set off in this deluge to find a garage, leaving me . . . *leaving us* . . . in the truck. And the rain kept coming down, drumming on the roof of the truck, and you kept squirming inside me, and just when I thought I was going to have you right there on the front seat, I saw a light—"

"Dad?"

"No, it wasn't your dad. There were three women, out there in the rain. I knew immediately they weren't from town. The way they looked, for one thing. An old woman, one of them, with long gray hair."

"Diamanda . . ." Candy said softly.

Melissa looked astonished. "You know her?" she said.

"A little," Candy said. "Diamanda, Mespa and Joephi. They're all Sisters of the Fantomaya. That means they're women who know magic. I don't mean the Las Vegas kind of magic—"

"I know what you mean," Melissa said. "At least I can guess. Oh, Lord, why did I let them come *near* me? I should have just run."

"How could you?"

"I should have tried. But instead I just sat there. And the door opened, and . . ." She paused, and a sudden anger came into her eyes. "We were going to have a perfectly *ordinary* life," she said. "A perfectly happy, easy life, until they came along with their *magic*."

"Tell me the rest, Mom. The door opened, and then what?"

"The old lady Diamanda had a box, which she was carrying as though whatever was inside was the most precious thing in the world. And when she opened it—" Melissa closed her eyes for a moment, and Candy heard the sound of sobbing. She looked over her shoulder to see that her mom was crying in her sleep, moved to tears by these memories. Candy felt a pang of guilt for what she'd done, dredging up the past this way. But she needed these answers. More than that, she *deserved* them. She'd had this secret kept from her for too long.

"Go on," she gently urged.

"She opened this box, and there was light inside. Not just a light. *Life.* Something alive in the light. And whatever it was—this bright thing—it came *into me*, Candy. Through my skin, through my eyes, through my breath."

"Were you afraid?"

"Not at the time. At least not for myself. You see, I knew the moment it began to move through my body that it wasn't *me* the light and life wanted." She opened her eyes finally, and mother and daughter looked at each other, dreamer to dreamer. *"It was you,"* she said. *"The light wanted you."*

24

HUSBAND AND WIFE

"MELISSA! GET UP! I'M hungry!"

Candy's father was standing at the back door, his shirt pulled out of his pants and hanging open, his beer-swollen belly shiny with sweat. He was pointing his finger at Melissa, who was still asleep in the chair. Candy could remember all too easily how it felt to be close to him when he was in a mood like this. The threat of him, the stink of him; the sickness he exuded. How many times, over the years, had he caught her looking at him, caught the contempt in her eyes and beaten her for it?

But right now his wife was the subject of his rage.

"Wake up, you lazy cow!" he yelled. "Didn't you hear me? I'm hungry."

"Oh, *shut up*," Candy said through gritted teeth. "Don't wake her up yet. We haven't finished talking."

"Too late," Melissa murmured to her, her voice growing faint as her husband's summons stirred her. "He hates seeing me sleep. I guess because he doesn't sleep well himself." Her image was flickering now. "He has nightmares."

Bill was striding down the garden now, yelling at his wife as he went. *"Melissa, damn you, WILL YOU WAKE UP?"*

He raised his fist as he approached. Candy didn't doubt for a moment what he intended to do —

"I'm warning you, woman!" he growled.

Instinctively Candy stepped into his path and raised her arm to block her father's intended blow. She wasn't sure what kind of effect she would have, if any. After all, she was only a *dreaming* presence. But she carried some weight here, even in her present condition. The moment her father's arm made contact with hers, he let out a shout of shock. He dropped his arm, narrowing his bloodshot eyes.

"What the hell—?" He waited a moment, then moved toward his sleeping wife again. He was still ready to do harm.

"No, you *don't*," Candy said. This time she didn't simply block his blow. She put her hand in the middle of her father's chest and she *pushed*. A hard push. Her father stumbled backward, reaching out to catch hold of the chair in which Melissa was still sleeping. But Candy casually knocked his hand away, and down he went, falling heavily. For a few seconds he lay sprawled in the unkempt grass. Then he got to his feet and retreated two or three steps, the fury on his face entirely fled now, replaced by a look of sudden superstition.

"What's going on?" he said, half to himself. Then, to Melissa:

"Open your eyes, woman! Open your damn eyes!"

Slowly Melissa answered her husband's summons, and as her eyes flicked open, the image of the dreamer to whom Candy had been speaking went out like a blown candle.

Melissa shook her head and got to her feet, looking around the yard as though she half expected to still see Candy standing there. What she saw instead was her husband, scanning the yard nervously.

"Is there something here with us?" he said to her. "Is there?"

"What are you talking about?"

"Something pushed me," he muttered. Then more loudly: *"Something pushed me!"*

It took Melissa only a moment or two to make sense of what he was telling her.

"Candy . . ." she said softly, looking around as she spoke. "Are you here?"

"Candy?" Bill said, his hands instinctively closing into fists. "You think she's here? If she's here, why the hell can't I see her?"

Melissa glanced down at her husband's white knuckles and tried to put on a smile.

"It's all right, Bill," she murmured.

"You said: are you here? Why'd you say that? Tell me! And don't you start lying to me. If there's one thing that makes me mad, it's *liars*."

"I was dreaming, that's all," Melissa said lightly. "I was dreaming about Candy, and when I woke up I was confused. I thought she was here."

"But she's not?"

Melissa put on a look of puzzlement. "How could

she be?" she replied, daring Bill to put words to his fears. "I mean, look. There's just you and me."

"Yeah . . ."

"It was just a dream."

"Damn girl," Bill muttered. "We're better off without her."

"You don't mean that."

"Don't tell me what I mean."

"I know it was never easy between you two," Melissa said. "But Bill, she's still our daughter. Remember how excited we were the night she was born?"

He grunted.

"That was quite a night, Bill. Do you remember any of what happened the night Candy was born?"

"Who cares?"

"I do."

"Well, *I* don't."

He turned away from his wife and walked off toward the house. Melissa followed him, talking to him as he went, gently reminding him.

"It rained, Bill. Do you remember how hard it rained? And you left me in the truck—"

"Oh, now we come to it. Billy-boy forgot to put gas in the truck, so poor Melissa was left in the cold for hours and hours and—"

"Will you let me finish?"

"Poor Melissa. Of course she should never have married him in the first place, isn't that what everybody tells you?"

"Shut up a minute, will you?"

He turned on her suddenly, as though he was going

to hit her. But he was still nervous after what had happened, and he kept himself from doing it in case he felt another push from that invisible hand.

"This isn't about you or me," Melissa went on. "This is about Candy. I tried so many times to tell you what happened that night, but you would never listen. You thought I was crazy. But what happened that night was real."

"And what was that?" he said.

"Three women appeared. They came from another world, Bill."

"Stupid."

"Abarat, it's called."

He sneered. "Never heard of it."

"Well, it's where our daughter is right now."

"According to who?"

"According to *her*, Bill. I saw her in my dream. I talked to her."

Bill rolled his eyes.

"Believe me—"

"You *are* crazy, you really are." He put his finger to his temple. "It's all in your head."

"No."

"Yes! Yes! Yes! Yes!"

"Candy even told me the names of these women."

"Oh, did she?"

"Diamanda, Joephi and Mespa. They're from a sisterhood called the Fantomaya."

"You know, you should write all this nonsense down. You could probably sell it."

"I'm not inventing it, Bill. Candy's there, in the

Abarat. She's seen these women. They're helping her."

"All right!" Bill said. "Enough! I don't want to hear any more of this crap." His voice filled with genuine revulsion. "You and your stupid women! As if there aren't enough damn women on the planet." He turned his back on his wife and headed for the house. But after a few steps he stopped and looked back at her.

"You know what?" he said. "One of these days I'm just gonna pack my bags and get the hell outta here."

"And where would you go?"

"I got places. I could go to Denver, see my brother. Back to Chicago. Anywhere but here." He turned from her and went to the back door. "I should have gone a long time ago."

And with that he disappeared into the house, leaving Melissa standing in the yard, despairing. She'd tried to get through to him, but he was a wall. What was it going to take for him to believe her?

She looked up at the sky. Small fleets of clouds were being driven northeast by the wind.

"Candy?" she said, hoping her daughter was still within earshot. "If you can hear me, darling, please take good care of yourself. Maybe one of these days we'll get a chance to see the Abarat together. I miss you, honey."

Then she put her sadness away, where Bill wouldn't be able to see it, and she went inside the house to fix her family some hamburgers for lunch.

25

FATES

MALINGO HAD BEEN ON some amazing trips in the weeks since he'd escaped his servitude, but none was as breath-snatching as the journey he took over the crowded boardwalks of Babilonium. The blue fabric that had snatched him up didn't seem to have much substance to speak of: it was a robe without a visible body to occupy it. But the woman who possessed it spoke to him clearly enough, and did her best to reassure him.

"Just keep calm," she said. "I don't want to drop you on these poor people's heads. They came here for some fun, not to be brained by a geshrat."

Malingo looked down through the folds of fabric. They were now a long way off the ground and moving at considerable speed. If he were to fall, he thought, it wouldn't be the folks below who would suffer most; it would be he.

"Who are you?" he said.

"Later."

"I just need to know: did Wolfswinkel send you?

Are you taking me back to Ninnyhammer?"

"No, no, no. Perish the thought."

"Only he used to beat me for the pleasure of it."

"Oh, I've heard about the cruelties of Kaspar Wolfswinkel," the woman in the cloth said. "And he'll pay dearly for them, by and by. You be comforted, my friend. All hurt is repaid in the great round. Trust me."

"I do . . ." Malingo said quietly, sounding a little surprised at himself.

"Hang on, now!"

They were coming to the edge of the Carnival, where the brightly lit boardwalk gave way to murk and mud, and thence to a rocky landscape which rolled away toward the sea.

Their flight had carried them north, he judged; the sky was darker over the straits that lay ahead than they had been behind them. Evening was turning to Night.

"Where exactly are we going?" he yelled over the rushing of the wind, which became steadily louder as they sped toward the coastline.

"You'll find out in a few moments," the woman in the robe yelled back. "Get ready! We've got some tricky maneuvering ahead of us. It may get a little bumpy."

Malingo peered a second time through the snapping folds of his carrier and instantly regretted that he'd done so. They were speeding toward a solid rock face.

"What are you doing?" he hollered. *"You'll kill us!"*

"Then don't look!" the woman said. "Keep holding tight!"

Malingo couldn't keep himself from looking, despite the woman's advice. They flew directly toward solid rock at a speed that surely meant they would be splattered against it, but at the last moment the spirit in the fabric swerved and carried them through the narrowest of fissures in the rock. His bearer knew her way. She speeded him through the crack in the rock without incident, though at times it seemed to get so tight he was sure they wouldn't make it. Still he clung to the cloth— what choice did he have?—and he was finally rewarded with the sweetest smell imaginable: the clean smell of salt sea air.

"Take courage!" the woman in the robe announced. "We're almost there!" and a few seconds later they started to slow down. Emerging at last from the fissure, they came to rest on a wet rock.

"Be careful now," the woman warned. "I don't want you to get swept away."

She had brought them down to a spot that was no more than three or four yards from the sea, and the waves beat against the boulders in a white frenzy. Within a few seconds of coming to land, Malingo was soaked from head to foot.

"That's cold," he said.

"A little seawater isn't going to hurt you," said the old woman, and as she spoke blue fabric parted and she stepped out of new folds, her occupying spirit becoming solid and visible. She was old, perhaps very old, her unpinned hair rising around her head as the wind caught it. "Lordy Lou, geshrat," she said. "That was hard work. You're heavier than you look."

"Well, thank you for the rescue," Malingo said. "But why?"

"Well, I didn't do it for the good of my health," she replied. "Or yours, come to that. I did it for—"

"Let me guess: Candy Quackenbush."

"Very good, geshrat."

"If it's any comfort to you, I would die for that lady."

"It is a comfort," said the old woman. "And believe me, I know that you would. That's why I'm sending you after her now. To prevent a double tragedy."

"That doesn't sound good."

"It isn't," the old lady said. "But time is of the essence, so can we hurry along?"

"Hurry where?"

"Turn around."

He turned and saw that in the blue murk there was a small two-masted vessel, which was being kept from dashing itself against the shore by the crew, who were wielding lengths of roughly hewn timber to prevent the ship from being carried against the rocks.

"Quickly! Quickly!" the woman in the blue robe said, directing Malingo to a plank that lay between land and boat. He gave her a doubting look. The plank was narrow and slick with water. But the old lady hurried Malingo across it so quickly his doubts were over in a heartbeat, and he was received into the beaming company of a young woman with dark skin and bright orange hair. Beside her was a third woman, fine boned but severe. She had a coat for him, which was certainly welcome.

"Let's go below and get you some nourishment," she said, a suggestion with which Malingo gladly complied. The women led him down into the hold of the ship, where a large fire was burning in an enormous iron grate. Malingo was offered a chair, but he said he preferred to sit near the hearth. The room quickly filled with the pungent smell of drying geshrat. The promised nourishment quickly came in the form of a four-decker sandwich made of slices of well-seasoned *ropa-ropa* and jabal pâté. Malingo was halfway through the sandwich when the old woman— now wearing clean, dry robes—came back in and sat in one of the chairs close to the fire.

"Better now?"

"Much," Malingo said. He set down his sandwich. "You're Diamanda, aren't you? Of the Fantomaya?"

"I am."

"And you"—he pointed to the woman who'd given him the coat—"you must be Joephi, yes? And you Mespa, yes?"

"All correct," said Mespa.

"Is that all Candy told you: our names?" said Joephi.

"She didn't say much more," Malingo replied. "She's a complicated one, that girl. She goes deep. I don't even think she understands the mysteries she contains."

"I doubt anybody does," Diamanda replied with great gravity.

"We'd been traveling together for almost eight weeks," Malingo went on, "and I was beginning to think we would stay together, but then she goes and runs off the way she did."

"She was protecting you," said Mespa.

"But that's a two-way street. She protects me, and I protect her. How can I possibly protect her if I don't know where she is?"

"You'll find her again," Diamanda said. "Your story together has a long way to go."

"Yes?" said Malingo, so relieved to hear this that tears welled in his eyes.

"Absolutely," said Diamanda. "Tell us now, did she display a good command of magic?"

"Not as much as she wanted to," Malingo said. "She knew I'd learned some minor conjurations from Wolfswinkel, and she was always pushing me to teach her what I knew."

"And did you?"

"No. I resisted for a long while. And then, once I agreed to do it, the opportunity was snatched away."

"Why did you resist?" Mespa wanted to know.

"It's as I said: she goes deep. I was afraid of what I might unleash in her. I didn't know how she'd end up if she got real power."

Diamanda sighed. "None of us do, Mister Malingo," she said, with a note of quiet unease.

"Not even Candy?" said Malingo.

"*Especially* not Candy."

"I think we can be certain of one thing," Joephi said. "Whatever she learns, whatever she *becomes*, she will affect the fate of these islands in ways we can none of us begin to know."

"So what do you want me to do? Besides find her."

"That entirely depends on how things have changed for her when you *do* find her."

"Am I going on my own?"

"On the first part of the voyage, yes," Joephi said. "But once you get to the Nonce, you'll hook up with a group of fine, good people."

"Can't you come with me?"

"We wish we could," said Mespa. "But events are hurrying us all along in different directions, I'm afraid."

"So it falls to you to find her, with the greatest possible speed, and bring her to a place of safety," Joephi told him.

"What place?"

Diamanda shook her head. "I don't know right now," she said, her voice raw with despair. "What we tell you now might not be true in half an hour. There are strange things happening on just about every island, Malingo. Powers stirring that we had hoped never to see the likes of again. Things rising out of the deep. Things dropping out of the high heavens. There are no *certainties*, I'm afraid. None. No places of safety, no things we know to be true now that will be true in the next heartbeat."

Malingo looked grim. "Can I ask—?" he murmured, then stopped.

"Say it," Diamanda told him. "If you've got a question, ask it now. There may not be another time."

"Well, as you put it *that* way," Malingo said. "What's the worst thing that could happen?"

Diamanda sighed heavily. "I'm afraid that's all too easy to answer," she said. She glanced at her sisters, then back at Malingo. "The Twenty-Fifth Hour is where our enemies will attempt to strike. If they put that Hour in jeopardy, then *our very existence* will be in question."

"They could do that?" Malingo said. "They could take the Twenty-Fifth Hour?"

"In sufficient numbers," said Diamanda, "and with the right kind of strategy, yes. Let's be in no doubt: the forces assembling against us are formidable. Mater Motley has been creating an army of stitchlings for years, hidden by the darkness of Midnight. If she unleashes them, and Odom's Spire falls to her army—if the mysteries that the Twenty-Fifth Hour contain become vulnerable to attack and desecration—then the way we live our lives—both here and in the Hereafter—will be destroyed forever. A profound chaos will descend, and everything that made life possible in these islands—all the joy, all the love, all the *meaning*—will be extinguished. It would be as though we—and our world—had never existed."

Malingo put his head in his hands. Though he was close to the fire, he was suddenly deathly cold.

"How's that possible?" he said. "All these terrible things going on and nobody even knows." He lifted his head a little. "Listen!" he said. "You can hear the Carnival music from here! Tens of thousands of people dancing and singing and . . . all *ignorant*."

"Oh, they know," said Diamanda. "People across the Hours have known for a long while now that matters of great consequence are in the air. They've woken from their slumbers, weeping and afraid, and they've not known why. They've been moved to kiss their children, suddenly, as though they feared they might not see them again."

"Yet they don't speak up about it," Malingo said.

"A few have," Joephi said. "But Houlihan took care of most of them. They disappeared, suddenly."

"Terrible," Malingo said.

"As for the rest—the ordinary men and women of the Hours—they just have to live their lives. Love their children. Grow old peacefully. So they turn their backs on what they suspect."

"Is there any hope?"

"Of course there's hope, geshrat," Diamanda said fiercely. "But you have work to do. I'll leave you in the company of my sister Mespa. She has her instructions. It's been a pleasure talking with you, Malingo Geshrat. Joephi, would you come with me? We have a great deal to do."

The two women left, and for a moment or two Malingo stared into the fire, meditating on the conversation they'd just had. Finally Mespa said: "Whenever you're ready, my Captain . . ."

"I'm sorry?" Malingo said. "Your *what?*"

"It was Diamanda's instruction," Mespa explained. "You are to be Captain of this ship. It's called the *Lud Limbo.*"

"Why me?"

"Because Diamanda trusts you."

"But I don't know how to captain a ship."

"Well then, you'll learn as we go, yes? Candy has faith in you and so do we. Do you want to come up on deck?"

They headed up into the soft starlight. There were lanterns lit everywhere around the vessel, and the flames illuminated a great crowd of folks, some human, many not, assembled in the middle of the deck. As soon as Malingo stepped into view they raised a mast-shaking cheer, much to his embarrassment.

"Your crew, Captain," said a Sea-Skipper, wearing a water-sodden uniform. He was a thin, quizzical creature, and looked nervous. "I'm Deaux-Deaux, your first mate."

"Oh," said Malingo, still too surprised by his sudden elevation in the world to think straight. "Good to meet you."

"So, do you want to make a speech to the crew?" Deaux-Deaux said.

"About what?"

"About our destination, perhaps? Or about what we're going to do when we get there?"

"Before you say a word," Mespa said. "Let me wish you bon voyage, Captain—"

Malingo took Mespa's arm and gently escorted her out of his first mate's earshot. "I can't do this," he said. "I can't captain a whole ship."

"Of course you can," she said to him, looking him straight in the eyes. "There'll be a lot more outlandish demands made on you before this war's finished, believe me. Take courage. You are part of something great and good, Malingo."

So saying, she wrapped her robes around her, and in the moment that she did so the fabric folded itself up and was gone, carrying its wearer away with it.

Malingo watched her vanish, hoping against hope that she might still return and announce to everyone that this was just a joke. But she had indeed gone. And

with her departure the crew's eyes—*his* crew's eyes—
were all turned on him, waiting, obviously, for him to
say something.

He had to speak. For better or worse, he had to
speak.

He silently counted to three. On the third beat he
took his eyes off the empty sky and looked down at his
assembled crew.

"Good evening," he said. "I am Malingo. I am a
geshrat. And your Captain . . ."

26

KASPAR IS VISITED

KASPAR WOLFSWINKEL REMEMBERED with painful clarity the girl who'd come knocking on his door not so very long ago. He had been foolish enough to open the door, foolish enough to let the brat in. He'd thought for a while that he'd outwit this poor lost child and persuade her to poison the tarrie-cats who were his warders on Ninnyhammer. He couldn't do it himself because the wretched animals were immune to his illusions. Nor could he escape them while they lived. And what better way to rid himself of his watch-cats than to have the innocent girl-child who'd come to his doorstep feed them poisoned fish?

But it hadn't been as simple as that. *Nowhere near.* For one thing, the girl was not as stupid as she looked. She'd quickly realized that he was plotting something. And then, to make matters worse, she'd taken it into her asinine little head to inspire his geshrat slave to free himself. She'd fired up the creature with a lot of inflammatory talk about liberty and such, and Wolfswinkel had retaliated with some serious wizardry, which had unfortunately gotten out of hand. When the business was over and done with, Wolfswinkel's house on the hill had been trashed; Malingo the geshrat, along with his liberator, Candy Quackenbush, had escaped. And the tarrie-cats had not been poisoned.

His life under house arrest, which had been plenty miserable *before* the girl had come knocking on the door, was a good deal more miserable when she'd gone. He'd lost his slave. Now he had to dust his own furniture, serve his own rum and tidy his own books. Worse than that, he missed the simple pleasure of beating the geshrat and humiliating him. He was alone and bored, and the girl was to blame.

He had complained to the High Court of the Hours about how unfair all this was, but none of the judges wanted to give him a hearing. In fact, matters only got worse. The court sent in a battalion of soldiers to patrol his hill, with the tarrie-cats lending them the benefit of their undeceivable eyes. It was distressing for a man who had as high an opinion of himself as Wolfswinkel to be treated like a petty criminal. And it had all started when he'd taken pity on a stranger. He cursed the moment he'd done it. And more, he cursed *her*. There was no revenge harsh enough, no punishment merciless enough, to satisfy his fulminating rage. He spent hour after hour, half pickled in rum, inventing things he would do to the girl when he finally got his hands on her.

And he would. Of that he had not the slightest doubt. *He would.* His present circumstance had somewhat limited his options, but eventually a way out of this wretched prison would present itself. And when it did, his first act as a free man would be to find the Quackenbush girl and make her regret she'd ever seen his front door, much less come knocking on it.

Tonight, however, he had something else besides revenge to claim his attention. Ninnyhammer stood at Ten O'clock, so it was always dark on the island, and usually quiet. But tonight he'd heard a lot of odd noises. First there'd been a good deal of shouting—some of it panicked—down by the harbor. Then some shots had been fired. For a brief time after that there'd been silence, then a second eruption of firing and further shouts, coming now from not one but several directions.

Wolfswinkel had gone up to the great dome that was perched on top of his house to see if he could get a better look at things. The dome worked much as a telescope lens worked, allowing him a close-up view of events; it also had night vision capabilities. Thanks again to the intrusion of the Quackenbush girl, the dome had been severely damaged, but he could still see a good deal more through it than he could with the naked eye. Sipping from his glass of rum as he went, he wandered around the cracked dome, peering out at the moonlit landscape of Ninnyhammer. There were more shouts, closer to the house this time, and beams of light piercing the evening darkness.

"What *is* going on out there?" he asked himself.

That was the same question—or a variation of the same—that was being asked by the soldiers of the

Ninth Hobarookian Cavalry, who were out searching the slopes and copses of the island's interior. They were looking for an enemy that had come out of the sea half an hour before and launched a surprise attack which had caused a dozen fatalities and twice that number of woundings in three minutes. And that was just the soldiers. Their mounts, purebred white carramasi, were being struck down in equal numbers.

The question was: who was doing the attacking?

It was Sergeant Massoff, who had just seen three of his comrades murdered in front of him, who offered Captain Cruss the most detailed reply.

"There's only three of them, as far as we can make out," Massoff replied. "They're not even that large: about five or six feet tall when they get up on their hind legs. But their heads are covered in bone; naked, shiny yellow-white bone. And they just drive into our carramasi and knock us off."

"Well, why don't you remount?"

"Can't, sir," said another of the men, who had blood streaming down the side of his face. "The blow to the animal stops its heart. They die instantly. Half the fatalities have been men trying to get out from under their mounts."

"So these creatures do the same to the men? One strike to the heart?"

"No, sir," said Massoff. "The bone hood swings back for a minute, and that's when you get a glimpse of the face. Well . . . I say *face*; it's just a mouth, really. All lined with teeth. That's what kills the men, sir.

The teeth. It's horrible, sir, what these things do. I mean, it's—"

"Yes, Massoff, yes. I saw for myself. Clearly we have a problem. We don't know what these creatures are, and they're slaughtering us."

There was a heart-clutching cry from somewhere out in the darkness. "We also need to know what they want. What have they come for?"

"They're coming for me!" Kaspar said, dancing a little anticipatory jig of glee. "That's what's going on out there! Somebody's finally come to *set me free*!"

"They will *not* make it past our defenses," said Jimothi Tarrie.

He, the most humanoid of the tarries, was standing in a copse of witch-pyre trees, staring down the slope toward the approaching monstrosities. Behind him were thirty or forty tarrie-cats. They stood on four legs while he stood on two, but they had this in common: they were all battle-hardened warriors. "Whatever we have to do, we must stop these *things* from getting to the wizard's house." He turned to his troops. "Has anyone seen anything like this before?"

The assembly of tarrie-cats was silent. This enemy was something new.

"I suspected as much," Jimothi Tarrie said. "If none of you have seen beasts like these in your many lives, I must assume such beasts did not *exist* until recently. Some form of perverse magic made these things." His huge green eyes grew sad. "For those of you who are approaching your ninth life, take care out there! And you young ones, with lives to spare, throw yourselves at these things with all your strength but be aware that you could well use all of your lifetimes fighting and still not succeed in stemming the tide. So don't be heroic for the sake of it. If you hear me call retreat, then *you will retreat*; do you all understand me? I sense we will have bigger battles to fight in the near future, I'm afraid to say, and I will not have you throwing your lives away unnecessarily."

He looked up the hill toward the dome. Kaspar Wolfswinkel's face, vastly magnified and grotesquely distorted, was pressed against the unbroken portion of the glass.

"On the other paw . . ." he said. "I don't like the idea of that thing up there"—he jabbed a claw in Wolfswinkel's direction—"escaping into the Abarat. If the whispers I hear these nights are true—and they come from all directions, telling the same terrible tales—then we cannot afford to let a villain such as Wolfswinkel go out into the islands if we can prevent it. There will be far too much trouble for the likes of him to cause."

"What have you heard, sir?" one of the tarrie-soldiers asked Jimothi.

"Oh, just that the forces of the enemy grow bigger every hour. And that in the end it may be the presence of one soul on either side who will make the difference between the winning and losing of the coming war."

"War, sir?" said another tarrie.

"Yes, war. And its first open conflict will be here,

tonight. So acquit yourselves well, tarries. This one is for the history books!"

There was no time for further talk.

A noise in the darkness suddenly grew louder, and the witch-pyre trees shook till their blossoms came down in a red rain, as the enemy surged toward the company of tarries.

From the dome Wolfswinkel watched the grisly spectacle like an eager child, talking to himself in a dozen languages—nonsensically mingled—in his enthusiasm.

"Lookee yum! *Yiefire!* 'Sblud, 'sblud on das tally-man. An' then a flick! An' then a flack, yeah! Lookee Malanin. Tarrie—pus die, tarrie—pus die! Laodamia tee; ewe et taud. Blebs a merrio, huh? Wanton! Blebs a merrio! Sool a salis pidden. Zuberratium! Ha!"

He beat a jubilant tattoo on the window whenever one of the tarrie-cats went down for the last time (having used up all of its nine lives), yelling the same sickening phrase over and over again:

"Tarrie—pus die! Tarrie—pus die!"

It wasn't hard, even from a distance, to work out how the battle was going. It was a massacre. The soldiers who'd been defeated on the slopes retreated to swell the ranks of the tarries, but the bone-headed beasts that had done such bloody work down on the shore were quick to carve their murderous way through the ranks of the tarries. Wolfswinkel's glee grew in direct proportion to the number of bodies, human and tarrie alike, left in the long grass.

But the battle was not yet over. Seeing that the tree line could not be held, Jimothi Tarrie had led a small contingent of tarries away from the slaughter, intending—Wolfswinkel guessed—some kind of final surprise attack. Jimothi was clever, Wolfswinkel had to give him that. He stalked his enemy with the greatest care, using his familiarity with the lay of the land to aid his strategy. There wasn't a gully or a boulder or a shrub on the hillside that Jimothi and the cats didn't know. They shadowed the bone beasts with utmost caution, the mingling of firelight and grass stalks concealing their striped fur.

But finally they had to attack; and for all their courage and their skills as warriors, they couldn't oppose the terrible efficiency of the bone beasts. One by one, the tarrie-cats fell. And those that rose to spend another life and another and another finally ran out of resurrections, and did not rise again.

Finally Jimothi conceded the inevitable. The tarries had lost the battle. The bone beasts, whatever they were, had gained the hill. To fight on would only cause further purposeless slaughter. Reluctantly he sounded the retreat; and reluctantly the surviving tarrie-cats, no more than a handful, left the field, carrying their wounded away with them.

"The beasts have Wolfswinkel all to themselves," Jimothi said. "For what he's worth. And damn them all to hell for this hour's bloodletting."

As soon as Wolfswinkel realized that the tarries were retreating, and that it would only be a matter of time before his liberators came to his threshold, he went to get ready. He had let his appearance deteriorate of late; or so the mirror told him. His beard had grown long, and his hair was a rat's nest. His yellow suit was dirty (luckily he had nineteen, all of identical color and cut) and the front of his vest was caked with pieces of poppy pie and leech ice cream, along with the inevitable rum stains.

He had no time to bathe, so he splashed on pungent cologne he'd bought in an emporium in Commexo City just before his arrest for murder. Then he put on a clean suit, did his best to hurriedly trim his beard, and—placing all six of his hats on his head (thus increasing his power tenfold)—he headed to the front door to await his visitors.

Before he could reach it, however, something slammed so hard on the door that the hinges gave way and it flew off, spinning across the tiles and missing Wolfswinkel by inches. As the cloud of dust cleared from the air, a creature stepped over the threshold and into the house. It was one of the bone-helmeted beasts that had shed so much blood among the soldiers and the tarrie-cats. Wolfswinkel retreated a few steps, afraid of what the thing might do to him. Where was its master? And why were threads of darkness spilling from its fingertips, weaving themselves into elaborate configurations around the beast?

This wasn't the only mystery. Two more creatures now came into view, to the left and right of the first. Each had a hand that bled darkness into the air, knotting itself with the configurations from the beast in the center. They were subtly *connecting* themselves.

Wolfswinkel was intimidated. But he knew better than to show it. He stood his ground.

"What do you want from me?" he said.

The trio responded by throwing back their bony heads in perfect unison and expelling long, eerie sighs. Their skulls seemed to lose rigidity and they too issued filaments of shadow-stuff, which knitted themselves together. The three were becoming one, their bony heads congealing into a single being, its identity unmistakably human.

So this is their master, Wolfswinkel realized. There was one mind; one will divided among the three of them, which was now making itself apparent. Its humanity was no great comfort to Wolfswinkel: it still exuded an air of threat, and he was a coward to his marrow. But he had nowhere to run. He could only stand and watch as the process continued and the face of the three beasts folded into a single entity. The eyes, when they became clear, were gray and unforgiving, the mouth a tight, thin line. Smoky folds of fabric enveloped its body from head to foot, and there seemed to be small, smeared faces in the weave.

Finally, a voice emerged from the still-transforming shape: a woman's voice.

"My, my, little wizard," she said, the words making everything shake a little. "You live in chaos!"

Wolfswinkel looked around. The woman was right.

"It's not my fault," he said. "I had a slave once. A geshrat. But he was taken from me. . . ."

"Yes, I heard."

The three forms had been entirely subsumed into a single body now. The bone beasts had disappeared completely and had been replaced by an old woman dressed in what looked like a garment made of antiquated dolls.

"Do you know who I am?" she said.

"You're the woman with the needle and thread," the wizard replied. "You're Mater Motley."

The old lady smiled. "And you are Kaspar Wolfswinkel, the murderer of the five members of the Noncian Magic Circle." Kaspar opened his mouth to protest his innocence, but Mater Motley waved his protests away. "Frankly I could not care less whether you killed ten magicians or a thousand. I haven't come here to hire an assassin."

"Oh? What then?"

"I don't know how much you know about my plans," she said. "I keep most of my business hidden from sight. I find it's safer that way. Otherwise people start to interfere. Even so, perhaps you've heard a little?"

"More than a little," Wolfswinkel said. "I can't do much locked away up here, but I can certainly listen."

"To what, exactly?"

"Oh . . . you of all people know how many scraps and fragments are out there. On the wind. In the way the stars fall. In the shapes of the clouds. I study these things very carefully. I haven't got much else to do."

Mater Motley was surprised. She had expected to find more of a bumbler in Kaspar Wolfswinkel. But behind that ugly, embittered face, with its raw stare and downturned mouth, was somebody she might well make more use of than she'd first supposed.

"You'd be surprised what I hear," he continued. "But I have ways of doing what you do." He smiled. "Threading things together."

"Oh, so that's what I do, is it?"

"It's what I hear," he said. "I hear that you live in the Thirteenth Tower of the fortress of Iniquisit; you and your seamstresses sew all the time. Night on Night on Night. Never sleeping."

"I sleep occasionally," Mater Motley said. "But I sew even then."

"You're making stitchlings."

"Yes."

"An army."

"Yes."

"So that one of these Nights—"

"Enough, wizard. You've proved your point."

"But just so I understand, it *is* your intention to conquer the islands?" Mater Motley didn't reply. "You can trust me. I swear," Wolfswinkel said.

"I trust only my seamstresses."

"Not your grandson?"

"I can't quite. Not at the moment. He has some problems of his own, you see. Which is the matter that brings me here."

"Of course I'd be only too happy to be of assistance, but I'm locked up here."

"You've just been liberated, wizard."

"The tarrie-cats?"

"Forget about them. You and I will walk away from

this prison of yours without being challenged."

"But they'll send more troops to recapture me." He proffered a smug little smile. "I've murdered five people."

"Let them send troops. I don't care. I'm in the mood to spill more blood." She stared at the portrait paintings on the wall. "Are these your victims?"

"Yes. They were magicians. All their power was in their hats—"

"So you murdered your friends for their hats?"

"Yes."

"Cold, wizard, cold. Frankly I'd heard you were an hysteric and a drunkard, but this episode with the Quackenbush girl seems to have toughened you up a bit."

"I'm ready for anything."

"Are you ready to swear allegiance to me?"

"Of course. Of course."

Wolfswinkel dropped to his knees in front of Mater Motley and snatched up the heavy hem of her dress, pressing his face into its folds.

"I'm yours!" he said. "You have only to command me."

"I need you to watch over my grandson. Keep a casual eye on him for me. I don't trust his instinct where this girl from the Hereafter is concerned. I swear she has some kind of hold over him that I don't understand."

Wolfswinkel's expression grew sly. "Well . . . I've heard things . . ."

"About the girl?"

"Scraps and fragments."

"Well, I've no interest in rumor," Mater Motley said. "When you can come to me with hard evidence, then I'll listen. Just don't go back to your old ways, wizard. No drink. No murder, unless I sanction it. I'm hiring you to watch. Not gossip. Watch. If I sense for a moment that you are pushing beyond the limits of your usefulness, then I will dispose of you. I won't give you back to the tarries. I'll have you skinned and stuffed with Todo mud. Do we understand each other?"

Again Wolfswinkel kissed the hem of Mater Motley's dress. "I understand. Absolutely. Just instruct me."

"Well, you can start by letting go of my garment."

"Oh. Yes."

"Now get up."

Wolfswinkel scrambled to his feet. "What do you need me to do?"

"Here's a letter. Take it to a man called Julix Mirethak. He lives in Churngold, on Soma Plume."

"How will I get there?"

"Take the smaller of the two boats you'll find down at the little harbor on the early side of this Hour. The letter instructs both you and Mirethak how to proceed. We will meet in a day's time, at a place I've named. Move quickly and without undue show, Wolfswinkel. If I hear you've broken the bond of silence between us—and I *will* hear if you do so—it's a skinning for you. Now take the letter and get out of my sight."

Kaspar claimed the letter from Mater Motley's

hand, stepped back and made an extravagant bow. Then he opened his mouth to make one last profession of his undying devotion, thought better of it and instead departed the house in haste, lingering on the lower slope of the hill just long enough to see where the blood of the tarrie-cats, his sometime captors, glittered in the grass. Then, whistling tunelessly to himself, he went to find a boat, a free man.

27

ABDUCTION

WHEN CANDY OPENED HER eyes, all she could think was how much she wanted to put her arms around her mother; to hold her tight and to be hugged in return. It was such a simple thing, but at that moment there was nothing she wanted more.

She sat up on the cook's bed where she'd been napping and looked around. The kitchen was very still. The wind had died away while she was slumbering, so the leaf- and blossom-laden branches no longer churned overhead. There were no birds chattering or singing up there: they'd either fled or were keeping their tunes to themselves. And strangest of all, perhaps, was the absence of any sound or opinion of the newly resurrected tribe of Totemix. They had been making a happy din when she'd gone to sleep, as if to announce: *we're alive and free!* Candy couldn't imagine a happier sound. But now their noise had been silenced.

"Filth?" she said. "Where are you?"

Again, silence. Something had happened here while she slept: but what?

"Filth?" she said, raising her voice. "Are you there?"

There was no response, so she headed off in search of him. The same eerie stillness she'd woken to in the kitchen had taken grip of the whole of the Twilight Palace. Passageways and chambers alike were silent. It wasn't that the birds weren't up in the branches; they were, she could see them. They'd just decided to stop singing for some reason.

"Filth?" she called again. "Where are you? Filth!"

At last she heard the sound of a muted cry, and following it from chamber to chamber, she discovered the munkee lying on the ground with his mouth gagged, his arms tied tight behind him and his legs bound at the ankles. She unknotted the gag.

"Lordy Lou!" he said, spitting out the taste of the gag. "I thought that was the end of me, I really did."

"Who did this to you?"

"Never mind about me. It isn't me he's come for, it's you!"

"Again: *who*?"

"I don't know his name. Some young man with a nasty look in his eyes. You have to get out of here!"

She untied his hands, and the first thing he did was push her away from him.

"Go!" he said.

"Not without you."

"That's very noble of you," Filth said. "Really it is. But . . . to be perfectly honest, I don't think you're the safest of people to be hanging around with right now. Not with that beast-boy after you. He's lethal, that one."

"You *do* know who he is," Candy said.

"I have my suspicions," Filth admitted. "But this isn't the time or the place to discuss them. You have to go before—" He stopped in midsentence. Then he said: "Oh, dear."

"What?"

"We're too late. He's here."

Candy looked all around. "I don't see anybody."

"Oh, he's a clever one. He knows how to use the shadows." As Filth spoke, his eyes darted in all directions, seeking out the "clever one," whoever he was. "Will you go?" he said, giving Candy another small push.

"Which way?"

"Any which way! Just get going!"

Candy began to back away from him, but as she did so, out of the corner of her eye she saw somebody starting to move toward her. It was just the briefest of glances. She caught sight of his pale face and the long dark hair surrounding it, but that was all. Then she turned on her heel—"*Run!*" she heard Filth yelling— and she did just that, following the winding path that had first brought her to the Twilight Palace.

Her pursuer was fast, however. After ten or twelve strides she heard the sound of his bare feet slapping on the mosaic, getting louder as he gained on her.

She didn't like the idea of being struck down from behind. So she came to a halt and spun around to face him. It was worth the risk just to see the look of shock on the young man's face: his deep-set eyes suddenly grew almost comically big. Then he seemed to recover

himself, and he came running at her again, pulling
something from his jacket. Thinking it was a knife, she
raised her hands to keep the blade away from her body,
but he lifted the object—not a knife, a bag!—up over
her head and pulled it down.

She started to yell and thrash around, but there was
something in the bag that smelled like the scent of rotted flowers, and its power made her head swim.

"Just relax . . ." she heard the voice of the young
man say. "You're going to be all right. Just let go,
Candy—"

(*"Candy,"* she thought. *He knows my name! How
does he know my name?*)

And then, as she shaped this question in her mind,
the perfume played a strange trick. She heard a voice
in her head say: "You have to sleep now."

"No . . ." she mumbled, her tongue somehow thick
and heavy in her mouth.

"Just for a little while," the voice replied.

And the next moment there was no next moment.

She knew how long she'd been asleep, precisely,
because the voice of the perfume was there when she
awakened to tell her.

"It's been thirty-seven minutes and eleven seconds
since you went to sleep. Wake now, if you will."

She didn't need a second invitation. She reached up
and fumbled with the drawstring, which had tightened
the bag around her neck. Loosening it, she pulled the
bag off her head. She was no longer in the Twilight
Palace. The sky was dark and full of stars. Indeed, she

could not remember a time during her voyages when there had been more stars visible than there were right now. They were so beautiful that it took a great deal of effort to take her eyes from the spectacle overhead and look around at the place where her abductor had brought her.

She was in a small, single-masted boat, which was bobbing along before a gusting wind. At the other end of the vessel, sitting spread-legged on the floor of the boat and making some conjurations with his hands over a large map of the archipelago, was her abductor: a young man who looked more or less Candy's age. His hair was a glossy black and hung in greasy ringlets.

"What are you doing?" Candy said.

The young man looked up, his expression a little nervous. "I'm . . . conjuring a route for us," he said.

"A route to where?"

"To where we're going," he answered with a bright but far from trustworthy smile.

"Well, wherever you think you're taking me," Candy told him, "I demand that you take me back where I came from."

"Oh, you do, do you?"

"Yes," she said. "I do."

"Why?"

Candy looked incredulous. "What do you mean: why? Because you kidnapped me, and I don't appreciate it."

"Oh, come on, you didn't want to stay in that old place."

"No, you come on!" Candy said, getting up from

her seat, making the boat rock. His casual attitude made her furious. *"You put a bag over my head and kidnapped me!"* she reminded him. *"You should be put in jail for that!"*

"I've been in jail. Plenty of times. It don't scare me none." He got to his feet; he was a little bit shorter than she was, Candy noticed. "Anyway, I was just obeying orders," he said.

"Oh, very original. Like that's an excuse nobody has ever used before. All right," she said. "If that's where you want to start, let's start there. Whose orders?"

"I can't tell you that," he said.

"Oh, can't you?" she said, approaching him down the boat. Her sudden movement made it rock even more wildly.

"Be careful!" he yelled. "You'll overturn us!"

"I don't care. I can swim!"

"So can I, but these waters are dangerous. So stop it!"

Mimicking his own irritating tone, she said: "Why?"

"Because—" He stopped, realizing he'd been set up. "You're crazy!"

Candy put on a wild-eyed look. "I've been thinking that myself lately," she said, deliberately making the boat rock even more violently.

"He didn't tell me you were crazy!" the youth said, grabbing the sides of the boat so hard his knuckles went white.

"Who didn't tell you?" Candy said, threatening

with her stance to making the rocking still worse. "Come on, spit it out!"

"My employer. Mister . . . Mister Masper."

"And how much is this Mister Masper paying you to get me on this little boat trip?"

"Eleven paterzem."

Candy looked disappointed. "I'm only worth eleven paterzem?" she said.

"What do you mean? I've never had eleven paterzem in my life. It's a fortune."

"I don't even know any Mister Masper."

"Well, he knows you. He's a very powerful man. Very influential. And very curious about you. He heard all these rumors about you. And he wants to meet you in the flesh."

"So you put a bag over my head and knocked me unconscious."

"Was the perfume not polite?" the youth said, looking genuinely concerned. "I used it because it's polite."

"Whether it was polite or not isn't the point. And stop putting on that big-eyed I'm-so-sorry look, because it doesn't work. You see, I've got two brothers. So I know every trick in the book of boys. *He did it. Somebody told me to. I'll never do it again.*"

"Not impressed, huh?"

"No. Now turn the boat around and take me back to the Twilight Palace. You can tell Mister Masper he'll have to be happy with the rumors."

"I can't control the boat. I put this conjuration on it, and now I can't undo it. I wasn't really planning the route when you woke up. I was trying to slow us down. You can see how fast we're moving."

Candy had indeed noticed the speed of the little boat. It was fairly racing over the water. But she wasn't buying his excuse any more than she was the lost-little-boy expression.

"If you put a conjuration on the boat," she told him, "then you can take it off again."

"I haven't been taught how to do that yet," the young man replied.

For a moment she just looked at her lunatic-con-juror-kidnapper in frustrated silence. Then she said: "Tell me you're kidding?"

"No. I swear."

"You . . . you *fool.*"

"I am not a fool," the youth protested. "My name's Letheo."

"So, Letheo, if you don't know how to slow this boat down, what's going to happen when we reach our destination?"

"Well . . . uh . . . I was assuming that . . ."

"Yes?"

"That is . . . I was . . . hoping . . ."

"Yes?"

". . . that the boat would know."

"The boat would know what?"

"That we were at the end of our journey. Then it would slow down of its own accord. And put us on the beach . . . gently."

"I don't know much about magic yet, but what I've seen so far has been pretty violent. I don't think we're going to be *put* anywhere gently."

"Stop looking at me that way," Letheo said. "I didn't *think*. I just wanted to get there quickly. I thought maybe that way he'd pay me more paterzem. You know, a bonus for quick delivery."

"Give me the map, Letheo."

"Why?"

"Because in case you hadn't noticed, your boat is still picking up speed, and if we don't figure something out before we reach land, it's going to be journey's end in more ways than one."

She could see by the way his eyes darted around that he knew she was right.

"Oh, by the Towers," he said, half to himself. "What have I done?"

"Give me the map."

Letheo pulled the map from under his foot and handed it over to Candy. The speed of the boat made the map flap around like a panicked bird. She had no choice but to go down on her hands and knees, lay the map on the waterlogged boards at the bottom of the boat and examine it as best she could from there.

"Where's it taking us?" she yelled to Letheo.

He went down on his hands and knees on the other side of the map and jabbed a finger at one of the islands.

"Efreet!" he said. "It's one of the Outer Islands!"

"Yes, I know about Efreet. I met some people who live there. Do you have any way of knowing our exact position?"

"I'll show you," Letheo said. "Here's a bit of magic I do know. Hold the map down."

Candy did her best to oblige, but it was difficult. Even in the belly of the boat, the wind kept getting under the map and making it bow.

"What are you going to do?"

"Watch." Letheo grinned. He spat on his hand and rubbed his palms together vigorously. Then he made a crude pipe by making loose fists of his hands; and setting one on top of the other, he blew down them, hard. A mote of red light (the same red as the boat's hull) sped from his hand and struck the map.

"That's where we are," he said, not without a measure of pride in his achievement.

Candy peered at the red mote—which was moving over the bucking map rapidly—with a mingling of curiosity and unease. Even at such a reduced size, the boat was closing in on the island of Efreet at an extraordinary rate.

She looked up over the edge of the boat. It was dark, of course, but she thought she could vaguely see the shape of the island ahead. And there was no sign of the vessel slowing. In fact, it continued to pick up speed, hitting the waves with such violence it seemed only a matter of time before one of the waves simply struck it so hard the boat would come apart at its creaking seams. Were that to happen, they'd be in serious trouble. The spray that was hitting her face was icy cold. If they were dropped in the water, hypothermia would soon take its toll. And if it didn't, well, there were always the usual predators. The gluttonous mantizacs; the vicious little jigsaw fish, called jiggers by the fishermen.

"We are in such trouble!" she said, staring at Letheo with a mixture of rage and frustration. "You're going to get us both killed, just because you wanted a bonus for delivery!"

He had nothing to say. He looked away from her at the rocks close to the island. "Oh no . . ." he said softly. "Kythrus." She followed his gaze to see that the rocks were inhabited by some flipper-footed creatures that were watching them with hungry eyes. One by one they slipped off the rocks and into the frigid water, making their way to the boat.

Candy went back to the map. Was there some conjuration *she* could do that could get them out of this mess? She scanned the map from left to right and top to bottom. But the signs on the map meant nothing to her. She felt none of the sensations she knew were connected with power. Her tongue failed to summon any magic words; no sudden knowledge leaped into her head.

"What are you doing?" Letheo yelled over the din of water and wind.

"I'm trying to figure out some way of using my own magic."

"You have magic?"

"A little."

"Then save us! *Please!*"

Candy glanced up again. It was snowing on Efreet: the landscape was gray and white. And the wind brought icy flakes against her face.

"I wasn't expecting snow," Letheo said.

Suddenly there was a roar from the water, and the

next moment the boat struck one of the kythrus, head
on. Candy caught a glimpse of the beast's yellow eye
as the boat rolled sideways. She grabbed the seat to
stop herself from being thrown out. As she did so, the
boat struck another of the animals, which seemed
intent on throwing them over, because it lifted itself
out of the water beneath the boat's hull. Letheo let out
a howl of terror as the boat flew through the air.

"Hold on!" Candy yelled.

She saw his face for a second as they dropped back
toward the water, all trace of manipulations scoured
from it. He was just a terrified boy—

Then the boat struck the water, its hull cracking.
Sprays of freezing water came up through the cracks.
And then they were off again, careering through the
kythrus, their speed seeming to increase the closer
they got to their destination. Any hope Candy might
have had of saving them with magic was forgotten
now. The map had gone. She could scarcely keep hold
of the boat.

And then they hit the beach. The bow cracked like
an eggshell and snow began to come in as the open end
of the little vessel dug into the drifts like a huge shovel. The deep snow was the saving of them. It steadily
slowed the boat's progress, weighing it down with its
freight. They were still moving when the boat reached
the tree line, but at a fraction of the speed they'd been
going when they hit the beach. Candy peered up out of
the chaos of splintered timbers, snow and ice shards in
which she lay just in time to see a tree dead ahead.

"This is it!" she yelled to Letheo, though she could

no longer be sure he was still in the boat. Then she put her arms around the seat in the middle of the boat and held tight. There was a tremendous crash and the boat broke open, and she was peppered with pieces of wood. Then she felt the boat tip up, and she lost her grip on the seat, sliding down into the snow. She lay there sprawled for a few moments, catching her breath. Then, spitting out particles of ice and pieces of shredded leaf, she reached up and wiped the snow out of her eyes.

"Lucky, lucky, lucky," she told herself as she checked her limbs for any sign of broken bones. There was apparently no serious damage done, however, which was a near miracle given the speed at which the boat had been approaching the island. Indeed Letheo's initial spell had still not deserted a few of the larger boards scattered between the trees. They twitched and rolled as if they were still good to go.

As for the spell-caster himself, the impact had apparently thrown him a long way clear of the wreckage, because Candy could see no sign of him. What she *did* see was a path of demolition that led back through the trees and across the beach to the water's edge. Were there guardian angels in the Abarat? Because surely she had one.

Her eyes had already become accustomed to the strange light here: starlight off snow. It showed her a forest that stretched off to the limits of her sight. It was odd to see trees that apparently flourished in darkness and bitter cold, as these did. Many were in full blossom, their fat fire-colored flowers undeterred by the snow.

Then came Letheo's voice, calling her name.

"I can hear you," she called back. "Keep talking."

"I'm here!" he yelled, as though she should know exactly where "here" was.

She followed his frail voice to the limits of the scattered wreckage and found him lying at the bottom of a shallow incline, curled up in a sorrowful bundle.

"You're alive," she said. "I can't believe that we both came out of this alive."

"Well, we haven't yet," he said.

"What do you mean? We're here, aren't we? We're safe."

"No, this is Efreet. There are five Beasts on this island. Terrible creatures."

"Like the kythrus, you mean? They weren't—"

"No, not like them. They're just . . . animals. These are monsters."

"Oh, that's right," she said, remembering what Mizzel had told her on Babilonium: *We've got some fierce beasts live up there,* he'd said. "Well, I don't see anything," Candy said hopefully. "Maybe we're on the wrong side of the island?"

Letheo shook his head. "They're here," he said. "They're just watching from a distance, figuring out who gets to eat who."

"Will you shut up?"

"It's true!"

"Well, I don't want to hear. We need to get moving before we freeze to death."

"My ribs ache and my head too."

She looked first at his head. He had a large, deep

wound above his right ear. "You're going to have a nice scar."

"It won't be my first," Letheo replied matter-of-factly. "Anyway, isn't scar tissue stronger than ordinary skin?"

"Hmm," Candy said. "If that's supposed to be some weird recommendation for getting hurt, I don't buy it. Now let me look at your ribs."

"No, thanks."

"Yes," she said forcefully. "Don't worry, I've got brothers. It's no big deal to me. You're just another boy."

He somewhat reluctantly unbuttoned his shirt, and Candy realized why he was being so coy. There was a strange pulsing coloration on his torso, which was dark turquoise in places and purple in others. With each flush of color his skin turned from smooth to scaly. In addition to the scales he had several crude tattoos on his thin arms. "So now you know," he said, wincing as his skin twitched and transformed. "I've got a bit of beast in me."

"Does it hurt?"

He lightly touched his reptilian belly. "Yes. When it takes me over completely, it's horrible. See, the thing is, Mister Masper has a medicine that makes this go away."

"And he gives it to you—"

"When I follow orders."

"But you don't always want to?"

"No," said Letheo. "Not always."

"So when do you need the medicine again?"

"Soon . . ." Letheo's eyes remained averted. "Perhaps Mister Masper will have some in the house for me."

"I don't see any lights out there. Is this house of his big?"

"Huge."

"The boat must have delivered us to the wrong beach."

"Or maybe we're early," Letheo said, slowly getting to his feet.

"What do you mean?"

"Maybe we're early," he said, as though the sense of this was obvious. "Maybe the house hasn't arrived yet."

"It moves," Candy said.

"Yes. It moves. If we're lucky we'll see it coming in to land."

Lordy Lou, Candy thought to herself. It always seemed that just as she thought she was coming to the end of the Abarat's amazements and nothing could astonish her, it had something more to unveil.

"Listen," Letheo said.

"What are you hearing?"

"We have visitors."

Candy listened. Letheo was right. There were animals nearby. She heard a long threatening growl. And there was a sharp smell in the wind suddenly, as though the beast was marking its territory.

"We're in trouble, yes?" Candy murmured.

"We're dead," Letheo said.

"They haven't got us yet."

"It's only a matter of time—"

"Then we'd better move," she said. "Let's go."

Letheo winced as he walked toward her.

"Sorry it hurts," she said. "But being eaten is going to hurt a lot more."

28

A SUMMONING

THE THREE WOMEN OF the Fantomaya sat in three high-backed antique chairs on the south shore of the Twenty-Fifth Hour and watched a storm move out of the shadows of Gorgossium to stalk the straits between Midnight and the island of Ninnyhammer. Joephi, thanks to the incredible eyesight of the squid whose vision she was presently sharing (the animal clamped to her face like a pair of living spectacles), could see a great distance. All the details of the storm and its effects—the thunderhead spitting lightning as it moved west, the ships in the straits as they plowed through the mountainous seas—were clear to her. And she was reporting everything she saw to the other two.

"What's going on at the wizard's house?" Mespa asked her.

"I'll take a look," Joephi said, and focused her attention upon the heights of Ninnyhammer. News of Kaspar Wolfswinkel's escape had reached them only a short time before. They had come out here to see what could be seen and to debate precisely what was going on.

"I can see a lot of bodies laid out at the bottom of the hill," Joephi said.

"Tarrie-cats?" said Diamanda.

"And some regular soldiers."

"Who would have done a thing like this?" Diamanda said.

"Well, it won't be difficult to puzzle it out," Mespa remarked. "Wolfswinkel had very few friends. If *any*. It's hard to imagine anyone risking their necks to liberate him."

"Well, somebody did," Joephi observed. "And just because he was locked away doesn't mean he wasn't working in secret. Plotting. Assembling a gang of some sort. He was a clever man, as I remember. Ugly and charmless, of course, and a terrible drunkard. But clever."

"All right," said Diamanda. "Let's for the moment accept your theory. He was plotting with somebody. But who?"

"Somebody who wanted the help of a wizard . . ."

"Why assume they took him because they liked him?" Mespa said.

"Meaning what?"

"He murdered five good people. For the possession of their hats. Maybe somebody related to one of them decided his punishment wasn't severe enough."

"What? And took him away to execute him?" Joephi said. "Absurd."

"I'm just saying—"

"That's a ridiculous idea—"

"Ladies, ladies—" Diamanda started to say. But she

didn't finish. Instead she rose unsteadily from her chair, her expression stricken.

"Oh . . . no . . ." she murmured.

Joephi gently eased the squid from her face. "What's wrong, Diamanda?"

"Candy."

"Candy?" said Mespa. "What about her? You think she has something to do with this Wolfswinkel business?"

"No, no, it's not that. I suddenly had a clear vision of her! What *does* the girl think she's doing?"

"Where is she?" Mespa said.

"I don't exactly know," Diamanda replied, closing her eyes. "It's dark, wherever it is; very dark."

"Well, that's a start, I suppose," said Joephi.

"And there's . . . feathers . . . no, no, not feathers . . . *snow.*"

"Heavy or light?" said Joephi. "Can you tell? There were flurries on Speckle Frew within the last couple of hours."

Diamanda's eyes scanned the scene she was seeing with her mind's eye, her pupils flickering back and forth as they searched for clues. At last she said: "This is heavy. The snow's deep."

"Is she high up?" Joephi wondered. "In the Pino Mountains, maybe? The Isle of the Black Egg?"

"No, that's not it either. There are trees. A lot of—"

All three sisters spoke the name of Candy's whereabouts together.

"*Efreet.*"

"What in heaven's name is she doing there? The

place is crawling with monsters."

"Well, that's where she is," Diamanda said flatly. "And the sooner we get her off the island and away from those beasts, the better." She walked away from her sisters a couple of steps, quietly muttering a common conjuration to herself as she did so. The color of her robe became suddenly uncertain of itself. The black and purple in its threads gave way to blue and white and more blue. The hem fluttered as though it had been entrusted to a flock of small, invisible birds.

"You're going somewhere?" said Mespa.

"To Efreet, of course," Diamanda replied. "Whatever our Candy is doing there, she's going to need help."

"Then we should all go," said Joephi.

"No, no, no. You two need to find out what's happening on Ninnyhammer. Wolfswinkel should be severely reprimanded if he has some hand in this violence. So investigate this closely. Find out the facts."

"Are you sure you can deal with Efreet on your own? You know how you hate the cold."

"If that's a *polite* way of asking me if I'm not too antiquated to be going off facing the Five Beasts of Efreet on my own, let me remind you what St. Catham of Dette says: *'We will bring the Infernal Enemy to its knees with wisdom, not sticks.'*"

"Diamanda, dear. St. Catham was eaten alive from the toes up, over a period of nineteen days. I don't think you should be quoting her."

"All right. Then I concede the folly of going. And if I meet a terrible death while I'm there, I promise one day I'll come back to this very spot and you can take my ghost to task for it. Meanwhile, you go to Ninnyhammer and let me go to Efreet, so we can get this wretched problem solved."

Her sisters plainly weren't convinced, but Diamanda wasn't about to change her mind. "We need to move quickly and with the minimum of attention being drawn our way. I want as few people knowing about Candy's presence as possible. She's in a very delicate place right now. I'm sure her visit to the Twilight Palace must have been confusing, to say the least."

"She won't be confused for very long," said Joephi. "She's not a stupid girl."

"No, she's not."

"Sooner or later she's going to put all the pieces of the puzzle of her young life together, and when she does we're going to have a lot more to deal with than mixed emotions."

"You think so?" said Mespa. "If I were her, I'd *love* to find out that I—"

"No, you wouldn't!" Diamanda said. "You'd be furious! You'd feel *lied to* and *cheated* and *used*. And you'd want to know who was responsible."

"Hmm," said Mespa. "Maybe."

"So what do we do about it?"

"What *can* we do? What's done is done. Anyway, I'm not sure I'd change a thing, if I had the choice to do it all over again. Yes, we took risks. But they were for the right reasons. We have nothing to apologize for."

"Let's just hope the girl agrees."

That remark silenced the three women for a time, and they stood staring out at the water for a few minutes while the gulls wheeled overhead, uttering their soul-stricken cries.

Finally Diamanda said:

"All right. I can't linger here. I've got work to do."

She wrapped her now blue robes around her and muttered a word of activation. They suddenly billowed, filling with wind —

"Just remember—" she said, imparting some last words of wisdom before the robes carried her away. "Work delicately. We're dealing with people's *lives* here."

"It seems to me," Joephi remarked, "that we should have considered that a long time ago."

Diamanda had no opportunity to reply to this. The motion of her sky blue robes became more urgent, and she was carried away in a heartbeat, her flying form lost against the bewitching skies that surged like a mirror of the tide above the Twenty-Fifth Hour.

PART THREE

A TIME OF MONSTERS

Sent out of Paradise Garden for their sins,
the First Couple stole fruits from every tree they passed
on their way to the gate, so as to spite their Creator.
And outside the Garden, crouched against the Wall,
they gorged upon the Fruits, eating one after the other,
until their bodies sickened with the excess of it,
and they puked them up.
And the Seeds of the Fruits were spilled in the dirt,
And from them came Monsters of the World,
Who were born in filth,
And never knew there was such a thing as Love.

—From *The Holy Book of Fiafeefo*

29

THE CAPTAIN CONVERSES

DESPITE HIS INITIAL RELUCTANCE
to take the helm of the good ship *Lud Limbo*, Malingo
very quickly came to understand the advantages of
such a position. A captain is a king on water, and
though his elevation brought considerable responsibilities with it, it also provided significant comforts.
Within ten minutes of the ship having left Babilonium,
Captain Malingo was sitting in an extraordinarily
plush chair in his exquisitely decorated cabin, being
poured an absurdly foamy mug of Micklenut ale. At
his new captain's instruction, Deaux-Deaux was
describing in detail the circumstances that had brought
them together on this voyage.

"It was the witches' idea," he said. "They have
these prophetic spasms, you know, when they see a little bit of this and they glimpse a little bit of that. Of
course they never see *all of everything*. That would be
entirely too convenient. There always has to be some
ambiguity. It's never straightforward."

"But they gave you a prophecy of some kind?" Malingo said.

"Yes, indeed."

"Which was—?"

"Well . . . when we'd decoded it, we realized it meant that there was going to be one last war."

"Hmm."

"I know. We all could have predicted that. But we didn't. They did."

"A war between us and Night, like the old times?"

"Presumably."

"Any mention of who'd be leading the opposition?"

"No. But can there be any doubt? The enemy is Christopher Carrion. He's the one who has the most to gain if Night wins the day . . . so to speak."

"Did they give you any idea what he's planning?" Malingo asked.

"Just a little, but it's—"

"What?"

"Let me finish. It's so preposterous that I think it's just a lie, a rumor that Carrion and his grandmother started."

"Why would they do that?"

"As a distraction from what they're *really* planning."

"Huh. So what's the rumor?"

"Well, it's simple enough," said Deaux-Deaux. "It appears they have some plan for creating permanent Night."

"What?"

"Yes. You heard right. Permanent Night on all the islands . . . for all time."

"How do they intend to achieve that?"

"I don't know. But the women of the Fantomaya seem to think it's a reality. That's why they want us to get everybody who's on the side of Day together. That way, we can all face the enemy side by side."

"Hence this voyage."

"Exactly."

"So who are we going to find?"

"Some very important people, according to the sisters. There was once a band of fighters under the leadership of Finnegan Hob."

"Hob? You mean the young man who was going to marry the Princess Boa?"

"Yes. He didn't marry her, of course, because his beloved princess was murdered—"

"—on their wedding day."

"Right."

"Whatever happened to Finnegan?"

"He began a Holy War against the whole race of dragons, swearing that he wouldn't be satisfied until he'd exterminated every last one of them; no small oath, of course. There are a lot of dragons out there. And some of them—well, you know how they can go to ground. They can stay hidden for generations."

"So is he still searching?"

"Nobody's very sure. Apparently a bunch of his friends decided that, what with all this news of war in the air, they should go look for him. They hired a boat called the *Belbelo*, captained by a fellow called Hemmett McBean. They left from the Yebba Dim Day just about eight weeks ago."

"And?"

"And they haven't been heard of since."

"That's not good."

"No, it's not."

"What do the Fantomaya say?"

"They don't believe they're dead."

"Why not?"

"Because they've seen enough of the future to believe that Finnegan Hob will play a major part in it. So will several of the folks who went out to find him."

"Who were they?"

"There was a warrior called Geneva Peachtree, from the Isle of the Black Egg. There was a friend of Finnegan's called Two-Toed Tom and another fellow—a gambler—by the name of Kiss Curl Carlotti. Though according to the witches he does *not* feature in their dreams of tomorrow, so who knows what will befall him. Or already has."

"Who else?"

"Let me see. There's apparently a girl called Tria, a waif, possessed of some strange powers. It's through her, I think, that the women of the Fantomaya made contact. And the others are a family I got to know just a little when he was swept in from the Hereafter with Candy—"

"John Mischief and his brothers?"

"Precisely."

"Candy told me all about them."

"The brothers live on the horns on his head, you know?" Deaux-Deaux said. "Besides Mischief, there's John Moot, John Pluckitt, John Slop, John Sallow,

John Drowze, John Fillet and John Serpent."

"So taken altogether this is quite a gang."

"Yep."

"And the women don't know if they found Hob?"

"No, at least not when I last spoke to them. They only know from Tria that the gang was headed toward the Nonce."

"The Nonce, eh? What's it like there? I mean . . . Three in the Afternoon . . . it should be siesta time."

"Oh, I don't think anyone on the Nonce gets much rest," said Deaux-Deaux. "It's a very unpredictable place, as far as I understand. Everything is in a constant state of flux. Things grow in a heartbeat and die in another. I don't know if anybody has ever properly mapped the island, because it always seems to be changing."

"You seem very sure that we're going to get there," said Malingo.

Deaux-Deaux gave Malingo a big grin. "Of course we will," he said. "We've got a wonderful Captain."

"You're too kind," Malingo said, and laughed.

When the Sea-Skipper had left the cabin, Malingo stayed there for a while, turning over the strangeness of recent times. Who would ever have thought that he'd be a captain of a vessel sailing the Izabella, and in such exciting, frightening times. Even if he weren't the Captain of the *Lud Limbo* for very long (and something told him he wouldn't be making it a lifelong career), at least he would have a grand adventure. What a change there'd been in his life! And he owed it all, of course, to one person and one alone: Candy Quackenbush. If she hadn't come to the domed house on the hill in Ninnyhammer—and more, if she hadn't challenged Wolfswinkel—Malingo would still be under the magician's thumb.

Picturing her now, facing off against the monstrous magician, Malingo felt a surge of yearning for Candy's company. There hadn't been a moment in the days they'd spent together when he had wanted to be anywhere but right there beside her, listening to her expressions of wonder and outrage, making up silly jokes and sharing songs and slices of pilgrim's pie. She had become in that short time his dearest friend, and now he missed her.

He gazed out of the cabin at the wild, wide waters of the Izabella.

"Wherever you are, my lady," he said, "take care of yourself. We're going to have some pretty amazing stories to tell each other when all this is over."

30

THE BEASTS OF EFREET

"**I**S THERE ANY WAY I can get you to move a little quicker?" Candy said to Letheo.

He wiped a trail of blood from the corner of his eye. "Yeah," he said. "Carry me."

"Very funny."

There was a roar from the snowy wastes behind them, its reverberations powerful enough to shake a dusting of snow off the branches above their heads.

The sound made Letheo cast a fearful backward glance.

"A Waztrill," he said.

"You can identify an animal by its roar?" she said, her teeth starting to chatter with the cold.

"I've told you—"

"Yes, they're not animals. They're Beasts of Efreet. Monsters."

"That's right. There's a difference."

"I'm sure you'll explain it to me if we get out of this alive." She dropped her voice to a whisper. "What does a Waztrill *look* like?"

"Their heads are usually bright red. Their bodies are mottled and their tails—"

"—have black spines?"

"That's right. How do you know?"

"Because there's one of them standing about fifty yards away," she said, nodding past Letheo's left shoulder.

"Oh. My. Lordy. Lou."

Very, very slowly Letheo followed the direction of her gaze. The Waztrill in question was a mighty specimen of its breed. It stood ten feet tall to its belly, and seventeen or eighteen to the crown of its head. Its breath erupted from its nostrils in clouds of gray air. On its back several sharp-billed birds were digging under the scaly plates of its armor for the edible parasites that thrived there.

"It's looking at us," Candy said. The monster's eyes were tiny white pinpricks in the grotesque scarlet mask of its head. But Candy had no doubt that its look was fixed upon them.

"Do we run, or climb?" she asked Letheo.

"It's no use climbing. It'll shake us out of a tree. And if we run it'll catch up with us in a few bounds."

"So what do we do?"

"I suggest we *very slowly* walk in the opposite direction. It's probably going to come after us, but maybe—just *maybe*—if it thinks we don't believe we're dinner, then it won't think we're dinner either."

"If you say so."

"Keep looking at it. Don't take your eyes off it for a moment."

"Don't worry," said Candy. "I have no intention of looking the other way."

"Would you . . . do me a favor?"

"What?"

"Take my hand?"

"Oh . . ." She couldn't help smiling, despite everything. "Sure."

They began their very cautious retreat, their clammy hands locked together. The snowfall had started to thicken in the last few minutes, making the Waztrill look like a ghost of itself.

Very slowly it began to come in steady pursuit of them, its motion causing the birds on its back to give up their search for parasites and rise into the icy air.

"I wish we had some place to *go*," Candy murmured softly.

She'd no sooner spoken than there was a deep resonant boom in the air, which shook the snow down from all the branches and blossoms in the vicinity.

"There!" said Letheo, pointing up into the air. "I told you!"

Overhead a large, elaborate geometrical shape appeared in the sky, illuminated by what little light was thrown up from the snow-covered ground.

"The house," Candy said.

"The Dead Man's House," Letheo said.

The shape kept falling, getting clearer and clearer as it tumbled out of the air. It was immense, and it was clearly going to fall perilously close to them.

"It's going to crash," she said, her fear of the pursuant Waztrill forgotten in the shadow of this almighty descent. And still it was falling, its size more and more breathtaking.

"It's not going to crash," Letheo said. "It does this all the time."

He was right. As the house reached a point about a hundred feet above the treetops, it seemed to discover its equilibrium. Its velocity slowed, and it rolled over so that its foundation was turned earthward. Then it began a controlled descent the rest of the way. Only now could Candy get any real sense of the size and the strangeness of the house. There was no building in Chickentown that it faintly resembled; nor any, she thought, in the state of Minnesota. Everything about it was extreme. Its windows were tall and narrow, like the windows of a church almost, only taller still, and narrower. The doors were even more emaciated and the vast roof absurdly steep. She was not surprised in the least that this was called the Dead Man's House. It was like a vast mausoleum that was coming down in the forest, its weight smashing to tinder those unlucky trees that lay where it had decided to put itself down. As it settled, its ancient beams creaked and a sigh came from its ancient stones. Then it was at rest, and the snow covered it as it fell on the entire scene. After a few seconds it seemed the house had been there forever.

"Well, that's something you don't see every day," Candy remarked.

"We should go," Letheo said. "Mister Masper will be expecting us."

"Oh yes. And you need your eleven paterzem,"

Candy said, claiming her hand from his.

She glanced back at the Waztrill. The beast seemed to have been just as unnerved by the descent of the Dead Man's House as she had. Any interest it might have had in Candy and Letheo had been postponed, at least temporarily. She'd no sooner shaped this thought than the beast threw back its head and let out a terrible din. It echoed back and forth between the trees and off the walls of the Dead Man's House.

"What's that all about?"

"At a guess it's summoning some of its friends," Letheo said.

Candy was in no mood to wait around and see what the rest of the clan looked like.

"If it comes after us we'll split up, right? That way, maybe we'll confuse it."

"You go to the front door and get Masper to open up. I don't want to be out here with that thing. Or its friends." She nudged Letheo, who was staring at the Dead Man's House, his teeth chattering.

"Do you understand what we're going to do?"

"Yes. I'm not stupid."

At that moment somebody inside the house began to light the lamps; and through window after window a warm light came, falling in amber pools on the snow. "Well, it looks welcoming enough," Candy said to herself, and she and Letheo headed toward it, keeping a wary eye on the Waztrill as they progressed.

The beast followed them with its piggy gaze, and several times it looked as though it intended to make a move in their direction but then changed its mind. The reason soon became apparent. From several other directions there came the cries of other beasts, which the Waztrill answered with a bellowing of its own.

"We've got company," Candy said, nodding toward the creatures that were appearing between the trees. She might have expected the Waztrill's cry to have summoned creatures from the same clan, but no. Each of the four creatures that appeared was of a different species. Letheo, the monster expert, had a name for each. The purple beast with a small head and huge bugeyes was a Thrak, he said, while the serpentine creature with a head like a mechanical shovel was a Vexile. The shaggy beast whose hide was seething with red parasites was called a Sanguinius; and finally the fat beast that walked on its hind legs, its head opening and closing like an enormous fan, was a Fever Gibe.

Here they were, all assembled: the Beasts of Efreet.

Keeping her eyes fixed on the quintet as best she could, Candy started to retreat toward the Dead Man's House. The snow was coming down more heavily now. Her feet were numb with the cold, and they weren't obeying her very well. Letheo was no better; he winced with every step he took. Surely the beasts would come after them at any moment. But no. Step by freezing step she and Letheo got closer to the house, and still the beasts didn't move. Were they afraid of the house; was that it? Whatever the reason, they were keeping their distance.

"Can I . . . lean on you?" Letheo said, his voice slurred.

"Of course," Candy told him, and murmuring gentle words of encouragement, she led him toward the door.

They were within perhaps thirty yards of the house when the Sanguinius, which, of the five beasts, had seemed the least interested in Candy and Letheo, suddenly unleashed a titanic bellowing. It didn't wait for a response from the other creatures. It had apparently overcome its fear of the Dead Man's House, because it now lowered its head and proceeded to charge.

Candy caught hold of Letheo's arm.

"Run!" she yelled.

The Sanguinius had obviously been watching them surreptitiously, because it now charged directly at them like a speeding truck, cutting a swathe through the trees. Letheo attempted to put on a burst of speed, but he slipped and fell heavily on the frozen dirt, sliding fully ten yards over the ice and into a thicket.

The Sanguinius instantly understood its victim's distress. It came to a quick halt—its huge hooves kicking up fans of snow as it did so—and turned its horned head toward the spot where Letheo had fallen. He was making a desperate attempt to get up, but the thicket was barbed, its thorns catching on his clothes, hooking themselves through his jacket and trousers; even his hair. The more he struggled to free himself, the more they pricked and hooked him.

"Candy!" he yelled. "I can't move!"

She half ran, half slid over the icy ground to help him. "Stop struggling," she said. "You're just making it worse."

She reached the thicket and began to unhook him from the thorns, one by one. It was a painful and difficult process. The barbs were serrated, which made them doubly hard to separate from the weave of Letheo's clothes. Candy's fingers were soon bleeding.

"Wait," Letheo said. "Listen. It's stopped."

The Sanguinius had *not* stopped, but it certainly slowed its approach, as though it knew its prey had no hope of escape and it could afford to take its time. With its eye fixed on Letheo, it began a final advance toward him, planting its huge hooves hard and heavy in the snow. Poor Letheo couldn't see the beast; the knotted thicket was too dense. He was almost delirious with fear and pain, his whole body shaking.

"Don't leave me here," he begged Candy. "Please, please, stay with me."

"Shush," Candy said gently. "I'm not going to leave you."

"No?" he said, his voice suddenly growing calm.

She glanced up from the labor of freeing him to find that he was looking down at her with a strange, almost puzzled, expression in his golden eyes.

"No," he said. "You're *not*, are you?"

"No I'm not. I'm going to stay."

"Most people would leave; just run."

"I told you: *shush*."

"They'd save themselves."

"And watch the beast eat you? No, thanks. Now pull on your left arm. Go on. Pull!" His arm came free. He laughed weakly.

Candy looked back at the Sanguinius. The beast was getting closer and closer.

"Okay, you're more or less free. Are you ready to run?"

"Yes. What are you going to do?"

"I'm going to distract it."

He caught hold of her hand. "Don't. It'll kill you."

"You just get to the house. I'll see you there."

"No."

"Wish me luck."

Before he had a chance to say anything, she made a dash from the thicket, yelling as she went.

"Hey, lunkhead!" It was an insult her father used when talking to Ricky and Don, and why it would spring to her lips now she didn't know, but it did. *"You hear me, lunkhead?"*

The creature stopped in midstride and looked up at her, a frown knitting its thuggish brow.

"Yeah, I'm talking to you!" she said, pointing at the beast. "Lordy Lou, you are *so ugly*."

The beast seemed to know it was being insulted and drew down the corners of its immense maw and uttered a low irritated growl.

"Well, come on then," she said, beckoning to it. "I'm right here."

She quickly glanced at Letheo, who was up and out of the thicket. Then she ran. The Sanguinius instantly came in pursuit of her, the weight of its vast body making the ground shake beneath her. She zigzagged through the trees in the hope of confusing the thing, which seemed to work, because she gained a few yards of ground. She chanced another look toward Letheo, but she'd lost sight of him. Hoping he'd already reached the house, she raced toward the door, putting every last drop of strength into outrunning the beast behind her.

The closer she got to the house, the more encrusted it looked: every window frame elaborately carved, every stone busy with lichens and mosses. Even the *smell* that came off the place—the cloud of antiquity in which the house sat—was complicated. Sweet like summer smoke, but with some bitterness beneath.

As she got within ten yards of the house, the Sanguinius roared again, and she looked back over her shoulder to see the creature come powering around the corner, moving so fast the parasites flew off its matted hide. It clipped the edge of the house with its shoulder as it came, and several shards of stone flew off. Candy put on a spurt of speed and raced on to the back of the house. There were two doors, she saw. She tried the first of them: it was locked. She rattled the handle anyway, and was sure she heard somebody moving around inside. But nobody opened the door. She glanced back toward the corner. The beast had not yet appeared. So rather than run on to the next door, and risk that being locked also, she beat her fist on the door.

"Open up! Quick! Quick!"

She could hear the Sanguinius just around the corner; it would be upon her in a matter of seconds.

"Please!" she yelled. *"PLEASE!"*

"I gave up saying please a long time ago!" said a voice behind her.

She turned.

And there was Diamanda, of all people, dressed in blue and smiling at her through the snow.

31

NEWS IN NONCE

THE LITTLE COMPANY OF adventurers
from the good ship *Belbelo* had been wandering the
Nonce for several weeks now, in search of Finnegan
Hob. So far they had little reason for optimism.
Though all reports had said he was here at Three in the
Afternoon, hunting down the last of the dragons, they
had caught no sight of him. The weather was uncommonly hot for the Hour, humid and oppressive, and it
was beginning to take its toll on everyone. Perpetual
Afternoon could be exhausting; it left folks panting
like tired dogs, their tongues hanging out. Right now
they were all sitting under the enormous leaves of the
jackoline tree, while the monsoonal rain—which came
regularly but did very little to clear the air—pelted
down. The jackoline tree was in full blossom (what, in
the Nonce, was *not* in blossom? Stones gave forth
flowers here), and the rain, when it struck the blooms,
made them ring like chimes. To those in a happier state
of mind, the sound might have been welcomed as pretty. But nobody in the company was in any mood to get

up and dance along to the jackoline's unpredictable melody.

"Damnable flowers," said John Moot, who was usually one of the better-tempered of the brothers John. "And this brain-bruising rain! I am sick to death of rain and flowers!"

"Not to mention the fecundity!" said John Drowze.

"Oh yes," said John Serpent. "The endless fecundity!"

"Can you shut your kin up?" Geneva said to John Mischief. "They're starting to get on my nerves."

"They might live on my head," Mischief said, "but I'm not their master. They have their opinions—"

"And the right to speak them," said John Fillet.

"Peace, peace," said Two-Toed Tom. "It's no use arguing. It just makes everybody sweat more. We may as well get along with one another because we're not leaving here until we find the man we came looking for. Finnegan's here somewhere. This"—he lifted up the short stabbing sword they had found wedged between two rocks—"is proof of that."

"It could have belonged to anybody," John Serpent said.

"But it didn't," said Tria without a trace of doubt. "It was *his*."

"Far be it from me to agree with John Serpent," Captain McBean said, "but we really have no proof. And you know what? This place is starting to take its toll on me too."

"What's wrong with this place?" John Mischief said. "I think it's paradise."

"You can have too much of *anything*," McBean replied. "Even paradise."

"And the way the flora changes every half hour," said John Moot. "It's bewildering. The rain comes down, washes half the plants away, and something completely new pops up. You know I saw a fruit hanging from a tree that looked like a face? That's just not natural."

"Who are we to say what's natural?" Two-Toed Tom remarked.

"Well, I might have known *you'd* be saying that," John Serpent snapped back. "You with your weird little household. Talk about unnatural!"

Thomas said nothing. He simply *leaped,* his thick muscular legs carrying him high into the air above the company.

John Serpent squealed in terror. "Don't let him hit me!"

But Tom didn't have fisticuffs in mind. Instead he caught hold of three of the giant leaves above the Johns and tipped them. They were like jugs filled to brimming with water. It came pouring down on the brothers, soaking them all.

"Typical! Typical!" John Serpent said, spitting out the rainwater. "The man can't take a simple little remark about his—"

"Other half," said Tom, still swinging from the thick stalks of the jackoline leaves. "His name's Tidal Jim, by the way. He's an oyster harvester. And he has my heart and I have his, and it will be that way to the end of the world."

"Well, now we know," said McBean.

"Will we meet him one day?" Tria said.

"You're all invited, as of this moment, to come and eat with Jim and me and our pets."

"You've got a lot of animals?" Tria said.

"Nineteen on the last count. A coyne bird we call Lord Egg. A wise old hog hound called Saint Bartholomeus, who is the worst-tempered dog in creation. An old tarrie-cat who wandered in one day. All kinds."

"Sounds like a madhouse," Serpent remarked.

"Well, *we'll* all go in and eat with Jim and Tom and their animals," said John Mischief. "And you can wait outside."

"Ha. Ha," said Serpent sourly. "I am convulsed with laughter."

"No, you're not," said Tria.

"That was *irony*, little girl," Serpent snapped.

"Tria, take no notice of him," said Geneva. "He's—"

"Just a miserable bad-tempered and completely unpleasant man," Tria said, her plain speech leaving everybody astonished. "I'm not afraid of you, John Serpent. I may still be a 'little girl,' but I know the difference between a man who has something real in his heart, that I should listen to, and a phony like you, who just says the first poisonous thing that comes into his head. By the way, you look silly with your mouth open like that. I'd close it if I were you."

Serpent said nothing. He was comprehensively hushed.

"I think the rain's stopped," said McBean.

The rest of the company now emerged from the cover of the jackoline tree to see the flawless blue of a Noncian sky appearing above their heads; the rain clouds receding to the northeast. And as the sun warmed the waterlogged Hour, the charmed dirt of the Nonce staged another Genesis, bringing forth a new generation of flora and fauna: their scents sweet, their colors and shapes written from a limitless alphabet of hues and forms. The company had, of course, witnessed this phenomenon many times now, but since no two verses from this Book of Beginnings was ever the same, they invariably found fresh reasons for wonderment. This time was no exception.

"Look at that," said John Drowze. "The purple-and-yellow flower!"

As he spoke, the blossom he'd been pointing at flapped its petals, raised its antennaed head and took to the air, inspiring a host of its petal-winged brethren to do the same thing.

"Maybe we're going to be like those flower flies one of these days," said Tria.

"What do you mean?" said Geneva.

"Oh, it was just a silly thought."

"No, tell us."

Tria frowned. The words seemed hard to come by. "I just meant that maybe one day—if we stay here long enough, and get rained on often enough—maybe we'll all change. Maybe we'd just take off on the wind . . ." She stared at the sky, eyes bright and wide; the idea obviously enchanted her. Then she seemed to realize that everybody was watching her, and she suddenly became embarrassed. "What am I yabbering about?" she said, looking from one of her companions to the next. "I'm just being silly," she said. "I'm sorry."

"It's not silly," John Moot said. "I've thought some of the exact same things while we've been here. I think we all have. I've even talked about it with my brothers."

"I think your memory must be misleading you," John Serpent said snottily. "I was never a part of a conversation about anyone turning into a bloody insect."

"Forget him," Tom said to Tria. "Go on with what you were saying."

Tria shrugged. "I've said what I was going to say," she replied. "Except—"

"In heaven's name, *what*?"

"I don't think it's only here on the Nonce. There's change happening everywhere."

"Big deal," said John Pluckitt. "So things change. What's so important about that? It stops raining, it starts raining—"

"It's not the kind of change I mean," Tria said.

"Well, can you be more specific?" Geneva asked her.

Tria shook her head. "Not exactly," she admitted. She went down on her haunches and gently plucked a tiny flower that was nestled in the mud at her feet. It came out of the earth complete with a pale green root that squirmed gently, as if reaching back toward the earth. "Maybe these changes will all seem small at first," she said dreamily, as though she didn't really understand what she was talking about. "But their effects will be enormous."

"And what about us?" Geneva said. "Are we a part of the changes?"

"Oh yes," Tria replied. "Whether we like it or not. The world is going to be turned upside down."

She tenderly returned the eager plant to the earth, where it sank into the ground with a kind of polite gratitude, turning its petaled head up toward Tria as it did so.

"Will you listen to that?" said Tom.

"I don't hear anything."

"I do," said Tria.

Everybody fell silent now. But they heard nothing.

"I could have sworn I heard a voice," Tom said.

"Maybe an echo of us."

"No, it wasn't one of us," Tria said. "Tom's right. There's somebody nearby."

Geneva scanned the landscape carefully, looking for any sign of a presence.

Tria did the opposite. She *closed* her eyes and stood absolutely still, focusing her attention minutely. Finally she said: "He's somewhere off to the left of us." Her eyes still closed, she pointed. "He's very close."

Then she opened her eyes and looked in the direction in which she'd pointed. The landscape wasn't entirely empty. The area had obviously been washed clear in the last cloudburst, but already bore new growths, which were appearing everywhere to carpet the ground.

"I don't like this," John Moot said. "I think we should get out of here."

"It's not a dragon," said Tria.

"How can you be so sure?"

"I'm not. I just don't think it is."

"Finnegan?" said Geneva.

"Well, where is he?" McBean said. "If he's close, why don't we see him?"

Tria was staring at the ground. "Down there . . ." she murmured.

"That's why we haven't found him," Geneva said. "He's underground!"

"Underground?" said Tom.

"Yes."

"Maybe he's using the tunnels and caves under the island to creep up on the dragons?"

"Yeah, or else he got lost down there," said John Drowze. "And now he can't get out."

"Either way, we're going to discover the truth," said Geneva. "We haven't come all this way to turn back because he's underground."

"Let me lead the way," Tria said. "I'll find a hole in the ground, and we'll go after him."

"All agreed?" said Geneva.

"Anything to get off this island," said McBean.

32

EVENTS AT THE THRESHOLD

DIAMANDA LOOKED WEARIER THAN Candy remembered her looking, but she was certainly a welcome sight.

"I heard you were in a bit of trouble," the old lady said.

"You could say that," Candy said.

She glanced past Diamanda, to see the Sanguinius rounding the corner of the house. It had apparently already sniffed the presence of power in its vicinity, because it had slowed its approach and now came cautiously, its teeth bared like a crazed dog.

Diamanda raised her left hand, and with an elegant flourish she said:

> *"Be still—*
> *Thing!*
> *That's my will—*
> *Thing!*
> *Or I will make you mourn—*
> *Thing!*

The day that you were born—
Thing!"

The simplicity of the spell brought a smile to Candy's lips; but simple or not, it did the trick. The expression on the Sanguinius' face grew suddenly peaceful and pleasant, and it sank dutifully down to the ground, its head laid on its front legs. Despite its enormous size, it suddenly resembled some domestic animal, lying down beside the hearth.

"There are four other beasts around here," Candy warned Diamanda.

"Yes, I know. But by the time they come looking for us, we'll be away, back to the Twenty-Fifth."

"I've got so much to tell you."

"I'm sure you do."

"But before we go . . ."

"Yes?"

". . . the boy who brought me here—his name is Letheo—is somewhere around here, and he's hurt."

"Well, we'll have to leave him to the tender mercies of some passing Samaritan," Diamanda replied. "I can't risk anything happening to you."

"Can't we take him with us?"

"Are you fond of this boy?" Diamanda said in her usual straightforward manner.

"No. I just promised I wouldn't leave him, that's all. And I don't like breaking promises."

"As it happens, I know of this boy. He has a curse in his blood, did you know that?"

"Yes. I saw. He needs to take medicine, he told me."

"Was this before or after he kidnapped you?" Diamanda said.

"He didn't mean to hurt me. I'm sure of that."

"You have quite a capacity for forgiveness, girl, I'll give you that. I suppose it doesn't surprise me, given what I know about you. Still"—she smiled indulgently—"you must be careful with kindness. It's usually mistaken for weakness by stupid people."

"I understand," Candy said. "I won't—" She stopped and studied the Sanguinius. "I could swear it blinked," she said.

"That's impossible."

"It did, Diamanda. It—"

Before she could finish speaking, Diamanda's gaze was also distracted: not toward the beast, but up to a window high above them. She caught sight of somebody moving away from the sill.

"Damn!" the old lady said. "Somebody in this House just undid my spell! We're in trouble, girl—"

An instant later the Sanguinius let out a roar and rose up from its supine position. Instantly its eyes locked on Candy and it came at her, its mouth gaping as though it intended to simply scoop her up and swallow her.

She backed away, one step, two steps. But that was as far as she could go. The locked door of the Dead Man's House was hard against her spine.

The Sanguinius let out a fetid breath. Candy put her hands up to ward off the creature, but its attack was a feint. Just as it seemed the jaws would close on her, the creature swung around and instead snapped up

Diamanda. It all happened so fast that Candy had no time to yell a warning, much less do anything to save the old lady. One moment Diamanda was standing right beside her, the next the Sanguinius had taken the incantatrix in its jaws. Candy had never witnessed anything so horrible. It struck some nerve deep inside her to see this. She let out a sob and threw herself at the creature in a fury of frustration.

"Give her back!" she yelled.

But the beast had no intention of relinquishing its meal. Instead it retreated from Candy with a curious caution in its step. Was it nervous of her? Why? Because she had power in her. Yes, perhaps. She'd sent the zetheks packing from the hold of the *Parroto Parroto*, hadn't she? Perhaps the same word would work now.

Too angry to be afraid, she pursued the Sanguinius, calling up the word—and the power that it contained—into her throat. But before she could unleash it, the beast casually closed its vast maw, its teeth skewering Diamanda in dozens of places.

The Sister of the Fantomaya did not cry out. She simply let out a shuddering sigh, and died. Then the Sanguinius turned and sauntered off, with Diamanda's limp body hanging out of its mouth to left and right, her blood staining the snow.

Shaking from scalp to sole, Candy sank back against the locked door, her hands pressed against her face.

"No more . . ." she murmured, "please . . . no more . . ."

Too much had happened; she was overwhelmed. First Babilonium, and losing Malingo, then the mysteries of the Twilight Palace and her abduction; now this. To lose one of the few people in this troubled world who seemed to understand her and who she was. Gone, in a few terrible seconds. It was too much, too much.

After a minute or so she looked up through her fingers. The blizzard was getting worse with every gust of wind. The thickening veils of snow had already virtually eroded the Sanguinius and its victim. As Candy watched, it disappeared from sight completely.

There came a sound from behind her, the harsh grating of a bolt being drawn aside. She started to get up and step away from the door, but she wasn't fast enough. As the door opened, she stumbled backward, flailing. She reached out for the door handle to steady her fall, but her hands were too numb, her body too weak, her brain too overburdened. She caught the briefest of glimpses of the world into which she had fallen; then her besieged senses gave up, and she willingly let darkness take her away from the world.

33

A VISIT TO MARAPOZSA STREET

IN THE DEPTHS OF her unconscious state,
Candy caught glimpses of Diamanda. On the shore of
the Twenty-Fifth Hour, smiling at her. On a boat, sitting calmly, watching the waters, still smiling. And
finally—much to Candy's surprise—walking in the
streets of Chickentown, unnoticed by those who
passed her by. The dream, or vision, or whatever it
was, reassured her. It seemed to say that Diamanda
had already moved on about some new business, the
hurt of life—and of her death—forgotten.

Candy murmured the old lady's name in her sleep,
and the sound of her own voice woke her. She was
lying on a huge bed in one of the strangest rooms she
had ever seen. It was dominated by a massive mantel-
piece, which was carved from black marble. A small
fire guttered in the hearth, its pale blue flames barely
big enough to tickle the dark throat of the grate. And
yet there was light in the room, even if it didn't come
from the fire. It bled out of the cracks in various
objects around the room: from a vase, from under the

door of a wardrobe, even up between the polished wooden floorboards. And where the strands and fili-grees of light crossed, which they did in perhaps three dozen places, they threw off sparks like fireworks. The flickering filled the immensely tall room with dancing shadows.

Candy got up off the bed in which somebody had kindly laid her and did her best to orient herself, but the constant motion of the light made that difficult: everything had an eerie animation in it, thanks to the sparks, as though all the objects in the room were alive. But after a minute or two, her eyes became accustomed to the dance of light, and she began to ten-tatively explore the room. On a chair near the fire were some clothes, which had obviously been left for her. A pair of dark blue shoes with bright red laces. A baggy pair of trousers, which were dark purple. A blouse that was close to the color of the trousers. And a loose jacket, which seemed at first glance to be decorated with abstract designs, but which a second and third glance revealed to be representations of creatures from some Abaratian Eden; fish and fowl, bird and beast, all parading around the coat together.

She was grateful for the gift. Her present clothes were torn and damp. As she put on the new stuff, she found it was all made of extremely friendly material: fabric that seemed to be eager to comfort her.

Dressed in her new outfit, she felt much more pre-pared to meet the owner of this house, even a little curious. She opened the door and stepped out into the corridor. It was lit much the same way as the room behind her—light leaking from cracks in everything, criss-crossing and sparking. The passageway went on for a long way in both directions and was filled like a warehouse with bric-a-brac. For the third time in recent days—once in Babilonium, once in the Wunderkammen in the Twilight Palace—she was aware of the curious *abundance* of the Abarat. Sometimes it seemed to be a kind of encyclopedia of possibilities; an A to Z of things wonderful and strange, brimming, overspilling itself in its eagerness to be All and Everything and More Than Everything. And somewhere inside that ambition, she knew, lay a clue to what it really was.

Maybe her host would know. She called out.

"Hello? . . . Anybody? Hello!"

There was no reply but the echo of her voice, so she turned right and ventured down the corridor, continuing to call. As she went she noted a few of the oddities along the way. The stuffed head of an animal whose mouth was a seething nest of tongues. A screen covered with carved birds that seemed to rise up as she approached. A table with a game that had perhaps three hundred pieces laid out on it, in the form of two armies: Day and Night.

There were signs from both above and below of other presences in the house. Somebody seemed to be hammering on the floor above, and nearby somebody was singing in a high, thin voice. It was a sad, peculiar song: one that she knew from Malingo. It told of a man called Tailor Schmitt, who had been, the words claimed, the best tailor in the Abarat. The trouble was that he was a little crazy. And the idea soon came into his head that the sky was like a badly fitting suit, and soon the buttons that kept the sky in place would pop.

> *"Tailor Schmitt, poor Tailor Schmitt,*
> *Thought the sky wouldn't fit—"*

The poor tailor was terrified of the consequences of this, the song said, because then whatever was lying in wait *behind* the sky—monsters, perhaps, or simply a devouring oblivion—would break through from the other side and spill into his world. So, according to the song, he spent the rest of his life making buttons so that the heavens could be buttoned up again, and made safe.

> *"—thousands of buttons, bone and*
> *lead,*
> *The tailor made till he was dead.*
> *Perhaps now Tailor Schmitt has*
> *died,*
> *He knows what lies on the other*
> *side,*
> *But we remember him in song,*
> *And pray to heaven that he was*
> *wrong."*

This was the sorrowful little tune that accompanied Candy as she moved through the house. Every now and then she'd open a door and look into one of the rooms. There was plenty of evidence of occupancy. In one room there was a large bed, which had recently been slept in, to judge by the shape of the sleeper's head on the pillow. In another room there was a small table on which a large egg stood, recently hatched, the creature coming forth from it a sentient plant.

She continued to call out as she explored, and finally found somebody to talk to. A diminutive woman dressed in black, with an elaborate ruff around her neck, came hurrying down the corridor toward her. She beckoned to Candy.

"Are you the person who brought me here?" Candy asked her.

The woman shook her head.

"Do you know who *did*?"

"Mister Masper," the woman said softly. "And I know he would like to talk to you."

"Oh. So where will I find this Mister Masper?"

"Come with me," the woman said, her eyes skipping over Candy's face, all curiosity: studying her eyes, her mouth, even her ears and forehead.

"Is there something wrong?" Candy asked her.

"No no," she said. "It's just . . . you're not the way I expected you to be."

"And how was that?" Candy asked.

"Oh, you know. A woman of power—"

"Me? You must have the wrong—"

"Oh, no. You're the one. You wouldn't be here if you weren't."

"Speaking of being here . . ."

"Yes?"

"There was a boy outside the house."

"Letheo. Yes, we found him."

"Is he all right?"

"He's under Mister Masper's protection now," the woman said. "Please go on."

"So he *is* all right?" Candy pressed.

"I told you—"

"—he's under Mister Masper's protection."

With that the woman turned her back on Candy and started along down the corridor.

"What's your name, by the way?" Candy said.

"Mrs. Kittelnubetz," the woman replied without turning. "It is my honor to work for Mister Masper." She paused at the door, and respectfully, even a little cautiously perhaps, opened it. "Enjoy," she said, ushering Candy in.

"Enjoy what?" Candy said, looking into the room.

"The dreaming street," said Mrs. Kittelnubetz.

And as she spoke, a light came on in the middle of the room (which, unlike the other rooms, and the passageway, had been in darkness). The light illuminated an odd-looking wooden device that sat on a table there. It was round, perhaps eight or nine inches high, and two feet or so in diameter. Its outer wall was highly polished, suggesting somebody took great care of this device. Whatever it was, it had slits in it, each no more than a quarter of an inch wide.

"What is that?" Candy said, glancing back at Mrs. Kittelnubetz. But the passageway was empty. In the fifteen, perhaps twenty seconds since Candy had taken her eyes off the woman in black she had gone, leaving Candy's question unanswered.

"Weird," Candy remarked.

She hadn't seen *anything* yet. When she looked back at the device, she saw that it had begun to go around, as though a small clockwork motor in its base had been activated. And visible through the slits there was a growing *brightness*. Fascinated—and thinking there could surely be no harm in a clockwork musical box, or whatever it was—Candy approached the table, bending down as she did so and peering through the slits into the circling drum.

Whoosh, whoosh, whoosh —

There was something almost hypnotic about the sound, and about the motion too. A contented smile came onto her face, and the more relaxed she felt, the brighter the light in the center of the drum seemed to burn.

Whoosh, whoosh, whoosh —

Was there something *moving* in there? It looked as though there was. She narrowed her eyes, trying to focus her gaze on whatever was inside the spinning drum. There was a name for old-fashioned devices like these, she remembered. They were called zoetropes, or something like that. They had pictures inside that were arranged to create the illusion of movement.

"That's cool . . ." she said, leaning closer.

And still the drum picked up speed, until the slits spun by so quickly that they all blurred together into a single window.

And what was the picture on the other side? She'd been expecting something simple, but no: there was a sunlit *street* there in the drum. And the houses and the sidewalks, the roofs and sky weren't painted: they were perfectly realistic. And sauntering up and down the street, as though this were a real day and a real world, were men, women (even an ape or two); black people and white, golden skinned and scarlet. What they all had in common, however, was the extraordinary things they wore on their heads. These didn't appear to be hats or hairpieces; they were strange fantasias rising like many-layered towers from their skulls.

Candy stared at the spectacle in astonishment, her gaze still being gently coaxed through the spinning window into "the dreaming street" vision the drum contained. She could almost feel it *pulling* on her, seducing her with its brightness and its beauty, to keep looking, keep looking, while the drum spun, *keep looking*—

She had by now guessed what she was seeing. Mrs. Kittelnubetz had named this mystery for her: *the dreaming street,* she'd called it. Its formal name, which was Marapozsa Street, was written on a sign on the wall, but its nickname was surely more accurate. Here on this bright thoroughfare the people were not simply wearing entertaining nonsenses on their heads because it was the fashion. These were their *dreams* they were carrying. A man wandered by with what looked like a single-windowed tower on his head, burning fiercely. On another there was built a cell in which some poor soul was bound up; yet another (a man with a large fish under his arm, which he was presumably taking home to dine on) had a tiny theater poised on his pate, with a skull-headed creature standing center stage.

But the illusions contained in the device were only just the beginning. Her sight was still being drawn into the midst of the spectacle; there were new visions to be seen around every corner, through every doorway and open window: glimpses of lives that weren't being performed, the way a play is performed, but were going on quite naturally as she casually watched. A woman was studying at an upper window with her hair like a thicket filled with little colored birds. In another place stood a striped beast about the size of a middle-sized mutt, long lashed and stubby tailed, which had on its head a little building, no more than a dome supported by six pillars: the humble animal equivalent, perhaps, of the elaborate towers that the two-legged occupants of Marapozsa Street boasted.

The zebratic dog seemed to be staring straight at Candy, its gaze so direct that it drew her attention still more deeply into the world of Marapozsa Street. Suddenly it seemed to become uncomfortable having her staring at it, and it turned tail and ran. She followed it with her eyes, down an alleyway that ran off Marapozsa Street. Again she had that uncanny sensation of being *drawn* into this little world, but why not, she thought? Where was the harm? The animal led her away down streets that steadily grew narrower the farther from Marapozsa Street they strayed. But at every corner, however narrow the thoroughfares became, and however decrepit the buildings, there were still oddities and wonderments to be witnessed.

A pale man stood at one corner, looking down with bliss on his face at the child he held in his arms, even though the infant had tentacles for limbs. In another place a woman sat with a very large and succulent slice of pizza (pepperoni, mushrooms, olives; no anchovies) on her lap.

Candy had lost sight of the animal she'd followed from the dreaming street, but she didn't much mind. She had plenty more to see, like the man who looked as though he had the blood of clowns running in his veins and was painting something fanciful on the walls. Or the patchwork animal that stood patiently in a piece of sunlight, feeding her infants, two of whom were suckling from her greedily, while a third clung to her leg in an ecstasy of love.

Clowns. Mothers. Dreamers. What a strange world this was she'd been drawn into. She was beginning to feel a little overwhelmed by the experience: not just by the sights but the sounds and smells of the place. It was time to turn back, she decided; time to unglue her sight from this place and return to the room where she was standing. But how? She'd come this far following the path of her curiosity. But how did she retrace her steps?

Perhaps if she simply closed her eyes, she thought, the illusion would somehow vanish and she'd be back in the room with Masper, watching the device from a safe distance.

But that didn't work. Though she closed her eyes and waited in darkness for a few seconds, when she opened them again she was still standing in the same place, trapped inside the device.

"What's going on?" she said to a pregnant woman

with a small forest sprouting from her head. "Why can't I get out of here?"

The woman looked at her with a puzzled expression on her face, as though she didn't understand a word Candy was saying.

"Can't somebody tell me what's going on?" Candy asked.

It was the red-faced ape that finally proffered an answer: "Where are your dreams?" he said. "Everybody wears their dreams on their heads here."

"But I don't belong here," Candy protested. "I came from outside."

"Outside?" said the bearded man with the fish under his arm. "There is no outside!"

"Oh yes, there is," Candy replied. "I've been there."

She looked up at the "sky," hoping there'd be proof of the room beyond this artificial world. But she could see no sign of her confinement. Only a flawless blue.

She felt a spasm of panic. Suppose the journey she'd taken into this world was strictly one-way? Perhaps the dreaming citizens of Marapozsa Street had once all been, like her, guileless visitors to this place. Visitors who found that once they were in this strange world they couldn't get out again. And as time passed they had forgotten that they'd even had a life beyond Marapozsa Street.

Well, it might have happened to them, but it wasn't going to happen to her! She hadn't taken a journey through the wonders of the Abarat—risking life, limb and sanity in the process—to end up a prisoner in some artificial world.

"I want to get out of this place!" she yelled. *"And*

I want to get out NOW! Somebody has to be able to hear me."

She threw back her head. "Mister Masper! Are you there? MISTER MASPER!"

"Just show us your dreams," said the man wearing the burning tower on his head. "Come on!"

"No!" said Candy.

"Don't be perverse," said a stately woman with an elaborate pillar of dream fragments on her head. Her voice, curiously, sounded not unlike that of the man with the burning tower. Strange.

"Show us," said another of the wanderers, his voice an echo of the others. "We want to see your dreams!"

"I'll keep them to myself," Candy said.

"Show us," said the man with the fish, moving toward her.

"Don't make us force you," said the ape.

"Keep away," Candy said.

The man took no notice of Candy's warning. He reached around behind his back and snatched hold of the tail of the fish, as if he intended to hit her with it. She didn't give him the opportunity. She snatched the fish out of his hand and aimed a strike at the dream things he had perched on his head. They were fragile. The pieces flew in all directions.

The man unleashed a howl of horror.

"My dreams!" he yelled. "Look what you've done to my precious dreams!"

The cry was instantly taken up all along Marapozsa Street, as those who'd witnessed Candy's blow and its consequences sent up their own cries.

"Make her show us!"

"Let's see your dreams, girl!"

"Right now! Let's see them!"

They were advancing on her from all sides, their once placid faces now twisted up in fury. She attempted to protest her innocence, but they weren't interested in listening to her. Her only option was to turn her back on them and run. She looked back over her shoulder. The news wasn't good. She was prevented from leaving the street by a wall of darkness. The sight was accompanied by a familiar sound.

Whoosh! Whoosh! Whoosh!

The spinning slits were passing in front of her, perilously close to her face. If she chose the wrong moment to jump, she'd surely hit the solid partition between the slits, which would not be good news. But how was she to know when it was best to jump? It was like trying to get aboard a fast-spinning carousel. If she mistimed her jump, she risked being knocked senseless; or worse, caught in the mechanism somehow, and carried around and around and—

"Just do it," she told herself, and the next moment she was in the air, flying and falling. There were a few seconds of pure terror when the world became a blurred place filled with the din of grinding cogs and uncoiling springs. She feared her nightmare had come true and she'd fallen into the spinning mechanism. Behind her she heard the dreamers yelling to her that she was going to die, stupid witch, and good riddance, because she deserved to die. The sound of the cogs and springs became so loud she had to put her hands

over her ears to shut it out. Even that didn't work. The noise still bled through, making her head throb.

"*Stop it!*" she yelled.

Perhaps her demand was heard; or perhaps it was simply good luck that brought her through the spinning slits. Whichever it was, she was released from the wracking din of the mechanism and fell forward, through the slits and out the other side. The sound suddenly ceased, and she found herself lying on a threadbare carpet, her head aching.

"Hello," said a voice.

She looked up. There was a man, dressed in dark gray, standing close to the door. "Are you all right?" he said.

"Yes . . . yes . . ." she said, doing her best to get to her feet. From the corner of her eye she saw the device, still spinning. She could hear the whoosh of the device, as powerful as ever. And more distantly, voices from Marapozsa Street.

"Did I . . . ?"

"Did you what?" the man said, offering a hand to help her get to her feet.

"It felt as though I was drawn into that thing." She shook her head to see if she could rid herself of the sense of dislocation. Only when it had receded a little did she trust herself to raise her head and look at the man who was standing in the room with her.

"I'm Mister Pius Masper," he said to her. "And I own this house."

34

SECRETS AND MEAT LOAF

ACROSS THE IMMEASURABLE DIVIDE between the Abarat and the Hereafter—in Chickentown, Minnesota—things were calmer than they had been of late. The curiosity and the concern that had been stirred up by the anonymous wall defacer at the Comfort Tree Hotel had cooled into general indifference, its position in people's order of gossipworthy subjects overtaken by the fact that the town's mayor, Harold Meadows, had been accused of taking bribes to overlook certain infringements of health policy (specifically that the runoff from the chicken factory's slaughterhouse should empty directly into the town's drains, making the taxpayers of Chickentown liable for the cleaning of the clogged pipes). As a result of this scandal, Harry Meadows was performing a rather humiliating dance of denial so as not to be thrown out of office, and his "I-didn't-do-it" two-step had the town's eyes on him.

There were a few exceptions, a few stalwarts who still patrolled outside the hotel night and day, watching for some evidence of supernatural manifestations. And there were even two officers at the police department who gave an hour a day to investigating the disappearance of Candy Quackenbush. But the truth was that these were no longer urgent issues. The citizens of Chickentown had other stuff to debate.

Even at 34 Followell Street—at the Quackenbush residence—talk of Candy had become such a source of irritation to Bill Quackenbush recently that Ricky and Don had taken the path of least resistance and simply never talked about her within hearing distance of her father.

And then, one day when they had all sat down for supper and Bill had drained a couple of cans of beer, he said: "I got some news for everyone."

"What about, Dad?" Rick wanted to know.

"About all of us," Bill Quackenbush said, cracking another beer. "I was talking to your mom about me leaving Chickentown. Going to Chicago or maybe Denver. But now I'm thinking we should *all* leave. As a family."

The boys both started talking at the same time.

"Chicago!"

"When would we go?"

"What about school?"

Melissa raised her hands to hush the excitement. "We're not going anywhere," she said, looking fiercely at her husband. "Not until Candy comes home. Not until we're a family again."

"She ran away," Bill replied, enunciating the words

as though he were speaking to an imbecile. "And Melissa, she is not coming back; at least no time soon. Maybe she'll come knockin' on the door in a few years with three kids and no husband. But right now she's gone, and the quicker we quit thinking she's gonna turn up again anytime soon, the quicker we can all get back to living regular lives again."

"But Dad—" Ricky said, his eyes brimming. "We can't just *forget*—"

"Don't you start cryin'," Bill said, pointing to his son. "You hear me, Rick? I swear, if you start bawlin' like some dumb-ass girl I'm gonna give you somethin' to bawl about."

Ricky sniffed hard and by sheer effort of will kept the tears from coming.

But Don, who was completely dry-eyed, had some arguments of his own. "Suppose she comes back here," he said. "And we're not here. How will she find us?"

"She ain't *that* stupid," his father said. "She'll ask around until she finds a neighbor who knows where we went."

"I don't want to go to a new school in a new town," Don went on. "I like my old friends."

"You'll make new friends," Bill said. "And one school's just like the next."

"You've obviously thought all this through," Melissa said coldly. "Exactly when were you going to tell the rest of us? Or were we just going to wake up one morning all packed and ready to go?"

"I'm the head of the household," Bill replied. "I get

to make these important decisions. If I don't make 'em, who will?"

"Oh yeah, that's you, Bill," Melissa said. "Mister Responsibility."

"Can I leave the table now, please?" said Ricky, staring down at his congealed macaroni and cheese and his dried-up meat loaf.

"You haven't eaten anything, honey," said his mother.

"I'm not hungry."

"Neither am I," said Don.

"All right, you're excused," said Melissa.

The two boys couldn't get away from the table fast enough.

"I'm not changing my mind about this," Bill said after he drained the can of beer. "I'm not going to rot here. Day after day with nothing to do."

"Then get a damn job, Bill."

"There aren't any."

"There are plenty."

"None that I want."

Melissa shook her head. "Well, you know what? You can plan all you like, but I am not going anywhere without Candy."

Bill said nothing for maybe a whole minute. Then he got up and went to the fridge and brought out another can of beer. "Why don't you just admit it to yourself?" he said, not coming back to the table. "She's *gone*. We both know it. She never belonged to us in the first place."

Melissa's eyes suddenly filled with tears. She pressed the heels of her hands against her sockets, to try and stem the flow. "How can you say that? She was our baby. She will always be our baby."

Bill leaned against the fridge, staring out into the darkened backyard. "No," he said. "I don't think she was ever really ours."

"What are you talking about?"

"Oh, come on, Melissa. She was a weird kid, right from the start. Her eyes, for one thing—"

"Lots of kids have eyes that are different colors," Melissa said, her tears suddenly dried up by anger. "And she isn't weird. The only problem is that you never really loved her."

"I did my best." He shrugged.

"That was your best?" Melissa shook her head. "Whole months would go by and you'd barely speak to her."

"Okay, we never got along."

"You're her father, Bill."

"Am I?"

Melissa stared hard at him. "What are you suggesting?"

"Well, you were the one who said it. Something happened the night Candy was born. Three women . . ."

"Oh, so now you want to talk about it."

"Are you going to tell me or not?"

"I'll tell you. But only on one condition."

"And what's that?"

"You *listen.* You *believe* me."

"That's two—"

"Bill."

"All right. I'm listening. Tell me what happened."

For ten, twenty, thirty seconds Melissa said nothing.

"Go on," Bill said. "I'm not kidding, I want to know."

Melissa drew a deep breath. "All right . . ." she said. "You know some of it already. The women who came to the truck when you'd left. I told you about them. They just appeared from out of the storm. I asked them where they'd come from and they said they came from another world. A place they called Abarat."

"And you believed them?" Bill said.

"Yes. I did. I don't know why but I *knew*, I absolutely knew, they were telling me the truth." Bill shook his head. "You told me you wanted to know what happened that night," Melissa snapped. "And I'm telling you. *So listen.*"

She paused, allowing her spurt of anger to subside. Her eyes glanced over the kitchen as if she was listing the duties that still needed to be done. Trash to be taken out; dirty dishes to be washed; the dead geranium on the windowsill to be dumped. The labor of listing calmed her. When she picked up her account of that rainy night again, the rage had drained out of her. She spoke quietly, so quietly that Bill had to listen hard to catch all she was saying.

"I don't know to this day if it was just an accident that they found me there," she told him, "or whether they'd somehow tracked us. I *do* know they were afraid that they were being followed by somebody from their world. What they were doing was probably against the law in the Abarat. But they were desperate. They had something to give me, they said. No, not to me. To the baby that was to be born. *They had something to give the baby.* And it would change her life forever. That's what they said. Nothing would be the same because of what they were here to give to her. . . ."

35

TWO IN NINETEEN

H<small>ENRY</small> M<small>URKITT</small> <small>DIDN'T SLEEP</small> anymore. Since his failed attempt to raise the folks of Chickentown from their televisions and their gossip, he was haunted night and day by the terrible prospect of what lay ahead for the town that had once carried his family's name.

The dreams that had begun this haunting didn't cease just because Henry no longer slept. Instead they took the form of daylight visions, which were in some ways more terrifying than ordinary nightmares. He would be standing at the window of Room Nineteen, peering through the dirty glass at the unremarkable people going about their unremarkable lives, when suddenly a shadow seemed to loom over the street, like some lethal judgment that would soon wipe them all away. He wasn't frightened for himself (what did a ghost have to fear from death?), but he was afraid, horribly afraid for the innocents he saw going about their business, realizing nothing.

* * *

"You look melancholy."

Henry turned around from the window, and his eyes grew wide with astonishment. Standing across the room from him was a face he hadn't laid eyes upon in a very long time.

"Diamanda?" he said. "It isn't you."

"Yes, it is, Henry."

Oh, but the years had been kind to her! Though her hair—which she'd always worn long—was now gray, and her face was decorated with a tracery of fine lines, the bones on which her flesh sat were still as elegant as ever. She had been beautiful in those distant years when she'd been his loving wife, and against all expectation she was beautiful still. It was easy to remember, in the first few seconds that his eyes were laid on her again, where his love had sprung.

"Is it *really* you?" he said, scarcely breathing the words for fear this lovely mirage would dissolve and leave him alone again.

"Yes, Henry," she said. "It's really me."

"But why . . . after all this time?"

"To be honest, Henry, death caught up with me, just a little while ago. And you know, as I was floating above the scene of my demise (which wasn't pleasant), I found my thoughts turning instantly to you. Of *all* people! *It's Henry I want to see,* I thought. The rest can wait. I came to make my peace, I suppose."

"You came, that's all that matters. You came. How did you know where to find me?"

"Well, that's both a very long story and very short one. The short version is: I've got eyes in my head and I looked."

"What happened to your fancy man in Chicago?"

"My *what*?" Diamanda laughed.

"Your . . . fancy man. Everybody told me—"

"Let's get a few things straight from the get-go, Henry Murkitt. Whatever you heard from the gossip-mongers, I did *not* have a fancy man in Chicago. Or any other place, come to that."

"Truly?"

"Henry. I wouldn't come back from the dead to tell you a petty little lie, would I?"

"No, I guess not." He expelled a contented sigh. "As a matter of interest," he went on, "why *did* you come back?"

"First, Henry Murkitt, to do *this*."

Diamanda walked over to Henry and laid a light kiss on his lips. Then another six, for good measure. It was the first human contact he'd been able to feel in many years.

"Oh my Lord, I've missed that . . ." he said. "So we're just two ghosts now, huh?"

"As you say: just two ghosts."

"How did it happen to you? That you died, I mean."

"I was trying to protect a girl from your world, Henry, a runaway called—"

"Candy Quackenbush."

"So you've heard of her?"

"She was here in this very room, just a few weeks

ago, working on some school project. A charming enough girl, she seemed."

"Miss Quackenbush turns out to be a very powerful young woman."

Henry looked puzzled. "Really? You surprise me. She seemed pleasant but quite ordinary. Where did you two meet?"

"In a world we have never spoken about till now," Diamanda said. "The Abarat."

"Ah! The fabled Abarat. I may have been locked up here for the past half century or so, but even I heard a little about that place. If there's more, tell me."

"There's always more where the Abarat's concerned. It's a world without limits."

He looked mystified, so Diamanda attempted to explain, keeping the description simple. But the more she told him, the more he wanted to know, and she was soon explaining the whole tale to him. How she'd gone off to voyage the Abarat; how she'd first met a woman of the Fantomaya, and been taken, after much preparation, to Odom's Spire, the Twenty-Fifth Hour, to be initiated into the mysteries of Time out of Time. Though it was an extraordinary story that she told, he didn't once doubt her truthfulness. He knew her too well. If she was telling him that there was an archipelago where every island existed at a different hour of the day, then he was obliged to believe her. It was only toward the end of her account, when she spoke about her involvement with magic, that he grew more cautious.

"You know what the Good Book has to say about witchcraft," he said. *"Thou shall not suffer a witch to live."*

"Those old hypocrites. They talk about killing witches but the Good Book's full of magic. Turning the Nile to blood and parting the Red Sea. What's that if it's not good old-fashioned magic? Want a little water into wine? No trouble! How about raising that dead man Lazarus? Just say the word!"

"You're walking on thin ice, Diamanda!"

"No, I'm not. I'm just telling the truth. And anyone who loves the Good Word loves the Truth, right?"

Poor Henry looked thoroughly confounded. In a matter of seconds Diamanda had run theological circles around him. She saw the puzzlement on his face and finally took pity on him.

"Think of it this way," she said. "Magic is about connecting things. Seeing how the power runs through the world. From you to that crack in the wall, to the spider in the crack, to the song in the spider's head, singing praise to God—"

"Spiders don't sing."

"Everything sings its praises in its own way, Henry. That's what magic is. The singing of praises. And the verses all connecting up, *till the power flows* . . . I'm going to have you listen one of these times, Henry Murkitt, and I swear you will hear such a magical hallelujah. . . ."

Henry shook his head. "I don't know who's the craziest. You for saying this stuff, or me for half believing it." The tentative smile that had come onto his face now fell away, and he said: "I've been having *dreams*. Terrible dreams."

"About what?

"I guess they're about the end of the world. At least, the end of Chickentown."

"You believe them?"

"Yes, of course I believe them! I even tried to warn folks about what was happening." He pointed to the wall where his message remained scratched in the plaster.

"Higher Ground?" Diamanda read.

"I know it's sort of vague," Henry said. "But it was the only thing I could think of at the time. Unfortunately, these people don't want to listen."

"Maybe we can *make* them listen, between the two of us."

"I hope so."

"I must say, Henry, you've changed your tune. I thought you *hated* Chickentown."

"I guess when I lost you I didn't have anything else to love. It was Chickentown or nothing."

"Listen to yourself. You sound so sad."

"Well, I am. I should have spent my life with you."

"Well, now you can make up for lost time. We've found each other again. You're a good man, Henry Murkitt. You deserve some happiness. Some freedom. How often do you get out of this darn room, anyway?"

"Actually . . . I've never left it."

"You're kidding me!"

"No. I felt I sinned when I took my own life. I guess I thought I deserved to be in here until the Last Judgment."

"Well, that's utter bull poop, Henry. And I think you know it. So we are gonna go out together. Out into the sun."

"We are? When?"

"Now, Henry! We are going right now!"

So out they went together: the Phantom of Room Nineteen and Diamanda Murkitt, the love of his life, walking hand in hand. They weren't visible to most of the eyes that casually turned in their direction, except perhaps as vague shadows or a subtle disturbance of the air that might have nudged people as they passed.

Their voices, however, were another matter. They weren't as clear as ordinary voices, but they were still perfectly audible. They sounded like whisperers, exchanging gossip at a nearby corner. It was the subject under debate—the imminent destruction of the town—that made people listen more closely. Several times as they walked and talked, they caught sight of people looking back at the spot where they stood, with puzzled expressions on their faces.

"Do you think our message is getting through?" Henry asked Diamanda as they stood beneath the pigeon-bespattered statue of his great-grandfather, the town's founder.

"Well, they can certainly *hear* us," Diamanda said. "But whether that means they're actually paying attention is anybody's guess. I mean: what are we to them? We're just some voices muttering at the back of their heads." Henry didn't reply. He just stared at Diamanda as she talked. "It's interesting. Have you noticed how the babies and the dogs seem to be quite happy to accept our presence? I think Chickentown's future would be perfectly safe if it were left with the babies and the dogs." She paused, returning Henry's stare. "What are you looking at?" she said.

"You. I'm looking at you. You're still very lovely."

"This is no time for flirtation, Henry."

"If not now, then when? After the time we've waited . . . don't we deserve to tell each other the deepest secrets of our hearts?"

"You old sentimentalist," Diamanda replied fondly.

"And very proud to be one!" Henry said. "Lord, Diamanda, the world might end at any moment. We should speak our minds. You are lovely. There. It's said." He smiled, and shielding his eyes from the sun, he looked off down the length of Main Street. "What do you think will be the first sign?" he said. "I mean, of what's on its way?"

"Rain in the wind," Diamanda said. "Salt rain."

"It sounds like you've been through something like this before."

"Something similar. And let me tell you, it will *not* be pretty. The more we can do to get people up and out of this town, the less weeping and wailing there's going to be when it's all over."

"Any suggestions?" Henry wondered.

"Well, to speed things along we ought to split up. Keep to the major thoroughfares. And while we go, talk to people. Drop our warnings into their ears. Tell them to get out of town. Only do it so subtly they don't even know it's us. Let them think these are their own thoughts."

"Clever," Henry said.

"Tell them not to pack anything. They just need to *leave*."

"How long do we have?" Henry said.

Diamanda looked up at the sky, studying it for clues. She apparently failed to find any, because finally she said: "I don't know. Hours, not days." She returned her gaze to Henry. "We must do whatever we can to save these people, Henry, or we're going to have a lot of angry spirits pointing fingers."

"Well, we don't want that," Henry said. "Not when we just found each other again."

Diamanda smiled. "I must say, it *is* good to see you, Henry. Very good. Now let's get back to work."

"Spreading the word," he said.

"Spreading the word," she replied.

36

THE BRIDEGROOM UNEARTHED

THE VOICE THE COMPANY had located beneath the fertile dirt of the Nonce grew louder sometimes, sometimes fainter. But there was no doubting the strength in it, and the rage.

"Spread out!" Geneva said. "Look for some way down into the ground."

"But be careful," Mischief said. "Whoever it is down there, he sounds a *little* crazy."

Walking cautiously so as not to further anger or disturb the man beneath them, they fanned out, looking for a route down into the tunnels.

"I've found something!" Tria said.

She had indeed: the tunnel was oppressively narrow, lined with roots and alive with a lot of many-legged dirt dwellers, quillimedes and yard lice and scorpits. The sight of it brought a variety of responses.

"It's suicide to go down there," John Moot stated bluntly. "If we don't get bitten to death, the tunnel will almost certainly collapse on us."

"And anyway, we'll frighten the Lordy Lou out of

whoever's down there," said John Drowze.

"But this is what we came to do," Geneva pointed out.

"Not to get buried alive, we didn't," Serpent replied.

"All right," Tom said to the brothers. "You lot stand out here and guard the entrance and the rest of us will go in." He made a move toward the entrance.

"Wait!" said Tria. "I'm the smallest. I should go first."

"Before anyone gets *too* enthusiastic about going down there," John Mischief said, "shouldn't we consider the situation a little more closely? Let's assume it *is* Finnegan Hob, the great dragon hunter, down there in the ground. Let's ask ourselves *why* he's down there."

There was silence by way of response. Everyone exchanged grim looks.

"Yes, that's right, ladies and gentlemen, he's probably down there with a *dragon*."

"Well, if it's as vulnerable as the beast we killed at sea," said Tom, "then I don't think we've got a great deal to fear from the thing."

"Don't get too confident," Geneva said. "Seagoing dragons have delicate constitutions. A lot of things can kill them. But your earthworm, on the other hand, is a good deal stronger. They live to be a thousand years old, some of them, and their skins just get tougher each time they shed."

"I heard the same thing," said John Moot.

"Hush," said Mischief.

"Don't shush me!" Moot protested.

"No, Moot," said John Fillet, who was looking the other way. "It's for your own good."

"What?"

"Everybody . . ." Geneva said to the Johns. "Duck down."

"Why?" Mischief muttered.

Geneva took the dagger she'd been polishing in her grip and spoke two syllables: "DRA. GON."

"Where?" said Tom.

Standing on the same spot, Geneva turned fully through three hundred and sixty degrees, pointing outward with her sword as she did so. "All. Around. Us," she said.

"Oh Lordy Lou," Mischief breathed.

"An ouroboros," said Tria.

"What's that mean?" John Mischief wanted to know.

"The serpent that eats its own tail," Tria whispered.

"That's why it's all around us," Geneva said, her voice so soft everyone had to strain to hear it.

"I don't see it," said Tom.

"Yes, you do," said Tria.

Her voice had a curious clarity to it despite the tiny volume. "It's there." She pointed to a gold-green slope. "And there." To a ridge which seemed to be infested with cacti. "And there. That blue-green rock . . ."

"It's breathing . . ." said Tom, his tone more astonishment than fear. "I hear it."

"Does it know we're here?" said John Serpent.

"Why don't *you* tell us that?" Moot remarked. "Serpent to serpent."

"Ha, ha," said Serpent, very unamused.

"In other words, you don't know."

"At a guess," Serpent replied, "it *knows*. It's just trying to work out how many of us there are."

As he proffered this reply there was a fresh outburst of shouting from underground.

"I think the earthworm has cornered him down there," Tria said grimly.

"That's why he's making such a din," said Two-Toed Tom. "He's trying to draw its attention. Trying to stop it from coming after us—"

He'd no sooner spoken than the ground around them shook violently, and great walls of dirt and plant life flew up into the air. Ten, twenty feet it flew, and then came down again in a rattling rain.

"She's right!" John Serpent yelled. "It's all around us!"

Geneva was no longer whispering. She was yelling at the top of her voice. "Arm yourselves!" she hollered. "It knows we're here! Get ready to fight!"

Those who had small weapons wielded them in readiness, while the rest searched on the ground for something—*anything*—to fight with. Even as they did so the earth *lurched*, and the worm's head—shaped like a giant shovel, flat and wide and ferocious—rose up out of the ground. Its head was of such size that its neck had difficulty bearing it up. There was nothing elegant or beautiful about it. A great mass of plant life sprouted from its skull, and a mud-clogged beard of roots hung from its lower jaw. It gave off a rotted smell as though its body had gone to corruption from lying in the wet earth for so long. Clumps of matter fell from the underside of its body as it raised itself up, but it was impossible to discern whether it was the dragon itself that was falling to pieces, or whether it was simply bits of dirt and decay that were dropping to the ground.

"Distract it!" Geneva yelled, and while Tom and McBean attacked the dragon's forelegs, Geneva went for the snout with the little dagger she had, piercing it as deeply as she was able. The blade barely penetrated the scales, however, and there was no sign that she was doing the beast much harm. Still, it knew it was under attack, and it fought back, opening its ragged mouth as though to swallow her. With a born warrior's speed, Geneva feinted to the left, then struck to the right, digging her blade into the tender flesh around the dragon's nostril and pulling down, opening a long wound. Viscous blood spat from the place, giving off a fierce heat along with the eye-stinging stench of excrement.

The worm was hurt, no doubt of that. It reeled back, letting out something that sounded not unlike a sob. But the sound was its own kind of feint, for it had no sooner made the complaint than it came back at its wounder with surprising suddenness, landing on the ground with such force that it cracked the earth open. Dirt and rock dust rose up into the air in a choking cloud. For a few moments the dirt obliterated everything: all anybody could do was stand and wait for it to clear.

And then, disaster. From somewhere in the dirt

cloud came a noise of rushing earth, and then a cry from Tria.

"Where are you?" Tom yelled.

"I see her!" John Mischief called out, and pointed through the clearing air. The ground had given way beneath poor Tria, and she was slipping down into the darkness.

Wounded though it was, the dragon quickly realized it had been offered a victim. The creature nosed toward Tria, growling in its throat, suddenly moving like a snake, belly to the ground.

Tom threw himself in its path, but it casually batted him away with its snout and went on with its weaving pursuit of Tria.

"It'll get the child," John Mischief said, sitting down on the edge of the slope and preparing to launch himself down at it.

"John?" said Moot. "Are you crazy?"

"We don't even know what's down there!" Serpent protested.

"*Tria's* down there!" Mischief replied.

"Oh, spare me the heroism!" Serpent said. "She's dead for certain—"

Mischief didn't waste time arguing. He simply pitched himself and his brothers down the slope where Tria had gone, and into the murk.

The dragon raised its humongous head on its gnarled neck and scanned the scene, its eyes burning in its mud-caked visage. It had fixed its gaze upon McBean now. The Captain had fallen badly when the earth gave way, and now he was having difficulty getting up again. He was sitting a little distance from the hole, rubbing his leg, obviously in considerable pain.

"McBean . . ." said John Drowze. "Be careful."

"I know, I know. It's my leg—"

"No, Cap'n, I'm not worried about—"

Before Drowze could finish speaking, the dragon opened its mouth like a tunnel and rushed at McBean, approaching him so quickly that he had no time to defend himself. The dragon's lower jaw pushed beneath the Captain, who fell backward into the throat of the thing. He cried out as he fell, a small boy's cry that echoed against the roof of the beast's mouth.

"Nythaganius Pejorius!" somebody yelled.

The dragon paused in midswallow. Tom, Tria, Geneva and the Johns looked down into the ground, from which direction the voice that had named the beast had come. There was a young man standing at the bottom of the fissure, his skin dark, his eyes a luminous green, his hair, a mass of dreadlocks, bright red.

"Do you see me, Nythaganius Pejorius?"

The worm cocked her head like an irritated parrot, and her pupils dilated as she sought out her namer.

"Yes, I see you," the worm said, petals being shaken off the flowers around her mouth as she spoke.

"Do you see also what I have under my foot, *Nythaganius Pejorius?*"

The man with the red dreadlocks lifted his bare foot a little higher, so that the worm would be in no doubt as to what she was looking at.

"Yes, I see . . ." she said with an icy rage in her voice.

"Then speak what you see."

"Finnegan, why do you infuriate me?"

"I said *speak*."

"It's an egg, Finnegan Hob. It's my egg."

"Your only egg."

"Yes! Yes! My *only* egg!"

"I could crush it."

"No! You wouldn't. Not my egg."

"Then spit out the man you just ate."

"Me?" said the worm, attempting a look of pitiful innocence. "I didn't—"

Finnegan raised his long, bare foot above the egg and made it twitch and quiver as if he were barely preventing himself from bringing it down.

"Monster!" the dragon roared.

"*Regurgitate*, worm. I'm counting to three. One—"

"Godless monster!"

"Two—"

"All right! All right! Have it your way."

The worm made a repeated scooping motion with her head, and a retching sound emerged from her throat. So, seconds later, did Captain McBean. He slid down the dragon's tongue and out of her mouth, landing with an undignified thump in the dirt that all this commotion had stirred up. He was covered in a thick layer of dragon spittle, but other than that he looked unharmed.

"Now, Finnegan Hob," the dragon said. "Keep your side of the bargain."

"Geneva Peachtree," Finnegan yelled. "That *is* you, isn't it?"

"Yes, it's me!"

"Then I want you to get your friends, including *him*"—he pointed to McBean—"out of here. This regurgitating worm and I have business to finish. And it will end with the death of one of us; that is for certain. So please . . . *Go!*"

And so saying, he broke his promise and drove his foot down on the dragon's egg.

37

THE OWNER OF THE DEAD MAN'S HOUSE

Mister Masper was almost certainly the most normal person Candy had encountered during her whole journey in the Abarat. In fact, he vaguely resembled a man called Mr. Wippel, who worked at the drugstore back in Chickentown: both meek looking, with pale, rather sad faces and round spectacles. Like Wippel, Mister Masper was losing his hair (the last few strands of which were plastered to his pate from ear to ear). He wore a dark, rather shabby suit and there were food stains on his gray tie; all in all, he was a forlorn sight. But his very ordinary appearance was in fact rather welcome after the wild ride Candy had just taken through Marapozsa Street.

"I'm glad to see you back," he said to her.

"What is that thing? It felt like I was trapped in it."

"Oh, it's just an antique, called a momentary. I really should put it under lock and key, where it can't do any harm."

"Is the place inside it real?"

Masper took off his spectacles, and teasing a white handkerchief from the breast pocket of his jacket, he cleaned the lenses as he spoke. "To be honest, I don't know whether it's real or not. I've always been of the opinion that such things are of little importance. What matters is the effect it has upon you."

"Well, I didn't like it. Everybody was asking me where my dreams were."

"Well, it was all perfectly harmless," Masper said. "You look fine."

"Well, I'm not!" said Candy with a sudden flash of anger. "I lost my friend Diamanda outside this horrible house of yours. And you had Letheo kidnap me to get me here. I don't like that!"

"Well, aren't *we* direct?" Masper said, the first subtle hint of discourtesy creeping into his voice. As he spoke, he went to one of the absurdly tall and narrow windows and stared out at the bleak landscape of Efreet. The snow was coming down heavily now, the wind blowing the flakes so hard they burst against the window.

"I had to get you here somehow. I apologize if the method was a little crude."

"Why did you need to get me here? I don't know you."

"But I know you, Candy. Was Letheo cruel to you?"

"No."

"Because if he was—"

"I said no," she replied. "Now when can I get out of here?"

"Well, it wouldn't be wise to try right now. It's *very*

cold out there, as you can see." He went to the door and called out: "Letheo! Come in here, please."

A few seconds later Letheo appeared. He looked entirely changed. Though his head wound was still raw, he had cleaned his face and combed his hair and was now wearing a black jacket and trousers; the jacket set off with shiny silver buttons, which held it closed all the way up to his Adam's apple. He stood at the threshold and clicked the heels of his shiny black boots together.

"Look at him," Masper said proudly. "The first soldier in a new army."

"Whose?"

Masper gave her a tiny smile. "I think we should leave that discussion for another Day, Candy, don't you? Or better, another Night."

"May I have a moment of your time, sir?" Letheo said. "Alone."

"What, now?"

"Yes. It's urgent."

The mask of benign indifference slipped from Masper's face for a moment, and anger flared there briefly. "Don't be wasting my time," Masper said.

"Of course not, sir."

"Then quickly . . ." Masper said. He turned back to Candy: "Stay here, will you? This will only take a moment." He walked past Letheo and out into the corridor. As soon as he'd gone, Letheo whispered: *"Get out."*

"What?"

"Trust me—just get out. Break the window if you have to, but go. He means to kill you—"

"Letheo . . ." Masper called from the hallway.

"I'm coming."

Masper returned to the doorway with a faintly amused look on his face. "What do you think you're doing, boy? Making a suicide pact?"

He stepped back into the room, and to Candy's eyes he seemed to shake, as though he were standing in the middle of a heat haze.

"I was just—"

"I know what you were doing, Letheo." He shook his head. "You really are going to have to learn: you can't be on both sides at the same time." He shook his head. "Enough of these *games*," he said. "I thought I might get your dreams from you the easy way. But I see after our little conversation that you're too willful to be persuaded and too clever to be tricked. So we'll have to do it the hard way."

As he spoke, it seemed to Candy that Masper's eyes were deepening, darkening, and his mouth was growing wider. His hand went up to his face, and he took off his spectacles, which *melted* in his hand and ran off, between his fingers, the matter from which they'd been made evaporating into nothingness.

"What's happening to him?" Candy said to Letheo.

"Just go . . ." Letheo replied.

"Just a few dreams," the man-who-used-to-be-Masper said. "Was that so much to ask? Just to see what's going on in that head of yours? But no. *No*." He reeled around on Letheo, jabbing his finger at him. "As for you—" he said, "—I warned you what would happen if you betrayed me. Didn't I? Well, *didn't I*?"

The haze intensified as he spoke. His shape wavered, and the illusion that was Mister Masper began to fall away around him. The plain jacket dissolved, revealing robes of black and gold. His features—which had flickered, as though there were lightning *behind his face*—began to dissolve and on the third or fourth flash disappeared completely, revealing a very different man. Rising from his shoulders was a kind of translucent collar, which covered the lower half of his face. It was a reservoir for a dark fluid, which he inhaled as easily as a fish might breathe water. Something moved in the fluid. No, not moved, *seethed*, like a congregation of angry eels. They flashed with electricity intermittently—that was the lightning she'd seen flicker—and threw an uncharitable light on his face.

And oh, that face! He was a portrait of living death. The muscles had half withered away, leaving his bones to jut through his parchment skin. His eyes had sunk into his sockets, and the flesh around them had become translucent and was filled with tiny tics. When he turned a little, she saw that the fluid in his collar (or else the creatures that lived in it) was being siphoned out of the back of his nearly hairless skull. It was horrible to see. And even more horrible, she saw, to *live in*, to pass every moment of every Day and Night trapped inside!

The rest of his body was strong, as if in compensation for the frailty of his head; the suit of black and gold so designed that it seemed to amplify the anatomy beneath. His hands were bare, but huge: long fingered and pale. He wore a ring of elaborate design upon every finger—and upon his thumbs—and the middle finger of each hand was covered in exquisitely wrought silver sheaths, with needlepoints for nails.

She did not need him to tell her his name. She knew it the instant the mirage of innocence was dissolved. *This was Christopher Carrion, the Lord of Midnight.* She had been in his company without knowing it; he'd almost charmed her, in his way. But never again. Not now that she saw him clearly, *never*, she swore to herself, *never again.*

"Take hold of her, Letheo," Carrion said. "I want to ask her some questions."

There was a moment of hesitation, when it seemed Letheo might not do as he'd been ordered, and Candy seized her opportunity. She made a dash for the door, her shadow thrown up against the wall by the flickering beasts in Carrion's collar.

"Don't waste our time trying to get out of here," the Midnight Lord said to her. "Even if you *did* get out of the house, which is very unlikely, what's waiting for you outside? Death by snow? Eaten by a Waztrill or a Sanguinius? And ask yourself: why are you running? I'm not even *hurting* you, am I?"

"I'd still prefer to take my chances out there, thank you very much."

"Stupid, stupid girl," Carrion said. "Letheo, for the last time. *Take hold of her.*"

Letheo looked away from Carrion and glanced at Candy. She saw the signal in his eyes. He was telling her to *go.*

She did just that. She ran.

"STOP HER!" Carrion roared.

For the briefest of moments she glanced back and saw that Letheo was stepping into his master's way as Carrion moved toward the door. With one mighty backhanded blow, Carrion knocked Letheo across the room. Letheo struck the window, which shattered, and in a hail of glass shards he disappeared from sight.

"Now," Carrion said, calling after Candy. He lifted his hand and clenched his fist, which caused all the lamps in the room and corridor to go out at once. The only source of light was now the creatures in Carrion's collar. Their ghastly luminescence threw his shadow up against the walls.

The Lord of Midnight shook his head and proffered an indulgent little smile. "Enough, lady," he said. "Come here. Come."

As he spoke he lifted his arms, as if to summon Candy into an embrace.

"All I want to know is a little about your dreams," he said.

"So you trap me in that thing—"

"The momentary? It's usually quite painless. But you? You're quite a piece of work, Candy Quackenbush. I hear all kinds of stories. Everywhere you go you seem to cause trouble." He advanced toward her, his eyes transfixing her, as though he had the capacity to hold her with his gaze. "Well, you're not going to cause trouble to me."

"No?"

"No. You've done all the traveling you're going to

do, Candy Quackenbush. The only place you're going now is a hole in the ground. Believe me, I'm being kind. You wouldn't want to be here when Midnight comes—"

"Midnight?"

"Absolute Midnight. The last great dark, covering the islands from dawn to dusk, and through the Hours of darkness an even deeper darkness. No moon. No stars." He smiled, and his smile was a death's smile. "You're better off in the ground. There'll be no terrors there. Just worms."

Candy tried to put out of her thoughts the horrible images his words laid in her head. If she survived this encounter, she'd want to try and make sense of what he'd said; pass his words onto others; warn them about his plans. So the more she knew about those plans, the better. She just had to find a technique for getting the information out of him.

"I don't see how you could ever put the stars out," she said, feigning a dismissive tone. "That's just ridiculous."

"Not if you have the right allies," he said. "An innocent like you wouldn't have heard of the sacbrood, of course—"

"Sacbrood. No. What are they?"

"You'll never know," he said.

She shrugged. "Fine."

"Don't think I don't know what you're trying to do, girl. I'm not stupid." Again, that smile. Horrible beyond words.

"Oh?" Candy said. "What am I trying to do?"

"Goad me. So I'll say, in an unguarded moment, something you can report to your friends. Except . . . who are you going to tell? Nobody. You are alone. Utterly alone."

It was strange, but for some reason this idea—that she was alone—suddenly seemed so wrong, so stupid, that all she could do was laugh. Which she did.

"What's so funny?"

"I'm not alone," she said, not even really under-standing what she meant by this, but knowing more certainly than she'd known anything in her life that it was true.

Her laughter infuriated him. *"Shut up,"* Carrion said.

She kept laughing.

"SHUT UP! HOW DARE YOU LAUGH AT ME?"

For just a moment his rage seemed to erupt in him, and the creatures around his head spat claws of light-ning against the confines of his collar. Their brightness apparently took him by surprise, because he closed his eyes against them.

She took her chance. Turned from him and ran, the flickering brilliance that spilled from her enemy light-ing her way. She slammed the door behind her and turned the key in the lock. Then she plunged into the darkness of the corridor, not caring that she bumped into things as she went.

There was a lamp burning ahead, beyond the limits of Carrion's darkening reach. It illuminated a stair-well: a spiraling staircase that either led down into another inky blackness or up toward the roof. Once, at the very beginning of these adventures, she'd climbed a spiral staircase and escaped death. Perhaps it would work a second time. Behind her, Carrion tore at the locked door, and off its hinges it came.

Candy didn't look back. She just climbed.

38

MIDNIGHT'S HEART

SHE TOOK THE STAIRS two, sometimes three at a time until she reached the third floor. Here the flight appeared to stop, though she guessed that the house had five stories at the very least. So where were the stairs that led on and up? The landing she'd come to had a number of paintings hung on the walls, none of them pretty, and three doors. She did her best to ignore the paintings—one of them, depicting a creature eating another creature, that was eating a third, which was eating a fourth, and so on, in a vile series of devourings, was particularly distressing—and went to the doors, opening them one after the other until she found the connecting staircase.

She glanced back over her shoulder. Carrion was on the landing below, watching her from behind his collar of glass, his eyes turned up in his sockets to watch her, almost as though he were dead. She shuddered, silently swearing that she would die rather than let him lay his clammy hands on her.

"Just leave me alone!" she yelled down at him,

though of course she knew it wouldn't drive him away.

Then she turned and continued to climb, her lungs and legs burning. The stairs got narrower as they spiraled upward, and more unstable with every step she took. She was reminded again of the climb that had begun this cycle of adventures: how she'd stumbled up the spiral staircase in the lighthouse, with the putrid Mendelson Shape coming in spider-limbed pursuit of her.

"*Slow your step, child,*" Carrion yelled after her. "*You're not going anywhere.*"

"I'm not afraid of you!" she yelled back.

"Are you not?" he said. Then again, more slowly and softly: "*Are . . . you . . . not?*"

As he spoke, the lights that illuminated the staircase flickered once, and then suddenly went out. For a few heartbeats she was in total darkness, then—and this was in some ways worse than the darkness—shafts of icy light came darting up the stairs from below. She felt their touch, as though Carrion was reaching out through their brightness and caressing her skin. The contact revolted her. She tried to avoid it by pressing herself against the wall while she continued to ascend.

"I don't want very much from you," Carrion said as he came up after her. "I just want to see what your dreams are like. Is that so much to ask? I feel if I knew your dreams then it'd be like having you close by me all the time."

"Why would you care?" Candy replied. "You don't even know who I am."

"You're Candy Quackenbush from Chickentown.

But there's more to you than that. You know there is."

"No, I don't."

"Oh, come now . . . all the things you've done, the trouble you've caused, the lives you've destroyed—"

"I didn't—"

"Don't waste your time protesting your innocence," Carrion said. She glanced back down the stairs and there he was, his face floating in darkness, lit by the sickly glamor of his nightmares. "We both know there's more to you than meets the eye. Why don't you tell me what's going on in your head?"

"Tell you what," Candy countered. "Why don't you stop chasing me first?"

"Agreed," Carrion said, much to Candy's surprise. He stopped on the stairs. "Listen to me," he went on, his tone calm. "You must have realized by now that you're not here by accident. For some reason or other, your life is bound up with the destiny of these islands. Don't ask me why. I don't understand anything about you, except that from the first moment I knew of your existence I also knew that some part of who *I* am is tied up with some part of who *you* are. And until I understand why, I cannot let you go."

"But if you did solve the mystery, I'd never have to look at you again?"

"Don't sound so happy about it," he said, sounding hurt.

"Then ask me your questions," Candy said. "Just don't come any closer."

"Thank you," Carrion replied, smiling his death's-head smile. "Well, where shall we begin? What are your first memories? The first sky you remember seeing? The first song you heard?"

It almost made her laugh, to hear him asking such simple things. Was there any harm in answering them? She could see none. "I remember a very cold wind," she said. "I think . . . it smelled of the sea. But that's not really possible," she added, half to herself. "There's no sea in Minnesota."

"But there is," Carrion reminded her. "You summoned it just a few weeks ago. Shape told me."

"I'd almost forgotten Shape," Candy said. "What happened to him?"

"He died," Carrion remarked casually. "He fell down some stairs, actually. The missing foot, you know, it made him—wait, wait! What am I doing talking about Shape? Ha! You're a clever one, girl. Go on with your memories. Tell me about your life."

"It was boring. At least until I came here."

"There must have been signs. Clues. Mornings when you woke up thinking: one day I'll be in a different world."

"No."

"You're holding something back from me."

"I'm not, really."

"Well, this is no good. You said you'd *talk*." He raised his hands, showing his palms in a kind of mock surrender. "You know you have nothing to fear from me. Really. I'm sure there are a lot of people who've told you terrible things about me. . . ." He let the observation hang, waiting for her to agree or contradict. Candy did neither. "Well, they may be right," Carrion said finally. "I had no one to show me a better way, a kinder way. To inspire me, if you like. All I had was my grandmother, Mater Motley. Not the kindest of women."

"Where is the rest of your family?"

"Nobody ever told you the story?"

"About what?"

"The Carrion Night Mansion?" Candy shook her head. "I had twenty-six brothers and one sister. And we had a huge mansion on Pyon, with a great orchard of smyrion trees on one side of it. My sister, Theridia, was very fond of the fruit. She was forever sneaking out into the orchard and stealing it."

"Pyon is a Night island."

"So?"

"There were fruit trees there?"

"Of course! In the Hereafter it always takes the sun to ripen fruit, yes?"

"Yes."

"But some of the finest fruit in the Abarat is moon ripened. Smyrion fruit, for instance. Anyway, Theridia ate one fruit too many. The stone in the fruit caught in her throat. She choked on it and died there in the orchard."

"Oh, God . . ." Candy breathed.

"There's more. Do you want to hear the rest?"

"Yes . . ." Candy said softly.

"My father had a terrible temper. We were all deadly afraid of him. He didn't stop to mourn for my sister. His first thought was to punish the culprit. In this case, a tree. He sent all of us children into the mansion and then he went out with the servants and set fire to the orchard. . . ." Carrion halted, and took a deep breath. The nightmares coiled in the waters of his collar had retreated now, their brightness dimming. "There isn't much rain on Pyon," Carrion went on. "At least there wasn't in those days. I believe Pixler has a weather machine that brings rain to clean Commexo City once every twenty-five hours. But back then it was very dry. Once my father had started the fire, the flames quickly spread from branch to branch, tree to tree. My father, in his fury, didn't see that the sparks flew up into the air and were carried to the mansion. He had locked the doors, to keep his children from getting too close to the fire. He never imagined that the fire would come to us. The mansion went up in a matter of minutes! Only two of us escaped. Me and my grandmother. I was just a baby. She snatched me out of the cradle and carried me to safety."

"But your mother and your siblings?"

"All dead."

"What about your father?"

"He disappeared after the funerals, and we never saw him again. I suppose he may still be alive somewhere. Who knows?"

"That's so *sad*. . . ."

"Life goes on. You try to make sense of it, but in the end you think: why bother? There *is* no sense in it. Life. Death. None of it means anything." He paused. "And then, out of nowhere, something remarkable happens. You meet somebody who could help you make sense of your sadness, if you could only have that person at your side. . . ." He had dropped his gaze from Candy, but now he looked at her again, and his eyes were full of such feeling it was hard for Candy to meet them. "Maybe, you think, she could help you stop the nightmares. Do you understand what I'm saying?"

"I don't think . . ."

"It was her, at first. The Princess Boa. She was the first one who I thought might save me. She was so good, you know? So gentle. So full of love." His voice suddenly transformed. It grew harsh, and his eyes burned with fury. "But she didn't care about me. All she wanted was her pretty boy Finnegan, her darling with the dreadlocks. I begged her. I said: *I need you more than he does. My pain is deeper.* And of course when the time comes for changes to be made in these islands—*and it will come, very soon now*—I would have put her on a throne beside me.

"But no, no, no. It had to be Finnegan, always Finnegan. I wasn't handsome enough for her. I wasn't princely enough for her. I wasn't heroic enough. Finally she tired of my importuning and cast me aside." His voice dropped to a gray growl. "I think she probably lived long enough to regret her decision."

"She was killed, yes?"

"Yes. A terrible accident. On her wedding day, of all times. A dragon murdered her!" He drew a deep breath. "So in the end we both lost her. Finnegan and me. And when she was gone, I thought I would never again feel the hope that being with her had brought into my life." He frowned deeply, as though puzzled by his own words, his own thoughts. "But I was wrong," he said. "I feel that hope again. Thanks to you."

39

DRAGON BONES

THE EGG BENEATH FINNEGAN'S foot
was not full of dragon yolk; the infant inside it was
fully developed and quite capable of defending himself against his attacker. Sleek as a snake he wove his
way up Finnegan's leg in two or three seconds, and
then bit down on his flank. Finnegan let out a yelp of
pain and pinched hold of the infant at the base of his
skull, wrenching him left and right to unseat his grip.

While he was doing so, the adult rose up on her
massive body, and spoke.

"You should know better, Hob. We dragons are born
with the capacity to kill a man! Bite down, child! Suck
out his guts!"

Nythaganius Pejorius was too interested in her offspring's labors to take note of what her other assailants
were doing. Geneva leveled her sword and ran at the
worm as though the blade were a very short lance. It
entered Pejorius' belly, and Geneva thrust it all the
way to the hilt. A red fury erupted. The worm thrashed
and convulsed and spasmed and shrieked, her violence

causing earth to slide down into the hole where Tria had tumbled.

Seeing Tria's jeopardy, Mischief went to her aid, throwing himself and his brothers deeper into the hole.

"Slow down!" John Moot hollered.

"You'll get us all killed," Serpent complained.

"And watch out for that baby worm!" John Drowze put in.

The baby was indeed a danger to them, because Finnegan had now succeeded in wrestling his jaws from his flank and had thrown him down among the fragments of the shell. With the taste of human blood in his throat, the infant was now nosing around for fresh meat. He fixed his hungry gaze on Tria, and with the fearless abandon of a newborn thing he flung himself down into the hole beside her.

"We've got to distract him!" John Mischief said.

"I know!" John Drowze said. *"The Pugwit song!* All of you! Same order as always! Go!"

And with that Drowze broke out into a ridiculous song.

> *"Zoomit! Zeemit!*
> *Kila Kala Kuumit!"*

The nonsense words were taken up by John Slop after two lines, but he began at the beginning, while Drowze sang on.

> *"Shamshu! Sheshu!*
> *Shalat Shom!"*

And now John Serpent and John Fillet started to sing, beginning the song afresh, while Drowze continued.

> *"Pugwit! Wugwit!*
> *Wila Wola Wagmit!*
> *Chumshu! Chashu!*
> *Cholat Chom!"*

By this time all the brothers were singing this absurd round, and the result was the most wretched cacophony. It did the trick, however. The infant dragon was thoroughly confused by the noise. He forgot Tria, at least for the moment, and watched as the brothers sang their hearts out, making a threatening growl in the back of the throat.

Unfortunately the sides of the pit were becoming unstable—what with all this singing and dancing, and the earth now began to slide down into the hole.

"We're in trouble!" Moot yelled.

"I know! I know!" John Mischief replied.

"Girl!" John Drowze yelled to Tria. "Hold on!"

Tria took the brothers' hand, and with her free hand caught hold of Finnegan. Then they all struggled up the fast-collapsing wall of the hole, with only seconds to spare.

"You're wounded," Geneva said to Finnegan.

"It's nothing that will slow me!" he said. "But I've dropped my sword. Do you have one?"

"It's there," Geneva said, pointing to the place in Pejorius' belly where she had been obliged to leave the short blade.

"I need that—" Finnegan said, stumbling back toward the thrashing worm.

"Don't!" Geneva yelled.

Pejorius realized what Finnegan was up to and curled back her rotted lips, baring her fearful teeth.

"You ridiculous *clown!*" she hissed, her rage deepened by the agony Geneva's blade was causing her. "Come here! I dare you! I'll swallow you up and keep you alive in my belly for a year or two, dissolving you by degrees. How's that for a death, Finnegan Hob? You can die in the dark, slowly, slowly, slowly. . . ."

If Finnegan heard any of this loathsome speech, he made no sign of it. He crossed the churned earth zigzagging and bent double, like a soldier under fire, so as to confound the dragon's murderous eyes; and so doing he reached Pejorius' belly and seized hold of the hilt of the sword. He began to pull immediately, but most of the hard work was done by the dragon, who withdrew her body from the skewering blade with a roar louder than any din she had so far made. It disturbed a dunce-headed juffet bird in the red-and-purple thicket, and it rose up complaining: *"Juffetjuffetjuffetjuffet—"*

"Did you hear that, Deaux-Deaux?" Captain Malingo said.

They were standing on a road of yellow-white rock, which snaked off up into the interior of the Nonce.

"I think it was a juffet bird," Deaux-Deaux replied.

"No, just before the bird," Malingo said. "There was a roar. It came from somewhere along this road, Deaux-Deaux. We should investigate."

"Shouldn't we go back and get some help?" the Sea-Skipper said.

"There's no time. You *did* hear that roar, didn't you?"

"Maybe."

"It was a dragon, wasn't it?"

"Um . . . maybe."

"A very irritated dragon? And please don't say maybe!"

"Possibly."

"Then let's go. Where there are dragons, we'll probably find Finnegan Hob. And hopefully he won't be alone."

"All right," said Deaux-Deaux. "Just give me a moment." He went into the thicket and picked two very large thine nuts, which he cracked together. "This is hot weather for a Sea-Skipper to be without a little wet-down now and again."

The nuts drizzled their cool clear milk on his face and shoulders.

"That's better!" he said.

And he was off down the road, with Malingo following him.

"What a peculiar road," Malingo remarked as they leaped. "These stones are—"

"Begging your pardon, Cap'n, but I don't think these are stones."

"What are they then?"

"They're *bones*."

"Dragon bones?" said Malingo.

"Of course. You've heard, surely, of the Dragon

Road? It's the skeleton of the enormous worm that murdered the Princess Boa. Its head lies no more than fifteen yards from the door where it had gained entry to the cathedral and unraveled its tongue—"

"How was it that nobody saw it?" Malingo said.

Both he and Deaux-Deaux were gasping now, from the effort of leaping from vertebra to vertebra, but Malingo wanted answers.

"A lot of people have wondered about that over the years. I think the people outside the cathedral were murdered by assassins so they could not raise the alarm when the dragon approached. As for the deed itself, the dragon was very sly. It didn't enter the cathedral, you see. It pushed its snout against the door, and then its tongue, which was the true weapon in this murder, slid up the aisle. It was fully thirty foot long—"

"A tongue thirty feet long? Why didn't it choke itself on the thing?"

"Who knows how these beasts live? Or why they do what they do? The point is that the creature was well informed. It knew that the Princess' train reached to the door and that it could weave its tongue up through its folds, threading itself through the bows and the flowers. Nobody was looking down at the ground, you see. Everybody was watching Boa and Finnegan. They were just getting ready to exchange their vows."

"Which they never got to do."

"No. The creature waited until the very last moment—just before the Princess said: *I do*. The words were on her lips. But before she could speak, the dragon's tongue slipped around her throat and—"

"Yes, yes. I can do without the details," Malingo said.

"Sorry. You asked."

"Tell me who was responsible for this. Somebody trained the dragon, presumably?"

"No doubt," said Deaux-Deaux.

"So who?"

"Nobody knows. It would have taken a creature of great cruelty. Dragons only respond to hurt in their training, or so I've heard."

"Huh. After all these years . . . nobody knows? Amazing. And what about the dragon? Was it interrogated?"

"No. Finnegan killed it in a fit of fury. Caught it before it could get ten yards."

"How did he kill such a monster?"

"Oh, he was fearless. He leaped into the dragon's throat and allowed himself to be swallowed. Then he stabbed all its vital organs from the inside and hacked a hole in its flank and exited the corpse that way! There was a lot of talk about what to do with the body, I believe, but in the end it was decided to leave it here to be picked clean. In time it became a road. And a kind of monument."

"And nobody was ever brought to justice?"

"There was never proof enough to accuse anyone," Deaux-Deaux said. "Though I don't think there was ever much doubt of where the true guilt lay."

"Where?"

"In the House of Carrion," Deaux-Deaux replied. "The old woman, Mater Motley, was probably the chief culprit."

"But she was never questioned?"

"No. And there wasn't a judge on the Great Council who would dare stand up against Mater Motley. They'd be too afraid of waking up in the middle of the night and finding a stitchling sitting at the bottom of the bed, sharpening its tail."

They were almost at the end of the Dragon Road now. Climbing a shallow ridge, they came in sight of the great mass of churned earth where Pejorius had appeared out of the ground and the pit, over which a pall of dirt hung.

"Well, well," said Malingo. "Look at this. We've found who we were looking for. Now all we've got to do is stop them from being eaten alive."

Deaux-Deaux drew a long, slim knife.

"Have you ever fought a dragon before?" Malingo asked him.

"No," said Deaux-Deaux. "You?"

Malingo shook his head.

"But there's a first time for everything," he said, and letting out a bloodcurdling cry, he raced down the incline toward the pit and whatever had come up out of it.

40

A TALE OF ENDLESS PARTINGS

THE DRAGON, THOUGH HORRIBLY wounded, had not finished with her mischief. She continued to knot and unknot her body in its final convulsions, spitting out an insane catalogue of nonsenses, interspersed with eerie periods of lunatic laughter and speaking in tongues. Then, suddenly, she would recover her lucidity and lunge out at whoever was within range of her jaws. Mischief was the next victim. She snatched hold of the brothers and threw back her head so as to swallow them in a single gulp. But Mischief was in no mood to be swallowed. He braced his feet against the animal's lower jaw and his hands against her upper, nicking fingers and toes on the teeth of the thing as he did so. Then, making his body as stiff as a board, he simply refused to let the dragon close her mouth.

Had Pejorius been completely healthy, this maneuver would not have carried the day. The worm would simply have snapped her mouth closed, cracking Mischief's spine and swallowing him bent back in two. But the wound she had sustained from Geneva's sword was weakening her. Now that the blade was no longer in the wound, the dragon's blood ran freely from the hole, into which they had now all pitched themselves. The bitter stench of sin and corruption filled the air.

"We can't hold on here forever!" Mischief hollered. "Will somebody please—"

The last word was uttered by Fillet, Drowze, Moot, Slop, Serpent, Sallow and Pluckitt at the same time as Mischief, a brotherly chorus of: "HELP!"

As they loosed this shout, Deaux-Deaux appeared at the edge of the pit, with Malingo at his side.

"Who are you?" Finnegan said to them.

"The Fantomaya sent us!"

"Then HELP US!" the brothers yelled again.

"Let's just finish the beast!" Finnegan hollered. He waved to the newcomers. "If you've got a weapon, use it!"

Deaux-Deaux unsheathed his dagger and jumped down into the pit, and on a cue from Finnegan, the Sea-Skipper, Tom, Geneva and Hob pitched themselves at the dragon, thrusting their knives into her throat at the same time. There was no shriek, not even a sigh. The dragon's eyes simply emptied of life, and she sank down on the ground in her own blood.

"Gone," said Tria, very quietly.

Mischief's body—which was still wedged between Pejorius' lower and upper jaw—suddenly slipped, and for two or three fearful seconds it seemed the brothers would slip down the dragon's dead throat. A chorus of cries came from the Johns. McBean was the first to their aid.

"Hold on, hold on!" he yelled, reaching down to catch hold of John Mischief's arm. There was a second chorus (this of gratitude) from the brothers, and then applause from everybody when Mischief finally jumped down onto the ground.

"That was entirely too close for comfort," John Moot remarked.

"What happened to the infant?" Finnegan said, looking around.

"He slithered away," said John Fillet.

"You saw him go?" Finnegan went on. "Why didn't you stop him?"

"We were in the jaws of his parent at the time," Fillet replied.

"He won't get far," Malingo replied. "Besides, what harm can he do? He's alone."

Finnegan looked grim. "I'll tell you what he can do. He can make more of his species, when he comes to breeding age," he said. "Dragons are hermaphrodite. As long as there's one, there will be many again in time. What's your name, by the way?"

"Malingo," said the geshrat; so began a round of introductions and explanations and thanks and welcomings. By the time it was all over, the dust of conflict was beginning to settle. As it did so, a sprightly melody rose from somewhere in the thicket, which was picked up quickly from other places. The animal life in the vicinity was singing for joy, it seemed, now that the reign of Nythaganius Pejorius was over.

In fact, the real reason for this sudden chorus was rather more pragmatic; it was a summons to a feast of dragon flesh. In a matter of half a minute, birds came flying in from every direction: some as small as hummingbirds, some the size of vultures, some as elegant as herons, some as ungainly as penguins. Dozens at first, then hundreds, until there was a chattering assembly of several thousand birds covering the carcass of Pejorius from snout to tail; pushing their beaks under the scales of the beast to first fetch out the mites and lice which thrived upon the dragon's body, and then pecking through the skin to get to the rich, gamy meat beneath.

The noise of their dinnertime conversation was so loud that it drowned out all possibility of any exchanges between the company, so at Finnegan's suggestion they left the flocks to their gluttony and followed him to a small house made of white stone, which had been his residence while he was searching for the dragon. It was a spartan dwelling: a mattress on the floor, with a threadbare blanket and a comfortless pillow; a fire guttering in the grate with the remains of a pot of stew left on the hearth. A map of the Nonce was pinned up on the wall, with an extensive network of lines upon it, tracking Finnegan's various journeys around the Hour. And in pride of place above that uncomfortable bed, a simple painting of a pale-skinned, dark-haired young woman in a turquoise and orange tunic, roughly nailed to the cracked plaster.

"Who is the lady?" said Deaux-Deaux. The question earned him a dig in the ribs from Malingo. "What did I say?" Deaux-Deaux asked.

"That's *my* lady," Finnegan replied, staring up at the picture. "My Princess Boa."

"Oh . . . yes . . . of course," said Deaux-Deaux.

"She's beautiful," said Tria.

"The painting shows nothing of her true beauty. It's just an echo of an echo. She changed the air she breathed; she changed the earth she walked upon. She changed everything she saw, so that the world became new." Finnegan looked away from the picture and out through the window, though the view was partially obscured by a mass of plant life that had sprung up after the last rains. "The only way I can make sense of her passing is to be the destroyer of the race that murdered her. Only when every dragon is dead will I let my life go."

"Let your life go?" said Geneva, horrified at what Finnegan was implying. "How could you ever do such a thing; even *think* of it?"

"Because my life isn't here, in the Hours. It's with her. I want to be wherever my Princess is. I'm impatient to be gone, away, forever. But not until all the worms are cold."

"Well, there can't be many left," said John Mischief brightly.

"You're right," said Finnegan, with something like pleasure coming into his voice. "The job's almost done. I regret losing that infant . . . that was my stupidity. I should have known he would slip away. But if I go now, and quickly, the creature will not have grown too big."

"But you're injured," said Geneva.

"I heal fast. And I've been dealt worse wounds than this and survived, believe me. There's no time to be wasted. When dragons are high up the royal line, as that infant is, they grow fast. If they have the right nourishment, they can double their size in an hour."

"You're joking."

"I don't joke a lot any longer," Finnegan said with a tone of regret in his voice. "Certainly not about worms." He turned his sad eyes on the rest of the company. "Please rest here if you would like," he said. "There's food, which the Kadosh tribe who live hereabouts bring me: michelmas cake and curried meejab, in the pot. Plenty for all. You'll forgive me if I do not play host."

"Please wait a moment," Malingo said as Finnegan went to the door. "I was given strict instructions to fetch *everybody*, including you, Mister Hob. The women of the Fantomaya led me to believe that you are vital to how things will go if war is declared."

"I have already declared *my* war, Mister Malingo," Hob said. "And I've been fighting it for the better part of fifteen years. I spent a year on the slopes of Mount Galigali, tracking the dragons that live in the laval rivers. That was a difficult campaign. I was almost fried on several occasions when the volcano vented its fury. But I killed the worms. Sixteen of them. And then at Spake, which is a green and beautiful place— like the Nonce without the strange evolutions every time it rains—I hunted the five members of the Kaziamia clan, wretched, murderous things. Small for dragons, but vicious. That took more than a year. On Autland there was only one, but it had taken possession of the ruins of a palace, and it was *worshipped* by the local peasants, who swore a drop of its blood cured just about every kind of sickness. All nonsense, of course. But they can be very clever, very deceitful. . . ."

"I should have thought by now you would have made your point," said John Drowze.

There was a long silence. Very, very slowly Finnegan looked at the brothers.

"My point?" he said. "My *point*? And what, pray, do you imagine that might be? Would I have made it with ten worms dead? Ten times ten? Or would the death of one have sufficed, in your opinion, *to make my point*?"

Drowze opened his mouth to reply, but John Mischief quietly put his forefinger to his brother's lips and very quietly said: "Be quiet, John."

Geneva now stepped into the middle of the conversation.

"Mister Hob," she said with great respect. "I think what we want you to hear is that we *need* you. Right now, there's only us, and the women of the Fantomaya—"

"And Candy," said Malingo.

"Well, perhaps," Geneva said. "But we're few, that's my point. And Carrion is very strong."

All eyes were on Finnegan, everyone waiting for him to give them an answer. He stared out of the window.

"Let me go and think on this for a little while,"

Finnegan said. "Please, help yourself to the meejab and michelmas cake. . . ."

So saying, he inclined his head slightly, and left.

"Strange fellow," John Moot remarked.

"He's not going to come," Tria said.

"He *must*," Malingo said. "Diamanda was very insistent. I think she believes he's the key to everything, for some reason."

"Oh, look," Tom said. "More rain."

He was right. A few fat spots of rain were bursting on the windowsill, and the downpour could be heard on the roof as well.

Malingo went over to Geneva. "Do you think I should talk to him?" he said.

"To Finnegan?"

"Yes."

"You could try. But I wouldn't hope too hard."

Malingo stepped out into the warm rain. Finnegan was standing several yards from the house, his face turned up to the downpour. He glanced around at Malingo for a moment, then went back to his rain bath.

"Do you know the legend of this Hour?" he said.

"No, I don't believe I do," Malingo replied.

"Apparently, somewhere on the Nonce (though I've never seen them) is a tribe of winged creatures called the Fathathai. A gentle, shy people: almost like angels. There are very few of them on the island because"—he looked at his feet—"because they don't find love very easily, and so a Fathathai wedding is a rare event. But anyway, the legend goes that there was one of these creatures by the name of Numa Child, who *did* fall in love."

"Lucky him."

"Well, yes and no. You see, he fell in love with a woman he met here on the Nonce, called Elathuria. She was, he thought, the most beautiful woman he had ever set eyes on. There was only one problem."

"What was that?"

"She wasn't flesh and blood as he was."

"What was she?"

"As you know, this island is home to some very strange life-forms. And Elathuria was one of these strangenesses." He paused, then looked up at Malingo as he said: "She was a plant."

Malingo only managed to suppress a laugh because there was such a look of deadly seriousness on the dragon killer's weary face. And though he *did* manage to suppress it, Finnegan nevertheless said: "You think I'm joking."

"No . . ."

"I've learned only two things in my life. One, that love is the beginning and end of all meaning. And two, that it is the same thing whatever shape our souls have taken on this journey. Love is love. Is love."

Malingo nodded. "I've had no . . . personal experience of this," he said to Finnegan. "But . . . I've read books. And all the great ones agree with you." Finnegan nodded, and for the first time since they'd met, Malingo saw something resembling a smile come onto the man's face. "Please tell me the rest of the story," the geshrat said.

"Well, when Numa Child first met Elathuria she was in full bloom. She was perfection. No other word for it."

"Extraordinary."

"It gets stranger still, believe me. Did I tell you Numa Child fell in love in a heartbeat? I mean, literally, it was that fast. He saw Elathuria, and that was it. His fate was sealed."

"Love at first sight."

"Absolutely."

"Do you believe in that?"

"Oh, certainly. It happened to me. The very moment I set eyes on the Princess Boa, I knew that there was no other soul I could ever love. No other, to the end of the Hours." Finnegan looked up at the rain, which was beginning to ease. He licked some of the raindrops off his lips, then he went on telling the story.

"So Numa Child told Elathuria instantly. *'Lady,'* he said. *'I will never love anyone the way I love you.'* And much to his surprise, Elathuria invited him to kiss her.

"*'Quickly,'* she said. *'Because the sun is hot and the hour is passing.'*

"Numa didn't think very much about the significance of this. He was simply happy to be invited to kiss his beloved. And as they kissed and talked and kissed again, the hour of the Nonce ticked away. . . ."

"This isn't going to end happily, is it?" Malingo said.

Finnegan didn't answer. He just went on with his story. "When Numa Child kissed her again, there was a little bitterness on her lips.

"*'What's happening?'* he said to her.

"She told him: *'Time is passing, my beloved.'*

"And to his horror, he saw that her blossoms, which had been so bright and beautiful when he'd first set eyes on her, were now beginning to lose that brightness, and her green leaves were beginning to turn gold and brown."

Finnegan's voice, as he told this part of the story, grew soft and full of sadness.

"Finally she said to him: *'Don't leave me, love. Promise me you'll never leave. Find me again, wherever I go. Find me.'*

"Of course, Numa didn't understand what she was telling him. *'What do you mean?'* he asked her.

"But it soon became clear. She was leaving him. The wind had risen, and it was shaking her, the way it would shake a tree, so that its blossoms and leaves fall, and its beauty is carried away. That was what was happening to Elathuria. She was losing her very being, right in front of his eyes. It was terrible."

Malingo heard the catch in Finnegan's throat as he spoke and looked up to see that there were tears running down Finnegan's cheeks.

"Elathuria was still strong enough to speak to Numa. *'Look for me wherever the wind comes,'* she said, her voice getting more and more hushed. *'I will grow again from the seed that is carried away from this place.'*

"Numa was, of course, happy to hear this, but his mind was filled with questions and doubts.

"*'Will it really be you?'* he said to her.

"'*Yes*,' she told him. '*It will be me in every particularity. Except one.*'

"'*And what's that?*' Numa asked her.

"'*I won't remember you,*' she replied.

"Even as she spoke these words, a breath of harsh wind sprang up and shook her violently, so that she was entirely shaken apart—"

"No!" Malingo said. "Had she gone?"

"Well . . . yes and no. The wind had scattered the seeds over a considerable distance, but Numa was determined to find some trace of her—*any* trace—so he searched like a wild man, not resting until his search was rewarded.

"At last, after a long time searching for her, he finally found her, rooted in a new place. She was still growing, but he knew her immediately, and fell in love with her again, just as he had the first time."

"And she with him?"

"Yes, of course."

"Even though she didn't remember him?"

"Yes. She was still the same soul, after all. And so was he. . . ."

Now Malingo began to see the significance of what he was being told. It was no accident that Finnegan was the bearer of this story; he was, after all, here on this island because he had lost the love of his life. It stood to reason that this legend would capture his imagination as it so clearly did.

"So history repeated itself?" Malingo said.

"Indeed it did. Not once, but over and over. Though Numa Child swore his undying devotion to Elathuria, the hour would always pass, and the wind would always come and she would be carried away to some new place. Sometimes he would find her quickly. Sometimes not."

"And so do you really think they're still out there, loving each other, and then being separated, and him finding her again, only to be separated again?"

"Yes. I do," Finnegan said.

"What a terrible way to live."

Finnegan considered this for a moment. "Love makes its demands, and you listen. You can't bargain with it. You can't fight it. Not if it's really love."

"Are you still talking about Numa Child and Elathuria?" Malingo said.

Finnegan looked up at him. "I'm talking about *all* lovers," he said.

"Ah," said Malingo. "I see. This is your way of telling me that you won't be joining us on our voyage."

"No, no. You misunderstand me. It's my way of telling you I *will*. But that I must come back here to the Nonce when our work is done."

"To kill what's left of the dragons?"

"To keep searching," Finnegan said. "Let's leave it at that, shall we? Just to keep searching."

41

AN AMBITIOUS CONJURATION

"**W**E HAVE TO GO!" Tria said when Malingo and Finnegan came inside.

"What's the hurry?"

"She had a vision!" said Deaux-Deaux.

"It was very impressive," John Drowze observed.

"One of the women of the Fantomaya," Geneva said. "The old woman, Diamanda. She's dead, Malingo."

"By whose hand?" Malingo asked grimly. "Surely the war hasn't already begun?"

"No, no. Apparently she went to the aid of Candy Quackenbush and was killed by one of the Beasts of Efreet. Not a happy death."

"So she wants us to kill the beast that killed her?" Finnegan said, his bloodlust roused.

"*No!*" said Tria with more agitation in her voice than anyone had heard before. "This isn't about avenging Diamanda. It's Candy we have to save. She's in the Dead Man's House, on Efreet."

"What's it doing there?" John Mischief said.

"The Lord of Midnight brought it there," Tria reported.

"As a trap?" said Mischief.

"Yes."

"Which the Quackenbush girl, of course, fell into," said John Serpent.

"How was she to know?" said John Moot.

Serpent made a moan. "Why does everybody *always* defend her? I'm telling you, that girl is *trouble*. She was trouble right from the very beginning, and she will—"

"Shut up!" said Tria. Her volume, not to mention the uncharacteristic vehemence in her words, instantly silenced Serpent.

"Yes," said Malingo a little more quietly. "Well, that's you told. Now we have to do something about getting Candy out of the Dead Man's House before Carrion . . ." He shook his head, unable to voice the worst.

"It's a long way down to the ship," Deaux-Deaux said grimly.

"And when we get there, we have to plan a course—" said McBean.

"Pray for a favorable wind—" said Tom.

"There's no time for ships!" Malingo said.

"What do you have in mind?" said Geneva.

There was a little silence into which Malingo gently lobbed two words.

"A glyph."

The ripple effect spread across the room, bringing to each face its own combination of doubt, confusion and a tiny breath of hope.

"Where would we *get* such an unlikely means of transport?" John Mischief asked Malingo.

"It takes *magic*, surely," said McBean.

"Big magic," said Geneva.

"But it can be done," Malingo said. Then, with a show of confidence he didn't exactly feel, he added: "I can do it."

"You can?" said Geneva.

"I did it before. Just once."

"And did the glyph fly?" said Finnegan.

"Yes. It flew. Of course it was only a two-seater. This one would need to be much bigger."

"We'll help," said Tria. "All of us can work together."

"I think it's our only choice," said Finnegan. "If getting this girl is such an urgent business, then the ship's not going to get us there in time."

"Well then," said Tom. "We should start."

"First we need to clear a space outside," Malingo said.

This being the Nonce, of course, there was greenery everywhere. But Tom quickly took charge and organized the clearing of an area of ground about twenty yards wide. It was hard, hot work in the eternal Afternoon of the Nonce, but they got the job done quickly, Finnegan and Tom laboring with particular gusto.

Malingo, meanwhile, took himself off a little distance from the clearing and meditated on the task that he was about to undertake. When he came back, John Mischief said: "How does this conjuration actually *work*? I've seen a few pieces of big magic in my time, but I've never actually understood the principle of it."

"Neither do I," Malingo admitted. "It's a spell I first read in one of Kaspar Wolfswinkel's books."

"So if something goes wrong . . ."

"We just have to pray that it won't."

The ground had now been cleared, and everybody was waiting—not looking at Malingo necessarily (well, perhaps from the corners of their eyes)—and wondering when he was going to begin the conjuration. As for Malingo, he was jiggling from foot to foot as though he were in need of a toilet.

"Are you all right?" Deaux-Deaux said.

"Yeah . . . just a bit nervous, that's all."

"You'll do just fine," the Sea-Skipper reassured him. "We're in this together, right?"

"Right."

"But we should start, my friend. Time's a-wastin'."

Malingo nodded. "I know. I know," he said. "I was just getting limbered up." He wiped the beads of golden geshrat sweat from his brow with his arm and went to stand in the middle of the cleared ground.

"I'm going to need all your concentration," Malingo said. "We need to act as one mind. All pull together."

"To do *what*?" said John Moot.

"There's a summoning chant, which I will start reciting. I want everyone to join in with me."

"And this helps the conjuration?" Mischief said.

"No, I'm just embarrassed to do it on my own," Malingo said with a big grin. "Yes, Mischief, it would help greatly. When I start circling and throwing air—"

"Doing what?" said Tom.

"You'll see," said Malingo. "You just fall in step and copy what I'm doing. Now, everyone spread out in a rough circle. That's it. There's nothing to be worried about. If the conjuration doesn't work, we simply won't get a glyph."

"And Candy's left there to the tender mercies of Christopher Carrion—" said Mischief. *"No."* He looked intently from one person to the next until he'd completed the circle. *"This has to work."*

"Let's do it," said Malingo, and closed his eyes. In his mind's eye he saw the scene on Ninnyhammer when he and Candy had performed this ritual together. It was wonderfully clear in his head. He took a deep breath, raised his hands over his head and clapped three times.

Then he began to recite the words of the spell.

> *"Ithni asme ata,*
> *Ithni manamee,*
> *Drutha lotacata,*
> *Come thou glyph to me.*
> *Ithni, ithni,*
> *Asme ata:*
> *Come thou glyph to me."*

The syllables came easily to his lips, and once he'd established their rhythm, he opened his eyes and began to walk around the circle snatching at the air *outside* it and tossing it in.

"Ah," Two-Toed Tom murmured. "So that's *throwing air.*"

Geneva was the first to join in with what Malingo was doing, adding her own powerful voice to that of the geshrat. Then, one by one, the rest picked up on the process and added their voices and gestures to the conjuration: all circling as they spoke the words and caught the air.

"When will we know whether it's working or not?" McBean whispered to Mischief somewhere between the fourth repetition and the fifth.

"Oh, I think we'll know," Mischief said.

He had no sooner replied than a few sparks ignited in their midst, their colors intense, even in the brightness of midafternoon. They weren't just red and blue, as the sparks had been the first time Malingo had performed this ritual. Now they were also violet and lime and gold. They wove around and around like delirious fireflies, leaving trails of color behind them as they quickened.

"*Yes!*" Malingo said. "*It's happening.* Don't stop, everyone. Keep the ritual going."

The beauty of this display gave the novice magicians confidence. Their voices became stronger, their snatching at the air more rhythmical. And in turn, as their confidence grew, so did its effect. The dance of light became more ambitious, the colors beginning to weave an elaborate shape in the Noncian air. Malingo let out a whoop of pleasure, seeing his ambitions for his second glyph were going to be realized. He could already recognize the immense curve of its bow, and the backward sweep of its cabin.

And still the number of fireflies grew, and their

elegant dance became more elaborate, so that everyone in the circle of conjurors (even the resolutely unimpressed John Serpent) wore expressions of pleasure, seeing word become fact in front of them.

"We can stop now," Malingo said after a certain point. "It will finish itself."

The novices stood back and watched in delight as the glyph did as Malingo had predicted. The points of light apparently knew their own way from here on, weaving themselves an invisible loom, back and forth and around and around, until the shimmering vehicle stood completed, shining in the afternoon sun and steaming ever so slightly from the heat of its coming into being.

"I dreamed this once. . . ." Finnegan said to himself as he stared in amazement at the craft. "Long ago . . . I dreamed it flew down from another galaxy."

"We should get going," said Tria.

"Indeed we should," Malingo chimed. "Candy needs us."

"Does anyone have a map?" said McBean.

"I've got an old copy of the *Almenak*," Tom volunteered.

"We won't need a map, actually," Malingo said. "The glyph will take direction from our thoughts."

"Clever piece of work," Deaux-Deaux remarked.

"It really *is*," Geneva said. "Amazing."

She opened the door and ducked her head down to step inside. She was not easily impressed, but the iridescent gleam of the glyph, contrived from air and syllables, had her smiling. "Congratulations, Malingo," she said. "It's a fine thing."

"Don't go congratulating me too soon," Malingo replied cautiously. "We haven't got it flying yet."

But there was little doubt that the glyph was ready for its duties. It looked visibly excited at the prospect of its maiden flight. Thousands of tiny motes of energy flickered through its form, starting at the nose of the craft and surging through its frame in schools of flickering particles, which then assembled at the other end of the glyph in what was apparently the engine: a ball of light and force, which was in constant chaotic motion. As everybody climbed into the craft, the engine picked up power. It gave off a noise like a choir of several thousand people all whispering a poem in some secret language. The glyph vibrated slightly. The doors closed with a soft sigh.

"Are we ready?" Malingo said.

"No!" said John Mischief. "I don't like this thing!" He started to pull at the door. "It's going to kill us all!"

"Calm down!" said Deaux-Deaux. "We're quite safe."

"No, we're not! *We're not!* I want to get out!"

"Well, I don't," said John Moot.

"Neither do I," said John Fillet.

In two seconds a chaotic argument erupted, with all the Johns throwing in their opinions at the same time.

"It's too late to leave," Geneva yelled over the din of angry voices. "We're moving!"

"She's right!" said Tom. "We're off!"

"Hold on!" Malingo yelled.

Before he could finish speaking, the vehicle rose straight up into the air.

"Yowza!" yelled John Moot.

"I'm warning you all," John Serpent said. "I'm going to be sick!"

The glyph came to a halt about thirty feet off the ground and began to spin around, pointing its nose first at Noon, then to the Twenty-Fifth Hour, then Midnight.

Halfway through all of this, John Serpent opened the door and made good on his promise.

"Be careful, son . . ." McBean said, speaking with a captain's caution. "Slowly does it."

"I don't have any more control over it," Malingo said. "I think it senses how impatient we are. It wants to get us there! Double quick!"

"Well, let's go then!" said Finnegan, standing up to peer out of the front window. "I'm suddenly looking forward to this fight with Carrion!" He turned to Malingo. "Does it hear me, geshrat?"

Malingo didn't need to supply an answer. The glyph did so. Its whole structure seemed suddenly to erupt with larval waves of iridescence.

"This is it!" said Deaux-Deaux.

With that the glyph took off toward Efreet, leaving the sky above the Nonce with such speed that it caused a spontaneous monsoon in the air above its creation space, which filled the ground they had worked to clear with a steamy little jungle of new birds and blossoms.

42

THE HIGH MAZE

O F ALL THE SHOCKS and amazements of her journeys in the Abarat, surely this meeting on the narrow stairs was the strangest! Standing on the steps below her was the Lord of Midnight, the terror of the islands. She had heard him talked of as though he were the very Devil made flesh. But now she wasn't so sure. He was ugly, certainly, and dangerous too. But there was also something pitiful about him. She did not doubt that behind that broken face of his there was suffering and sorrow.

He stared up at her, his eyes drained of color. "You know, of course, that I'm supposed to kill you in this house?" he said. "My grandmother believes you are a disruptive force in the Abarat. She believes that unless you're stopped you'll cause our plans to be . . . inconvenienced."

"Your grandmother hasn't even met me."

"Oh. Are you suggesting that if she did, she'd change her opinion?"

"Look at me," Candy said. "I'm no danger to you,

or anyone. I'm just a girl from Chickentown who got lost here by accident."

"Is anything really an accident?" he said.

"Of course. Things happen all the time that . . ." She was going to say weren't supposed to happen, but she realized as she was about to say it that she no longer entirely believed it to be true. The words trailed away.

"Finish your thought."

"It doesn't matter."

"Well, if it's any comfort, I'm lost too. Lost and alone."

"What about your grandmother?"

"She's not much of a comfort to me," he replied, with a thin smile. "Nor I to her, I suppose. Though we are the last of our line; you'd think we'd have learned to take solace wherever it can be found." He fell silent for several moments, the creatures in his collar slowing their motion as if matching his melancholy mood. "But no," he said finally. "I have looked and looked for someone who would understand me. Just a little. That's all. Just understand, a little. The night is very dark sometimes. And in Gorgossium, of course, it's endless."

Was the sorrow in his voice and expression just an act, Candy wondered? Somehow she didn't think so. The creature standing on the stairs was confessing something true here. But why? She had her answer in his next words.

"Perhaps you would understand . . ."

"Me?"

"You said you were lost. Perhaps we have more in common than it might seem."

She wanted to tell him he was crazy, that there was nobody either in this world or the Hereafter she could imagine having *less* in common with. But she kept her thoughts to herself. It was safer that way. Instead she tried to return the conversation to the subject of Mater Motley.

"I thought you said your grandmother wanted me dead."

"I'll change her mind for her," he replied confidently. "I'll show her that we've nothing to fear from you. That we understand each other."

It was strange to hear the Lord of Midnight talking about *her* as the one people might have reason to fear, not himself.

"You look perplexed," Carrion said.

"Yes . . . well, I guess I am," Candy admitted. "I just don't know what it is your grandmother—or you, come to that—see in me. But whatever it is I'm supposed to be . . . I'm not."

"No?" he said, very softly.

He smiled and reached up to take hold of her hand. No doubt it was a perfectly innocent gesture, but there was something about the way that the smile made his face look—*like a death's head, grinning in its rot*—that made Candy pull her hand away so that he couldn't catch hold of it.

His response to her rejection was instant, and *terrifying*.

The nightmares that had been quieted in his collar suddenly became bright as lightning, and he reached for her with a burst of speed. This time she wasn't fast enough to outmaneuver him. His fingers knitted with hers. And the moment they did so, all was changed.

The horrors she'd thought she'd glimpsed when he was sloughing off the face of Pius Masper (and which she'd convinced herself she had *not* seen) appeared in all their repulsive glory around her. A procession of monstrosities—*all gloating, glaring, gaping*—rose around her the moment Carrion locked his fingers with hers; it was as though the Devil had unleashed every beast in the asylums of hell and put them to dance around her.

"No!" she yelled, and mustering more strength than she thought she possessed, she pulled her hand free.

For a terrible instant it seemed their separation would not free her from the infernal dance, and the creatures continued to lope and caper around her. Then the sickening spectacle began to gutter like a dying firework, and finally it went out.

She was standing on the stairs again, as though nothing had happened.

But of course it had.

Now she knew the truth. She had just been granted a glimpse of the real Christopher Carrion. Not with her eyes, but with her mind.

Carrion knew perfectly well what had happened. His bluff had been called; the rot in his soul had been laid out for Candy in all its vile detail.

"I . . . am . . . ashamed," he said.

"Yes . . ." Candy replied, slowly backing away from him. "I don't blame you. I'd feel pretty bad if that was what *I* really looked like."

He had one last manipulation to try.

"It's terrible," he said. "To live with this . . . this . . . *grotesquerie* in me. Until I saw you, I had given up on the hope of ever being healed. But perhaps you can help me change."

It didn't take Candy long to summon up an answer.

"I'm sorry about that, whatever you called it—"

"Grotesquerie."

"Yes, that. But I can't help you." She kept her tone as reasonable as possible, all the while retreating from him slowly, afraid that he'd suddenly rush her, suddenly catch hold of her again, and the parade would return to flood her mind. She couldn't bear it. Not again. Behind her, however, was a closed door. This house seemed to have so many of them. She'd had her back to a locked door when she'd tried to get *into* the house, and now here was another when she wanted to get out.

"Listen to me, Candy," Carrion said, his tone all comfort and sweet reason. "I know what you're afraid of. And I swear, I *swear*, you'll never again see what you saw a few moments ago. That was unforgivable. And yet—knowing that it was unforgivable—I ask you nevertheless to forgive me. Can you do that? No, I know that you can. The question is: *will* you?"

She didn't answer him. She simply turned and put her shoulder to the door. The lock was rusty, but the wood around it was dark with rot, which gave her the tiny hope that she might still escape him.

"What are you doing?" he asked her, as if he genuinely didn't know.

Candy didn't waste her breath on replying. Instead

she threw her body against the door. There was a cracking sound as the rotted wood around the lock began to give out.

"*Think*, please," Carrion whispered. "Even if you open that door there's nowhere for you to go. There's just snow up there. You'll freeze to death in a matter of minutes."

"There are worse things," Candy said. Then, with one last heave, she threw the door open. The wind carried a stinging wall of ice shards and snow against her face.

She glanced back at the Lord of Midnight one final time—just long enough to meet his despairing gaze. He looked as though he was about to say something to her, to make one last appeal, but she didn't give him the opportunity. Squinting against the chilly blast, she stepped out onto the roof and she slammed the door behind her, though she knew of course that it wasn't going to keep Carrion from following her for more than ten seconds.

It was even less than that.

A mere heartbeat later, the door was shoved open, and the foul light that pulsed from his nightmares came pouring out across the snow, catching her in its vivid spill.

"Candy!" he shouted to her. "Stop this foolishness! You'll fall and break your neck!"

She looked ahead. The steeply gabled roof was slick with wet snow. No easy escape route presented itself.

"*Come back here,*" said Carrion. "I'm not going to

hurt you. On my life, Candy. I would *never* hurt you. Don't you see: you're my salvation? Don't you understand? *My salvation.*"

Candy ignored his contradictions and pushed on through the snow. It became thicker the farther from the door she ran. Soon she was up to her ankles in it. And apart from the spill of light from the nightmares, which brightened and dimmed depending on how far ahead of her pursuer Candy was able to get, there was no illumination to guide her over the treacherous maze of slates and gargoyles and guttering. But what choice did she have? If she stopped for a moment, he'd catch up with her. She had to *move*, risking her life with every benighted step.

Carrion continued to call to her, of course; continued to try and bring her back to him. He'd given up talking about salvation now. He had moved on to naked threats.

"You want me to leave you out here?" Carrion called to her. "There's another storm front moving in from the northwest. The snow will be ten feet deep in an hour or two. And you'll be buried underneath the snow, small and blue and dead. Is that the way you want your life to end, Candy? You, who could have been so *much*?"

Still she didn't reply to him. She wouldn't give him the satisfaction of glancing back over her shoulder at him. Nothing he could say—not the threats, not the flattery, not the appeals to sentiment—could put the images she'd seen of his true self out of her head. However civilized his talk might be, he was a monster down to the depths of his soul.

So she kept running. The roof was like an enormous labyrinth, rising dark against the sky to either side of her, the passageways between them zigzagging crazily. At every other turn she would encounter one of the stone gargoyles, its shape horrible. The gargoyles seemed to watch her as she passed them by, as though at any moment they might pounce on her. It was when she came upon the same gargoyle, its head split open and lined with teeth, that she realized she was running in circles.

She had hoped that her footprints would keep her from moving in circles, but the snow was coming down so fast now it erased her steps.

She might have wept with frustration if she'd had the energy, but she didn't. It was all used up. Her legs were numb with cold. So were her hands and her face. All she could do was stumble on, looking for some way out, with Carrion's threat—*you'll be underneath the snow, small and blue and dead*—echoing in her head.

A gust of wind raised a strangely brightened cloud of snow, and she was momentarily blinded. She wiped the stinging particles from her eyes and suddenly—there was Carrion! Somehow he'd outmaneuvered her in the darkness, gotten ahead of her or climbed over one of the roofs.

"The chase is over," he said. "Come here." He opened his arms. "Look at you! You're frozen! I said: *come here.*"

He reached out for her again. She had so little

strength left in her she could barely draw breath to speak. But she found it somewhere.

"Once . . . and for all . . . LEAVE ME ALONE!"

Her voice echoed off the roofs and came back to meet her sounding unlike herself: thin with exhaustion and shrill with fear. The strangeness of the sound saved her from his grip at least for a moment longer. He stared at her in that moment, as though there was something *inside* her that he wanted to pry out before he put an end to her. There was time, in his hesitation, for Candy to turn from him and look back the way she'd come for some last route of escape.

There was only one possibility. Off to her left there was a steep roof, with a narrow metal ladder, almost concealed in the snow, laid against it. She called up the final dregs of strength from her numb limbs and made a stumbling run for the ladder, throwing one quick look over her shoulder at Carrion to see if he was giving chase. He was. In desperation she threw herself toward the roof, and seized hold of the iron rungs. Then—trying not to think of what pursued her, or of what choices awaited her when she reached the apex of the roof—she started to climb the frozen ladder.

43

THE DARK DENIED

"**M**Y GRANDMOTHER WAS RIGHT!" Carrion yelled up at her as she ascended. "You *are* crazy! Crazy and dangerous! Why are you putting off the inevitable? *Give in,* little girl. This is just adding pain to pain. I've told you over and over: *there's nowhere left* to run!"

Candy was a little more than halfway up the ladder, and she could see from here that Carrion was right: once she got to the top, she would have nowhere left to go. All Carrion would have to do was catch hold of her and unleash that ghastly parade of monstrosities so it could invade her head.

"Are you listening to me, Candy Quackenbush?" Carrion yelled.

Candy glanced back down at him. From this curious angle, his head looked as though it was floating in a pot of some kind. He stared up at her from the fluid that bubbled around his face like the prize serving in a cannibal's stew. Exertion, or rage, or a combination of the two, had turned the whites of his eyes a dark purplish

color. His irises, by contrast, had become nearly colorless.

"Give it up, girl," Carrion said. "You just cause
trouble wherever you go. Unhappiness. Suffering.
Death. It's time it ended. You're better gone, for everybody's sake."

The words stung Candy more sharply than the ice-
pricked wind. There was too much truth in them; that
was why they hurt so much.

Back in Chickentown she'd lived a boring but
blameless life. She'd done no harm to those she came
in contact with, but then neither had she improved
their lives in any way. Whereas here in the Abarat, for
some reason, whatever she did seemed to carry more
significance. Wherever she'd gone on her journey—to
the Yebba Dim Day, which stood at Eight in the
Evening, to Ninnyhammer, to the Time Out of Time at
the Twenty-Fifth Hour, to Babilonium, to Scoriae and
even Efreet—the effect of her presence had had some
real influence on the lives she had touched. She had no
idea why, but things *happened* in her vicinity: strange,
unpredictable things. The established rules of the
world into which she'd come were overturned.

It wasn't always disastrous. Sometimes she'd
helped people, Malingo, for instance. But she feared it
was only a matter of time before something truly tragic happened. Not to her, most likely, but to some innocent whose path she had crossed.

All this went through her head at lightning speed in
the time it took Carrion to climb perhaps three rungs of
the ladder. He would be able to reach her in a matter of

seconds. She could no longer climb with her back to him, she decided. Moving slowly, for fear of losing her footing on the icy rungs, she carefully turned around on the ladder, so that she could ascend the rest of the way with her eyes on her pursuer. If he got too close, she could still kick at him, she thought. In fact, his face looked vulnerable right now staring up at her, despite all she knew about the horrors that lay in wait behind it. Yes, damn him, she would kick hard, if it was the last thing she did.

He watched her watching him.

"What are you thinking?" he wondered aloud. "You're a mystery, girl."

She climbed as he talked to her, her feet constantly threatening to slide on the rungs of the ladder. But her caution paid off. She reached the apex of the roof without incident, and looked down the other side. It was her last frail hope that there'd be some way to get back into the house on this side of the roof. But no. The news was bad, all bad. There was just a steep roof awaiting her; and off the roof, straight down to ice-hardened ground below. It would be a quick death, she supposed. But death it would be.

"What did I tell you?" Carrion said, seeing any remaining glimmer of hope fade from Candy's face. "Nowhere left to go."

He reached up to her. "Come. I'll make it quick. I promise."

"Wait—"

"What?"

"Suppose—"

"What?"

"Suppose I promised I'd go?"

"Go where?"

"Home," she said. "Back to the Hereafter."

"Bargains now?"

"You don't want to kill me."

"How would you know what I want?"

"I don't know *how* I know, but I do. Maybe you're right. Maybe we do understand each other somehow. I know you don't want to kill me, whatever Mater Motley says. You don't want it on your conscience."

"Ha! Listen to her! I'm a Carrion, girl. I don't *have* a conscience."

"I don't believe you," Candy replied with steady certainty.

"Well then, let me prove it to you," Carrion said, his face knotted up with so many conflicting emotions Candy couldn't read it clearly.

He started up the ladder toward her, but as he did so a gust of wind came sweeping up the roof behind him, gathering a freight of ice shards as it came. It flew in Candy's face, and for a moment she was blinded. She flailed, attempting to keep her balance, but the ladder was too slick beneath her feet. Her hold slipped and she started to topple backward. For just a few seconds, she almost managed to regain her equilibrium, but it was a short reprieve. Her left heel slid off the top of the roof, and back she went.

For a long terrifying moment she fell through empty air, not knowing sky from ground. Then she hit the roof, faceup. The thump knocked the breath from her, and she started to slide down the slates headfirst. Somewhere high above her, she thought she saw something passing between the snow-laden clouds—a bright shape that appeared for no more than a heartbeat and was then obscured again, its coming and going so swift she was not entirely certain that she'd even *seen* it.

The moon, was it? No, the moon didn't move so fast—

An instant later she hit a waste pipe that had been run across the roof, and the impact swung her around. Her body moved faster than her mind. Without even thinking about it, she reached up and caught hold of the pipe. It creaked, but it didn't give way. She clung there for several seconds, desperately trying to catch her breath. It was hard to do, stretched out on the roof as she was, hanging on for dear life. And then, as if she didn't have enough to trouble her, she heard the sound of motion behind and above her, and looked up to see that Carrion had clambered up the ladder onto the apex of the roof and was standing there, his arms spread, as if welcoming the snowstorm in all its killing fury.

"What a view!" he said. "The sky. You. The drop."

He squatted down, balancing on the top of the roof with uncanny ease. Then he reached down toward her.

"I could practically push you from here," he said.

"There!" said Finnegan. *"Down there!"*

"I see her!" Malingo yelled.

The glyph responded instantly to their thoughts. It

swooped out of the clouds toward the roof of the Dead Man's House.

"We're not going to make it!" John Slop yelled. "She's going to fall!"

"I can't look," said John Drowze. "Mischief! Cover my eyes!"

"Down!" Finnegan willed the descending vehicle. *"Down!"*

The glyph immediately did as it was instructed, but dropped with such suddenness that it slipped past Candy.

"Up! Up!" Finnegan was now yelling. He beat his fist against the roof of the cabin. "Damn machine!"

The glyph rose again, reeling. The travelers were buffeted around, knocked from one side of the glyph to the other, but nobody complained, not even John Serpent. Everyone was concentrating on the sight now coming into view: Candy clinging by her fingertips to the pipe on the roof.

Finnegan opened up the top of the vehicle so as to be ready to catch hold of Candy as soon as she was in reach. Deaux-Deaux went one step further and actually clambered past Finnegan and stood on the roof. He was unconcerned by the glyph's motion. He was a Sea-Skipper, after all; he was used to walking on the sides of waves. He balanced on the rolling glyph like a surfer on a tilting board.

"Candy!" he yelled.

She chanced a quick look over her shoulder. Even managed a smile.

"You're going to have to let go, lady!" Finnegan said.

"I'll fall!"

"We'll be here to catch you!"

"Trust us!" the John brothers yelled.

Candy looked up at Carrion one last time. Whatever happens next, she thought, I hope I never see his face again.

Then she let go of the pipe.

"Catch me!" Deaux-Deaux yelled to Finnegan, then threw himself forward, catching hold of her hand. It was an act of pure trust. If Finnegan hadn't been fast enough to grab hold of Deaux-Deaux's foot and arm, both Candy and the Sea-Skipper would have fallen to their deaths. For a few perilous moments, they clung to one another while the glyph tipped and rolled.

Meanwhile, up on the roof, Carrion was pointing toward the glyph, muttering something. Malingo let out a low moan, but nobody really heard him in the confusion of the moment.

"Lend a hand here!" the Captain yelled to Tom, and together they hauled Finnegan back into the glyph, while Geneva helped Deaux-Deaux and Candy. There were a few gasping moments of laughter and relief. Then Malingo moaned again, his hands going up to his face, and a heartbeat later, the glyph went crazy, pitching itself from side to side with incredible violence.

"Close the roof!" McBean yelled. "Before somebody falls out!"

Finnegan slammed the roof closed, and just in time. The glyph flipped over, and over again; and again, reducing everybody inside to sickened and bruised confusion.

"What's happening?" Mischief yelled to Malingo. "Can't you stop this?" He managed to keep the geshrat in view long enough to see the cause of the problem. "Malingo looks really sick," he yelled.

Geneva caught hold of Malingo's arm. He was rigid, his eyes glazed.

"It's Carrion," Tria said. "He's got Malingo under his control."

Malingo was obviously attempting to fight Carrion's hold on him, but it was causing him pain to do so. His teeth were clenched, and a dribble of blood ran from each nostril.

The glyph now began a series of suicidal maneuvers, pitching and spinning and flipping like a plate in the hands of a mad juggler. Inside, everyone held on as best they could as the craft moved away from the house, shearing off branches as it sped through the trees. On the roof below, Carrion followed its chaotic path with hands outstretched. Clearly he still had possession of the glyph. Nor was there any doubt of his intentions. He steadily lifted his hands, instructing the glyph to climb and climb, until it was perhaps two hundred feet above the ground. There, for a few tormenting seconds, he let it hang, giving everyone inside time to fear the worst.

Then it happened. Carrion dropped his hands, and the glyph obeyed his instruction. It fell out of the sky like a stone.

"Oh, dear . . ." John Mischief remarked.

As they fell, Candy slipped her arms around the geshrat from behind and clung to him.

"Malingo," she said. "It's me."

She couldn't see his face from her present position, but Geneva could, and her look was grim.

"You have to fight him," Candy said.

She glanced at Geneva, who shook her head. "Fight him, please," she said. "For me. For all of us!"

Finally Malingo seemed to hear her. His head swung lazily around.

"Candy . . . ?" he said.

"Yes!" she said, and smiled at him. At that instant the glyph struck the top of the branches and pitched sideways, its descent slowed by the impact. There was no time for anyone to redirect it. The vehicle hit the ground, smashing into a drift of snow, and sped on for another thirty or forty yards. With each yard its speed slowed, and it finally came to a juddering halt with its nose lodged between the sprawling roots of a tree.

Several seconds passed filled only with gasps and grunts and groans. Finally all the John brothers spoke at the same time: "Is everyone alive?"

There was a chorus of affirmation from all corners.

"Candy?" said Mischief.

"Yes. I'm alive!"

Her reply was followed by an outburst of joyful welcome from Mischief and his brothers, even John Serpent.

"Alive! Alive! Candy's alive!"

"Hug us!"

"Tighter!"

"Tighter!"

"Oh, we've missed you!"

"I've missed you! All of you! Thank you so much, everyone, for getting me out of there!" She turned her attention to Malingo, who was still in the pilot's chair. "How are you doing?"

The leathery fans on either side of his head were spread wide and shaking. "I'm okay . . ." he said, ". . . I think. I'm sorry, everyone. He got control of me, and I couldn't shake him off."

"He was in your head?" Geneva said.

"Yes," Malingo replied. "It was horrible."

Why, Candy wondered, had Carrion not tried to do the same thing to her? It would certainly have brought a quick halt to their chase if he'd simply *ordered* her to give up. But then perhaps he'd tried, and failed. Perhaps her human mind presented a different kind of challenge to him than that of the geshrat.

"Uh-oh," said John Fillet. "Carrion's not finished with us."

Candy looked up.

"There," said Geneva.

She pointed through the cracked window at the back of the glyph. The elaborately carved front door of the Dead Man's House stood open, and out over the threshold strode the Lord of Midnight. He had put on an enormous black coat of sleek fur. The mummified heads of the animals that had supplied their skins for this garment were arranged in a collar (all gazing up at him in sightless adoration). In his left hand he carried a staff that was fully half as big again as he was, and on top of it squatted the skeletal remains of a huge winged toad. Light burned in its eye sockets and shed a demonic glow into the snow-filled air.

"Here comes a man with murder on his mind," said Finnegan very quietly.

"Who's the brat in the uniform behind him?" said Mischief.

"His name's Letheo," Candy said.

The last time she'd seen Letheo, he'd been knocked through a window by his furious master. But he had apparently been forgiven his trespasses against Carrion, because he was back in Midnight's shadow.

"You know him?" said Tom.

"He's the one who brought me here. Carrion's got him under his thumb."

"Well, Carrion looks as if he's spoiling for a fight," said Finnegan, taking his short sword out of its sheath. "So let's give him one."

"He means to kill us, Finnegan," said Geneva.

"He can try."

"This isn't the time or the place."

"She's right," Candy said.

"Well, what do you suggest?" Finnegan said, turning on Candy with rage in his eyes. "We run away? No. I'm not afraid of him."

"Nor am I," Two-Toed Tom said, rolling up his sleeves as though he was planning a round of bare-fisted boxing.

"Nor me," said Deaux-Deaux. "Just because he's the King of the Dark Hours or whatever he calls himself these days." He shoved open the door and started to clamber out of the craft. "You want a fight?" he yelled to Carrion.

Candy caught hold of him.

"Don't," she cried.

"It's time somebody stood up to him."

"Deaux-Deaux, *please*," Candy begged. "Diamanda was already killed here, right in front of me. I don't want to be responsible for anybody else getting hurt."

"Candy's right," said Tria. "This place smells of death, Deaux-Deaux. We don't want to be here."

"We don't have any other choice," Finnegan said. "What are we going to do? Lock ourselves in the glyph and hope Carrion goes away? He's not going to do that."

"I can get the glyph moving," Malingo said, wiping the blood from his nose with the back of his hand.

"Then do it!" said Mischief. "But be quick about it."

In fact, Carrion wasn't in any great hurry. He seemed to believe—why would he not?—that he had them all trapped, and he could take his time to deliver the killing blow. But Candy, who had been so close to the enemy minutes before, could already feel his proximity. The air in the glyph had a bitter tang to it.

"He's ten strides away," Candy murmured.

"Don't worry," Malingo said. "We're going. Pull the Sea-Skipper back inside."

"Finnegan!" Candy said. "Will you get Deaux-Deaux down from there?"

Finnegan threw Candy a look of frustration. He obviously wanted to face Carrion now, whatever the dangers or consequences. But he also realized that the weight of opinion was against him and put up no further protest. Instead he reached out and grabbed Deaux-Deaux around the waist, saying:

"Another time, Skipper! We're leaving!"

He'd no sooner spoken than a surge of energy passed through the glyph, though it was by no means as smooth as it had been before the crash. The engine sounded more guttural now, and the luminescence that passed through the craft flickered like a lamp that was on the verge of failing.

Candy kept her eye on Carrion. She knew he'd respond the moment he saw Deaux-Deaux get pulled back into the glyph, and she was right. He instantly picked up his pace, yelling something back to Letheo as he did so. The beast-boy began to run, producing a long-bladed knife as he did so.

Malingo reached out and caught hold of Candy's hand.

"Help me do this!" he said. She put her arm around him. "We need to put our thoughts together," he said. "And get this thing flying." He leaned close to her, so as to speak to her more confidentially. "He muddled all my thoughts up and now I can't quite think straight."

"Don't worry, I'm here with you."

He smiled at her. "I know."

"Let's get this thing flying. Everybody *hold on*!"

Again Candy glanced back at Carrion. He was four, five strides from the glyph, muttering something as he came. A spell, was it? A few words to undo by magic a thing that had been made by magic?

"Are you ready?" Malingo said to Candy.

"As I'll ever be."

"Rise," Malingo murmured.

She saw the word in her mind's eye.

"Rise," she said.

Nothing happened.

"Why isn't it moving?" Tria said. "Candy. Make it fly!"

The Lord of Midnight was almost upon them, his hand extended toward the craft as though he intended to simply hold it in its place, while in his other hand he lifted his staff in preparation for striking the glyph like an egg—

"We have to do this together," Malingo said.

"Yes," she said. "One breath—"

They inhaled together, and let the word out in the same breath.

E."

S

I

"R

This time the glyph obeyed, lifting into the air with surprising smoothness despite its wounded condition. Carrion struck it with his staff, but he was too late. The glyph was already ascending. The travelers were given a jolt, but the glyph was unfazed. It rose up beyond Carrion's reach, cracking the branches as it cleared the trees.

The moon was waiting for them. The blizzard had

moved off northward, and the sky was wide and bright.

"I can't believe it," Candy said, her voice raw.

"What, the moon?" said John Mischief.

"No. Being alive. I'm alive! Thank you, thank you; thank you all: I'm alive! We're all alive!"

44

THE PRINCE
AND THE BEAST-BOY

CARRION RETURNED TO THE Dead Man's House in a blind fury.

"Letheo!" Carrion yelled. *"Come here! NOW!"*

Letheo had seen the Prince of Midnight's temper tantrums before. They were unpleasant in the extreme. But he couldn't run away. For one thing, there was nowhere to run, and for another, he felt sick and weak. The sickness in his blood had taken a powerful hold on him now; and his only hope of a cure, however temporary, was the medicine that Carrion possessed. Without it, Letheo would be reduced to a blood-hungry, reptilian thing.

He had no choice, therefore, but to answer his Lord and master's summons. He found Carrion climbing the stairs, trailing his great coat of candlemas skins. His staff was smoking, giving off an acrid stench that filled the hallway. Sensing that his servant boy had appeared at the bottom of the stairs, Carrion glanced back over his shoulder.

"This is a conspiracy," he growled. "How did they know she was here? Who told them? And who were they anyway, besides *Finnegan*?" He bared his teeth as he spoke the man's name. "Did you see him striking poses? Always the perfect Prince. So handsome, so brave. No doubt she thinks he's flawless."

"You mean Candy?"

"Yes, Candy. Who else?"

Exhausted and trembling, Letheo leaned against the wall.

"Just forget her," he said. "She's nothing."

"Nothing?"

Carrion slammed his staff on the stairs. The flames in all the lamps guttered, and for a moment Letheo was afraid that they would all be extinguished and he'd be left with only his master's nightmares for light. But the moment passed. The flames brightened again. "Don't be so stupid. That girl can be our undoing. I see that now. The Hag was right. There's something powerful in the girl."

"What, Lord?"

"I don't know what it is, and I don't care to know. I just want her dead. *I must have her dead, Letheo, before I can sleep again.*"

"Yes, Prince."

"I know what you're thinking, beast-boy."

"Do you, Prince?"

"You're thinking she can somehow save you—"

"No—"

"Shut up!" Carrion said. "I saw the look in your eyes when you came back from the Twilight Palace.

You thought you'd seen your salvation. You'd heard the stories about how she'd saved Wolfswinkel's little geshrat, and you thought maybe you'd be the next soul marked for liberty. But I have my eye on you, beast-boy. The change is upon you again, isn't it?" Reluctantly, Letheo nodded. "Soon you'll be a monster, with a monster's appetites."

"Please, Lord, I don't want this in me."

"No, I daresay you don't," said Carrion, slowly descending the stairs. "You want *this*, instead." He dug in the deep recesses of his robes and brought forth a vial of the medicine, called green thuaz, which would reverse the inevitable process of Letheo's sickness. The youth's breath quickened at the sight of it. The sickly sweat of need bloomed on his brow and cheek and chest. "Well, say it," Carrion instructed him. "Tell me this is what you want."

"It is, Lord. You know it is."

"And what if I gave it to you, Letheo. What if your bestiality retreated for a time? What would you dream of then, boy?"

"Of serving you, Prince."

Carrion descended the rest of the flight in two strides and struck the beast-boy on the shoulder with his staff.

"Liar!"

Letheo slid down the wall.

"Why does everybody lie to me? Everybody turns their hearts away! Even that girl. I tried to show her some sights her narrow little head could not have *conceived* of, but she fled from me. *Fled! From! Me!"*

Again the staff came slamming down, this time an inch or two from Letheo's nose. "You will not let her escape again, will you?"

"No, Prince," said Letheo. "She is to be yours and yours alone." His voice had become raw and ugly in the space of this brief exchange. There was less and less of the dark-eyed boy left in Letheo's scrawny face, and more of the monster. "Now, Prince, may I have—"

"This?" Carrion said, twisting off the tip of the vial of green thuaz with his thumb.

"Please. Please."

"A drop, only," Carrion said. "Just enough to keep you capable of rational thought."

"But it hurts me."

"Well, you'll have more when the Quackenbush girl is dead. Do you understand?"

"Yes, Lord. When the girl is—is dead . . ." Letheo's voice was barely comprehensible now.

"Roll, boy."

Letheo obediently rolled onto his back.

"Open wide."

Letheo put his hand to his mouth and opened it. Carrion carefully allowed a drop of the thick fluid to fall from the bottle onto the youth's tongue. Letheo's response was instantaneous. He curled up into a little ball, gasping, sobbing.

"Gratitude, gratitude," Carrion said.

"Th . . . th . . . thank you. Lord."

"Better."

The spasm finally passed, and Letheo lay still.

"Now listen to me, boy," Carrion said.

Letheo made a soft, pained sound, which was almost *yes*.

"We Carrions have a warship, called the *Wormwood*. I have ordered it to meet us at the coast. We will pursue Candy Quackenbush until we catch up with her. If she is given safe haven in any place, that place will be destroyed." He reached down and caught a handful of the boy's hair, hauling him to his feet. "Now stop looking pitiful, boy. This is going to be amusing. We're going to take lives. Isn't that what you came into my employ to do?"

Letheo nodded, tears of agony and relief in equal measure pouring down his face.

"Good. Maybe I'll even let you take the life of Candy Quackenbush herself, if I am feeling generous. Would you like that, Letheo? Well? WOULD YOU LIKE THAT?"

Again, that pained affirmation.

"Then we understand each other. Go pack my books."

He pushed Letheo toward the door.

"Oh, and *boy*?"

"Yes, Lord?"

"Never contemplate betrayal again. If you ever do—*look at me, Letheo*—"

The boy turned at the door and stared with a strange defiance at his Lord.

"If it ever passes through your head for a moment to betray me—" Carrion said, *"that moment will be your last."*

45

A DECISION

WITH CANDY AND MALINGO piloting the glyph, the craft quickly moved away from the snow-blanketed landscape of Efreet and out over the Izabella. There was a glimmer of the morning in the east, but above the travelers' heads the stars were still bright. For a little time no one said anything: each was lost in their own little sphere of meditation.

At last Candy felt a presence at her side and glanced around to see a handsome but tired young man with dark skin, bright green eyes and bright red dreadlocks standing beside her.

"We weren't properly introduced," he said, very quietly, so as not to disrupt the contemplations of their fellow travelers. "I'm Finnegan Hob."

"It's nice to meet you," Candy said. "I'm Candy Quackenbush."

"Thank you for what you did back there," Finnegan said. "You saved all our lives."

"You saved mine," Candy replied. "Thank *you*."

"What were you doing on the roof of the Dead Man's House?"

"Trying to avoid being killed by Christopher Carrion."

Finnegan shook his head heavily, as though he was tired of the whole monstrous, murderous world. "Did he tell you why he *wanted* to kill you?"

"He thinks I'm going to upset all his plans."

"Plans to do what?" Finnegan asked.

Candy thought hard, trying to remember precisely what Carrion had said to her.

"He told me he was going to bring—what were the words?—oh yes: *the great dark. Absolute Midnight.* And he talked about *sacbrood*. They were going to help him, he said. No moon. No stars."

"Sacbrood?" said Finnegan. "They're extinct."

"I beg to differ," said Two-Toed Tom. "There were sacbrood nests found when Pixler dug the foundations for Commexo City."

"Really. Did he kill them?"

"No. I heard he sold them to Carrion. For his private zoo."

Finnegan shook his head. "Well, that was clever of him. Pixler likes profit. Doesn't care where he makes it."

"But I don't see how the sacbrood would help him put out the stars," Finnegan said.

"No," said Mischief. "He's crazy."

"You agree?" Finnegan said to Candy. "Carrion's crazy?"

"I wouldn't be so sure."

"What about the way he came after you?" said

McBean. "That seemed like insanity to me. You're not even a real threat to him."

"Well, even if he thinks I am, I won't be a threat for long," Candy replied.

"What do you mean?"

Candy gazed out over the exquisite patchwork laid below: light and dark, landscape and sea. After a few seconds she said: "Because I won't be here."

Feeling the strange intensity of Finnegan's stare, Candy looked back at him again. The light from the east had found its way into his eyes; their green had flecks of gold in it. For a moment they held each other's gazes. There was something familiar about him, she thought. About the green and gold. Was it possible that somehow they'd met before? Had she passed him on the street in Tazmagor, or in the Yebba Dim Day, and met his gaze, as she was meeting it now, if only for a moment? She wanted to ask him, but she didn't know how to say it without sounding strange.

"Hey, watch the road, will you?" said John Mischief, waving his hand between Candy and Finnegan as though to stir them from a trance.

Blushing, Candy returned her attentions to piloting.

"So tell us," John Moot said chattily. "Where have you been since last we met?"

"All over the place," Candy told him. "Babilonium, Scoriae—"

"What were you doing on Scoriae?"

"It's a long story," Candy replied. "I'm going to write it all down when I get home. I'll find a way of sending you a copy."

"When you get home?" said Malingo. "What do you mean?"

"I've been doing some thinking," Candy said. "And I've decided to go back to the Hereafter."

"In the name of Lordy Lou, why?"

"Because wherever I go in the Abarat, things happen that probably shouldn't. People get crazy. People get hurt. I think it would be . . . safer, I guess . . . if I just went home."

There was silence in the glyph for several seconds. Finally Malingo said: "You don't mean that. You can't."

"Yes, I do. I really do. I've given it a lot of thought, and I'm not going to change my mind, Malingo, so *please* don't try."

She heard a deep, sad sigh from Malingo, and he slipped into the seat beside her. "Of course you must do whatever you think's best," he said softly. "It's your life. But I'm going to miss you so much."

"And I'm going to miss you. But didn't we both know I'd have to go back one day? I miss my family, Malingo. Well . . . at least I miss my mom. And I've got a life back there, believe it or not."

"Not like this life, surely," said Two-Toed Tom.

"No. Nothing like this life. I don't have magic in me. Or if I do I don't know that I do. Nobody tries to kill me. I suppose you'd say it's a very *boring* life compared with this. But I can't run away from it forever."

"Maybe you weren't running *away*," Finnegan said. "Maybe when you came here, you were running *toward* something. Have you thought of that?"

Candy shook her head wearily. "Maybe I was. I don't know anymore. It's too much. It's all too much."

"Let me pilot for a while," Malingo said gently. "You're tired."

"Yes," Candy said. "Thank you. I am tired."

"You have every right," Malingo replied. "The things you've done in the last eight weeks . . ."

"You'd better take us back to the *Lud Limbo*," Captain McBean said to Malingo. "If the young lady feels that it's time to go, we should honor her wishes."

Candy said nothing. She just stared out of the window at the stars, remembering her astonishment when she'd first discovered that the constellations here were different from those that hung over Minnesota. *I'm in another world,* she'd thought, and her heart had been filled to brimming with all kinds of contradictory feelings: awe and fear, excitement and bewilderment. But it was time to let it go. Time to go back to 34 Followell Street and be an ordinary girl again (if that was possible); to get up and go to school every weekday, and on the weekends do her best to stay out of her father's way. In truth, some part of her was a little afraid of being here in the Abarat, afraid that staying would be the death of her, sooner or later. And yet . . . and yet . . . there were so many people here who'd become dear to her; it made her heart ache already to think of being parted from them.

"You're sad," said John Mischief.

Candy nodded. "I guess in my heart of hearts I don't really want to go," she admitted.

"Then don't," said Finnegan. "If it hurts to leave, then stay."

"I think if I do that I'll end up hurting even more."

"But why?" said Geneva. "You've made quite a name for yourself here. Back in the Hereafter, what would you be?"

"Not much," Candy admitted.

A star fell overhead, silently arcing across the purple darkness. Candy watched as it hit the water, its brightness continuing to burn as it coursed its way into the depths.

"So many wonderful things . . ." Candy said softly, ". . . so many *new* friends . . ." She drew a deep breath. "But if I stay, and any of you were to be hurt . . . or worse . . . I'd never forgive myself."

There was no arguing with this, of course, and nobody tried. Except for little Tria, who had not piped up until this moment.

"I just want to say that I think you were born to be here," she said. "And I think if you were to stay you would somehow change the Abarat forever."

Candy answered in a near whisper.

"Maybe that's a part of what I'm afraid of," Candy said. "I think I should leave things the way they are, instead of getting mixed up in Abaratian life."

"Too late," said John Drowze with a fond smile.

"In the end it's your decision," said John Moot. "But for the record, we brothers are of the same opinion as young Tria. You should stay. If there are risks to take, we'll all take them together."

Candy was utterly bewildered now, her thoughts in

turmoil. There was so much love for her here. But then, wasn't that why she couldn't risk staying?

Finally she said: "My mind's made up."

"In which direction?" said Mischief.

"I need to go back."

"If that's your decision—" Geneva said, her tone suddenly businesslike.

"It is."

"Then the least we can do is escort you to the shores of the Hereafter."

"The Izabella doesn't flow that far," Two-Toed Tom said.

"There's a conjuration for the tide," McBean said. "It opens the way between the Abarat and the Hereafter."

"We know that one." Mischief grinned.

"The mariners used it in the old days," McBean went on, "when ships used to go over all the time. My grandfather taught it to me."

"You know some magic?" Tom said. "You astonish me."

"Oh, you'd be surprised what I know," McBean said with a chuckle.

"How long will it take us to get there?" Candy asked him.

"Once we get to the Nonce and on board the *Lud Limbo*? Eight hours. Perhaps nine. As long as there are no storms toward dawn."

While he was talking, Candy glanced in Finnegan's direction. He was still watching her, frowning slightly, as though he was trying to solve some puzzle. He smiled at her, and the smile made her heart ache more than ever, to think that somewhere in his head he had an answer to the question that she had only begun to ask once she came into the Abarat, and would never solve, she knew, once she left. It was the hardest puzzle that anybody had to solve:

Who am I?

PART FOUR

THE SEA COMES TO CHICKENTOWN

Do not blame the wind.
It carries whatever freight
It is laden with, fair or foul.
It brings gossip,
It brings laughter,
It brings prayers
And songs of love.
It brings the chatter
Of madmen and children,
Not knowing one from the other.
Do not blame the wind.

—by Zaosharan,
poet of the Totemix

46

DEPARTURES

THE GLYPH TRAVELERS REACHED the northern shores of the Nonce with only a short time to spare. The craft they'd conjured together under Malingo's tutelage was beginning to deteriorate rapidly, and they had barely landed on the dunes close to the *Lud Limbo*'s anchorage when the craft shuddered, its engine ceasing.

They all got out of the vehicle and stood back to watch their magical creation unknit itself. It was a melancholy spectacle: like watching a bonfire that had once blazed high and mighty reduced to guttering, and then dying out altogether. But they kept watching, to the very end, out of a strange loyalty to the thing they'd made. Only when the last of the once-bright motes had faded into the air did they leave the spot and head over the dunes and across the beach to the little rowing boat that would carry them to the *Lud Limbo*.

Candy was the last to get into the boat. She lingered on the shore for a minute or two, knowing that once she forsook Abaratian earth she would not step onto it again. She took the moment to remember all the places she'd been in her travels: the Yebba Dim Day, the island of Ninnyhammer, Odom's Spire and the wonders of the Twenty-Fifth Hour; the cold terrors of Efreet and the wild Carnival of Babilonium; Scoriae and the beauty of the Twilight Palace; the Nonce and its endless visions and mysteries. In all she'd visited twelve of the twenty-five islands; not a bad piece of voyaging for less than eight weeks of travel. But she knew she had only scratched the surface of what the Abarat might have shown her. There was so much that she hadn't seen, even on the islands that she'd visited. There were the ruined cities on the lower slopes of Mount Galigali, which she would have loved to have explored; and the miracles of evolution on the Nonce, which were glories unto themselves; not to mention the endless possibilities that were concealed behind the mirages of the Twenty-Fifth Hour. And of course there were thirteen islands that she had not even stepped upon, nor now ever would. Her heart was heavy at the thought. So many wonders she was leaving unwitnessed.

There was a gray rain cloud taking shape over a patch of dense jungle not far from the beach, the conditions for its formation so perfect that it swelled up even as Candy watched it, and then unleashed a monsoonal rain. The treetops swayed and churned like a great, green sea, and watching it churn she was filled up with a great gratitude for all that she *had* been given a chance to see.

"Are you coming?" said Finnegan.

He had climbed back out of the boat and was standing just behind her.

"Yes," she replied reluctantly. "I just wanted to watch the storm a little longer."

"There are no storms in Minnesota?"

"Oh yes," she said. "There are *enormous* storms. But nothing quite like that. Look at it!"

"You know, you could still change your mind," Finnegan said. "We could go adventuring together. I'd keep you safe."

"I know you would. And thank you. But I've made up my mind. It's funny; back home people used to say I never made up my mind about things. I guess I didn't care one way or another about anything. But I think maybe I've changed. Being here has changed me. I found . . ." She halted, searching for the right words. ". . . something to care about."

The thought suddenly caught her heart, and she felt tears rising up in her.

"We should go," she said, doing her best to keep the tears from coming. "You folks have more important things to do than wait around for me."

Finnegan nodded. "If you're ready."

They waded out through the warm shallows, their feet making slow explosions of sand in the pristine water. Tria and Geneva had taken the oars and McBean the tiller. The boat breasted the waves with little difficulty, and they were soon beyond the surf and moving swiftly across the calmer waters that lay between the breaking waves and the spot where the *Lud Limbo* was anchored.

They were no more than a few yards from the red hull of the vessel when Tria stood up in the boat and pointed back toward the shore.

"Look! Look!" she yelled, her voice shrill with excitement.

All eyes followed the line of Tria's gaze. The cloud that had unleashed the monsoon had now thinned and had become a rising spiral shape, through which the bright sun poured unhindered. It wasn't the sun that was drawing Tria's attention, however: it was what that light fell upon. There, on a ridge on the shoreward side of the forest, a shape that was green and glistening—as though just born out of the rain-drenched ground—was swelling and shifting. It was a human form, no doubt of that. A woman, her dress lush and full and decorated with either dewdrops or jewels.

"Does anybody see what I see?" Tom said.

"A woman," Candy replied.

"Not just *any* woman," John Mischief said. "That's Elathuria."

"It *is*," Finnegan murmured. "By all the divinities of love, it is! Elathuria!"

"But where's Numa Child?" said Malingo.

"Who?" Candy wanted to know.

"The soul who loved her. Who would follow her around the island, waiting for her to be—"

"There!" said Candy, with a big smile appearing on her face. "I see him!"

And indeed there he was, climbing up the ridge, with his purple-blue wings folded neatly against his broad back.

"Numa Child," Candy said, turning the words over on her tongue to see how they sounded. "He's really an angel? I mean, from heaven?"

"Who knows?" Finnegan said. "But there they are, united again."

"Again?" said Candy, not knowing the story.

"It's a sad tale," Finnegan said. "And I think you're sad enough."

"Maybe another time," Malingo said, then realized that there would not *be* another time and fell into gloomy silence.

They all watched the scene play out on the now distant shore, Elathuria and Numa Child reunited for a brief time. Then the rain clouds broke a second time, and a veil of water concealed the reunion from sight.

Carrion went down to Faithless Harbor on the southwestern peninsula of Efreet to find that news of the *Wormwood*'s imminent arrival had spread through the islands and that large numbers of people had assembled there to witness the arrival of the notorious warship.

"What pitiful lives they must lead," he said to Letheo as he scanned the crowds—rich men and women warm in their carriages, the laboring classes dressed in whatever protection their meager earnings would provide (ratty old goatskins or rodent skins sewn together; straw coats on some, rope coats on others, and everyone wearing wooden clogs).

Carrion had no wish to go among this stinking multitude, even in some sort of guise that would prevent them from petitioning him. So he found a place a little way above the harbor, where he could sit and wait for the arrival of the *Wormwood*.

He didn't have to wait long. After just a few moments the surface of the sea—which had been placid up until now—became agitated, and fish began to appear in the waves: not the schools of melk and wretchen fish which would normally have populated these waters, but creatures that usually lived in deep sea trenches, called up from the darkness by some urgent summons. They were barbaric-looking creatures, some of them armored and spiny, while others made sounds as they broke the surface, speaking in fishy tongues as they cavorted in the surf.

And then out of the darkness came the sound of the ship that had summoned these scaly multitudes: of ropes and boards creaking, and then—as the vessel came closer to land—the voice of the first mate as he called the water depths (six fathoms! five fathoms!) and the sound of the crew singing a hauling song as they labored to bring the *Wormwood* into the harbor. Finally the titanic form of the *Wormwood* itself appeared from the darkness. The vessel was so terrifying a sight to some of those who'd assembled to witness its arrival that they fled in confusion, offering up panicked prayers of protection against its appearance. They had reason for their terror: it was in every way a hellish vessel. Smoke rose in columns of black and red from ports along its flanks and from its central tower. At the bow sat not one but two demonic figureheads, one looking heavenward, one into the depths of the

Izabella. At the stern sat their brothers in grotesquerie, looking out to port and starboard. The smoke swirled around them, lending them a terrible liveliness, as though at any moment they might unroot themselves from the structure of the ship and swim off to make some terrible mischief.

The *Wormwood* had not one but two means of propulsion. In the dark depths of its hold were slave giants: creatures from the mountains of the Isle of the Black Egg, who would live out the rest of their long lives chained to their oars of the *Wormwood*. But the greater power that pressed the *Wormwood* forward was the wind; and the sails that captured it were vast and purple: the final proof, if any more were needed, that this was a vessel that traded in cruelty and despair.

It anchored no more than a quarter mile from the shore. By the time Carrion, followed by a limping Letheo, had made his way down to the water's edge, a minor spell had created a pathway of solid water that allowed them to walk casually to the ship, in the hull of which a door opened to receive them. As they were about to enter, Letheo snatched hold of his master's cloak.

"*She's* here," he said. "Your grandmother."

Carrion's pace automatically slowed. He scanned the imposing bulk of the vessel, searching for some sign of Mater Motley.

He'd no sooner spoken than a figure *did* emerge from the darkness of the ship, accompanied by two members of the crew. It wasn't Carrion's grandmother, however. It was a wizard Carrion knew of by reputation: one

Kaspar Wolfswinkel. A ridiculous little man, he was dressed in a suit of bright yellow, which could not have contradicted Carrion's mood more profoundly. The wizard was all smiles, however: "Welcome! Welcome! Welcome!" He beamed.

"Wolfswinkel?"

"You remembered me," Wolfswinkel gushed. "How kind! How very kind! I had no reason to imagine you might know who I was, but still I hoped—"

"What are you doing on the *Wormwood?*"

"Your grandmother invited me to come aboard," Wolfswinkel said.

"So she *is* here."

"Oh yes, she's here," Wolfswinkel went on. "And she insists you attend on her at your earliest convenience."

"I'm sure she does," Carrion said sharply.

They were by now in the dark bowels of the ship. From someplace nearby, one of the giants was weeping in his chains, the sound reverberating in the boards of the ship. It made Carrion smile.

"May I show you to your quarters, my Lord?" Wolfswinkel offered.

"I'll find my own way," Carrion replied abruptly. "Take Letheo and get him something to eat."

"I was instructed to attend upon *you*, my Lord, not on this *boy*."

"And I'm ordering you to make my servant comfortable, wizard. Feed him and get him some fresh clothes. Those are orders."

"As you wish," Wolfswinkel said, doing his best to put a polite face on his ill temper. "But if you should need *anything*, Prince, please call for me. I am at your beck and call."

He proceeded to bow, deeply and flamboyantly. But Carrion had already gone off to explore the ship. He had very seldom had occasion to travel in the *Wormwood*, and he had forgotten what a masterpiece it was. The shipwright had been a man called Dyther Selt; and he had given his life, literally, for the creation of the *Wormwood*, the tasking of conceiving, designing and building the great warship so overwhelming that it had fatally exhausted him. His death was not the end of his presence on the *Wormwood*, however. Sometimes, Carrion had heard, sailors claimed they saw Selt's ghost on the deck close to where he had fallen, staring up at the wind-fattened sails.

"Welcome aboard," said a voice from the shadows. The nightmares in which his head swam grew suddenly agitated.

"Grandmother . . ." Carrion said.

The old woman stepped into view.

"Alone?" Carrion asked.

"No, no. I brought my sewing circle with me, so not a moment would be lost: we'll continue to make an army of stitchlings while we hunt the girl."

"I could have happily done it without you."

"Happily? You? When was the last time you did anything *happily*?"

Carrion raised an eyebrow. "Did you come here to contradict everything I say, or is there some other reason?"

"Oh, there's another reason."

"And what is that?"

"I don't trust you."

"Ah."

"You're too used to doing things your own way. Well, of course you are. You're a man. You think you're near as dammit perfect."

"What's your point?" Carrion said, his lip curling.

"We can't afford to let this girl live."

"It wasn't my intention—"

"Don't embarrass yourself with a lie," Mater Motley said. "You don't know *what* you would have done if she'd truly been at your mercy."

"What are you suggesting?"

"That you might have let her slip, for sentiment's sake."

"I'm not stupid!" Carrion snapped. "And I'm certainly not sentimental. So you go home, Grandmother. Let me do my work. You do yours."

"I think not. I'm going to stay. Sew. Watch."

"Then I'm disembarking," Carrion said. "If you won't trust me, then you can go to hell!" He turned his back on the old woman, furious.

Mater Motley suddenly reached forward and snatched hold of Carrion's robes. *"Don't you dare speak in that tone to me!"* she raged. *"I've always protected you! And now all you do is show me disrespect! I won't have it, Carrion! Do you hear me?"*

"And I will not be watched like an erring child, Grandmother. Do *you* hear *me*?" As he spoke he slowly raised his hand and disengaged the old woman's fingers from the haunted fabric of his robes. "I've seen enough of what the girl can do to want her out of our way, believe me."

"Then why did you let her slip in Efreet?"

"I was . . . distracted," Carrion said irritably. "It won't happen again. I've made up my mind to kill Candy Quackenbush and she will die if I have to chase her beyond the end of the sea. *She will die.* What do you want as proof? Her head? I'll bring you her head if that's what you want."

"No, thank you," Mater Motley said as though the very thought of such a gift nauseated her beyond words. Then: "Just the eyes."

"They are unalike. You know that? Different colors."

"Of course. They speak of her nature."

"If I bring you her eyes, you'll leave me in peace?"

"Here's what I'll do. I'll retire into the hold with my women and we'll sew. I'll leave you in the hands of Admiral Bloat and the wizard Wolfswinkel. If you should need me, I'll be close by. If not, I'll be invisible to you. How's that? Good enough?"

Carrion contemplated the compromise for a moment, then nodded. "By the way," he said. "Why did you free that damnable wizard?"

"He knows the girl. She got into his house and liberated his slave. I thought he might be useful. He's certainly devoted to her downfall. Use him as you wish. Promise him power if it helps. Then I'll put him out of his misery when the girl is dead."

"Do we know where she is?"

"She's on board a ship called the *Lud Limbo*, last seen leaving the Nonce."

"In whose company?"

"The usual suspects. The geshrat slave she freed from Wolfswinkel, Malingo. The revolutionary Geneva Peachtree, who was involved in several acts of aggression against the institutions of the Grand Council of the Islands. A comrade of hers called Two-Toed Tom and another called Captain McBean. Oh, and a young girl who would have made a fine member of my sisterhood had she not sided with these fools. The Peachtree woman found her. Her name's Tria. Then of course there's Mischief and his brothers."

"And Hob. You're forgetting Hob."

"No, I wasn't forgetting. I would never make that error. He's the one to watch, if it gets personal. He'd die for the girl. He doesn't know why, of course—"

"Well, we'll put that to the test," Carrion said, allowing himself a little smile. "Maybe he won't feel so brave when I have him in my nightmares."

"Maybe," said Mater Motley. "But I'd prefer not to fathom his devotion. Better just slaughter them all and be done with it."

"Finally, Grandmother," Carrion said. "We agree on something."

The winds were good and the currents favorable; the warship, for all its size, quickly picked up speed as it wove between the islands. Admiral Bloat, who was an unpleasant-looking man in a constant dull fury about that fact, predicted that they would catch up with the escapees in a matter of an hour or so. "We'll simply ram them, if you like," Bloat said to Carrion.

"That'll sink them quick enough. Then when they're going under, we'll pour a dozen buckets of goat's blood into the water. That always starts a feeding frenzy. They'll be eaten alive in two minutes."

"You speak from experience?"

"You don't become an admiral in the Gorgossian Navy by being a great lover of peace and justice, Lord," Bloat replied.

"No, I suppose not."

"Shall we have the goats slaughtered?"

"Yes. Why not?" Carrion said, faintly revolted by the Admiral's flushed enthusiasm for the coming cruelties. "Let's get this over and done with."

"The world will be a better place, Lord, with these felons dead."

"Will it indeed?" Carrion said, turning away from Bloat and losing his thoughts in distance. "Will it indeed?"

47

SOMETHING IN THE WIND

CHICKENTOWN WAS IN A strange mood that day. It had woken after a night of disturbed dreams: people up at two in the morning, three in the morning, sitting in their kitchens taking comfort from a bowl of ice cream or in their dens watching some old movie, but in fact not really tasting the ice cream, nor seeing the movie, because their thoughts were in other places entirely.

Rumors had been spreading through town, whispers and warnings that Chickentown was in the most terrible danger. Nobody, except the stone deaf, had been untouched by this talk. Schoolchildren had passed the rumors back and forth as they played; dog walkers had chatted lightly about it when they stopped to let their charges say hello to one another's bottoms; patients sitting in dentists' waiting rooms had turned the conversation to something worse than the subject of the drill, just for comfort's sake.

In the aisles of supermarkets, on the corners of streets, in the chicken factory, where there had been a record-breaking slaughter the previous day, even in the less friendly parts of town, where folks lingered suspiciously in doorways and there wasn't a lot of casual chat, people *talked* today; talked in ways they had perhaps never talked in their lives, nor ever would again. Talked of things they'd dreamed in recent nights, things that overshadowed every hope of tomorrow, or the day after tomorrow. Things that made them think that perhaps they should put off whatever they were going to do with the rest of the day—however pressing it had once seemed to be—and leave town for a little while.

And the more the whispers were repeated, the more plausible they began to sound. Folks began to make plans. It was time to stop worrying about what the neighbors might say (let them seek their own salvation) and simply pack a small suitcase, gather up the family and pets and carry them off to some safe place.

To *Higher Ground.*

So the exodus from Chickentown began. And the more people packed up and left, the more their neighbors took courage and did the same. Very soon Main Street was clogged for almost a mile, and a lot of folks, seeing that there was difficulty making progress up the street, had abandoned their cars and were proceeding on foot. Everybody was heading in more or less the same direction. There was, after all, only one piece of higher ground in the vicinity of the town, and that was the ridge that lay to the east of Chickentown, commonly called the Rise. It was probably no more than two hundred and fifty feet higher than street level, but obviously people's suspicious selves were telling them that this was a significant distance, because there were plenty of Chickentowners making the climb.

A few, it should be said, had been there for quite some time: about two dozen had made a little camp on the top of the Rise, setting up a ring of tents with a bonfire in its midst. It was a simple arrangement, but it seemed to serve its purpose; it became a focus for everyone who was thinking of doing the same thing. *Come up the hill,* the circle of tents and the smoky fire seemed to say: *come up the Rise onto Higher Ground.*

And as the day went on, more and more people came, forsaking their offices and their stores, their customers, their bosses and their homes.

"It's working," said Henry Murkitt as he and Diamanda wove through the town, assessing the effect of their campaign of whispers. The seeds of doubt that they had meticulously sown had come to fruition.

"What's going on in the Abarat?" Henry asked the incantatrix.

"Oh, do *shush,*" Diamanda said irritably. "I almost had a glimpse of Candy then, but it slipped away. She's on a ship, I can see that much."

"Alone?"

"No, no. She's got people with her. But none of them look too happy—"

Henry sighed. "I have a very bad feeling about all of this."

"You're not the only one," Diamanda remarked. "We're at the very . . . *edge* of things, Henry. Nothing's certain after this." She caught hold of his hand. "Except love."

"Are you afraid?" he said.

"For us? No. But for these people—these poor, confused people who don't believe that their lives have the least meaning—yes, I'm afraid for them."

"Afraid they're going to die?"

"Worse than that. Afraid the end will come and they'll be in terror, because they won't believe they have a heaven to go to."

"Maybe they're right," Henry said bluntly. "I mean, this is a cruel world. And I doubt the Abarat's much better. What is there to believe in, when you come down to it?"

Diamanda slipped her hand out of Murkitt's hand and turned to face him.

"Henry Murkitt," she said. "Listen to yourself, you damn fool! Anybody can shrug and say life is just some accident of mud and lightning. But Henry, it *isn't*. And I mean to show you, in the time we have together—whether it's an hour or a day or whatever it is—I mean to show you that you just have to open your heart and *look*—you hear me, *look!*—and you'll see every minute a hundred reasons to believe."

"Oh, will you?" Henry said, irritated by Diamanda's tone. "And where will I find these hundred reasons?"

"Everywhere!" Diamanda said. "Don't you see we're born into a pattern so huge and so beautiful and so full of meaning we can only hope to understand a tiny part of it in the seventy or eighty years we live with breath in our bodies? But one day, it will *all* come clear. And on that day I'd like to be standing right beside you and saying—"

They spoke the rest together:

"I told you so!"

And then they laughed, so loudly that for a moment those living souls who were within earshot of them looked around, puzzled, as though they had *heard* the laughter plainly enough but could neither see its source nor imagine what anybody would think was funny on this day of fear and whispers and unanswered prayers.

There had been no talk of leaving town at the Quackenbush house. Not since the argument over the meat loaf about the family relocating to Colorado. Today, in fact, the house was unusually quiet. The television was on, but muted; Bill was sitting in front of it staring with a vague expression of bemusement at the basketball. Melissa was in the bathroom obsessively cleaning it, a ritual she always performed when something was troubling her. She felt strange; removed from everything, as though she hadn't completely woken up from the dream conversation she'd had with Candy. She'd heard none of the whispers about Higher Ground that were all over town: she was too busy listening for her daughter's voice, and getting the bathroom clean. The boys were at Howie Gage's house, two blocks away, playing war games. Bill had let them go several hours ago. But now, without warning, Melissa appeared at the door and announced that she was going to go and pick them up.

"Why, for God's sake?" Bill said.

"I just think we should all be together as a family right now."

"Leave 'em to play their shoot-'em-ups," Bill growled. "There's no harm going to come to them."

"We don't know that," Melissa said, snapping off her yellow rubber gloves.

"What are you talking about now?" Bill said, with the martyred air of a man who thought his wife was probably crazy, and that it wasn't fair that he be left with the burden of her lunacy.

"Never mind, Bill. I'm just going to go over there and bring them back."

"Melissa—"

She dismissed any further debate with a shake of her head. Bill shrugged.

"Whatever . . ." he muttered, turning up the sound of the television.

Melissa didn't attempt to express her fears to him. She was just glad, for once, that he was playing the couch potato. She didn't have to worry about where he was. He was a hard man to love, but love him she did, and she wanted no hurt or harm to come to him.

She picked up the car keys from the kitchen table and went out the back door, down the side of the house to the street. As she came out of the shadow of the house and into the sun, two things happened at more or less the same moment: a gust of wind came from the direction of the street, and Karen Portacio, who lived next door, called to her. She didn't answer at first; her thoughts were on the wind and the smell it had brought to her nostrils. But Karen was talking at her insistently and plainly wanted a reply.

"I'm sorry, what did you say?" Melissa asked her.

"If you're thinking of driving somewhere, don't bother," Karen replied. "I just tried to get out onto Laurel Street, and it's impossible. I think there must have been an accident somewhere, and everything's backed up."

"Oh, thanks," Melissa said. "I was going to pick up the kids. I guess I'll just walk."

With that she pocketed the car keys and headed off down the street in the direction of the Gage house. After a few strides, Karen called after her: "Any news about Candy?"

As soon as Karen spoke Candy's name, Melissa realized what the smell was on the wind.

"The sea . . ." she said to herself.

"What did you say?"

But Melissa was already hurrying off down the street—running now, not walking—determined to have her boys back with her before it was too late, and her fears came true.

48

STIRRING THE WATERS

IT HAD ALWAYS SEEMED to Candy when she was younger that when she was going on a trip the *getting there* took forever, while the coming back only seemed to take half the time. Now, of course, she was no longer a child, and the place she was leaving wasn't some summer camp or a theme park where she'd spent a happy, thoughtless day. She was leaving her paradise, her wonderland, and the sense of loss she felt was tearing at her heart. She couldn't remember ever having a feeling like this before. No, that wasn't true. There had been one other time. Five years ago her canary, Monty, whom she'd raised from an egg and hand-fed till he was old enough to feed himself, had gotten sick and died suddenly. She'd found him lying on the bottom of the cage, cold and stiff. She had not gone immediately to tell her mom, wanting to spend a quiet moment saying good-bye to him before the whole family came in. She laid him against her cheek and told him she loved him; told him to wait for her because one day she would come to the place where he had gone, and they would start another life together, which death would never interrupt. The feelings she'd had, talking to him but knowing he didn't hear her, rubbing the back of his head but knowing he didn't know that she was doing it: the terrible twisting ache in her chest as she said her good-byes to him, had been a hint of what she was feeling now.

The trouble was, you never keep memories clear in your head for very long. Just as her memories of Monty had dimmed as the years passed, so, she knew, would her memories of the Abarat. What did she have to keep them fresh? The photograph she and Malingo had taken in Tazmagor? A copy of *Klepp's Almenak*? It wasn't much. As soon as she got home, she decided, the first thing she would do was write down everything she remembered—every last detail about the conversations she'd had and the things she'd seen and the food she'd eaten—

"What are you thinking about?" said John Mischief.

"Writing my memoirs," Candy replied.

"You're a bit young to be doing that, aren't you?" said John Moot.

"Well, this is a special situation," Candy replied. "I feel as though . . ." She stopped, because she could feel tears rising up in her again.

"Go on," said John Slop. *"You feel as though . . ."*

"If I don't remember all this now then maybe I'll lose it."

"You won't lose it," John Fillet said.

"Are you sure?" Candy said. "My aunt Jessica got this disease called Alzheimer's. And bit by bit she forgot everything in her life. We had to put signs up all over her house, so she'd be reminded to do even simple things. Locking the doors, turning lights off. Then she started to forget the names of her friends, and then her own family. It was horrible. For her, for everybody. Suppose the same thing happened to me, only all the things I forgot were all the things about Abarat?"

"But this is different, Candy. This is a two-way street."

"I don't understand."

"It's not just a question of you remembering Abarat. Abarat is also going to remember you."

Now the tears *did* fill Candy's eyes. "It will?" she said.

"Oh yes," said Mischief. "Tell her, brothers."

"Yes!" the John brothers all said in chorus. *"Yes! Yes! Yes!"*

The happy moment was interrupted an instant later by a yell from Finnegan, who had climbed the mast of the *Lud Limbo* to the crow's nest to get a better look at what lay ahead. It was not the vista that lay in front of the vessel that was making him raise the alarm, however. It was a sight that was coming up from behind.

"Vessel to stern!" he yelled down from the nest. *"Vessel to stern!"*

Everybody on board followed Finnegan's instructions and looked back. A patch of sickly yellow fog had formed on the surface of the Izabella, and as they watched the fog churned and divided like a great curtain and a vessel, fully ten times the size of the *Lud Limbo*, came into view. It was monstrous: in size, yes, but in detail too. There were cast-iron icons of mythic beasts everywhere over its hull; the sails looked as though they'd been sewn together from shrouds, some still bearing the stains of death, while from the bowels of the vessel came the moans of terrible suffering.

"It's Carrion's ship!" Two-Toed Tom yelled.

"The *Wormwood*!" Captain McBean hollered. *"Lords and ladies save our souls, we are being pursued by the* Wormwood*!"* He sounded almost disbelieving, as though his mind couldn't entirely accept what his eyes were showing him: that this, the most notorious warship that had ever sailed the Izabella, was right there behind them. "The *Wormwood*!" he kept saying. "The *Wormwood*! The *Wormwood*!" as though by some paradoxical magic the calling of the beast's name would unmake it.

But still it came. And the closer the two ships got to each other, the more the crew of the *Lud Limbo* realized their jeopardy. The *Wormwood* wasn't just a fearsome vessel, it housed a terrifying crew. Stitchlings of every horrendous shape hung from the rigging and the railings and skittered on the deck of the vessel. Some had been sewn together in parodies of nameable animals: a monstrous spider, for instance, made of brightly colored patchwork; another beast that appeared to be distantly related to a pack of wild dogs, snapping and growling as though rabid (which perhaps they were). In the rigging were stitchling birds that looked like a lunatic version of the pterodactyl. They hopped on the crossbeams, shrieking and snapping at one another.

Candy had spotted an absurdly overdressed figure, his cheeks rouged and his bald head tattooed, parading on the poop deck. "Who is that?" she asked.

"That's Admiral H. H. Bloat," said Captain McBean. "One of the vilest men ever to set sail on the Izabella."

"And beside him . . ." said Tria, her voice barely louder than a whisper. "That's *him*, isn't it?"

It was Candy who replied. "Yes, that's him," she said. "That's Christopher Carrion."

Tria had seen him before, of course, on Efreet; but he was no longer the ominous figure in furs hung with mummified heads. Now he wore magnificent decorated robes in black and gold and scarlet.

"Look away . . ." said a voice at Candy's side. It was Mischief. "Please. Look away."

"He can't hurt me here," Candy replied.

"Don't be so sure."

Even as Mischief spoke, Carrion made a hook of the finger of his left hand and beckoned to Candy. Again she heard John Mischief at her side. But she refused to be intimidated by Carrion's theatrics. She just kept looking at him.

"Lady . . ." Mischief said again.

"I'm not going to be frightened just because he's staring at me."

John Moot said, "It's not Carrion we're worried about."

"What then?"

"It's the wave."

"What wave?"

"If you'd just unglue your eyes from the Prince of Darkness for a minute, you'd see," said John Serpent.

With more difficulty than she'd anticipated, Candy took her gaze off Carrion. There was no missing what the Johns were talking about. In the half minute or so that Candy had been meeting Carrion's stare, a great swell of water had appeared from beneath the *Wormwood*, lifting her up on its foamy back.

"We're in trouble," Captain McBean said grimly.

The wave was growing in size and speed by the moment. Clearly it would soon possess staggering power, not only to carry the monstrous vessel forward, but to destroy anything that lay in the wave's path.

"I didn't realize Carrion had elemental powers," John Mischief yelled as he watched the Izabella become more and more frenzied.

"I don't think it's him," said Finnegan, clinging to the rigging of the *Lud Limbo* with one hand and watching the warship through a telescope, which he held in the other. "It's his grandmother! Mater Motley."

He had no sooner uttered the witch's name than there was a surge of blistering energy that rose up out of the bowels of the *Wormwood*, and the woman who had unleashed the Izabella rose into view. Her stick-thin arms were raised, and her gray hair swirled around her head.

As she appeared, everybody on board the *Lud Limbo* heard her voice, and for every person it was as though she were speaking to them and them alone. Her message was grim and simple:

The Lud Limbo is about to sink. When it goes down, you will all drown. Make your peace with death. And be quick about it.

As she finished her speech, the boiling body of water beneath the warship suddenly rose up like a tower of water.

"DROWN THEM!" the old woman yelled.

49

INTO THE HEREAFTER

As THE WAVE BENEATH Carrion's ship continued to grow, the power that was creating it summoned up from the depths great multitudes of fish, many of which were not designed ever to meet the light. Some blew up like balloons as soon as they surfaced, then exploded. Others, conversely, met the light in a state of writhing pleasure, as though they were in ecstasy to have themselves finally revealed in every repugnant detail. And repugnant they were, many of them, their flesh bloated and gray-green, their eyes ghastly lanterns; their mouths gaping and lined with needle barbs. Some were so far from being recognizable creatures that they lacked eyes and mouths but were just writhing shreds of life, roiling in the tumult like the skins of damned souls.

And all this was just in the froth of that frenzied sea. Beneath the bubbling surf was a massive body of dark, glistening water, which lifted the immense bulk of the *Wormwood*. First the stern, then the shuddering mass of the ship itself, which threw its shadow down on the *Lud Limbo*.

"We're in trouble!" Geneva yelled. "Look at all those stitchlings!"

A terrifying number of the creatures had issued from the bowels of the warship and were now climbing up into the rigging or lining the decks in some ragtag approximation of a military assembly.

"There's a couple of battalions of those damnable things," Tom said.

"We've certainly got a fight on our hands," said Finnegan.

"We're all going to die. That's the truth of it," said John Slop. "If we're not drowned first, of course."

"Whose clever idea was it to head back to the Hereafter anyway?" John Serpent said, casting an accusing glance at Candy.

"Belay that kind of talk!" said the Captain. "Or I'll throw the offender overboard!"

The other brothers all whispered *hush* in John Serpent's direction. They weren't going to suffer just because he couldn't keep his mouth shut.

"We all knew the risks of coming on this journey," Finnegan pointed out. "So let's just get on with it, shall we? We should prepare for hand-to-hand combat. Who has weapons?"

There was a show of arms. It wasn't a very encouraging sight. Mischief had a short-blade knife, as did Tom. McBean had two antiquated pistols and a rusty sword; Tria (surprisingly) had two thin, finely polished knives; Finnegan had what looked like a machete. The rest had only their bare hands and their will.

Before Finnegan could comment on this meager show of defenses, McBean yelled:

"Brace yourselves!"

Two seconds later, the *Lud Limbo* was struck from behind by the force of the waters Mater Motley's magic had stirred up. Everybody was thrown forward, and for a few perilous moments it seemed the little vessel might very well be swamped. Finnegan was pitched out of the crow's nest and would have hit the deck if he hadn't caught hold of the rigging on the way down and clung there. The *Lud Limbo* rolled and reeled, its boards complaining at the punishment it was taking. But McBean had captained ships in some of the worst tempests the Sea of Izabella had ever stirred up. He knew how to turn the power of this surge of waters to their advantage.

"Hold on for your lives!" he yelled, and swung the wheel around.

The *Lud Limbo* veered starboard. Foam-headed waves broke over the deck, and the vessel shook from bow to stern. But the maneuver worked. McBean had brought the boat into the path of a very fast-moving current. And it carried the vessel away.

"Clever," said Carrion.

He was standing in the bow of the *Wormwood*, his hands behind his back but spread wide, gripping his winged-toad staff. The distance between the *Wormwood* and the boat containing his prey was getting bigger by the moment, but he wasn't concerned. The

Wormwood had immense speed: a crew of giants in the hold, working their oars, and on deck Mater Motley and her witch-women seamstresses, whose power over the elements allowed them to bend the Izabella to their will. His grandmother and her terrifying entourage could raise tempests and water spouts; they could call up out of the deeps the ghosts of men drowned over the millennia: fishermen, pirates, admirals and cabin boys. And of course the monstrous creatures that made meals of the dead could also be raised up: species that made vile schools which had appeared so far like inconsequential things. The giant black-backed scorpion crabs that could cut a man in half with their claws; the tiny scalpel fish, who had been known to perform entire surgeries on drowning men, operations so immaculate that their bodies had been retrieved and studied by the doctors in Commexo City; furnace fish, which by some unknown means kept fires stoked in their five stomachs, where they cooked their catch before devouring it in the normal way through a sixth stomach.

But the presence of all these creatures caused problems. The frenzied waters were becoming so thick with roused life that the progress of the *Wormwood* was being slowed.

"Grandmother!" Carrion yelled.

Mater Motley failed to heed his summons. He yelled again, and still she ignored him. His fury rising, he sought out Admiral Bloat and found him at the railing, with two midshipmen providing primed pistols for him, firing down into the surf at creatures that were seething there.

"Admiral, what in hell's name are you doing?"

"Practicing my marksmanship," Bloat replied. "See that vicious thing with the blue stripes? I took it out with one shot!"

"We have more pressing matters than your marksmanship, Admiral."

"Such as?"

Carrion caught hold of Bloat's fat arm and snatched the pistol from his hand, tossing it overboard. "The *Lud Limbo*, Bloat!" he said. "Our enemies are getting away!"

"Then unhand me, sir," the Admiral said with a tone of annoyance. "I will not act to apprehend the *Lud Limbo* until I am treated with the appropriate respect."

Carrion released the man as though he was something faintly gangrenous and let Bloat step away from him. The Admiral took out his telescope and assessed the position of the *Lud Limbo*, and then, with a great deal of bowing and scraping, he approached Mater Motley. There was a brief exchange, which Carrion didn't attend to. Something else had caught his attention. There was a subtle shifting in the mists that covered the divide between the Abarat and the Hereafter. He could see, for the first time, glimpses of that other world: tall grasses, swaying and shimmering in the heat; and beyond the grass, the roofs of dwellings, and a steeple.

"Chickentown . . ." he murmured.

"Chickentown!" said Candy.

"What?" said Mischief.

"Where?" said Moot.

"There!" she said, pointing to the sight. "You see it?"

"*I* see it," said Malingo.

"That's my hometown."

"We came upon it quickly!" said Geneva.

"Look behind you, girl," said John Serpent to Candy, not without a little maliciousness. "The Abarat's going to be out of sight very soon. And you won't be seeing it again."

It was true, Candy realized. Her final glimpse of the Abarat was imminent. Bracing herself, she looked over her shoulder. The Outer Islands had all but disappeared from sight—they were just amorphous forms in the mist—but she could still smell the flower-sweetened air that came across the water from places she would now never see, with names she would now never learn.

She drew a deep sigh, her heart brimming with feelings for this farewell. Of regret, that she hadn't seen more places, of sadness that she hadn't met more people. And of bittersweet gratitude that at least she had lived to see as much as she had seen . . .

. . . the stone head of the Yebba Dim Day, filled to capacity with all manner of refugees, snatched from the waves . . .

. . . the beauty of Odom's Spire, which had been so haunted by visions of the past and the future she had never quite decided what was real and what wasn't . . .

. . . Ninnyhammer, where the night settled in the trees and tarrie-cats pierced the shadows with their all-seeing eyes . . .

. . . Babilonium, brimming with visions of the freakish and fantastic and the din of happy souls . . .

. . . Scoriae, where the evening star was always rising and Bilarki's sad songs wove between the misty trees . . .

. . . and always, when the sound of sad songs and happy souls was stilled, the wind had been there to bring her the music of the sea: the all-embracing Goddess Izabella, the unfathomed sea, mother of death and mystery. It was the Izabella that had first found her, and it was the Izabella that was delivering her home. She reached over the side of the boat and put her fingers in the water; then she lifted them to her lips. "Thank you," she murmured. Then—only with the greatest difficulty—she took her eyes off the place she'd been and redirected her gaze toward the place they were going, toward the Hereafter, toward home.

"Hang on!" McBean hollered.

The waves were breaking against the solid world that lay ahead, and their backwash struck the *Lud Limbo*, lifting the vessel up.

Candy grabbed hold of the railing to keep herself from falling. As she did so, she heard a noise behind her. A kind of chanted music was coming out of the *Wormwood*, its source, to judge by its shrillness, the women of Mater Motley's sewing circle. The sound they made was complex and strangely distressing. It made her stomach churn. It made the Izabella churn too. As the rhythm of the chant quickened, the sea became more frenzied, surging even higher beneath the *Wormwood* as though it were a watery mountain that was being summoned in a great spiral motion from the depths. As below, so above. The same chant that raised the waters brought down a spiraling cloud of slate and lightning, which took as its focus the main mast of the *Wormwood*. Now everything was in motion, except the great warship itself, which by some tremendous force of its own audacious will held steady while the sea and sky described vast, implacable motions around it.

"A storm?" Melissa Quackenbush said to herself. She let the dirty plate she was washing slip back into the gray water in the sink. Ricky came in, still sour-faced from having been brought back from the Gages' house, and took a container of orange juice out of the refrigerator. She glanced around at him.

"Take that scowl *off* your face right now," Melissa said. Ricky chugged the juice. "And for the thousandth time, *don't* drink out of the container!"

"Dad does!"

"Well, you're not your—"

She didn't finish the sentence. Two lightning strikes came in quick succession, bright against the darkening sky, followed by a loud crack of thunder. She slowly stepped away from the sink, staring down at it as she did so. The plates were rattling against one another, and the dirty dishwater was rippling.

"What's going on?" Ricky said.

"I don't know, honey. I think you should get away from the windows."

There was another flash of lightning that looked

like a crack in the sky. The thunder came immediately after, and it was so loud it shook the clock from the kitchen wall.

"Stay inside," she said to Ricky, and then defying her own edict, she stepped out into the backyard, her stomach convulsing.

She could feel the ground reverberating beneath her feet. Could this be an earthquake? They'd never had one before, to her knowledge. But the reverberations were getting stronger. Some old fence timbers propped against the side of the house fell over. There was a crash from somewhere upstairs as a vase or a can of deodorant danced off a shelf and hit the floor.

"Oh, my God . . ." she said.

Her eyes had caught sight of something glittering in the distance, at the very edge of town. No, *beyond* the edge of town. It seemed to roll as it came, turning its silver back to the empty blue sky, like a wave.

Like a wave.

"I don't believe it," she murmured.

Like an enormous wave.

"This isn't happening."

She backed away, toward the house. The reverberations were setting off car alarms all along the street.

"Bill?" she yelled. "BILL!"

As she came into the kitchen, Bill came from the other direction and tossed an empty beer can into the trash.

"What's all that noise?" he said.

Melissa pointed toward the window. For once she didn't need to explain anything to him. He saw.

"That's a damn wave," he said.

"Yes, Bill, that's exactly what it is."

"Where'd it come from?"

"Never mind that now. We've got to do something."

"This is the end of the world," Bill said, his voice a monotone.

"No, it isn't. It's just a flood, Bill. A dam broke or—"

"There ain't no dams around here."

"Whatever it is, it's coming this way."

"Then we'll drive."

"We can't drive. The traffic's backed up—"

People have been leaving, she suddenly thought; *I've been wandering around in a fog, and all the time people have been leaving.*

"It's too late," Bill said, still staring at the wave. "We're all gonna die."

"No, Bill. We have to go *up*—"

"Into the attic?"

"Onto the roof! Can we get out onto the roof?"

"I guess so. Through the attic window. I mean, I don't know how *safe* it is."

The windows were all rattling now; cups were coming off their hooks; things falling out of the fridge, which Ricky had left open. Eggs smashing, milk spilling and spreading its own little flood.

Melissa stared at the open fridge. "Food!" she said. "We have to take some food up with us, in case we're stuck up there for a long time!"

"Maybe I should get some medical stuff too," Ricky suggested.

"Yes! I'll get that stuff, you get the water. Don, get in here—"

"There's a wave—"

"We know," said Ricky.

"I'm getting a gun," said Bill.

"Just *hurry!*" said Melissa.

Everybody scattered. Melissa went upstairs to the bedroom to get the medical supplies and then went into the bedroom to pick up some warm blankets. The pictures on the wall beside the bed were all rattling. Her eyes went to them for a moment. There was one of the boys, and one of Candy in Florida, with Grandpa and Grandma. Candy was smiling, but not with her eyes. In her eyes there was a strange sadness. Melissa had looked at the picture hundreds, probably thousands of times, but she'd never seen that sadness before.

She had no time to study it. Ungluing her gaze, she returned to the business of finding blankets, glancing up just once to see that line of silver creeping closer, ever closer—

At one thirty-eight in the afternoon, the first wave from the Sea of Izabella entered the streets of Chickentown.

It swept through the streets like a great cleansing river. It uprooted trees and picked up cars like toys. It wasn't strong enough to level brick houses, but it took off their roofs and it blew in the windows and smashed in the doors, entering without invitation to wash away the remains of the lives that had been lived there. It

sluiced the cereal off the kitchen table and the tooth-
paste oozing from the tube on the bathroom sink. It
overturned the unmade beds and pitched the television
against the wall. It emptied the closets and the cabinets
and the goldfish bowl.

Street by street the waters of the Izabella took over
the town, moving between the houses as though it
were solving a puzzle, turning, turning, turning and
coming to meet itself as it rounded another corner—

The noise of this deluge was terrifying. The great
roar of water sounded the bass note, of course, but on
top of it were a hundred other noises of destruction.
Glass smashing, chimneys collapsing, doors splintering, car alarms whooping—

And in the midst of this chaos of advancing waters,
and the damage they were doing, there were *people*.
Not all that many, in fact. The campaign of whisper-
ings that Diamanda and Henry had undertaken had
paid off. Most of Chickentown's inhabitants were
watching the inundation from higher ground. But there
were still plenty who had not heard the call and were
caught up in the flood. Some, like the Quackenbush
family, had decided that the roof would be the safest
place to be, and had retreated there. Some had hurriedly created makeshift rafts of this and that (crates,
the kids' inflatable swimming pool) and a few actually had boats in their garages, which they climbed
aboard as the wave approached.

There would be plenty of tales to tell, for those who
survived this day of days! Stories of last-minute
escapes, of people going back into their houses for

some sentimental keepsake only to find there were fishes swimming in their living rooms; of folks who'd been carried away in their old mobile homes and deposited miles away. But there would also be many sad stories to tell. Lives lost in a moment of foolishness or indecision; people swept away by the foamy current as they made a dash to their cars, or caught by a surge of white water as they clung to the eaves of their houses.

And then there were those events that were neither happy nor sad, but instead could be filed only under the category of strange. The greatest of these events happened at one thirty-one, just seven minutes before the waters of the Izabella began their invasion of the Hereafter. An anonymous individual (in fact, Henry Murkitt) masterminded the mass liberation of the chicken coops. The result was not, unfortunately, a mass exodus to freedom and health. The animals had lived in a world of false dawns and excrement all their lives. When liberty came, they had no idea what to do with it. But at least they didn't drown locked up in their coops. In fact, their semistupefied state was the saving of many of them. When the water came, they let it carry them away and were swept out of captivity forever. It made for a memorable sight. Thousands and thousands of chickens, borne up by the magical water, staring vacantly at a sky that they had not known existed until now.

As for the *Lud Limbo*, it was carried into the midst of this maelstrom by the sheer governing force of the sea. The journey—which had been perilous enough so far—became more treacherous still once the boat started to encounter the trashed remains of Chickentown. All kinds of flotsam and jetsam careered around in the turbulent waters: street signs, bicycles, chairs, tables, sinks and fencing, the pulpit of St. Stephen's on Fuller Street, a truckload of pig carcasses, store signs, shrubs and on and on and on.

Every time something large struck the boat's hull, the *Lud Limbo* shuddered and rolled. "We just have to ride this out!" McBean yelled as the increasingly filthy scum spilled over the gunwales and onto the *Lud Limbo*'s deck.

Clinging to the railing so that she wasn't thrown out if the boat suddenly pitched, Candy made her way, hand over hand, to the bow. Before her lay a panorama of disaster: the roofs and upper stories of buildings emerging from churning gray waters littered with garbage. Tears blurred her sight. This had been her world until eight weeks ago: and there wasn't a street or store she hadn't known. Now, in a matter of a few minutes, the waters of the Izabella had washed it all away. Her mind almost refused the truth of it.

"This can't be happening," she said. *"This can't be happening."*

It was Finnegan who came to her and put his arms around her to steady her. She looked up into his face. There was such a depth of hurt in his eyes—a sadness so inconsolable—that her own pain suddenly seemed something she could bear. The ship pitched and rolled while they held onto each other.

"My family's out there somewhere," Candy said. "And this is all my fault."

He shook his head. "No," he said. "You didn't do this, *they did*."

He pointed back toward the warship that was still following the *Lud Limbo*. A veil of fog, green and gray, was spreading from the *Wormwood* to port and starboard, as though to cloak it. "Mater Motley brought all this about," Finnegan said. "She raised the wave. You didn't."

"Yes, but if I hadn't wanted to come back here, they wouldn't have followed."

"You'll make yourself crazy thinking like that," Finnegan said. "You might just as easily say it's all because you were at the lighthouse that day and you met Mischief. You might as well say it happened because you were born. But then you would never have come to the Abarat, and I wouldn't have met you."

"No . . ."

"We wouldn't be here now."

"No, we wouldn't."

"So who's to say what's for the best? We do what we do and we take the consequences. You just have to know this is *not your fault*."

He sounded so certain of what he was saying that Candy could put no argument up against it. At least not now. Perhaps there'd be another time, another place, where she could think of what he'd said and agree or not agree. Right now her thoughts went back to 34 Followell Street.

"I just hope my family all got away," she said.

"Do you have any idea where your house is from here?"

Candy turned back and surveyed the desolate scene. "Well . . . that's the clock tower of the old school-house, which is close to where I used to live." She pointed to a distant tower, emerging from the water. "Do you see it?"

"I see it." Finnegan yelled up to McBean, who was in the wheelhouse. "Captain? Do you see that tower in the distance, with the clock?"

McBean confirmed that he did.

"We need to get to it."

"It's going to be difficult in these conditions," McBean replied. "All this debris in the water. We're going to get hit by something big sooner or later. Have you seen what's floating out there?"

"Candy needs to find her family, McBean!" Finnegan yelled. "Are you going to help, or shall I take the wheel?"

"All right, all right, don't get your underwear knotted up! I'll do what I can. But if we sink—"

"We won't blame you," Finnegan said. "And while you're in such a happy mood, why don't you toss down your telescope?"

"One of these days—" McBean growled, pointing a threatening finger at Finnegan.

"Yes, yes! You'll teach me a lesson in courtesy, right? Just give me the spyglass, McBean. You can punch my nose tomorrow." McBean gave his telescope to Tom, who duly brought it down to Candy. "Or I'll punch yours!" Finnegan added with a grin.

Candy put it to her eye, focused it and began a systematic scanning of the water. It was a dreadful sight—the surface was so densely littered with the remnants of people's lives that it looked almost as though you could walk on it. Every now and again something would appear among the wreckage so personal—a little bicycle with training wheels, a bed floating by with the pillows still in place, an empty kennel—that Candy had to work hard to keep from crying. But the thing she'd feared seeing the most— the bodies of people who'd drowned—were few and far between. Very occasionally she'd catch a glimpse of something grim protruding from the foul waters that made her quickly look away, but there was very little to appall her.

"So few dead," she said to Tom.

"I think they were warned," Tom replied, and he pointed to the hill off to the port side. There were people up there, Candy saw. Not just a few, but hundreds, perhaps thousands. She could see smoke rising from fires and a sprawling collection of tents.

"They *were* warned," Candy said, feeling the first real surge of hope she'd dared feel since this catastrophe had started to unfold.

"Maybe your family is up there," Finnegan said, nodding toward the city of tents.

"I hope so," Candy replied. "But . . ."

"You don't believe it?"

"My dad never did anything anybody told him to in his whole life. In fact, the more people said he should do something—"

"—the less likely he was to do it," said Tom.

"Yep."

"My other half's just the same," said Tom, fondly patting the pocket where he kept a dog-eared photograph of his family.

"So you think we should search the water, not the hill?" said Finnegan.

"Keep searching till they catch up with us—" said Tria, who had joined them at the railing. She turned to look back at the *Wormwood*. "Where's the ship gone?" she said.

The *Wormwood* had disappeared from sight again, totally obscured by an eighty-foot-high wall of mist that had spread to conceal the warship, and a good deal of the Izabella too.

"I guess they're going to choose *their* moment," said Tom. The mist cloud was still growing, creeping over the littered waters toward the *Lud Limbo*. It was impossible to guess how far behind that wall the warship was hiding: two hundred yards; a hundred yards; ten.

"We'll be ready for them," Finnegan said. "Whenever they choose to come, we'll be ready."

50

FATHER AND DAUGHTER

"*I CAN SEE MY MOM and dad!*" Candy yelled up at McBean. "And my brothers! They're alive!"

The Captain scanned the scene ahead of the *Lud Limbo*, trying to fix his gaze upon the Quackenbush residence. But it was hard to do, when there were so many half-submerged buildings in the vicinity, several with small groups of survivors huddled around the chimney or squatting along the eaves like enormous bedraggled birds. Nor was the panorama clear. Several buildings had paradoxically caught fire when the deluge had descended, thanks to an electrical fault or a gas leak, and were now burning fiercely, the smoke they gave off muddying the scene ahead and making identification of the Quackenbush family harder still.

"Which ones are they?" McBean called down to Candy.

"You can't miss them," Candy said, pointing. "My mom and dad are the two yelling at each other."

Nothing, it seemed, had changed very much: her mother and father were indeed having a shouting match, their voices so loud and full of rage it was a wonder they weren't audible in the Abarat. Candy's mom was standing on the roof with Don, while her dad stood uneasily in a small rowboat (which was not painted red) with Ricky and several other passengers. Bill was clearly attempting to get his other son down into the boat, but Melissa wasn't allowing him to go. The more enraged Candy's father became, the more he rocked the boat, threatening to pitch the five other occupants of the little vessel into the churning waters. The presence of human food in the boat had attracted some interested fish; pop-eyed and stick snouted, they circled the trembling vessel like a flock of starving vampires outside a blood bank. Their presence was not lost on the people in the boat. One of them—a young man who worked in the garage where Candy's dad took his truck when it broke down—was staring into the water, his panic rising.

"There are *things* down there!" he said. "Oh, God in Heaven, there are huge fishes! *Sharks!* There are sharks! *There are sharks down there!*"

The response from the rest of the passengers in the boat was much as might have been predicted: a chorus of shrieks, howls and prayers.

"We've got to be quick!" Candy hollered to McBean. "There's mantizacs—"

"—in the water!" McBean prompted. "Yeah, I see them!"

"Tell your father to get everybody out of the boat!" Geneva called up to Candy. "Or somebody's going to get hurt."

"He won't listen to me," Candy said.

"Well, maybe he'll listen to us!" John Mischief said.

He took up a position in the middle of the bow, and from there he and his brothers proceeded to harangue the passengers in a multiplicity of voices. Terrified though they were by the circling fishes, the spectacle of this little man leaning over the railing and ordering them to *get off the boat before they were eaten alive* certainly claimed their attention. Bill's demands were drowned out completely by the noise of the Johns, and he gave up in frustration. He'd no sooner done so than one of the largest mantizacs Candy had ever seen appeared from the water close to the boat in which her dad was standing and assessed the smorgasbord on board. The human meal stared back at the fish with horror.

"Look at that damn thing!" yelled one of the survivors.

"Dad!" Ricky yelled. *"Shoot it!"*

Candy threw a panicked look at Finnegan, who cupped his hands around his mouth and yelled: "Don't do that!"

Bill looked up at the man who had just addressed him and an expression of contempt came onto his face.

"You giving me orders?" he yelled back at Finnegan.

"Dad, it's me! It's Candy. He's right. Don't shoot it!"

It wasn't her father who heard and answered her, however; it was her mother.

"Honey! You're alive!"

"Get them out of the boat, Mom. *Quickly!* The fish'll eat any boat that's not red!"

"What'd she say?" Bill yelled. "Who the hell cares what color it is? *Fish are color-blind!*"

At which point three mantizacs disproved the contention by taking sizeable bites out of the offending boat. Fountains of water sprang up instantly, and the little vessel proceeded to sink. There was a chorus of panicked cries from all on board, silenced by Melissa, who yelled:

"Shut up and get back on this roof! Ricky, you first!"

Ricky didn't need a second instruction. Every ounce his father's son, he elbowed Miss Holloway, the old woman who lived on the corner of Followell Street, squarely in the stomach to prevent her from getting out first and leaped up onto the roof and into his mother's arms. Cursing the boy in very un-Christian language, Miss Holloway clambered after him, followed by the other occupants of the sinking boat. Only Bill Quackenbush remained on board, still attempting to prove his marksmanship. He leveled his gun at one of the mantizacs that was chewing up the boat, and fired. At such a range he scarcely could have missed. The creature's brutish head erupted in a cloud of blood and fish flesh. Bill whooped with glee, and he fired a second and third time.

"Is that your papa in that boat?" McBean said to Candy.

Candy nodded.

"You have my condolences," the Captain said.

"You think he's going to drown?"

"No, I just think he's a damn fool," the Captain replied. Then, after reassessing the situation, he said: "Actually, I think he *is* going to drown if he doesn't get out of that boat double-quick!"

He'd no sooner spoken than the water started to slop over the sides of the little boat in which Bill Quackenbush stood. Candy watched the expression on his face change from delight to fear. Suddenly, for all his beer belly and his fierce expression, he looked like a little lost boy. *That's who he really is,* Candy thought. He wasn't the beer-slurred man sitting in front of the television; he was this forlorn figure standing in the chaos he'd made of his life, frightened and alone. All the anger she'd felt toward him over the years suddenly fell away. In its place there was a kind of dull sadness.

She looked at the people on the roof, who were much closer to her dad than she was, and to her horror she realized that none of them were intending to try and rescue him. Everybody, even Candy's mom, was just staring in horror at the scene in front of them: Bill Quackenbush standing there in the sinking boat, the body of the mantizac he'd shot turning its pale belly up in the water; the other fish devouring it from all sides, churning up the waves in the frenzy.

"We have to get closer to him!" Candy told McBean.

"I'll do my best!" the Captain yelled back, and steered the *Lud Limbo* through the crazed waters toward the little boat.

"Dad!" Candy called to him. "Get ready to jump!"

Her father's situation was getting worse by the second. The boat was disappearing fast, while the fish, big and small, were becoming steadily more ambitious, even throwing themselves into the little vessel in order to attack him.

With great care the Captain nudged the *Lud Limbo* close enough that Bill could risk a jump. But for some reason he refused to move.

"Jump, Dad, jump!" Candy yelled.

But either out of terror or stubborn pride, Bill stayed in the little vessel.

"I'm going to get him," Candy told Finnegan.

"There's got to be some other way," Finnegan said.

But Candy had already made up her mind. She clambered over the railing of the *Lud Limbo*, and without further word she launched herself into the air between the two boats. For a moment it seemed the current would carry the little boat out of reach and Candy would fall short, dropping into the fish-frenzied waters. But luck was on her side. A sudden surge caught the boat and brought it back in her direction. She landed, sprawling, in the small vessel. Fish flopped and jumped all around her.

"Well, aren't you just the little hero?" said Bill Quackenbush to her.

"Heroine," Candy replied.

"What?"

"Never mind."

"You gonna try and force me to jump too?" he said. "'Cause I'm not gonna."

"Don't be dumb, Dad."

"Don't call me dumb!"

"You don't want to be eaten alive any more than I do."

"Maybe I should just jump and leave you here?" Bill said. "After all, you're responsible for all this, aren't you? *Well? Aren't you?*"

Candy's gaze slipped past her father toward the *Wormwood*. Her eyes grew wide with amazement.

"What are you lookin' at?" Bill Quackenbush said. Getting no reply, he looked over his shoulder, following the line of his daughter's gaze.

A staircase, which seemed to be made of dust and darkness, had appeared and was growing and solidifying even as Candy and her father watched. And descending it, his arms spread in welcome to the girl in the sinking vessel below, was the Lord of Midnight.

51

INTO THE *WORMWOOD*

Behind her, Candy heard her dad utter a string of curse words, fueled by the terror he felt at the sight of Christopher Carrion.

"You're the father, I presume?" said Carrion as he approached, the stairs still being forged in the air ahead of him.

"Just leave him out of this!" Candy shouted.

"Why?" said Carrion. "Is he an innocent man? Somehow I doubt that. I think he's cruel and vicious. Would that be about right, Quackenbush?"

"Go to hell."

"Why don't you get down on your knees to me, Quackenbush?"

"I don't get on my knees to nobody."

"Do you not?" Carrion raised his hand slowly.

"Don't look at him, Dad!" Candy yelled.

But Bill had never taken a single piece of advice his daughter offered him, and he wasn't about to start now. Almost in defiance of Candy, Bill stared directly into Carrion's eyes. The Lord of Midnight smiled and closed his hand into a fist. Candy's father let out a sob of helplessness. Then his legs bent double beneath him, driving him down to his knees among the fish dying at the bottom of the boat.

"There. That's better," said Carrion. He turned to Candy, smiling. "Doesn't he look better that way?"

"Leave him alone!" Candy said.

Carrion looked back at Bill Quackenbush.

"Did you ever dream that your little daughter had such a rebellious spirit? No? Well, she does. In fact she's caused a great deal of trouble for me and for my friends. You see that man up there on the deck? It's all right, you can look."

Bill looked, as did Candy.

"His name's Kaspar Wolfswinkel," Carrion went on.

It was indeed Wolfswinkel who was up there, with all his hats buckled onto his head to keep them from being blown off in the escalating winds.

"Now, your daughter has caused that poor man incredible inconvenience, as I'm sure she'd be the first one to tell you. But you'll be pleased to hear that today's the day when she pays for all her troublemaking."

The staircase down which Carrion had been descending was touching the boat now, and Carrion had come to the bottom step. Suddenly he reached out, his reach uncannily long, as though his arms had suddenly grown to twice or three times their length, and caught hold of Candy.

"Say your good-byes," he said to her.

Candy looked back at her father. She'd never seen an expression on his face like the one that he was

wearing now. Confusion, anger and fear were all mingled together there. More than that, he seemed to be
staring at his daughter as though he were seeing her
for the first time; as though he couldn't quite believe
that she actually was his offspring.

From the roof of her house, Melissa began to yell to
her husband: "BILLY! DO SOMETHING!"

But Bill Quackenbush was beyond responding. His
frail imagination had cracked beneath the weight of all
that he'd seen in the last few minutes. He was left with
nothing to do but stare and gape and doubt his own
sanity.

On the deck of the *Wormwood*, the man in the yellow suit was applauding as Carrion dragged Candy
back up the stairs.

"Bring her up here!" he said, opening his arms.
"Please. Bring her to me! I've waited a long time for
this little reunion."

On the roof of 34 Followell Street, Melissa watched
in despair as the man with the death's head and the
sumptuous robes dragged her daughter up the spectral
stairs and into the looming ship. Had she come so
close to being reunited with Candy only to have the
opportunity snatched away from her again? It was
agonizing.

And to see her own husband standing idly by while
the abduction took place! That was the final straw. If
they survived this terrible day, Melissa thought, she
would file for divorce as soon as she could find a dry
lawyer.

There was only one tiny comfort to be had from these calamitous events: that it proved once and for all that the visions and the dream memories she'd had concerning the night Candy had been born were not her mind's crazed invention. There was a greater story here, of which she had glimpsed only a fragment: the daughter she'd known simply as Candy for all those years was somebody more. Part of a mystery she did not yet understand. Perhaps never would.

From the deck of the *Wormwood* Candy glanced back down at her mother—as though she sensed Melissa's stare. Then the Lord of Midnight pulled her away from the railing, and they both disappeared from sight, into the mystery of the ship.

Finnegan was the first into action. He flung himself off the *Lud Limbo* and landed on the stairs, which Carrion had ascended.

"*Come on!* Let's get up there before these stairs disappear!"

The rest of the gang were quick to pursue him, picking up whatever they could find by way of weapons and racing up the steep stairway in pursuit of their leader.

"Be ready!" Finnegan warned them as they entered the ship. "He knows we're coming after him."

They'd no sooner boarded the *Wormwood* than there was a yell from Carrion, which brought a ragged chorus of cries out of the bowels of the ship.

"I don't like the sound of that," Deaux-Deaux said.

"We have to do this *fast*," Finnegan said. "Let's find

Candy and get her out of this damnable place."

There was no further discussion. They went straight to the hold and threw it open. The grotesque results of Mater Motley's and her sisters' labors were waiting there, in all their horrible glory. Loosing a cacophony of shrieks and screams and caterwaulings, they poured out of the hold like a flood from a broken sewer pipe: stinking and repugnant.

They were not all human, not remotely. Some were huge: one a hybrid spider, its legs decorated with colored barbs and a woman's head set on its thorax; another a spine on which a hundred arms were sewn, like the limbs of a millipede, and at both ends raw wounds of mouths. Some were small: like crazed crabs, or eels with the heads of dolls. But whatever their size or shape, they were possessed by the same relentless rage. They shrieked and roared and chattered, dirtying the air with their obscenities.

There seemed to be no leader among them, nor strategy: they simply attacked. In a matter of seconds, the deck of the *Wormwood* was awash with mud and blood.

Finnegan fought his way through the battle to the wheelhouse, calling Candy's name every step of the way. There was no answer, however, nor any sign of her, which was troubling. He seized a round, ragged stitchling who was hanging upside down from the rigging, spitting on those below, and put the clean edge of his sword to its sewn-up throat.

"Where's the lady?" he demanded.

The creature giggled like an excited hyena. Finnegan pushed the blade into the stitchling's fabric.

A little arc of Todo mud spurted from the spot. "*Tell me,* filth," he said, "or so help me, I'll cut your stitches. Where did Wolfswinkel take the girl?"

The creature spat at him. Finnegan wiped the foul spittle from his face and pushed the blade a little deeper. More mud spurted. "All right! All right!" the stitchling said. "She was taken below. But you're not going to save her."

Finnegan withdrew his sword and was turning his back on the creature when he saw it pull a blade out of its pocket. He swung around on it, and with one swift motion he separated its head from its neck. The head hit the deck, still giggling, and rolled away under the feet of Geneva and a spider woman, who were locked in combat. Nearby, McBean, Tom and Deaux-Deaux were fighting a quartet of fiends whose heads were in their bellies. Mischief, meanwhile, had clambered up into the rigging where he was stabbing at a triple-horned monstrosity, which swung from the foresail with its claws hooked into the canvas and attacked the brothers with its venomous tail.

Nobody was having an easy time of it. But it was Malingo who was in the most imminent danger. As soon as he'd come aboard, he'd found himself surrounded by several of Mater Motley's seamstresses. Wielding their lethal needles, they had cornered him.

"We know who you are!" one of them spat.

"Giving aid to the enemy, weren't you?"

"Geshrat filth."

"Kaspar told us all about you," said the woman

closest to him, pricking his arm with her needle. "You're his little *slave*."

"Well, I'm not anymore."

"Once a slave, always a slave," said the woman, poking him again with her needle.

"No!" he said, knocking her hand away.

"How dare you touch me, *slave*," the woman seethed. "Prick him to death, sisters! First the eyes! Then the heart!"

Surrounded with needles, Malingo ransacked his memory for some defense against them. He threw back his head, staring up into the mass of ropes, sails and timbers. A spell! Quickly; something powerful—

Yes! A few words came into his head that might do the trick. They were from one of Wolfswinkel's grimoires, *The Testament of the Ninth Palamuudian*. He spoke it out, toward the heights of the ship; to the canvas and the rope.

> *"Come, unloving stuff.*
> *Take life,*
> *Take life!*
> *From this—"*

He blew into his hand, and threw the breath up into the rigging—

> *"And this!"*

He blew again, and threw—

"Take life!"

"What do you think you're doing, geshrat?" said one of the women, her voice oozing contempt. "Too late to be clever."

Malingo ignored her. He just kept staring up into the sails.

"Look at me!" the woman said.

Still he ignored her.

She slapped him hard across the face.

"I said, look at me, slave!"

Malingo had taken too many blows in his life to take even *one* more.

"You shouldn't have done that," he said very quietly.

The woman laughed and raised her hand to strike him again. But before she could do so, a rope snaked down from above and wrapped itself around her wrist. She let out a shriek of anger.

"What is this?" she screamed. "Undo this, geshrat!"

Malingo shook his head.

"Up," he said to the rope.

It obeyed on the instant, hauling the seamstress up above his head. She shrieked and slashed at him with her needle, but the rigging was alive to her malice. A second rope snaked down from among the sails and caught her hand, turning the needle against her and sinking it deep into her throat. For a few seconds she struggled. Then the struggles decayed into twitches, and the twitches ceased.

Seeing their sister dead, the women raised a vengeful chorus of shrieks.

"Death to the geshrat!"

"Tear him apart!"

"Eat his eyes!"

Needles glittering, they came at him from all directions. But the spell Malingo had breathed into the ropes and sails was only just starting its work. There was a great splintering of wood overhead, and the creaking of ropes being pulled taut; then a series of loud cracks and ripping sounds as the sheared timbers sliced through the sails. The women looked up, more puzzled than enraged, as the ropes snaked and wove and knotted and the canvas folded itself around the lengths of wood.

"What's happening?" one of the women demanded.

"It's him! He's doing it!" said another.

"Kill him, quickly!"

She'd no sooner spoken than there was a great din of snapping ropes above and a kind of makeshift creature—strange even in the company of the many strangenesses that littered the *Wormwood*'s deck—dropped into view. It had fingers of timber shards and its body was a toga of torn canvas, while its head looked like a nest of rope snakes, which rose up like cobras, flicking their frayed tongues at the sisters.

"Don't be scared of it!" came a voice behind the women. "It's nothing!" With a sudden rush of bitter air, Mater Motley swept into view. "It's just some nonsense this geshrat called up! Kill him, and *it* dies too!"

But the thing had already unnerved the women. It was half their height again, and the wind filled its sailcloth anatomy so that it swelled and snapped.

"Say your prayers, geshrat!" Mater Motley said, and slid two six-inch needles out of the folds of her soul-haunted dress. She wielded them like an assassin, striking to the left and right as she came at Malingo. He ducked and dove as she advanced, her needles getting closer and closer to his flesh. From the corner of his eye, he saw that the creature he had summoned from overhead was causing chaos among the Hag's sisters. Indifferent to their needles, it drove them to the railings and casually threw them over the edge into the sea.

"Damn you, geshrat!" Mater Motley spat. "I swear I'll make you bleed from a thousand wounds."

She stabbed at him again, but at the last moment he threw himself aside and the needles flashed past him, embedding their points in one of the two demonic figureheads that guarded the stern of the *Wormwood*. The old woman cursed ripely and worked her needles back and forth to try and free them from the painted timber. But even as she loosened them, there was a rumbling growl from the carving, and the great chiseled demon raised its horned head.

"That," it said, *"hurt."*

For an instant Malingo had the immeasurable satisfaction of seeing a flicker of fear cross Mater Motley's furrowed face. Then she governed herself, and the fear was replaced by a look of contempt.

"Idiot thing," she said, and turned on Malingo to finish him off. "Wood and paint don't scare me."

It was a mistake.

The pricked figurehead lifted a crudely carved fist

from its barrel chest, and with a casual flick of its hand it swatted the old woman across the deck.

Malingo didn't wait to see what damage the demon had done. He just offered up a silent prayer of thanks for his salvation, and—tempting fate to throw worse his way—he went in search of Candy.

52

THE SECRET OF SECRETS

THE DEEPER WOLFSWINKEL DRAGGED
Candy into the bowels of the *Wormwood*, the more terrifying his threats became.

"I bet you thought you'd never see me again, did
you? *He'll never do me any harm,* you thought. *He's
locked up forever.* Well, you were wrong. Don't they
say that everything comes to those who wait? And I
have been waiting—oh yes, waiting patiently—for the
chance to pay you back for my . . . humiliation. And
when you've gone, I'll find my slave and I will *make
him pay.* Oh yes. I will beat him till he has no more
tears to shed."

Candy didn't say anything. She just let Wolfswinkel
rant. "I'm not a prisoner anymore, you see. Oh no. I'm
a free man. She saw my importance, and she came to
get me personally."

"Who?"

"Who do you think? Mater Motley. She realized
that of all people, I'd be the one who knew how to deal
with you. How to find out all your little secrets."

"I don't *have* any little secrets."

"Oh, really." He laughed. "You don't know the half of it, you really don't."

As he spoke, there was a terrible din of screams and sobs from the deck overhead.

"You hear that yelling?" Wolfswinkel said. "That's your gang getting finished off. We're not going to waste time on anything fancy. We're just going to hang them all."

This was too much. Candy turned on him.

"You really are the scum of the earth, aren't you?" she said. "I thought you were just a nasty old drunk when I first met you. But the more I got to know you, the more I realized what a *hater* you are."

"A hater, am I?" said Wolfswinkel. "Well, listen to you! A few weeks in the Abarat and you've suddenly come over all high and mighty. I guess you think you've got the right, being a Princess and all."

"I'm no Princess."

Wolfswinkel turned to look at Candy with a puzzled expression on his face. "Didn't they tell you?" he said. Then, after a moment: "No, they *didn't*, did they? Well, isn't that something? I get to be the one to tell you. Ha! How perfect is that?"

"Tell me what?"

"I had a lot of time to listen while I was locked up in that damn house."

"Listen to what?"

"Whatever came my way. Like I said to Mater Motley, scraps, mainly. But if you're patient, you learn to thread them together."

"Am I supposed to know what you're talking about?"

"I'm not surprised they didn't tell you. What they did was against all the rules. And it was probably sacrilegious. You should never put power in the hands of women. It's asking for trouble." He grinned. "Especially those three."

"Diamanda and—"

"Joephi and Mespa. Yes."

"What have they got to do with me?"

"Think about it. Why do you think you're here?"

"It was an accident."

Wolfswinkel shook his head. "You know that's not true."

"What then?"

"I'm going to tell you this because of how much it's going to hurt you."

"Oh. That's nice."

"After what you did to me, girl, it's the least I can do." He looked at his nails, taking his time before he went on. "Do you know who Princess Boa was?" he said finally.

"Of course."

"So you also knew that she was murdered."

"On her wedding day, yes. By a dragon."

"By a dragon sent by Christopher Carrion, actually." Wolfswinkel looked up from his nails and studied Candy's face. "Are you surprised?"

"Not really," said Candy. "Why did he want her dead?"

"Oh, love, I suppose. At least that's the short answer. He loved her and she didn't love him. Not even a little. Instead she was getting married to Finnegan Hob, and Carrion couldn't bear the thought that he was going to lose his beloved to a half-breed."

"So it was better to kill her than to see her happy?" Candy said.

"Well, of course," Wolfswinkel replied, as though the logic of that was self-evident. "You don't believe me?"

She thought on it a moment.

"No. I believe you."

She'd seen the hatred that burned in Carrion's eyes. And the sorrow, and the anger. He was perfectly capable of destroying what he loved.

"Shall I go on?" Wolfswinkel said. "There's more."

"Yes . . . yes . . . go on."

"So the Princess Boa perished. And of course it was a terrible shock because she was supposedly this great force for good, and everybody thought that when she married Finnegan Hob there would be a new Age of Light and Love. In fact there were some stupid people who weren't willing to give up on that hope, even though she was dead."

"I don't understand."

"They thought that if they broke a few rules, they might still be able to save the soul of their beloved Princess."

"You're talking about Diamanda—" Candy said.

"—and Joephi and Mespa. Yes. The Sisters of the Fantomaya. Powerful, powerful women. Willing to risk—well, who knows what?—to undo the harm that had been done. They performed their magic over the body, and they brought forth the soul of Princess Boa."

"Who knew about this?"

"Just them. Like I told you, this was forbidden magic. Sacriligious. And the less people who knew, the less likely that whoever had ordered the murder of the Princess would hear that her soul had survived and attempt to finish the job. So the women worked their magic in the greatest secrecy. And when they were done, they took the soul of the Princess away from the Abarat."

"Where to?"

"Oh . . . I think you already know," Wolfswinkel replied.

"They took it to the Hereafter," Candy said softly.

The wizard smiled. "Indeed they did. They carried the soul of the Princess across the Izabella to the shores of the Hereafter. There was a terrible storm that night—which I suppose is only right and proper, given that such a massive crime against nature had been committed. The women's little boat was almost sunk. But they somehow got across to the other side. And do you know who they found when they got there?"

Candy already knew the answer. Knew it in her heart.

"My mother," she said.

"Yes," said Wolfswinkel. "Your mother: Melissa Quackenbush. She'd been sitting in a truck on an empty road. And of course she was very, very close to giving birth . . ."

". . . to me."

"Yes indeed. It was quite a night. And of course the

women of the Fantomaya assumed that all this was in the stars. It was meant to be this way, that they'd come ashore and find your mother sitting there in a broken-down vehicle."

"So what did they do?"

"What do you think?" Wolfswinkel said. "They *gave* Boa's soul to your mother for safekeeping so you and she would be brought up together."

"But I don't *have* a sister."

"She isn't your sister, Candy. Her soul is inside you. Sharing the same body."

"What?"

Candy's breath grew quick and shallow, almost panicky. She opened her hands and stared down at them, remembering as she did so how they'd looked in the Wunderkammen, when the Totemix were being freed. The golden light that had flowed through her skin and bone.

"In me?" she said. "The Princess is in me?"

"Yes."

Suddenly, so much that she'd experienced in the Abarat made sense. The countless moments when she'd had a feeling of familiarity; or when she'd known something she'd never learned in Chickentown (how to light a lamp that called a sea; how to say a Word of Power; how to speak to somebody in their dreams). It wasn't Candy who'd been doing all these things: it had been the Princess inside her.

"How did you find out," she said, "if it was all so secret?"

"You can't do anything so momentous in complete

secrecy," the wizard replied. "The earth hears. The wind hears. Rumors begin, and rumors beget rumors. Sooner or later somebody puts two and two together. There were you, appearing on my doorstep with more power in you than any child from the Hereafter should rightly have. What was I to make of that, huh?"

"So you worked it out?"

"It took a while, but yes, I threaded it all together. You, and the rumors I'd heard. Soon I was thinking the unthinkable."

"Who did you tell?"

"Nobody. Until now. Knowledge is power. I'm going to use what I know to get a lot of things."

"Suppose you're wrong?"

"But I'm not, am I? You see, I've followed your progress, Candy. I know what you've done. Battled zetheks. Unleashed Totemix. Killed the Criss-Cross Man. You're not an ordinary girl. Not remotely. In a way, I feel very honored to have some minor part in your undoing. You were the last hope of goodness in a darkening world. And when you're gone, there will be such a wonderful Night. *Such a terrible, wonderful Night.*"

The speech seemed to drain him, spilling out—as it did—so much that was poisonous and hateful.

"You pathetic little man," Candy said.

"Very possibly," he said. "But I am also your executioner."

"Shut your mouth, fool," said a voice out of the darkness.

Wolfswinkel took his eyes off Candy and squinted

into the shadows. "Who calls me a fool?"

"I do" came the reply. And out of the darkness stepped a creature Candy would not have recognized as Letheo but for the fact that he was wearing the same dark uniform she'd seen him wearing in the Dead Man's House. Otherwise he was completely transformed, his eyes huge and luminous, his mouth misshapen by teeth like needles. His body was covered with a fine coat of silver-gray scales. He was shaking from head to foot.

"What do you want, beast-boy?" Wolfswinkel said. "You've no business down here, you know that."

"I came for the girl."

"Well, you can't have her," said Wolfswinkel, moving toward Candy. "She stays with me."

Letheo stepped in the wizard's path, but Wolfswinkel moved with surprising speed for one of his weight. He caught Letheo a backhanded swipe that threw the changeling boy back against the wall of the passageway. The breath rushed out of him, and for a moment it seemed he would slide down the wall. Then a brightness flared in his eyes, and he leaped up off the wall as though something had pushed him from behind. The look in his eyes was suddenly crazed, like a rabid animal.

Wolfswinkel seemed to understand that he was in jeopardy. He began to issue a garbled spell—

> "Agrez monnifoe,
> Psych eye,
> Dremu dramu,
> Phorthigre!"

—the words creating a cage of spiraling energies around Letheo.

But the boy wasn't about to be made a captive so easily. He reached through the bars of his cage and caught hold of Wolfswinkel's throat.

"Let go of me, you freak!" Wolfswinkel shrieked, shaking Letheo violently.

"No!" Letheo hollered. "I don't think so."

Furious, Wolfswinkel reached up through the bars of Letheo's cage and clawed at his arm, opening wounds. Letheo yelled and struggled to hold on to his enemy, but finally Wolfswinkel's bulk carried the day. Wolfswinkel freed himself and retreated from the cage.

"You really have the most peculiar friends, girl," he said to Candy. "This one needs to be put out of his misery—right now!"

He spoke another word or two, and the energies that contained Letheo suddenly blazed like lightning. The boy threw himself back and forth in the cage to escape the pain.

"Stop this!" Candy said. "Please! Please!"

"It's over," Wolfswinkel said. He uttered a word, and the cage flickered out of existence, leaving Letheo to drop to the ground, his face knotted up in agony. Candy went to where he lay and stroked his face.

"I'd be careful," Wolfswinkel said. "He bites."

Letheo's eyes flickered open. "I won't . . ." he murmured. ". . . not you."

As she looked into Letheo's eyes, Candy saw Kaspar's reflection there—he was reaching down to grab hold of her. She was quick. She dropped onto her stomach and rolled over, kicking the wizard in his belly. He tottered backward against the wall. She was up in a heartbeat, and on him a heartbeat later, pulling at the buckle that secured his six miraculous hats to his head and knocking them off.

Wolfswinkel was not happy. *Not. Remotely. Happy.*

"NO!" he yelled, his face turning bright red in his fury. *"NO! NO! NO!"*

Letheo, meanwhile, had managed to get to his feet.

"Destroy the hats!" Candy yelled to Letheo. "Quickly!"

The beast-boy did as he was instructed, and with gusto. He seized the hats and tore at them with claws and teeth. Barbed spikes of power leaped from the torn material and burst against the walls and ceiling. The air smelled of fireworks. Wolfswinkel continued to holler his grief at the unmaking of his glorious millinery as pieces of headgear floated down like rainbow snowflakes. Even then Letheo wasn't finished. He seized the pieces out of the air and ripped them into even tinier pieces till there was nothing left but lifeless confetti scattered on the boards.

The destruction of the hats had somehow reduced Wolfswinkel too. He looked suddenly frailer. Even his clothes hung badly on his once well-fed frame, as though Letheo's attack upon his magic had made him a shadow of himself.

But it wasn't the beast-boy he was furious with. It was Candy.

"You," he said, pointing at her with a trembling

finger. "Right from the beginning you've tried to bring me to my knees. You . . . you . . . HELLSPAWN!" Flecks of thick white spittle erupted from his mouth as he worked himself up into a greater and greater fury. "All my *finest* plans! All my *dearest* dreams! YOU DESTROYED EVERYTHING!"

As he shrieked at her, a pained expression darted onto his face.

"WHY?" he demanded, his hand going up to his chest. "WHAT HAVE I EVER DONE TO YOU?" His fingers worked at his chest, the expression on his face getting more and more agonized. "I'M AN INNO-CENT MAN!" he yelled. "DO YOU HEAR ME? AN INNOCENT—"

He stopped there. The words. The breath. His heart. All of them stopped, right there and then.

His hand dropped away from his chest; he swayed for a long moment, then he fell sideways and hit the floor.

Very quietly Letheo said: "Well, will you look at that?"

A little trail of spit ran oh so slowly from the corner of Wolfswinkel's mouth, and then, like everything else, stopped.

Candy was astonished. This wasn't the way that she'd imagined a wizard (even a wizard as absurd as Wolfswinkel) dying: having a heart attack and keeling over.

But then the Abarat and its occupants had always been full of surprises; right to the bitter end.

53

THE WARSHIP UNMADE

STANDING ON THE ROOF of 34 Followell Street, Melissa kept turning and turning, and turning, looking for what? A sign that there was some purpose to this chaos and fear? Or better still, a glimmer of some miracle: the possibility that all these terrors would be swept away in a moment, and the hurts they had done be healed. But nowhere could she see any hint of salvation for Chickentown. The invading waters swept on past the roof where she stood, carrying an endless parade of flotsam and jetsam. Sometimes the sights she saw were so horrible that it was all she could do to keep herself from blotting them out, from crouching down beside the chimney and covering her face until the invading waters had cleansed the streets, carrying away their cargo of the dead, the living and the never-having-lived; only opening her eyes again when the house no longer shook as the current plowed against it.

But she couldn't avert her eyes. Not as long as she knew that Candy was still very possibly in the great dark hulk of the *Wormwood*. After all, she was responsible for what had happened to her daughter, wasn't she? If she'd had her wits about her that rainy night on the empty highway, when the three women had come from the Abarat smelling of souls and seawater, she would have locked the truck doors and windows against their magic, rather than curse her daughter with the terrible responsibility of another life.

But her wits had failed her that long-ago night. She'd been glassy-eyed with pain and fatigue; and when the old woman had opened her little box of miracles, and a wave of warm bright air had come to comfort her, Melissa had let it caress her, let it soothe her, and in so doing she had begun the brutal game of cause and effect which had in time brought the relentless waters of the Izabella down on the roofs and streets and innocent heads of Chickentown.

She took a moment to seek out the faces of her other children, including that most vulnerable of her infants, her husband, who had been pulled from the rowboat after Candy's disappearance and deposited on the roof. How were they enduring all of this? Shakily, it appeared. No matter. The boys were young and strong. And Bill? He'd find a way to tell heroic lies about himself tomorrow, if such a day ever dawned.

As she looked at her men, she heard a voice at her side.

"We should talk, Mother Quackenbush."

Melissa looked up, knowing even before she found the empty air that there would be nobody there to speak these words.

"Where are you?" she whispered, so as not to draw unwanted attention to herself.

"Here," the sorrowful woman replied. Diamanda was there to accompany her reply. She was like pale smoke in the afternoon light.

"Remember me?" she said.

Melissa nodded. "Of course."

"I know what you're thinking," the old woman said. "And whatever you do, don't regret the choice you made that night. It was for the best."

Melissa looked around at the chaos on all sides: the detritus of Chickentown's life left floating in the unforgiving waters of the Izabella.

"How can all this be for the best?" she murmured.

"It isn't always easy to see the greater purpose of things when you're trapped inside a single life."

"Who isn't?" Melissa said.

The old lady gave Melissa a strange smile, both sad and sweet.

"You'd be surprised," she said.

"So surprise me."

Bill interrupted the conversation there. He was staring at Melissa as though he thought she was crazy.

"Who the hell are you talking to?" he said, his lip curled with the old contempt.

Melissa was momentarily stuck for an answer, but the old lady whispered one in Melissa's ear.

"Myself," she said. Melissa smiled and furnished Bill with the same answer.

He shook his head. "Crazy cow," he muttered.

Melissa ignored him. She had better things to be

doing than trading insults with a man whose opinion she'd long ago given up caring about.

Instead she sought out the misty form of Diamanda. "Where were we?" she murmured.

Diamanda smiled. "*Surprise me,* you said."

"Oh yes, so I did."

"Well, I must tell you very quickly, though you may find what I'm about to tell you hard to believe, I swear on the Skein of Being that it's true—"

"I'm ready," Melissa said.

"Good. Then *listen.* The night we met. The night in the rain, on the highway. Do you remember?"

"Of *course* I remember."

"I had something with me. Besides my sisters."

"Yes. You had a box. It was filled with light."

"It wasn't light, Melissa."

"What was it?"

"It was a soul," Diamanda replied. "It was the soul of a dead Princess."

On the deck of the *Wormwood*, Christopher Carrion had watched the battle between the forces of Finnegan Hob and the stitchlings become steadily more destructive. The fabric of the ancient warship had taken a brutal hammering from the conflict. Decking and railings had been torn up, sails slashed and rigging brought down. A fire had been started at the stern of the vessel and rather than be burned alive by the flames, the two carved beasts that protected that end of the ship had wrenched themselves off their painted plinths and lumbered away down the length of the vessel, inspiring the figureheads at the bow to similar revolution.

The spectacle of destruction—any kind of destruction—had always given Carrion pleasure, from his earliest rememberings. The unmaking of the *Wormwood* was no exception. But now he had watched for long enough. It was time for him to find the girl from the Hereafter and finish her off. He was surprised that Wolfswinkel had not reappeared, but then perhaps he was taking rather too much time terrorizing the girl and would now need to be stopped.

Tearing his eyes from the pleasurable scene, he headed down into the hold. As he did so, a small figure darted across his path. He reached out and caught hold of the figure by the scruff of the neck. It was Letheo, looking thoroughly bestial.

"Thuaz," he managed to say (though his mouth was so misshapen that it could barely make the word). Then: "Please . . . Lord. It hurts me, being like this. I need . . . the green thuaz."

After luxuriating in the spectacle of the *Wormwood*'s unmaking, Carrion was feeling uncommonly generous. He let go of Letheo, who fell to the ground at his feet.

Again Letheo begged. "Prince . . . *please* . . ."

"Yes, yes," Carrion said, reaching into his robes and taking out the small bottle. "Why not?"

He tossed the vial from hand to hand a few times, enjoying the obsessive way that Letheo followed it with his eyes. Finally he let the boy snatch it out of the air. With trembling fingers, Letheo uncorked the bottle and took a swig of its contents. Then he swallowed the stuff, making a face at the bitter taste. He folded forward, his teeth chattering wildly. Carrion stood back and watched with a curious dispassion as the antidote took its agonizing effect.

"I wondered where I'd find you," said a voice from the shadows.

Carrion looked up from the sight of Letheo's twitchings and chatterings, and there was the girl from the Hereafter: his haunter, his nemesis.

"Well, well," Carrion said. "Did you give Mr. Wolfswinkel the slip?"

The girl shook her head.

"Wolfswinkel's dead," Candy said.

"How?"

"I'm not a doctor. But at a guess, his rage got the better of him. His heart just gave up."

"You're joking?"

"What would be funny about that?"

"Lord in Heaven. What is happening to the world?"

"Good question," Candy replied. She stared at Carrion for a long while as the *Wormwood* creaked beneath them and the fire consumed the sails above. "Why don't you tell me?"

"No," Carrion said. "You first. I insist. This was your plan from the beginning, wasn't it? You came into the Abarat to undo the very order of things. Lord, what a destroyer you are."

"*I* didn't plan anything," Candy replied. "But maybe the ghost in me might have done." She scrutinized Carrion and watched for some clue as to whether he understood its significance. But he looked genuinely puzzled, so she went on.

"I'm not Candy Quackenbush," she said. "At least . . . I'm not *just* Candy Quackenbush."

Still the puzzlement.

"The soul of somebody you once knew is inside me," she said.

Slowly it seemed to dawn on him what she was saying. His nearly fleshless face grew slack in its haunted pool.

"Boa?" he said, so quietly he was barely audible above the noise of destruction. "My Princess? My beloved Princess?"

"Yes."

Now it was Carrion who did the scrutinizing, watching Candy with a feverish stare.

"No. That's not possible," he said eventually. "I would have known."

"Not if she didn't know herself," said a third voice.

And there was Mater Motley, coming down the stairs to join them in her gown of the damned. Though Candy was scarcely happy to see the woman, the Hag's presence here was perfectly right and proper. Here they were, the four of them together for the first time. On one side, the Lord of Midnight and his grandmother. And on the other, the girl from the Hereafter with her Princess, joined in a single body: *the Two in One.*

"Is this all true?" Carrion said to his grandmother. "Does she have Boa's soul inside her?"

Mater Motley's stare was reptilian. There was no trace of human feeling in it.

"Yes," she said. "It's true."

"And all this time you *knew*?" Carrion said. "You knew that the woman I loved was just a touch away, and you didn't tell me?"

"How would it have helped?" Mater Motley said. "You think this girl would have loved you for what you did? You murdered Boa, child. And why? *Because she didn't love you.* As if love matters in the grand scheme of things."

"She loved me. She couldn't say it, she couldn't show it, but she loved me."

"Listen to yourself," the old woman said. "You sound like a lovesick adolescent! The time you spent besotted with her was time you could have spent planning and plotting. But no. You had to *dote*. You had to break your heart over some speck of beauty when anyone with eyes in their head could have seen that SHE DID NOT LOVE YOU!"

It was too much. Carrion couldn't bear to hear any more. He let out a cry of rage and frustration, the cry, perhaps, of a man whose heart had been truly broken. It resounded through the walls of the ship, scaring tens of thousands of tiny blue-backed roaches from their holes in the timbers. His nightmares were also agitated; they circled around, their bodies throwing off arcs of lightning against his collar.

Candy was tempted to make her escape while Carrion and his grandmother were distracted, but she couldn't bring herself to turn her back on this confrontation. Not when its subject was at least in some measure *herself*. Her life—past and future—was intimately bound up with the debate these two were engaged in.

The nightmares in Carrion's collar were continuing to get bigger, their forms becoming more and more grotesque. Carrion seemed not to notice what was happening to them. He was completely consumed by the feelings that had seized hold of him. With the greatest of difficulty, Candy took her eyes off Carrion for a moment and looked back at Mater Motley. The old woman was watching her grandson's agonies with undisguised satisfaction, as though this were a moment she had waited for, and she was determined to savor it.

There was a sharp cracking sound. The nightmares inside Carrion's collar—too big to be contained any longer—were fracturing the glass. The dark fluid in which they'd swum ran hissing down over the Prince of Midnight's robes. A flicker of concern came onto Carrion's face as he realized that his beloved night-mares were about to break out. Then he seemed to change his mind. For an instant something resembling a smile flitted across his lipless mouth.

Then the fracture in the collar gaped, and the flu-ids gushed out, hitting the boards at his feet with a wet slap. For the first time Candy saw Carrion's nightmares in all their lurid glory: they hung around his neck with their pallid, twitching lengths knotted and intertwined. But they didn't hang there for very long. No sooner had the collar emptied of fluid than they began to swell again, seeming almost to turn themselves inside out in their eagerness to be greater than themselves, skin following skin following skin, mottled one moment, scarlet the next; white speckled with yellow the next —

They had eyes, she saw. Clusters of long eyes, like the petals of shiny black flowers, and around the eyes there were trails of eggs, which were even now beginning their own horrific life cycle. They shook themselves free of the parent creature and went into freefall, but had only dropped a foot or so before they sent out a little hook which caught somewhere in the fabric of the robes. There the next generation rapidly swelled up and fattened, so that the Prince of Midnight became a kind of grotesque nursery, alive with all manner of mewling, spittling things; some made in an instant into the very image of venom and sudden death, others still sickly in their infant state.

Carrion had got beyond his furies now. He had begun to laugh—for no reason that Candy could properly comprehend—and the laughter quickly rose both in force and volume, so that it had a kind of insanity about it.

"Calm down, Christopher," Mater Motley said. "You're getting hysterical."

"And with good reason," he said.

"Oh?"

He began to advance on the old woman. "All along you've known . . ."

"What are you talking about?"

"About *her*," Christopher replied, and though he hadn't looked around at Candy since she'd begun her subtle retreat, he pointed toward her with unnerving accuracy. *"Her,"* he said again. "All along you knew what she was in her, and you didn't tell me."

From the corner of her eye, Candy saw Letheo crawl away on his belly, as though he sensed something apocalyptic was about to happen and didn't want to witness it, but Candy didn't move. Now all Carrion's attention was fixed again on his grandmother. The laughter, like the fury, had passed away. But they had left their echoes in him. His voice shook and his eyes flickered back and forth dangerously.

Candy could see by the look on Mater Motley's face that even *she*, whose bloodline ran in this man's veins, was a little afraid of him at this moment. She watched him very carefully, as though ready to act in her own self-defense in a heartbeat.

Meanwhile, as though there weren't jeopardy enough in the meeting of these two obscene powers, there came a din from above: the cries of attackers and wounded, the crash of falling timbers, the swelling din of conflagration. The fire was obviously spreading fast. Smoke was steadily thickening the air in the corridor where Candy, Carrion and Mater Motley stood; it couldn't be long before the air would become unbreathable.

Such concerns were very far from Carrion's thoughts right now, however. He was advancing on his grandmother, his voice filled with a cold fury.

"Do you have any idea of how much I have suffered?" he demanded. "Do you? The hours I have lain in an agony of despair because I longed for nothing more than to beg for her forgiveness? But how could I? I thought she was gone. I had paid a fortune to have the life choked out of her. What use were my *regrets*? I didn't know where her eternal soul had taken refuge." His voice rose in force and volume. "BUT YOU DID! ALL THIS TIME, GRANDMOTHER—YOU! DID!"

Suddenly, fueled by the agony and rage in Carrion's heart and unable to hold themselves back an instant longer, the nightmares leaped from Carrion's body and threw themselves toward Mater Motley.

The old woman was prepared for the attack. She raised her hands in front of her face, and for one extraordinary instant Candy seemed to see the eyes *burn through* Mater Motley's hands from the other side. Perhaps it was not an illusion but a piece of terrifying magic, because two hands made of light, ten times the size of the old incantatrix's hands, leaped forth to meet Christopher Carrion's nightmares. There was a massive release of energies as the two powers met: a force that momentarily threw itself around looking for someplace to escape and, finding a frailty in the ceiling, erupted in that direction, flying up with such power that it carried half the roof of the passageway with it.

Candy was helpless. Even if she'd had time to grab hold of something before the eruption caught her up in its blast, there was nothing to seize hold of, for everything was being uprooted.

The force of the energies caught her. Helpless to resist, all she could do was let it carry her up out of the passageway and deposit her in the midst of the fiery battlefield above.

54

THE LIVING AND THE DEAD

FOR A FEW SECONDS she lay on the deck in a daze, her consciousness almost knocked out of her by the blast. Sickened and dizzy, she sat up. There were eruptions of whiteness at the edge of her vision. She drew a few deep breaths, determined not to let her consciousness escape her. This would not be a safe place to lie in a dead faint, she knew. Not with the ship creaking and groaning around her as it prepared to die.

Finally, when the threat of unconsciousness passed, she hauled herself to her feet.

She could hear screams from the bowels of the vessel, the din of wholesale destruction. The lower compartments were flooding, and the slave giants who had worked the *Wormwood*'s oars were tearing up their prison in order to escape being drowned by the invading waters. Fires raged unchecked on the deck, columns of acrid smoke rising from the conflagrations. And everywhere she glimpsed, between the smoke and the flames, the litter of battle: stitchlings sprawled in pools of their life mud; a few of Mater

Motley's seamstresses, killed either by blade or by fallen debris.

And in one place, a heartbreaking sight: side by side, Captain McBean and little Tria lay, their eyes open and empty.

"Oh no . . . no . . ." Candy murmured.

She picked her way over and through the chaos toward the place where they lay, not wanting to believe what she already knew. Twice she lost sight of them: once when a column of fire erupted from the fractured deck in front of her, the other when—with a deafening crack—the deck opened so wide in front of her she had to run at it to make the jump to the other side. But finally, breathless and besmirched, she reached the bodies.

She saw immediately who the death bringer had been: the deck around Tria and the Captain was stained by a blast of energies that had surely emanated from Mater Motley. The Hag's hand was on this slaughter, no question of it.

She knelt beside the bodies, tears burning in her eyes. Gently she laid her hands on her friends' faces, and some voice in her (not entirely her own) quietly said thank you to them for being with her on this voyage, and wished them safe travels on the journey that they had now begun.

Then she stood up and returned the way she'd come—over the fissure, through the fire—to the hole in the deck through which the blast had first thrown her. The murderess was still below, to judge by the shock waves that continued to shake the deck. She quickly thought about what she was planning to do, and its possible consequences. One of them was that she would end up another victim of Mater Motley's power. But then why had the old incantatrix gone to such trouble to track Candy down and attempt to destroy her if Candy didn't pose some genuine threat to her?

There's power in me, Candy thought.

Maybe it was because of Boa; maybe it would have been in her anyway. Whatever its origins, it was real. She'd felt it inside her; heard its words from her own mouth; witnessed its effects. It was time now to accept it as her own. To possess it. To *wield* it.

She looked back through the smoke at the bodies of Tria and Captain McBean, to give force to her will, to empower whatever it was that was coiled in her.

As she fixed her eyes on them, the deck beneath her feet shook, buckled, and broke open, throwing her backward. A hail of dried tar and wood splinters came down around on her. And up out of the bowels of the *Wormwood* came Carrion and the Hag, locked together in a spiraling column of black flame. They screamed furies as they rose, unleashing waves of raw sound that broke against each other's faces like blows.

In a matter of seconds they rose high above the deck, out of Candy's reach. All she could do was watch while they battled, Carrion's nightmares arranged around him in a network of sickly pale monstrosities, Mater Motley's needles of dark venom spitting from her fingertips and from a slit in the middle of her forehead. They were a perfect match for each

other. Mater Motley piercing, Carrion smothering;
Mater Motley wounding, Carrion strangling; back and
forth, and around and around, and up and up, in an
ever more vicious exchange of hurts and hatred.

Scraps of wounded nightmares and shards of toxic
needles came down like an apocalyptic rain, some
piercing the deck, some falling away into the gaping
hole from which the two warring forces had emerged.

Candy was so intent on watching this grotesque
spectacle (*learning* from it, even) that she didn't notice
Malingo's approach till he caught hold of her arm.

"We have to get away from here!"

She tore her eyes from the locked warriors and
glanced at him. He appeared from the smoke looking
like a veteran not of one battle but of many: spattered
with Todo mud that had spurted from wounded stitchlings, his clothes singed by fire, and here and there
running with blood from the wounds he'd taken in the
battle. But he didn't seem to care. Not about his own
state, nor about the great struggle that was going on
above them. All he cared about was Candy.

"The *Wormwood*'s sinking—" he said to her.

"I know," she said, her eyes going back to the battle.

"If we don't get off it soon, we'll go down with the
ship! Are you listening to me?"

"Yes."

"So come on. Right now!"

"Wait—"

"Forget them, Candy."

"I want to watch!"

"What's to look at? Let them murder each other!"

"Could I have had that much power, do you think?" she said, half to herself. "If I'd stayed, I mean. Back in the Abarat."

"Would you want it?" Malingo replied.

Candy kept looking, almost afraid to answer the question truthfully. But then, if not to Malingo, then to whom? Hadn't he been there at the beginning of her self-discovery, in Wolfswinkel's house? And outside, in the wilds of Ninnyhammer, when she'd miraculously known how to call a glyph? She owed him an honest answer.

"I guess . . . if I knew I could use it properly . . ." she said. She looked his way again. "Why not have all the power you can get?"

"Well, you won't get it here," he said. "You'll just get death." He pulled on her arm. "Please, Candy. Come."

"But that damn woman killed—"

"I know. I saw."

"She deserves—"

"—to be judged. Yes! I agree. But not now. Not here. *And not by you.*"

Malingo had never spoken to Candy like this before: he'd always been aware, it seemed, of the debt of liberty he had owed her. But right now was not the time for niceties, and they both knew it. The ship was coming apart around them, its mighty structure unknitted by fire and battle and magic.

"All right," she said, finally allowing Malingo to coax her away from watching Carrion and the Hag. "I'm coming! I'm coming!"

They ran to the railings, and Malingo directed Candy's attention over the side. The *Lud Limbo* had been brought about by Deaux-Deaux and now scraped hulls with the listing bulk of the *Wormwood*.

"Do we jump?"

"We don't have much choice. See that pile of canvas and rope?"

"I see it!"

"Then let's go!"

He caught hold of her hand and grasped it hard. And together they jumped, landing heavily but safely on the heap of canvas. The breath was knocked out of her for a moment. She barely had time to catch it again before the *Lud Limbo* pitched sideways, and the canvas on which she and Malingo had landed slid to the edge of the deck.

The waters around the two vessels were filled with the fish that had accompanied the *Wormwood* here. They were now in a frenzy of hunger and anticipation. Candy and Malingo would have been delivered into the needle-lined jaws of these creatures had Candy not caught hold of a length of rigging with her left hand and kept tight hold of Malingo with her right. For a few terrifying seconds they swung back and forth while the monstrosities below snapped at their feet. Then the *Lud Limbo* tipped back in the opposite direction, and they slid back into the middle of the deck.

"We have to get away from here!" Malingo yelled to Deaux-Deaux, who was at the wheel of the *Lud Limbo*.

As the battle between grandmother and grandson escalated and death shudders passed through the *Wormwood*, the hull of the larger ship was striking the smaller, causing it to tip. This time Candy and Malingo were ready. They held on while the *Lud Limbo* rolled, then righted itself.

"The sooner we get everybody safely on board and get away from here—" Malingo began to say.

"Where're Tom and Mischief and Geneva and Finnegan?"

Malingo looked grim. "Bringing our dead," he said.

Candy sighed, nodded and glanced up at the *Wormwood*. In fact, she could see Geneva and Tom now, with a sad bundle in their arms, preparing to lower it over onto the deck of the *Lud Limbo*. She looked away, turning her gaze toward the roof of 34 Followell Street. Her father, she saw, was among the little cluster of people perched on the roof. They were safe for now, but their safety was by no means certain. The same fish that had surrounded the little rowboat could sense that their meal was now on the roof. The more ambitious of them were actually attempting to throw themselves up toward their victims. A few, possessed of rudimentary limbs, had even secured a tenuous hold on the eaves and had their shiny, wet eyes fixed on their intended victims.

Candy's family weren't the only people who were in trouble. Nearby were the remains of another small boat; this one overturned, its hull (which was white) holed in several places. Its occupants were perched on its barnacled hull. A huge mantizac circled the wreck-age, occasionally sticking its snout out of the water either to sniff at or terrorize its victims.

"How many people can the *Lud Limbo* carry?" Candy asked Deaux-Deaux.

"I don't know," said the Sea-Skipper. "Not that many."

"Well, we need to get my family off the roof. And the folks off that boat. And pick up any people in the water."

"Agreed. Enough people have died today."

Candy couldn't help but glance back up at the *Wormwood* again. Not at the removal of the bodies, but at Mater Motley and the Lord of Midnight, still high above the deck, locked in battle.

"Two too few in my opinion," she said coldly.

"Will you look at her?" Diamanda said softly to Melissa.

"I'm looking," Melissa said. "Believe me, I'm look-ing. She's changed. I mean, that's not the Candy who left here."

"That's truer than you know," Diamanda said.

"She doesn't seem to have any fear," Melissa said, watching in amazement as Candy, who was standing at the bow of the *Lud Limbo*, which was now halfway between the hull of the *Wormwood* and the roof of the Quackenbush house, supervised the picking up of the survivors from the overturned boat. The mantizac swam backward and forward in front of the rescue ship in frustration, staring up at Candy as though it knew that she was responsible for the removal of its dinner.

"I hope you're proud of her," Diamanda said.

"I am," Melissa replied.

Bill, who'd been listening to Melissa's half of the conversation, scowled at his wife.

"You *are* talking to somebody," he said. "Who is it?"

"You wouldn't believe me if I told you," Melissa replied.

Bill shook his head and turned away, muttering something under his breath.

"Was he ever charming?" Diamanda asked Melissa.

"Oh yes. He was charming. Good looking. Funny. I loved him. I still do." She saw Bill almost turn, as though he had something to say. But plainly he thought better of it, because he kept his silence.

"I should be going," Diamanda said.

"Must you?"

"Yes. There's work to be done. Souls to guide away to better places."

"The Abarat."

Diamanda smiled. "What, you think it's Heaven?" she said. "I'm afraid not. Maybe once it was . . . at least a *kind* of Heaven. But times change." She smiled. "Even there."

Reaching out, she touched Melissa's face with her phantom fingers. "Be strong, little mother," she said to Melissa. "I know you can be."

"Yes?" Melissa said a little doubtfully.

"Of course. Remember, I've seen you in *her*. And it's wonderful." She looked back toward Candy, and murmuring a good-bye, she left the roof and walked off purposefully across the water.

55

THE BEGINNING OF THE END

IT TOOK SEVERAL MINUTES for the *Lud Limbo* to pick up everybody in the vicinity of 34 Followell Street, and eventually get the people who were perched on the roof (Mrs. Hagen, from Number 37, and her dog, Rose-Marie, old Tom Shay from the corner house and the widowed sisters Lucy and Ruth McGinn, in addition to Candy's family) aboard the *Lud Limbo*. By the time everybody was safely on board and drying off in the afternoon sun, which was still warm, events on the *Wormwood* were reaching their grim conclusion.

To those watching the battle, it was unclear as to whether it was Carrion's nightmares or his grandmother's dark powers that were carrying the day. The fire had spread from bow to stern by now, and the ship was so wreathed in flame and smoke that all but a few glimpses were granted the spectators. But there was no doubting that the two forces were still colliding, catastrophically. Sometimes the vessel would erupt with blazing energies, as though a stray spark had gotten into a fireworks factory and everything was going off at the same moment. Then there'd be a curious moment of stillness as the sparks cleared away, and the folks on the *Lud Limbo* would see—or think they saw—two figures locked together as though only death would separate them. Then the flames and smoke would rise up again, to obscure the scene.

"Mater Motley's old," Malingo said. "Brittle bones."

"Yes," said Candy. "But I bet she's got more tricks up her sleeve."

By degrees it became apparent that she was right: Mater Motley *was* carrying the day. Though Carrion's nightmares seemed capable of re-creating themselves in fouler forms, the old woman was steadily laying them low. The once mighty Lord of Midnight seemed painfully exposed now that his collar had been destroyed and its fluids poured away. It was his skeletal features that looked brittle, not his grandmother. Though his monstrosities repeatedly put themselves between their master and Mater Motley's conjurations, the wounding spells broke through over and over again, steadily weakening and exhausting him.

Once in a while, he would launch a sudden sideswipe and catch the old woman a devastating blow, but she was uncannily resilient. She'd go down, howling, and Carrion would dispatch his nightmares to finish off the job, only to find that she was faking. She'd be up in an instant, tearing open her grandchild's creatures without mercy, spattering their vile matter in all directions.

"Surely he can't last much longer," Malingo murmured as Carrion appeared momentarily in the chaos, his whole body torn and broken.

"Maybe he wants to go down with the ship," Candy said.

"And take her with him?"

"Why not?"

"Couldn't happen to two nicer people."

"Oh, wait," Candy said.

"What?"

"There!"

As she spoke, she saw the Hag raise her hands, and a burst of power flowed from them toward Carrion. Candy saw him lift his own hands in a pitiful attempt to ward off the attack, but his defenses were extinct. As the assault came against him, he pulled his robes up in front of his head to shield himself. But it was useless. As Mater Motley's flow of power continued to strike him, she added words to her attack, calling out to him.

"I should have left you in the fire," she said to him. *"It would have saved a lot of wasted time."*

Her words seemed to mark Carrion's undoing. He let the robe drop from his fingers, and the assault strike him down. He dropped to the deck and for a few seconds lay there unmoving. Then, at a summons from their mistress, a horde of Mater Motley's stitchlings came out of the filthy smoke and picked him up. Doubtless at the old woman's instruction, they made certain that these last moments were as distressing and humiliating as possible. They vomited mud upon him as they tore off the last vestiges of his fine robes, uncovering his wretched, wounded body. Then they threw him up in the air like a plaything, dropping him and picking him up to do it again.

Candy watched all this with profound revulsion. Though Carrion had been her chief tormentor during her time in the Abarat, she still felt some residue of pity for him. She didn't know whether it was the Princess' heart that felt this surprising tenderness toward him, or her own. But in the end, she thought, did it really matter? A feeling was a feeling wherever it was born.

"Why can't they just get it over with?" she growled. "I hate stitchlings! And that woman. Most of all I hate that woman."

The creatures were bored with their tormenting now. They looked up at Mater Motley, who still hovered in the stained air on a column of churning motes, and she pointed to the railing. Hauling him like a sack of garbage, they carried their plaything to the side of the vessel and tossed him overboard. He sank quickly, and the water where his body disappeared became foamy and scarlet for a while as fishes converged on the spot to pick at the remains. But perhaps he was too toxic a meal even for the mantizac, because the feeding frenzy quickly died away.

"Was that who I think it was?" said John Serpent, looking toward the *Wormwood*.

"Not Carrion, surely?" said John Drowze, sounding quite scandalized.

"Like a piece of spoiled meat," John Slop said.

"Well, isn't that what he was?" said Deaux-Deaux. "What else is *Carrion*?"

Candy wanted to contradict Deaux-Deaux, but she knew any protest she made now would not be understood. Later, perhaps, when all these horrors were over and done with, she would confess to somebody that what little she had known of the Midnight Prince had suggested a man far more complicated than anything she'd ever heard said about him. But now was not the time for the truth to be told. People needed a villain today, pure and simple: and he was an ideal candidate. So she kept her silence.

Besides, there were other things to occupy everybody's attention. One fact in particular was now of pressing importance. *The Izabella was starting to recede.*

It began slowly at first. The flotsam and jetsam that was floating on the surface of the water turned around and was carried away. Mischief was the first to notice what was going on.

"All those who are going ashore ought to get going," he said. "Because after this, the next stop's the Abarat!"

There was sudden consternation on board the *Lud Limbo*. Mrs. Hagen was quite prepared to throw herself overboard rather than take a one-way trip to a country she'd never heard of, and was only dissuaded from doing so when Candy said: "Ropes! Everybody help me!"

"What are we going to do?" said Geneva.

"We'll hitch the ship to the chimney of our house till the water goes down a little—"

"That's risky!" said Finnegan.

"What else do you suggest? These people don't want to go to the Abarat."

"I do," said Ricky, glancing at his father. "That's where you went, right, Candy?"

"Yes, that's where your sister went," Melissa said. "But she had special reasons to be going. You belong here with your family."

"Aw, Mom—"

"Don't even *try* it, Ricky. You're not going anywhere."

While this exchange was going on, Candy, John Mischief, Geneva and Tom had all found ropes. Finnegan scrambled up the roof to the chimney stack and caught the ropes as they were flung to him, while they secured the other end to the mast of the *Lud Limbo*. None of the Chickentowners lifted a finger to help with this labor. They kept their distance from the Abaratians, as though only now—with the distracting spectacle of battle over—had they begun to realize what incredibly alien company they were in. Only Bill Quackenbush spoke up; and it was to make the most idiotic of complaints.

"I built that chimney!" he said, pointing his finger at Finnegan. "You'd better not do any damage—"

"Oh, for God's sake, Bill," Melissa said. "You didn't build it."

"It's still *my* chimney," he raged.

"Got no choice, sorry," said Mischief, leaning forward so that he and all his brothers' faces were inches from Bill.

"It's either that—" said Moot.

"—or you and your family—" said Slop.

"—get swept away—" said Fillet.

"—to places—" said Drowze.

"—you would not want—" said Pluckitt.

"—to end—" said Serpent.

"—up," said Sallow.

"They'd eat you," Mischief added. "Beginning with your nostrils."

All the brothers were most amused at this last remark.

"Nostrils, good one!" Drowze remarked amid the guffaws.

"Are you laughing at me?" Bill Quackenbush said. "You *freaks*!"

Bill threw a punch at the brothers, but somehow he missed all eight targets. Mischief put out his foot behind Bill and gave him a quick push. He stumbled backward and would have slid off the roof into the water had Ricky and Don not caught him.

"Let it go, Dad," Ricky said.

"We need some help here!" Candy said. "Everybody lend a hand."

Bill glowered and muttered to himself while everybody else put their efforts into hauling on the ropes and helping Finnegan secure them around the chimney. It wasn't an easy task. The receding water was exerting a powerful grip on the boat, and it took everybody hauling together to keep the vessel from being swept away. But with the combined strength of Chickentowners and Abaratians, the *Lud Limbo* was successfully moored to the Quackenbushes' house, at least for a while. As folks wiped the sweat from their brows or leaned over to catch their breaths, Tom said: "There's a sight," and everyone, either on the roof or on the deck, looked up to see the *Wormwood,* its structure weakened by the fire and magic and nightmares, now unknitted by the very tide that had carried it here. Its back broke in two places, and the forward section started to slide into the water, dragging the mast on the midsection with it. The mast came crashing down, rolling off the deck and into the sea, its rigging in turn dragging down the mast beside it.

"Can you see Mater Motley?" Finnegan asked Candy.

"She's there at the stern. See her?"

The only victor of today's battles wasn't alone. A few of her seamstress sisters had survived the engagement and, along with the stitchlings who had disposed of Carrion's body, were gathered around her. An ugly music was coming from the women: a chorus of unharmonious voices singing a song of power. Its purpose soon became plain. The sound produced a nimbus of skittering energies, which proceeded to cloak Mater Motley from head to foot.

"She's getting away," Finnegan said. He then let go a stream of Abaratian, for which Candy needed no translation. He was cursing.

The song spell was steadily growing more discordant.

The veil of transport now eclipsed the old woman entirely.

Finnegan glanced at Candy: "Can't you stop her somehow?"

"Me?"

"You've got magic. Stop her escaping."

"I don't know how."

"Damn her," Finnegan said, as though he were genuinely wishing the Hag to hell, deep in his heart.

"She doesn't escape unscathed, if that's any comfort," Geneva said. "I saw wounds upon her. Carrion left his mark."

The seamstresses' song spell suddenly stopped dead. And on the instant that it ceased, the flux it had summoned up folded into itself and disappeared. Mater Motley had gone with it.

"If there's any justice, her wounds will be the end of her," Mischief replied grimly.

"I doubt that they will," said Geneva. "But we can hope for the worst, I suppose."

56

DOWN AND DOWN

With Mater Motley gone, the remaining portions of the *Wormwood* now succumbed to the receding tide. What little remained of the deck collapsed, bringing down the final mast; and as it fell the once mighty vessel shuddered and folded upon itself, timber on timber, the waters of the Izabella extinguishing the flames as the ship sank and receiving the sad remnants into her embrace with something like a sigh. In a matter of a minute or so, the Sea had claimed the vessel's bones and carried them away, leaving only a dark scum of Todo mud, ash and splinters to mark the spot where the *Wormwood* had sunk.

Only John Serpent, of all people, had anything good to say about this grim scene.

"She was a great ship," he remarked. "Whatever terrible purposes she was put to. Mischief, salute her for us, will you? We should pay our respects. She was mighty in her way."

Candy gave Serpent a sideways glance.

"Of course if you think not, lady . . ." he said, his

tone distinctly more courteous than usual.

"No. Salute away. Personally, I'm glad it's gone."

"You're young," Geneva said softly. "Death doesn't move you so much, because you can't imagine it ever happening to you."

Candy contemplated this for a moment. "I think I can," she said finally.

Behind her, her father suddenly started yelling at the top of his voice. "Look at that! My chimney! I told you this would happen!"

Candy looked around to see that the chimney stack was beginning to crack under the pressure put upon it by the tugging of the *Lud Limbo*.

"It doesn't matter, Dad," Don said, quite reasonably. "We were going to move anyway."

"Shut up! I didn't ask your opinion!"

"I'm only saying—"

"And don't talk back to me!" Bill hollered.

He lifted his hand as though he intended to strike his son. Don didn't flinch, as he would normally have done. He just stood looking at his waterlogged father with a faintly amused expression on his face.

Bill suddenly seemed to realize that there were a lot of people watching him. He lowered his hand. Then he turned to Melissa.

"Are we going to get on this damn boat then?" he said.

She didn't bother to look at him. She was staring at her daughter. "What are you going to do, Candy?" she said.

"Well, first we're going to get you all to a safe, dry

place, where you can stay till the water goes down. There'll be help here soon."

"Yes, I know. But after that, honey? What will you do after that?"

"Oh. I'm staying," Candy said. "That's why I came back. It was time to come home."

A smile of relief came onto Melissa's face. "Oh, honey, I'm so glad. I've missed you. Lord, how I've missed you."

"And I've missed you, Mom," Candy said.

They put their arms around each other, as though they had only just been reunited, and hugged and cried, while everybody else on the roof tried to pretend they weren't looking. "Why didn't you tell me, Mom?" Candy said.

"I didn't know how to," Melissa replied.

"What the hell are you two talking about?" Bill Quackenbush demanded.

"Forget it, Bill," Melissa said.

"Oh no. Not this time. It's a conspiracy, that's what it is."

"Don't be stupid, Bill."

"I'm not stupid. I'm the only normal one here." He turned his rage on the Abaratians. "Look at these freaks."

"They're not freaks, Dad," Candy said. "They're my friends."

"Friends? These things? They're not even human." He pointed at the brothers John. "How can you call that your *friend*?" Now at Finnegan. "Or that . . . abomination. What kind of screwed-up thing is that?

Black skin! Red hair! Green eyes! That's not *natural*. I'm warning you. All of you. You'd better get your sorry butts out of this state before the water goes down, because I'm telling you, this is Chickentown. We don't mess around with weirdos like you here!"

"Stop it, Dad," Candy told him.

She didn't speak loudly, but she didn't need to. Her voice carried a quality she'd heard in it before: her father wasn't so dumb as to ignore it. He stopped his threats and looked at his daughter with a puzzled expression on his face. No, not puzzled. *Frightened.* For the first time in his life, Bill Quackenbush was a little afraid of his daughter. Candy could see the fear there in his eyes, and after all he'd said and done over the years, she couldn't help but feel a little rush of pleasure.

"You listen to me," she said to him. "One last time. *These are my friends.* They come from a place called—"

That was as far as she got. There was a sudden crash, and the chimney stack toppled, an avalanche of bricks and concrete tumbling down over the roof into the water. No longer moored, the *Lud Limbo* creaked and rolled as the receding waters tugged on it.

"This is it!" Finnegan yelled. "The boat's going back to the Abarat whether we like it or not."

Panic and confusion erupted, as everybody who'd been pulled aboard the *Lud Limbo* started to clamber off. They didn't know where the boat was going; they only knew they didn't want to be on it when it went. The roof of 34 Followell Street might be a shaky refuge, but at least they knew its address. People pushed, people cursed, people kicked.

Sickened, and a little ashamed of what her people were doing, Candy looked away, down into the water. Was there something down there, besides the ever-vigilant fish?

Yes, there was! A face, a human face, was looking up at her from the murk. She knew it too. The deep-set eyes, the mass of dark hair—

She started to retreat from the railing, but in the same instant the figure below her propelled himself out of the water, his hands reaching up to catch hold of her. The deck was wet and slick beneath her heel, and she lost her balance, falling forward. His hands grabbed her neck and shoulder. She let out a yell.

The creature smiled up at her for an instant, as though this was just some innocent game, and then she was dragged over the railing and into the fast-retreating waters of the Sea of Izabella.

57

"NEVER FEAR . . ."

HER ABDUCTOR WAS STRONG, and he carried her down and down, and though she fought him as best she could, his hold was too powerful for her to free herself. Once, just once, she managed to look up and saw the shape of the *Lud Limbo* far above her. The bullyings and persuasions of the tide were quickly carrying it away. Any hope of rescue was leaving with it.

She took her eyes off the dark shape of the vessel and looked down at her abductor again. It was Letheo, of course. She tried to signal to him that she needed to go back to the surface, but he shook his head. Was he crazy? Her lungs were ready to burst from the lack of air.

She struggled to release herself from his hold, desperate now, and this time, much to her astonishment, he loosened his grip and pointed toward a doorway. It was not just *any* doorway. Though she'd become momentarily disoriented in the rush of gray-green water and all the trash that it contained, she now understood where they were. He had brought her down to the front door of number 34, her own front door. It opened and closed eerily as the vagaries of the current caught it. Letheo pushed it open, and they swam over the familiar threshold and into a very *un*familiar world. Yes, of course she knew it all: the pictures from the family's visit to Orlando floating off the hallway wall, a school of beer cans floating past; the furniture and the threadbare rug. She knew all of it so well. But—as if in a dream—it had been made over by the waters: become a murky warren of rooms, and she floating through them, defying gravity.

Letheo was pointing upward now. Candy understood instantly what he was telling her, and she started to swim up the stairs. After thirteen or fourteen steps up, she broke surface. She drew a succession of gasping breaths, then climbed the rest of the stairs until she reached the top, where she sat, panting and coughing. Letheo had put his head out of the water now, and as soon as she'd caught her breath she said: "Were you trying to drown me?"

"No!"

"Well, why did you drag me off the boat like that?"

"Him." Letheo pointed up the stairs.

Candy looked over her shoulder. The door to her parents' room was open. She got to her feet, the water squelching in her shoes, and crossed the landing to the bedroom door.

She glanced back at Letheo, thinking he was going to accompany her. But he had stayed where he was, his chin just clear of the water. A box of cereal floated behind him, its soggy contents scattered over the water. Small silver eels picked at them.

"Go on," Letheo said, nodding toward the door. "He won't hurt you. He's beyond hurting anybody now."

She'd known the moment that Letheo had said *him* who he was talking about. She could hear a thin, whining breath from the bedroom. He was there. But was he really beyond hurting her, as Letheo claimed? She thought of her last sight of him, as he was thrown over the side of the *Wormwood* by the stitchlings. He'd been in no condition to harm anybody. She was safe from him. She pushed open the door a little wider and stepped inside.

This room had been her mother's sanctuary, her place of refuge from the kids and from the man she'd married. There was a double bed in it, but her father hadn't slept in it for five or six years. And now—*how weird was this?*—there was a man in that bed, and that man was Christopher Carrion. The Lord of Midnight was lying sprawled like a corpse in the middle of her mother's bed.

He was a mess. He had pulled up a sheet to roughly cover himself, but his wounds were already bleeding through it. His collar was of course shattered, leaving just a few sharp fragments around his neck. His nightmares had gone, dead or forsaken him.

But it was his face that was the really shocking part. His skeletal look, that living death's head of his, had always frightened Candy. But he was fearsome no longer. The battle on the *Wormwood* had cleansed all the venom from his expression; the cruelty had gone too; so had his intimidating stare. He didn't even seem to know that she was in the room. Finally she said:

"Carrion?"

His yellow-gray lids flickered, and his pale, pale eyes slid in her direction.

"So. Letheo found you. Good."

His voice was so small, so frail, that she could barely make sense of what he was saying.

"Come here . . ." he said to her. She didn't move. He raised his hand, the fingers barely more than bone, and beckoned to her. *"Please,"* he said. "Come here."

She took a step toward the bed. Some ragged scrap of a thing that had been brought into the room attached to Carrion's body crawled like a wounded crab away from her foot and took refuge under the bedside table. She shuddered. She was sorely tempted to leave now, before he spoke again. But then she'd never know what he had to say to her, would she? And she wanted to know.

He reached up, and very gently he took hold of Candy's hand. His flesh was icy cold, and damp. His thumb moved across her palm and came to rest in the middle of her hand. Then he seemed to summon a little fragment of energy from somewhere, and two pinpoints of brightness appeared in his eyes, focusing upon her.

"Princess?" he said. "Are you in there? I want to talk to you."

Candy started to pull her hand away. But for all his frailty, Carrion held it tight.

"Princess?" he said again. *"Speak to me. I beg you."*

Candy shook her head. Tears had sprung into her eyes, and she felt an agonizing ache in her chest. The air in the room—pressed into this little space by the water—made her blood thunder in her ears.

"Please," he said again. "All I want to do is speak to you one last time. Is that so much to ask?"

The reply came out of Candy without her even willing it to, her tongue shaping thoughts that her mind had not invented.

"I'm here," she told him.

It was true too. She could feel the presence of the Princess in her, almost as though they were standing side by side. But the stranger thing was this: there was nothing new in the feeling. She realized in that moment that the Princess had *always* been there with her, right through life, but her presence had been so familiar to Candy, so much a part of what it felt like to be Candy Quackenbush, that she'd never questioned it.

"I . . . see . . . you," Carrion said, his eyes narrowing. "By all the powers . . . *I see you.*"

There was a noise at the door, and for a moment Candy took her eyes off the Lord of Midnight and looked back. It was Letheo. There was something about the way he watched her that made Candy's heart quicken with unease. *You should get out of here,* said a voice at the back of her head.

Princess? Candy thought. *Is that you?*

Yes, it's me, the thought replied. *We have to get out of here, sister, while we're still able to do it.*

Can Carrion hear our thoughts?

No. But he'll guess soon enough. He's not stupid.

We have to get out. This time there won't be any women of the Fantomaya to save our necks.

Does he still mean us harm? Candy thought.

Of course, came the reply, *of course.*

"What are you thinking?" he said to her.

"Nothing important. Just talking to myself."

"Are you afraid?"

"No," she said with more certainty than she felt.

She deliberately kept her gaze averted from his, afraid that he would read something there.

"Princess?" he said. *"Forget the girl. It's me you need speak with."*

They had to have a plan, Candy thought while Carrion talked on. If they were going to get out of here alive, then they needed to be ready, if a moment presented itself, to seize it.

But it was hard to hold on to her thoughts in the oppressive bubble at the top of the house. The air seemed to be getting staler with every breath she took. Her head throbbed so hard she thought she would pass out. It was so hot up here; the air under such pressure—

Wait! There was something useful in that thought, if she could just make sense of it again. What had she just imagined? A bubble of stale air locked up at the top of the house; air that kept them breathing and also kept the water of the Izabella from invading the rest of the house.

Yes! That was it! *The air was keeping the water out.* The windows were all closed, and so the Sea couldn't get in. But if one of the windows were to break—

"What are you thinking about?" Carrion said.

"Me?" Candy said.

"Yes, you. *Look at me.* Let me see what's in your eyes."

Candy tried to laugh it off.

"It's just strange, that's all," she said, still keeping her eyes from meeting his. "To see you . . . uh . . . lying there like that . . . on my mom's bed."

"I said: *look at me.*"

There was more strength in his voice now. It wasn't a request, it was a demand.

Be careful, Boa warned. *He's not as weak as he's pretending to be. We're only going to get one opportunity to do what we're thinking. He means to die with us.*

"Why don't you look at me?" Carrion said.

She couldn't put off the moment any longer. Taking comfort from the presence of the Princess, she looked down at Carrion, and he returned the look: gaze meeting gaze meeting gaze.

"There you are," Carrion said softly, and Candy knew by the tender tone in his voice that it wasn't *her* he was talking to at that moment; it was Boa. She took immediate advantage of his distracted state, very gently slipping her hand out of the Dark Prince's grip. Then, still holding Carrion's gaze (or more correctly, letting the Princess hold it), she took a slow step backward from the bed.

His eyes flickered, like fire flecks in milk.

She held her breath, praying that he wouldn't wake from his trance of devotion but would keep staring at his Princess, keep adoring her.

She began to take a second step. But as she did so,

there was a sound from the roof above, and he made a small puzzled noise in his throat, as though he suddenly understood that he was being abandoned.

Oh so softly, he said:

"...*no*..."

Then he sat up in bed. The sheet fell away from his wounded body, and a foul smell came to Candy's nostrils. The stench she'd sometimes smelled behind the chicken factory, of dead and rotting meat.

She turned her back on him at that moment and ran toward the window, trying to keep her mind focused on what she'd been planning—

Behind her, Carrion spoke again. Not so softly this time. Nor to her.

"*Princess,*" he said. "*Where do you think you're going?*"

Candy squeezed her eyes closed until they stung, determined to ignore both the question and the questioner. But the Princess had a history here that she did not. She couldn't be quite so indifferent to this man. He had killed her, after all; or at least masterminded her death. That was a hard claim to casually shrug off.

"Come back here," the Lord of Midnight said. "And let's get this whole tired business over, once and for all. I've waited, Princess. And so have you. Even the girl from the Hereafter has waited, though she didn't really know what for. But it is very simple. We were waiting to put an end to this sad little game of hide-and-seek."

"*I'm sorry*..." Candy heard herself saying, though the words were not being shaped by her; they were coming from the other girl in her head, the Princess. Was it a trick the Princess Boa was playing on Carrion right now, distracting him with this apology while they'd plotted against him? Or was there something here Candy didn't understand? Something that the Princess had done to Carrion for which she was genuinely apologetic?

"Sorry isn't good enough, angel," the Lord of Midnight said. "You owe me more than that. You know you do."

Candy heard her mother's bed creak as the Lord of Midnight lifted himself up off it, which in his broken state must have taken an immense effort of will. She forced herself not to look around at him, even when she heard his dragging tread as he approached her. She just stared at the window, and at the fish on the other side, darting through clouds of silver bubbles.

He was right behind her now. She could feel his breath on her neck, even colder than the touch of his fingers. It was the ice of the Midnight Hour that was in him: the cold of Gorgossium's Hour, the Hour of madness and despair and sorrow everlasting. All of it was in his touch. She felt his fingertips graze her shoulder.

"Never fear, angel . . ." he said with a terrible tenderness. *"I've got you now. And for always."*

No, Candy thought: *No—*

He wouldn't take them. She wouldn't allow it. Not after the struggle she'd had to free herself from him; and understand who she was. She wouldn't let him put his hand on them and take them away to death.

The Princess seemed to hear her resistance. Candy felt Boa's presence, closer than close. In her, beside her: holding her hand, holding her heart. It gave her comfort.

More than that. It gave her power.

Together . . . she thought.

Together, the Princess replied.

"Angel?" Carrion said. The Princess didn't reply. Instead they drew a single breath, the Two in One, and unleashed a cry on the back of that breath, their voices one tremendous word-sound.

"Jassassakya—thüm!"

The force of the Word flew against the window. For a moment the glass simply rattled, its strength sustained by the force of the water on the other side. Then it cracked.

A second before it broke, Candy felt her legs go out from under her as the Princess dropped her down to the carpet. A heartbeat later the window shattered inward, and a rush of inky water flecked with silver fish poured into her mother's bedroom. Candy caught a glimpse of Carrion in the instant before the flood claimed him. She saw his white eyes widen and his mouth grow slack. Then the wall of water caught them all, and the image of the Lord of Midnight was erased as though a dark hand had been passed across it.

58

THE RETURN OF THE SEA

ON THE ROOF OF number 34, the survivors heard the sound of the breaking window and felt the house shake as the water rushed into it. But none had the least idea of what had gone on below; nor saw the three people—Candy, Carrion and Letheo—who were carried away by the force of the tide. They were too busy praying, or sobbing, or watching the skies in the hope of seeing some sign of rescue. Even if any of the survivors *had* glimpsed somebody in the flood, it's doubtful they would have recognized any faces in the rush of water. Not with so much else from the Quackenbush residence being carried along in the same tumult: the armchair which Bill had made his throne and the television in front of which he sat despairing of his life; the family photo albums and all the love letters Bill had written to Melissa while he was courting her; the kitchen table where they'd all sat as a family and eaten in unhappy silence. All of it washed away.

* * *

The same thing was happening throughout Chickentown: as the Sea of Izabella retreated, her waters carried the town's garbage away with her, scouring the streets of the weary town. Of course in the process they destroyed much that was of genuine value, and which could never be replaced. The town hall and all its records were washed away; the parks and cemeteries were turned to mud; whole streets were leveled, hundreds of vehicles carried away. Even the biggest structures in Chickentown, the coops that had housed the egg-laying treasures of the town, were brought to their knees by the fury of the waters.

But in spite of how terrible all this destruction was, there was remarkably little loss of life. Not only had a lot of people retreated to safe places before the inundation, but the waters themselves seemed to have treated with a supernatural courtesy those whom circumstance had put into their care. Stories would abound of how people were saved *from* the flood *by* the flood: how the waves seemed to conspire to bear them up rather than overwhelm, to lull them like infants in cradles of water, to be their protectors.

It was all so *strange*, people would say when they talked of this day in times to come: the Day of the Chickentown Wave. All so very, very strange. Tragic too, of course, and sometimes even terrifying, but mostly strange.

Needless to say, the retreat of the waters was scarcely the end of the matter. While Chickentown went about the business of accounting its losses and burying its dead, the authorities attempted to solve the question of where the waters had come from in the first place. The more preposterous suggestions—another dimension or world that could not be seen by the human eye—were immediately dismissed. Luckily, there were other, more plausible answers close at hand. Four days after the deluge, a group of geologists came from the University of Minneapolis with a clear edict from the head of their department that they find a rational explanation for what had happened in Chickentown. It didn't take them long. Forty-eight hours later they were able to report to the press that they had discovered the presence of subterranean tunnels that had undoubtedly provided the conduits for the flood that had inundated the town. There was, they surmised, a very large body of water deep underground, which, owing to some fracturing of the walls that contained it, had been suddenly and disastrously unleashed. The water lay too deep for anyone to reach it and offer photographic proof of its existence, but it was still the version of events that most people accepted. It had the stamp of science upon it, after all, and that lent it legitimacy. Of course there had been significant pieces of evidence suggesting an entirely different explanation: pictures of the lighthouse and the jetty taken by the *Courier*'s photographer, and several garbage bags full of dried fish and other detritus picked up in their vicinity. But the police records had been washed away. So, of course, had the lighthouse, the jetty and all that had been left at the high-water mark; erased by the coming and going of the Izabella.

* * *

Those same erasing waters had borne Candy away from Chickentown with great speed, their tumult quieting once the divide between the Hereafter and the Abarat was reached.

I'm going back—

Candy thought as the sky started to darken overhead and the unfamiliar constellations that hung in the heavens above the islands began to show themselves.

I tried to leave, but here I am, on my way back.

The thought made her smile. And the smile was still on her face when sleep overtook her. . . .

News of what had happened in the Hereafter had preceded her to the islands. Some of it was unsubstantiated rumor, some pure invention, but fact or fiction, it was the matter of the hour. There'd been a great wave, everybody agreed. It had traveled deep into the other world, breaching the divide between the Abarat and the Hereafter. There had been great damage caused, and many deaths. Possibly a great sea battle. Possibly (though this was widely dismissed as unlikely) the destruction of the great warship the *Wormwood*. Even less believable (though there were many who prayed it was the truth) were the reported demises of the matriarch of the Carrion clan, Mater Motley, and her lethal grandson.

Finally some solid facts emerged from this seedbed of possibilities. The first fact was the arrival of the *Lud Limbo* at the Yebba Dim Day, where the weary travelers—led, to everyone's astonishment, by a man the Abarat had long thought dead, Finnegan

Hob—presented themselves to authorities and requested an emergency meeting of the Great Council of the Islands. There was much to tell; much that the leaders of the Hours and their people needed to know. The council was quickly convened, and half a day later, in the three-domed Chamber of Decrees, on Soma Plume, representatives from all the Hours assembled to hear the tales that Finnegan, Tom, Geneva, the John brothers and Malingo (even Deaux-Deaux skipped in for the proceedings) had to tell.

"And what news is there of Candy Quackenbush?" the leader of the council asked when the testimonies had all been offered up. "She seems to be at the center of all this. Is she still alive? And if so, where or when?"

Only the Izabella knew the answer to that. With the tenderness of a loving mother, the waters carried the sleeping Candy through the channel between the Outer Islands of Autland and Efreet, protecting her from the bitter winds that howled around the latter island by calling up a current from thermal vents concealed in the coral shelves north of Qualm Hah. Occasionally Candy's eyes would flicker open, and she would catch a glimpse of some sight that reminded her that she was back in the Abarat. Once a huge red ship sailed past her with what was surely an entire town built on its decks: houses and churches and winding streets. On another occasion, she sleepily opened her eyes to see that she was traveling past a rock on which there stood a church with twin steeples made of the skull of an immense dragon. She smiled to herself in her dreamy state. There was so much more to see, she thought. So much more to learn. So much more to be.

Finally it was the sound of birds that woke her properly. She opened her eyes to see that the tide had brought her close to the shore of a tiny island, with an even tinier island set just a few yards from it. She didn't need to make any effort to reach the island; the current carried her straight toward it. These were no shallows; it rose straight up out of the water. But she had no difficulty hoisting herself onto the grass, which grew lushly under a large spreading tree, in the branches of which the birds Candy had heard hopped and sang, feeding on the fruit that hung abundantly among the foliage. Candy was too hungry not to try the fruit herself. She was glad she did. Not only was the meat of the fruit rich and filling, there was a pit at its heart that was filled with sweet water. Both hunger and thirst assuaged, she lay on the lush grass beneath the tree, thinking she would make some plans for the future. But her fatigue was by no means over. Again, a lovely drowsiness crept over her, and again she slept.

Over in Gorgossium, on the other hand, *nobody* slept. The Hour of Midnight had seen more horrors than most, but it was now in the throes of a new round of terrors. Though Mater Motley had returned to the island wounded, she quickly recovered from her injuries, and proceeded to put Midnight under a new rule of law: *her* law. The first of her draconian measures was to order the arrest and execution without trial of anyone she or her seamstresses suspected of being sympathetic to Carrion. He was dead, she announced, and any who had been loyal to him would now follow him to oblivion. No sooner had the guillotining begun than several battalions of stitchlings began the demolition of all towers but the Thirteenth, where Mater Motley had long resided, destroying in the process every piece of furniture on which Christopher Carrion had sat or slept; every book from which he'd read, every scrap of paper on which he'd written, every keepsake, every statue; in short, everything upon which he might once have laid his eyes or taken pleasure in.

The official reason given for this cleansing was that his grandmother was grief stricken by the loss and that she wanted to be rid of every object that put her in mind of him. But this persuaded few. They knew the truth. A new Night had begun, which would in time prove darker even than any that preceded it, and in its midst was the Hag Mater Motley, who nursed in her broken soul cruelties that even her grandson would have refused to countenance.

And alone in her tower, Mater Motley sewed and sewed, like a woman possessed, and while she sewed, she thought of how fine the orchard had looked the Night it had burned, and how proud she was of her fire. . . .

Again Candy woke.

This time it wasn't the birds that stirred her, it was

the crash of waves. She sat up. The sky that was visible through the branches was bright with stars now, and the moon, full and amber, was rising over another island, from the shores of which came the sounds that had awoken her. But how was that possible? The island hadn't been in view when she'd sat eating the fruit under the tree. Nor had it been Night.

There was only one plausible explanation. The little island on which she had found refuge had *moved*. Indeed, it was still moving, with its tiny attendant island in the lead, gliding through the waves toward the shore where the silvery surf boomed.

"Weird," she said, wandering down to the edge of her little dominion and looking out at the peaks of the approaching island. It was Huffaker, she guessed. Yes, Huffaker. She could see the enormous cave where she and Malingo had been washed out into the starlight, several adventures ago. But how had the island gotten here? Her question was answered as soon as her traveler islands reached shallower water. The tiny island ahead of her lifted itself up out of the surf, and the bushy green head of an animal with vast, kindly eyes turned back toward her and smiled.

She had no words. What do you say to a smiling island? All she could do was smile back. Then the beast returned its gaze to its destination and began to raise its immense body—on the back of which grew the sweet-fruit tree under which she'd slept so soundly—out of the waves and climb the shore.

There were lights in the woods that fringed the

beach, she saw. And people, emerging from the shadows of those woods and coming out onto the moonlight sand . . .

And in the Pyramids of Xuxux, and in the hives beneath, the sacbrood multiplied until there was nowhere left for them to breed.

And then they waited, knowing their time would come, and soon.

And on the shores of the Twenty-Fifth Hour, Diamanda introduced her sometime husband Henry to Mespa and Joephi, and sat down to talk about a future that seemed to have more darkness in it than light, and where even the light was uncertain, and flickered like a candle in a great wind.

And far away, in a motel room outside the flood-swept ruins of Chickentown, Melissa Quackenbush lay awake while her husband snored in the darkness beside her and thought of how it would have been if she had given herself to the retreating waters, as she knew in her heart Candy must have done, instead of staying here in this stale place. What sights she would now be seeing, what wonders filling her eyes. When instead there were only tears.

And on the shores of Huffaker, Candy slid off the back of the great island beast that had brought her here and saw to her great delight that she knew the faces of the people who had come out onto the sand. They were laughing and calling her name and opening their arms to her, welcoming her back with shouts and songs.

And so it was that Candy Quackenbush and the Princess Boa came home, at last, to the islands of the Abarat.

Witch, do this for me:
Find me a moon
made of longing.
Then cut it sliver thin,
and having cut it,
hang it high
above my beloved's house,
so that she may look up
tonight
and see it,
and seeing it, sigh for me
as I sigh for her,
moon or no moon.

—Christopher Carrion

So Ends
The Second Book of Abarat